Waiting for the Vote of the Wild Animals

CARAF Books

Caribbean and African Literature
Translated from French

Carrol F. Coates, Editor

Clarisse Zimra, J. Michael Dash, John Conteh-Morgan,
and Elisabeth Mudimbe-Boyi, Advisory Editors

Waiting for the Vote of the Wild Animals

AHMADOU KOUROUMA

Translated and with an Afterword by
Carrol F. Coates

University Press of Virginia

CHARLOTTESVILLE AND LONDON

Publication of this translation was assisted by a grant
from the French Ministry of Culture
Originally published in French as *En attendant le vote des bêtes sauvages*
© Éditions du Seuil, 1998

THE UNIVERSITY PRESS OF VIRGINIA
Translation and afterword © 2001
by the Rector and Visitors of the University of Virginia
Printed in the United States of America
First published 2001

⊗ The paper used in this publication meets the
minimum requirements of the American National Standard
for Information Sciences—Permanence of Paper for
Printed Library Materials, ANSI Z39.48-1984.

Library of Congress Cataloging-in-Publication Data
Kourouma, Ahmadou.
    [En attendant le vote des bêtes sauvages. English]
    Waiting for the vote of the wild animals / Ahmadou Kourouma ; translated
and with an afterword by Carrol F. Coates.
        p. cm. — (CARAF books)
    Includes bibliographical references.
    ISBN 0-8139-2022-1 (cloth : alk. paper)
    I. Coates, Carrol F., 1930– II. Title. III. Series.

PQ3989.2.K58 E613 2001
843'.914—dc21   00-068661

Contents

Contents

Acknowledgments

My sincere thanks go, first of all, to Ahmadou Kourouma, who graciously gave time for me to interview him when he was invited to speak at Wellesley College in March 1999. Mr. Kourouma has continued to consult in subsequent communications, and he was the one who commissioned Charles Dadié to paint a hunter's gathering for the cover of the translation.

A number of African and Africanist friends and colleagues have generously assisted and given me counsel as I worked on the translation. Eloise A. Brière and Juliana Makuchi Nfah-Abbenyi gave critical assessments of Kourouma's literary achievement in the early stages of the project. Karim Traoré, a hunter like Kourouma, has advised me on questions of the Mande languages and gave me early access to the manuscript of his thesis on hunters' narratives. Jean Ouedraogo, whose comparative study of Kourouma and Maryse Condé is under revision for publication, took time to read the entire manuscript and to engage in frequent discussion. The Nigerian novelist and my colleague Isidore Okpewho took time from work on his own forthcoming novel to read the first *sumu* as I was pushing to complete a draft of the translation. Various colleagues have consulted on details of language, traditional cultures, and political history as I worked—Rachid Aadnani, Kosongo Kapanga, Ambroise Kom, Cynthia Sims Parr, and Ruzima Sebuharara. I am sincerely grateful to these friends and colleagues and acknowledge that whatever lapses, lacunae, and obscurities may remain are purely my own responsibility.

Julie Candler Hayes, chair of modern languages at Richmond University, invited me to speak on the problems of translating multilingual texts in February 2000. The suggestion of one of her students to italicize African terms retained in the English version, for easier recognition, led me to reconsider my early intention to avoid such typographical devices.

As always, I am indebted to the invaluable services of the Bartle Library at Binghamton University. Without the help of the circulation

Acknowledgments

and reference departments, the research involved would have been far more arduous and costly, if not impossible. Once more, Cathie Brettschneider has seen my project through all stages, from proposed to production. Ellen Satrom has been perceptive and supportive in all of her editorial duties, including meticulous copyediting. My thanks to both of them and to the staff of the University Press of Virginia.

My wife, Clarisse, and daughters, Juliana and Lucie, have continued to support and humor their beleaguered husband/father, even when he was unavailable to provide the usual morning and afternoon transportation.

Waiting for the Vote of the Wild Animals

To you, lamented Uncle **Niankoro Fondio,**
my greetings and respect!
To you, lamented Papa **Moriba Kourouma,**
my greetings and respect!
To you,
my two emeritus master hunters, gone forever!
Your nephew and son dedicates these sumu
and solicits over and over
your protection and your benedictions!

First *Sumu*

Your name: Koyaga! Your totem: the falcon! You are a soldier and president. You will remain president and the greatest general of the Republic of the Gulf as long as Allah (may he spare us for years and years to come!) does not take from you the breath that animates you. You are a hunter! Along with Ramses II and Sundyata, you will remain one of the three greatest hunters of humankind. Remember the name of Koyaga, hunter and president-dictator of the Republic of the Gulf.

Now the sun is beginning to disappear behind the mountains. It will soon be night. You have summoned the seven most prestigious masters among the multitude of hunters that have come running. They are sitting cross-legged in a circle around you with their Phrygian bonnets and their hunting cloaks bedecked with gris-gris, tiny mirrors, and amulets. They all have their long slave rifles slung over their shoulders and a master's flyswatter in their right hands. You, Koyaga, sit enthroned at the center of the circle. Macledio, your minister of orientation, is seated on your right hand. I, Bingo, am the *sèrè*; I praise, I sing, and I play the *kora*. A *sèrè* is a minstrel, a bard who recounts the exploits of the hunters and praises their heroes. Remember my name, Bingo; I am the griot musician of the society of hunters.

The man on my right, the acrobat dressed in his outrageous costume and with his flute, is called Tiekura. Tiekura is my responder. A *sèrè* is always accompanied by an apprentice called a responder. Remember the name of Tiekura, my apprentice responder—he is an initiate going through the purificatory stage, a king's jester.

Here we all are, in the garden *apatam* of your residence. Everything is ready; everybody is in place. I will recite the purificatory narrative of your life as master hunter and dictator. The purificatory narrative is called, in Maninka, a *donsomana*. That is an epic. It is recited by a *sèrè* accompanied by a responder or *koroduwa*. A *koroduwa* is an initiate in the purificatory stage, the cathartic stage. Tiekura is a *koroduwa*, and, like all *koroduwa*, he plays the buffoon, the clown, the jester. He does anything he wants, and nothing he does goes unpardoned.

Tiekura—everybody is here, everything has been said. Add your grain of salt.

The responder plays the flute, wiggles, and dances. Abruptly, he stops and calls to President Koyaga:

"President, General, Dictator Koyaga, we are going to sing and dance your *donsomana* during five festive *sumu*. We shall tell the truth. The truth about your dictatorship. The truth about your parents and your collaborators. All the truth about your filthy tricks and your bullshit; we shall denounce your lies, your numerous crimes and assassinations."

"Stop insulting a great and righteous man of honor like Koyaga, the father of our nation. If you don't, malediction and misfortune will pursue you and destroy you. So stop it! Stop it!"

A festive assembly cannot be conducted without a theme as an undertone to the narration. Veneration of tradition is a good thing. From this theme will come the proverbs enunciated during the interludes of this first *sumu*. Tradition must be respected for the following reasons:

If the partridge flies away, its child cannot remain on the ground.

Regardless of a bird's long sojourn in the baobab, he will never forget the nest of the humble shrub where he was hatched.

And if one does not know where he is going, let him recall the place from which he comes.

1

Ah, Tiekura! During the meeting on the partition of Africa held by the Europeans at Berlin in 1884, the Bight of Benin and the Slave Coast devolved to the French and the Germans. The colonizers tried out an original experiment in civilization with the Black peoples in the zone called the Gulf. They went off to buy back slaves in America, free them, and settle them in these lands.

This was a vain effort, a complete failure. The freedmen are adept at only one profitable endeavor: trading in Black slaves. They undertake once again the hunt for captives and the sale of Blacks. This is a bygone commerce forbidden by international laws since the Berlin meeting. The colonizers are forced to get along without the freedmen.

They recruit warriors from local African tribes and undertake the subjugation of remote corners of their concessions by means of the cannon. These murderous conquests follow a normal course up to the day that, in the high mountain ridges of Africa, the Europeans find themselves faced with unknown, unexpected phenomena not covered in the Africanist treatises that serve as breviaries for explorers.

They find themselves face to face with the Naked people. People who are completely naked. No social organization. No chief. Each head of a family lives in his fortified village, and the chief's authority carries no farther than the range of his arrows. These are savages among savages with whom one can use neither polite language nor violence for purposes of communication. And besides, these savages are fearsome archers. They must be subjugated village by village. The territories are vast, mountainous, and inhospitable. A task that is impossible, unworkable with sparse columns of troops. The conquerors call in the ethnologists. The ethnologists give a name to the Naked people. They call them the Paleonegritic people—and, since the word is too long, let's be content with calling them by the abbreviation, the "Paleos."

The ethnologists recommend that the soldiers go around the mountains and pursue their victorious and bloody conquests among the costumed, organized, and hierarchized Black peoples in the savannas.

The Paleos are temporarily relieved from duties as bearers and forced laborers. (Forced labor was the required, unpaid service that other native peoples performed each year for the white colonists.) The Paleos are exempted and simply left to the priests. It's up to the priests to invent techniques, communicate with the Naked people, evangelize, Christianize, and civilize them. To render them capable of being colonized, administered, and exploited.

Each people, each community, each village has a hero—the man who is best known, most admired, the idol. He may be a singer or a dancer. One tribe in Senegal prizes the greatest spinner of yarns, the greatest liar. Among the Konate in Katiola (the brothers of the Kourouma clan in matters of joking), the favorite is the most gifted fart-maker. Among the Paleos, those Naked men who were left to the priests and the ethnologists, the most admired person is the *evelema,* the champion of initiatory combat.

In fact, one ceremony among the Paleos brings together all the young men from all the fortified villages of the mountains each year. These are the initiatory combats called *evela.* The best-known Paleo of all the villages and the most admired by all Naked people is this *evelema.*

At the beginning of this century, when the northern mountains of the Gulf were under the sole authority of the priests, there came a Naked man from the mountains by the name of Tchao, after Tchaotchi Mountain. Your very own father, Koyaga, became the most prodigious *evelema* in the long history of the Naked people.

Your father, Tchao, fought through all the mountain regions, behind all the fortified villages, season after season without having his neck pinned to the ground by another fighter. Finding no equal in the mountains, he went down to the plains and challenged the Peul, the Mossi, the Malinke. . . . There, too, he was unable to find a challenger in any nation of this African land. The griots praised him, celebrated him, and informed him that the French were seeking and hiring hero fighters.

This was an unfortunate semantic misunderstanding—it was not true. Neither the French nor Blaise Diagne, the first Black deputy of Senegal in charge of recruiting Blacks, was looking for fighters—what was needling them was more worrisome than the fire that makes the crocodile flee the backwaters. They were seeking and engaging Black warriors to send overseas. War was wasting French lands and villages, explains Macledio, the minister of orientation, who was sitting at the right hand of the general and master hunter.

Unfortunately, in the language of the mountain people, the same word means "brawl," "combat," and "war." So Tchao came before the commander of the colonial administrative group, seeking to go participate in a vast world championship of hand-to-hand combat that was taking place overseas. The French welcomed him and congratulated him for his patriotism:

He was the first Naked man to answer the pathetic call from the mother country, from endangered France, continues Macledio.

They signed him up and sent him to Dakar, to a regiment of Senegalese infantrymen that was leaving for Verdun in 1917. Tchao learned the difference between war and hand-to-hand combat when, in the trenches, his regiment came under the deafening and brutal shelling of German artillery. For three entire moons, the thunderous shelling continued with the same intensity. As an authentic Naked man, a real mountain man, Tchao was unable to sit back in resignation awaiting a muddy death and the chill in his bowels, explains Tiekura.

One morning, Tchao became angry and, despite orders from the sergeant, rushed into the facing trenches, surprised the Germans, and killed five of them. A sixth came in behind him, felled him with blows from a rifle stock, snatched up his body with the bayonet, and threw it up onto the terreplein. The French crawled forward, retrieved the body, and noticed that there was a little warmth of life in one of the mountain man's toes. They hovered over him and managed to bring him back to life and care for him. Here was a model, a true hero. They awarded him a military order and decorated him with four of the most prestigious French military distinctions: the Military Medal, the Croix de Guerre, the Legion of Honor, and the Colonial Medal.

The convalescent Tchao returned to the mountains without his strength but bedecked with medals. Back in the mountains, expert healers came running. With their leaves, roots, and magic, they succeeded in reviving all his faculties, even the dexterity and former courage of the fighting champion.

Only when he had completely recovered and wanted to go out did the former combatant realize the dilemma that he would face. He could get rid of his clothes and reassume his original naked state, but, in that case, he would be forced to go around without his medals. The medals could not be attached in his hair, on his neck or to his penile sheath: he would be unable to display his medals without wearing the tunic that the French army had given him. Tchao hesitated. One morning, he made up his mind and dared to leave the village enclosure clad in his tunic bedecked with medals for the entire village of Tchaotchi to see.

The elders gathered in the sacred woods and lavished upon him their counsel, followed by abundant threats. Nothing worked.

Still clad in his tunic and bedecked with medals, Tchao continued to parade morning and evening over all the roads of the mountains.

This was a transgression. A pernicious transgression for the Naked people because it was committed by the most prestigious combat champion of the country.

In its century-old history, the world of the Naked people had never been required to face anything other than attacks from the outside world. For the first time, this world found itself threatened in its very heart by an internal factor, explains Macledio. The brushfire that burns at the edge of the savanna can be contained; the one that burns in the center cannot be extinguished. You can survive the bullet that goes into a foot, but never the one that penetrates your heart.

The transgression of such an ancient and respected tradition as nakedness among the Paleos could not remain unpunished by Allah and the manes of the ancestors. Tchao paid dearly for his error; he paid with a hideous end, death under the most abominable conditions.

Tchao's transgression fulfilled the desires of the colonizers, confirmed their observations, and led them to make some momentous decisions.

With the perspicacity of civilized people, the French had observed every gesture and every habit of infantryman Tchao, in Dakar and at Verdun, and had even analyzed them by statistical means. Like other infantrymen, and often even better than those coming from certain peoples of the plains, Tchao the mountain man knew how to wear the red chechia, to wrap his belly with red flannel, to wind the puttee around his calves, and to tolerate footwear. With little effort he had learned to eat with a spoon and to smoke Gauloises. So the French authorities noted with delight that, once he was back in the mountains, he refused to reassume his state of nakedness. The administrators looked once more at the contradictory notes of the ethnologists who, even as they had requested the retention of a favorable regime for the Paleonegritic peoples, had demonstrated that the Naked men of the mountains had needs like every other human being.

The minister of colonies concluded with great authority that the Naked people could be civilized, Christianized, and conscripted for forced labor. That is to say, they could be constrained to labor for the White colonists three months per year. They could be constrained to pay the head tax. They were economically exploitable. It was profitable and feasible to civilize them. The cost of conquering the mountain regions would quickly be amortized.

One can fault the French for many things, but never for their great experience as conscientious and humane colonizers. When, upon careful examination, a conquest impresses them as profitable and feasible, they cease all procrastination and recall their mission to educate, nurture, and Christianize. They proclaim their principles loudly and immediately go into action.

They attacked right away. Before they had even finished with the Germans, the French encircled the mountain people with fairly seasoned regiments equipped with modern arms. Tchao, the champion fighter, was perforce the generalissimo of the armies throughout the mountains. He assembled archers, trained them in the guerrilla warfare of the jebel and in discipline. Fortified village by fortified village, the mountain men resisted. Throughout the winter season, murderous ambushes kept the French troops in the ravines, at a great distance from the villages. Unlike the Africans, the French did not go to consult the seers; they went to visit the ethnologists.

One is betrayed only by one's close friends. The ethnologists, great friends of the Paleos, advised the French command to cease frontal attacks. Frontal attacks against the Naked men of the mountains cannot be won. Patience is needed. The ethnologists cited to officers the Paleo proverb: a patient man can cook a stone until he drinks it as a bouillon. They told the soldiers simply to bivouac calmly and to wait for the harmattan. They asserted that nothing in the world could make the mountain men give up their initiatory combats during the good season. The colonial army command was right to listen to the ethnologists.

Waiting for the Vote of the Wild Animals

At the onset of the harmattan's first foggy mornings and the arrival of the first birds proclaiming the pleasant season, the warriors began emerging one by one from the mountain refuges and the trenches of the fortified villages.

And, in all tranquility, they headed for the edges of the sacred forests, states Tiekura.

With the impassiveness of civilized and Christian people, the French allowed them to assemble. Without stirring! They allowed the warriors to get rid of their poisoned arrows, as required by their code of honor, before entering the fight arena. Without blinking! Without crossing themselves! The signal strength of that civilized being—the White man —is not his repeating rifle, but his patience. The French conquerors stretched their patience to the point of allowing the fights to begin and to become animated. The invincible *evelema*, Tchao, entered the circle as the chants resounded and the tam-tam crackled.

Most assuredly, the Naked men, the fathers of all Black people in the universe, fashioned from music and dance like all Black people, had in the excitement of the game forgotten that they were at war, asserts Tiekura.

The French did not move a finger to fire a single shot. It would have been useless; one does not fire on guinea fowl caught in the net. The French troops merely had to make their appearance, to encircle the disarmed warriors, and to collect them along with their generalissimo, Tchao.

Tchao refused to go along and resisted the infantrymen like a wild beast. With a compulsive rage to avenge all the compatriots that the warrior had caused to pass from the land of the living to the land of the dead, the French did not skimp in applying various modes of torture. They bound him with leather thongs and slave shackles and dragged him to the central prison of the administrative seat of the mountain region, at Ramaka.

In prison, Tchao broke the thongs, cracked the shackles, and spread panic among prisoners and guards. His behavior obliged the French jailors to order chains specially forged in Paris for the rebel. They shackled him with chains that were embedded in cement on the floor and walls.

Attached to the back of his cell, in his own urine and excrement, Tchao still took three months to die of hunger and thirst. He died from the blows and the torture of the White men. Those same Whites for whom he had been a hero and a model.

Koyaga! It is by the physical suffering and the spiritual pain of ingratitude that Allah and the ancestral manes sanctioned that great transgression of your father.

Tchao, my father, should have given up the ghost within three weeks. He survived three months, thanks to my mother, adds Koyaga.

Nadjuma, your mother, planted herself in front of the gate at the prison where her husband was in irons. She was able to cook roots and useful decoctions, to use powerful spells, and to make solid friendships.

Your mother, Nadjuma, was generous and good.

With the collusion of the guards and the nurse, and, especially, thanks to the miracles for which only she knew the secret, her magic was able to pass through the impenetrable walls of the prison. The multiple actions of Tchao's wife gave him the ability to resist, to survive for three months.

Before taking his final breath and freeing his Paleonegritic souls one after another, your father sang and prophesied. For the French, he intoned evil spells that loomed greater than the Fouta Djallon.

He summoned you, his only son, when you were only seven years old. He spoke to you face to face. What did he say and explain to you?

He began by telling me, "The atrocious death I am undergoing is a punishment; it stems from the curse, the anger held by the manes of my ancestors." Answered Koyaga.

Then he took time to go beyond himself—he was exhausted and living his final hours. Like an inspired man, he spoke to me softly, in those flights of oratory that come from people speaking their last words. "My abominable end is the punishment visited on me for having violated the taboo against wearing clothes. The manes of the ancestors consider that my fault can only be atoned for by death, death in the most inhuman of conditions. I knew it. I sacrificed myself for you, first of all, and then for all the youth of our Paleo tribes. My travels to Dakar, in France, and to Verdun taught me that the universe is the world of people who wear clothes. We cannot enter that world without dressing, without giving up our nakedness."

"It is true that I am the first champion of hand-to-hand combat to know shame for my nakedness, to have dared wear clothes. It is true that our nakedness, and nothing else, protected us for millennia against the Mandinka, the Hausa, the Peul, the Mossi, the Songhai, the Berber, the Arab. Because of our nakedness, all the invaders and builders of empire, and proselytes of foreign beliefs scorned us and judged us too savage to be converted and exploited. Perhaps the French colonists would have shown us the same scorn. Perhaps, if I had not fallen into that madness, that stupidity of challenging the entire universe to combat and, especially, of covering my body with clothes, the French would never have violated our sanctuary and would never have Christianized us. But we would have put off the donning of clothes only for a few years. We would merely have delayed our entry into the civilized world and staved off our descent to the plains to become cultivators of more generous lands, put off sending our children to school. . . . We would merely have adjourned, delayed, been reprieved. . . ."

My father did not finish; he fainted in his chains, excrement, and urine. He died the next day.

The image of my father in agony, in chains at the back of his cell, will remain throughout my life. It will incessantly haunt my dreams. When I recall it or it appears to me in trials or defeat, it will unleash my strength; when it comes back to me in victory, I shall become cruel and I shall have neither humanity nor pity. Concludes Koyaga.

In every narration, it is necessary to take a breath from time to time. We are going to pause, announces the *sèrè*. For five long minutes, he sings a song accompanied by the kora, as his responder engages in a wild dance, then he stops. He takes up the same melody with the flute. The *sèrè* asks him to stop playing and to recite some proverbs on tradition.

The new rope is braided at the end of the old one.
One takes advantage of a feast day, but lightning speaks from its belly.
The dew does not get you wet if you walk behind an elephant.

2

Ah, Tiekura! After disposing of Tchao and mastering the reservoirs of the mountain people, the French were not content merely to collect head taxes, recruit riflemen, impose forced labor, and send their catechumens: they also demanded pupils. They wanted to recruit for their schools the sons of the traditionalists, the former combatants, the former combat champions, the *sinbo*, the griots.

Koyaga was in the first bunch recruited and sent to the school at Ramaka. He was ten years old at the time.

Before speaking of Koyaga's school years, we must recount his birth. The *donsomana*, the literary genre of the *donsomana*, requires that we speak about the hero from the instant that the germ was planted in his mama's womb. We shall recount later how Koyaga's germ was placed in Nadjuma. For the moment, let us begin with his gestation.

Tiekura, my dear pupil, *koroduwa,* and accompanist, listen carefully. The day following Friday is called Saturday. Koyaga was born on a Saturday. The gestation of a baby lasts for nine months; Nadjuma carried her baby for twelve whole months. A woman suffers from childbirth for two days at most; Koyaga's mama suffered from labor for an entire week. A human baby does not come out stronger than a baby panther; Nadjuma's child was as heavy as a baby lion.

What was the character, the truth, the nature of this child?

Everyone learned that when the mother was able to deliver herself of him and the infant fell on the ground at dawn.

Even the animals learned that the baby who had just come into the world was predestined to be the greatest killer of game among the hunters. The tsetse flies abandoned the distant bush and mountain and descended on the baby. Koyaga, you crushed those *Glossina* by the fistful. Crawling on all fours, you did not spare a single chick or agama pecking in your baby dishes. When you were five years old, the rats no longer knew security or tranquillity in their holes; you were a great and skillful rat trapper. The turtledoves could no longer rest peacefully in the tree branches; you were an adroit shot with the sling.

When you reached age nine, the distant brush and the mountains resounded with the distress cries of the beasts passing from life to nothingness; the animals saw their ranks irremediably thinned; countless young were orphaned.

You had already killed a panther, Koyaga, marked by your arrow, and you danced in the ranks of the master hunters during the evening assemblies when the Whites came looking to place you in their school. The wild beast cannot be domesticated; true wildcats will never be tamed. You, Koyaga, were fervent and impetuous; you were stifled between four walls. In order to breathe, you needed the open spaces, rivers, mountains, the perpetual challenges and dangers. You detested school; school made you sick to the stomach. You wanted to continue your life as a hero hunter and a champion combatant. You were already the best combatant of the fortified villages in your native mountains. School was boring; the teacher whipped and flayed.

Several moons after the beginning of school, the winds were whirling and bringing foggy mornings. On those implacably sunny days, whirlwinds roared over the distant and spacious brushlands. Leaves yellowed and the bare branches of the trees seemed to howl their distress toward a pitiless sky. At night, the horizons lit up with the glow of distant brushfires.

Another season had just come in following the rainy months, and that new season was the harmattan. The harmattan, season of combats, dances, and hunts in the mountains. A true Naked man cannot bear to experience the harmattan away from the mountains.

At the rural school in Ramaka, you roused the children who, like you, came from the mountains. At the moment the moon set, you deserted en masse and arrived at the foot of the Tchaotchi mountains before dawn. Singing, you threw off shirts, pants, and underwear. You covered your penises with sheaths. You armed yourselves with spears. You reclaimed your places and ranks in the various societies. You threw yourselves into the dances, ceremonies, and hunts. The excitement of the feasts of the harmattan in the mountains is catching and makes one forget everything.

Koyaga and his fellow students did not remember their role as pupils until a dozen weeks later, after the bad season had hidden the horizon and the mountains were covered with greenery. Unfortunately, it was too late!

Your teacher's name was de Souza, a descendant of emancipated Brazilian slaves. After taking note of their disappearance, de Souza had decided to get rid of all the turbulent, undisciplined little mountain savages. When you return, he refuses to let you back in the classroom. He goes up to the commander's office and presents the dismissal forms for signature.

The White man refuses, refuses outright and gives his reasons.

He likes the mountain Paleos, studies them, understands them. In his reports to the minister of colonies, he brags that he is the only colonial official who is teaching the young mountain Paleos to read and write in his school; he is alone in training the first literate Naked men.

Forced to accept the escapades of Koyaga and his fellow pupils, the teacher administered the regulation thirty lashes in punishment for the unauthorized absences of the mountain boys. Thirty lashes on the naked buttocks of these mountain scholars seemed like caresses to them. Such punishment did not discourage them: they continued to disappear time and again.

For six years, at the beginning of each harmattan season, Koyaga persuaded the other wild boys from the mountains to desert the desks at their boarding school in favor of the delights of the dry season in the mountains. Each time, they returned to their assigned places in school as soon as the first clouds covered the sky. And, each time, before returning to their benches, they climbed to the platform and presented their naked behinds so that Monsieur de Souza could administer the thirty lashes. The *tubab* held his ground. He never agreed to sign the order to expel the future Supreme Guide or his companions.

At the end of the seventh rainy season in school, Koyaga was granted the *certificat d'études,* and his written examination made him eligible for admittance to the next level. Unfortunately, the oral examinations took place during the harmattan. As a dutiful master hunter obeying the call to the mountains for the feasts and the ritual initiatory combats, he was absent. When the sky became gray, the trails disappeared, and the ravines filled with muddy torrents, Koyaga returned to class, where, without even a hello, he stored his arrows and his penile sheath.

With his usual serious demeanor, the teacher administered the thirty lashes, but he did not send Koyaga to his place in the classroom. Koyaga had finished his primary schooling at the rural school and no longer belonged there. Monsieur de Souza sent up to the office to declare to the commander that Koyaga should be sent back to the mountains.

The White man ordered him to keep the pupil in residence; Koyaga was not to go back to the mountains forever. France had a debt toward the son of Tchao. The father, the rifleman Tchao, had been placed in irons. The rifleman Tchao had killed five Germans during the Great War and had been the first Naked man to wear clothing. As a result, he had been the first to introduce the rudiments of civilization to the mountains. The commander felt it was his beholden duty to find a place for the son of Tchao. He wrote and sent telegrams to commanders in other *cercles,* to the inspector general, to the governor of the colonies, to the governor general of the Federation and even to the minister of colonies. He went on horseback to the administrative seat and maneuvered with such conviction that he arranged for the first mountain Paleo to graduate from the administrative domain of the mountains—that was you—a place at the Kati School for Military Children in the French Sudan.

When you arrive in Bamako, you are at Kati, which is not far away. At Kati, people still remember Koyaga. At Kati, there were students who were better than Koyaga at reading and mathematics, and Koyaga had his equals in racing, combat, and the rifle range, but nobody outdid Koyaga for brawls and indiscipline.

When the season of harmattan came, the character of the combatant and mountain hunter, who was already a hero, welled up within him. The only pastime that he engaged in seriously and consistently was his training as a hunter. In Kati, he had located a great master hunter, whose disciple, companion, and most faithful apprentice he became. When he was separated from the master hunter, upon return to school, he became an unbearable troublemaker.

In the dormitory, the dining hall, on the playing fields, in class, you were always the one who blasphemed, insulted, broke, struck, boxed, and felled. The lieutenant commanding the school was soon fed up with your wild behavior and sent you to the Saint-Louis School for Military Children.

Saint-Louis is close to the northern border of Senegal, at the mouth of the Senegal River; it was the capital of the colony of Senegal at that time. The colonel who supervised all the schools for military children in French West Africa resided in Saint-Louis. The colonel received Koyaga publicly. He loudly proclaimed his admiration for riflemen with healthy testicles between their legs, those riflemen who love a fray and battle. The colonel was amused by Koyaga's fights with his colleagues up to a certain harmattan morning: two comrades teased him at the moment when longing for the mountains was burning within the son of the Naked man and woman. The tormentors were quickly laid out; each got up with a broken limb, and the supervising general, who had attempted to stop the fight, went away with a fractured jaw. Still laughing, the colonel decided that Koyaga had already acquired the soul and physique of a warrior. He was the prototype of a good warrior and was wasting time in the classroom. The colonel locked him up for one month (as required by regulations). Upon Koyaga's release, the colonel expelled him from school and had him enrolled as a Senegalese infantryman second class.

Greetings, my dear *koroduwa*-responder! Greetings Mister Minister Macledio! Greetings to you master hunters and Mister Supreme Guide!

Transgression has the effect of a little coal thrown down on the great savanna at the height of the dry season. You see where the flame starts, but nobody knows where it will stop. Tchao's transgression did not simply bring about the schooling of the young mountain men: it resulted in the massive recruitment of mountain men as infantrymen. It made of the mountains a reservoir of infantrymen from which the French drew abundantly for all their wars.

The rapid adaptation of Tchao to the living conditions of the infantryman, to the subtleties of civilization, and, in particular, his scorn for danger led the colonialists to continue their experiment; they recruited a hundred mountain men whom they sent overseas. Upon their return, these veterans behaved like the great combatant Tchao; they began parading from one fortified village to another decked out in their uniforms. They strutted in that garb, adorned with red flannel over their bellies and red chechias on their heads. Anyone who knows the inordinate taste of the mountain men for adornment and color can imagine at once that the veteran combatants and infantrymen were immediately admired and beloved throughout the mountains and retreats of the Naked men of continental Africa. They will also understand that the mountain women wanted to possess them, serve them. Mothers abandoned husbands and children and let themselves be kidnapped according to the fine traditions of the Naked men—the tradition of abduction-marriage by the men coiffed and girded in red.

Ah! my responder, Tiekura! What happens when mountain men steal women has no equivalent in feverishness other than the unending roaming of sparrow hawks whose young have been kidnapped. The scorned cuckolds made up their minds to go after the boots, chechias, and red flannel of the White colonialists. They came down from the Tchaotchi mountains and showed up at the colonial seat of Ramaka wearing nothing more than their penile sheaths, hats, bows, and quivers. The commander understood that they had come to sign up and advised them to wait for the enlistment period.

After a certain time, all the mountain cuckolds finally came down and fell like salt into a gumbo sauce. The White man not only understood them, he congratulated them. The French army was recruiting Blacks by the truckload for Indochina. The Naked men were in particular demand. Their scorn for danger made of them excellent material for combat in the rice paddies. For months, regiments almost completely composed of mountain infantrymen were being formed and shipped off to the Far East. One last regiment, which was lacking only a French-speaking mountain man to serve as interpreter, had been waiting weeks on the wharfs of Dakar for the next ship. The colonel commanding the Saint-Louis School for Military Children had been informed of the postponement of this regiment's embarkation. You were assigned to it, Koyaga, you the best educated of those Paleos, the Naked men of the mountains.

The regiment disembarked at Haiphong. They took up their position at Post PK 204, not far from Cao Bang, on the Tonkin-Chinese border.

Waiting for the Vote of the Wild Animals

Let us state it right away. Water never fails to follow its former course; the leaping male antelope does not abandon its young. After his own fashion, Koyaga garnered the same distinctions in the rice paddies that had been bestowed upon his father, Tchao, in the trenches of Verdun. Like his father, he was to be decorated and repatriated in health.

The chief master sergeant of the regiment of Naked men at Post PK 204 was from the Koto people, people of the plains who were the traditional enemies of the mountain men. The proud mountain men had only scorn for the Koto. They called them impure and inferior. And here was an inferior, impure Koto, the Koto master sergeant, who was supposed to order the mountain infantrymen to give blood when the team in charge of collecting blood for the army arrived at the regiment in Cao Bang. From what race do the wounded men who are to receive the blood come, the mountain men asked the head nurse. It's for men of all races, all colors, all nationalities, the nurse told them. Those were tactless words, provocative words. He demonstrated ignorance of the traditions, magic, and logic of the mountain men. For those mountain men, for all Black animists, to give one's blood to somebody else is to surrender one's soul, to create with that blood their own double, to make another self. Any transgression of a taboo committed by that double can be attributed to the other self, and his death may cause our own. Giving blood to unknown people created, consequently, a danger for every mountain man. The sergeant major should have known that. He should also have known that an order by a Koto to give blood would be considered a provocation and an insult by the mountain men.

There was danger, Koyaga, and you understood it immediately. You gave long, very long explanations to the mountain men. But you did not manage to convince them.

They refused as a bloc to go along with the order. Deeply offended, the sergeant major became angry and dealt with them ruthlessly. He meted out severe punishments. The two leaders were arrested and locked up to await an appearance before the military tribunal. In the view of the mountain men, the sergeant major had added injustice to insult.

It is better to take the cub away from the mother lion than to act with injustice toward a mountain man. It is better to step on the tail of a desert viper than to act with unfairness toward a mountain man, adds Tiekura.

Injustice unifies the mountain men, and when mountain men are united against a foreigner, they are capable of committing the most inhuman acts, any or all acts of savagery. Every mountain infantryman considered it his duty to succor the imprisoned men, and they helped them escape. The two escapees hid quietly in a blockhouse and waited for the regiment to assemble on the parade ground for the report. The sergeant major arrived. The impure, insulting sergeant major arrived. The men lying in ambush executed him. They cut him down with a tommy gun and, along with him, killed thirty-five soldiers among whom (unfortunately, most unfortunately!) was a mountain twin. You cannot kill a twin in front of his brother; you must never kill a mountain twin in front of his brother.

The brother of the slain twin enters a trance, screams for vengeance, and calls his clansmen to his aid. First three, then four infantrymen join him, and they take over the opposite blockhouse. With one blockhouse against the other, both heavily armed, the mountain men begin bombarding one another; the crossfire from the submachine guns sweeps over the camp. Exchanges of fire between the mountain men resulted in numerous victims; the parade ground was covered with the dead and the fire continued.

The commanding officers decide to save those survivors who, flattened in hidden corners, have escaped the bloody savagery of the Naked men. Two regiments dispatched to stop the mutiny encircle Post PK 204 and accomplish their mission with flamethrowers, teargas, and napalm. Another good fifty mountain men are roasted in the flames. But nothing, absolutely none of the most deadly weapons, can dislodge the five mountain men from their blockhouse. For three nights and three days, they resist and hold out until an officer of indigenous affairs arrives from headquarters.

The officer suggests and carries out a different method: the *sumu,* an African *sumu.* He calls Koyaga and gives him the megaphone. In the manner of the mountain men, you intone the lament of the hero-hunter, executed in your honor when you dance in the circle of hero-hunters. The lament is followed by the song of the sacred forests; you recite sonnets and harangue the men. The miracle is accomplished.

The mountain men, with their fingers still on the triggers, understand that the man who is calling to them is the son of the most prestigious combatant champion of all the mountains and plains of Africa and is already a hero-hunter acclaimed in all the hunters' *sumu.*

You ask them to put down their arms, to come out of the blockhouses, and to surrender. The bodies of those slain can be shrouded, and their souls will be able to return to their native mountains to be assimilated by the ancestral gods. And the marvel takes place! Before the speechless French officers, the mutineers come out with their hands up, humming the same songs that you intoned.

The French take note of the sway that you, the son of Tchao, already a recognized master hunter, hold over your compatriots. They decide to do you honor: they cite you for the Order of the Army and promote you to corporal.

Ah, Tiekura! The bird who has never left his tree trunk cannot know there is millet elsewhere. Let us cease speaking for a moment of the savagery and stupidity of the Naked men and of Supreme Guide Koyaga in order to praise the warriors of Vietnam. The *donsomana* is a type of discourse, a literary genre for the purpose of celebrating the deeds of the hunter-heroes and all sorts of heroes. Before introducing a hero in a *donsomana,* the genre requires that his praise be sung. A hero is a tall mountain, and the performing *sèrè* is a traveler. The traveler perceives the mountain from far away, before approaching it, walking around it, and getting to know it. The Vietnamese warriors are heroes; they are like so many tall mountains. Their names have dropped into our narrative. We must pause a moment to sing their praise.

Ah! Tiekura, the Vietnamese are the Pygmies of Asia, frail Pygmies. They have chased all the great peoples of the universe from their lands. Peoples in great numbers, such as the Chinese; peoples great by their technical means, like the Americans; peoples great by their culture and their history, like the French. If the entire universe were to become allies in order to occupy Vietnamese soil, one might surmise that the Viets would be victorious and toss everybody into the sea.

The Viets sacrificed themselves in the mud, in the canals, in the mountains, in the rice paddies, and in the prisons in order to render a certain form of colonization impossible on that land. Through their combat the Vietnamese addressed a message, very strong truths, to all the colonized peoples—a message that has been heard.

A great nation can conquer only the small people unable to come together in order to resist aggression. A rich people can dominate only that poor nation whose inhabitants are unable to sacrifice themselves. A nation that has mastered technology can vanquish only the underdeveloped people lacking in cunning and courage. After the war in Vietnam, there are still some nations on the planet that take delight in colonization, but there is no nation that could not recover its freedom. Let us bow to the Viets.

The "Viets" is the derogatory name given by French soldiers to the

Indochinese guerrillas. Scorn for one's adversary, even if he is short and frail, is always a strategic mistake in combat; in an insignificant grove of trees, there is quite often a vine sufficiently strong to entrap us, explains the Supreme Guide.

The Viets were slender as climbing lianas—but short and resourceful, courageous and clever like little marmosets. The French looked down on them at first—but the Viets were to get the upper hand in the end. With the struggles between a swarm of flies and a herd of elephants, it is not necessarily the big fellows who win. The French would chase them out of the cities; the Viets would attack the French on the roads and would decimate them in deadly ambushes. The French would take over the main arteries with their tanks, burning and destroying villages while massacring their inhabitants; the Viets would take refuge in the rice paddies. The French would follow them into the swamps in order to drag them out of the canals like catfish and slit their throats; the Viets would climb into the trees like monkeys. With napalm, fire, death, and airplanes, the French would destroy the forests and every possible hiding place; the Viets would take off to burrows, retreats, and dens in the mountains. The French, trusting in their own know-how, would set up camp in a basin at the base of the mountains in order to cut off all the paths that the Viets use to harvest the paddies. The Viets, with the patience and perseverance that come from their religion, would wait for long days and nights so the French could gather their men, aircraft, and all the complex matériel of modern warfare in the basin of Dien Bien Phu. One night, after the moon set, the Viets came down the sides of the mountains, like countless ants from a multitude of anthills, surrounded the French, and destroyed them—with all the Arab and Black infantrymen from the plains and the mountains, with the cannons, aircraft, and other equipment.

It was with great shame that the final embarkation of the French lions took place during the night. After the French and the Americans, the invincible Indochinese warriors would add the Chinese to their hunting tally! Since then, no other invader has attempted to occupy Vietnamese lands.

Ah, Tiekura! That's who the Viets are, those heroes, those clever people who are uneasy and perplexed witnesses to the clan massacres that the Naked people of the day and of the night perpetrate on one another. The post is damaged by mutiny. The watchful Viets do not expect that all the defenses can be reconstructed in order to attack again. One night, at the setting of the moon, they attack with their powerful means. And, before dawn, everything has been overrun, taken, and burned.

Air reconnaissance reports that there are no survivors in the still smoldering ruins. All of us, comments Koyaga, every one of us from the post is thought to have died for the nation, for France—we all died honorably on the battlefield.

That report is cabled to the white commanders of the land of the Naked people. The white commanders announce the fatalities to the families. The mountain people weep, worship their gods and the souls of their ancestors as they sing and dance in interminable funeral ceremonies.

The Paleos, the mountain people, are a different kind. With any people other than the Paleos, after having heard of so many deaths, the recruiting offices would have been deserted and there would have been no more volunteers. Despite the announcement of so many Paleo fatalities, the volunteers flooded into the recruiting offices. At reception centers, the volunteers declared that they were eager to go to war, still eager to wear the red flannel sashes and the chechias demanded by Paleo wives in return for their conjugal fidelity.

There remains one of the great loves of your youth, General Koyaga, rarely mentioned by your official biographers. It is the great passion that you conceived for Fatima, a Moroccan prostitute in Indochina. Those who praise you pass over that adventure in silence. In this purificatory *donsomana,* we will speak of it in detail.

The colonial army considered the Senegalese infantryman, the Black soldier in the Far East, as a big child, as a great simpleton, and took him into hand as a hopeless case. The army worried about his correspondence with his wife, his parents, and the children still in Africa. It took charge of placing his savings. It looked after his preferred leisure-time activities (films and cartoons for children) and his pilgrimage to Mecca if he was a Muslim. And, above all, the colonial army was concerned about satisfying the infantryman's furious sexual drives. The officers in the colonial army claimed that the infantryman who had been stuffed with rice was only half useful as long as he had not spent time in the bordello.

Certain officers from the social and medical services of the army in Indochina had been sent to Casablanca, in Morocco. They had gone to the slums and recruited the most successful prostitutes, the leaders. These head prostitutes had been given a rank and military status. They had been shipped to Indochina, where they were assigned to camps and posts along the main arteries. Military patrols had organized sweeps through the neighboring Indochinese jungle and had captured some young Vietnamese women. These young Vietnamese women were placed under the orders of the head prostitutes, who set up and organized RMBs, rural military bordellos, for each camp or post.

In the military bordello of Post PK 204, there were two commanding Moroccan prostitutes and a half-dozen young Vietnamese women. The Moroccans were too far from Casablanca; they reminisced about the High Atlas plateaus in nostalgic songs. Commander Fatima, who was the more buxom, had touched you with her nightingale voice and had finally won your mountain man's heart, you the most educated man of the regiment, a soldier who was already a hero. With your humanity (what should I call it?), your compassion, your faithfulness, and your strength, you managed to console her, to steal and keep possession of Fatima's heart. After her daily work (satisfying some thirty infantrymen each evening) and her facial and bodily ablutions, she gave you the singular privilege of being welcomed into her bed until daybreak. Fatima was good-hearted and generous; she conceived for you feelings that were maternal and intensely loving. You could dip into her great bag of money according to your whims, and with no accounting. The surprise of the Viets had taken place while you were in your dulcinea's arms. You dressed swiftly and returned to your combat post. You fought like a lion. When the post was about to founder under the deluge of fire, you ran to help Fatima.

After the fall of Post PK 204, the high command of Hanoi carried out a number of air reconnaissance missions over the site, which continued to burn and smoke. The photos were developed, enlarged, and minutely examined. The report was that all the installations had been crushed, that everything had burned, and that there were no survivors, nobody saved, nor anyone who escaped. As required by regulations but without any great expectations, the high command of Hanoi dispatched some patrols from the area to the edge of the jungle. Those patrols were not content merely to operate at the edge: by way of paths and rivers, they ventured into the heart of the jungle. They observed conscientiously, they actively surveyed, waited, and listened for four entire weeks. At the end of the four weeks, the high command of Hanoi called off the patrol missions. They judged that, if anybody had escaped, they could not possibly have survived more than four weeks in the jungle, infested with beasts and Viet combatants.

The high command erred; it was grievously mistaken. The results of the aerial photo analysis were accurate—there could be no human being capable of living through such devastation, such chaos, or such fire. But Koyaga was more than a man—he was a hunter-hero, the son of a sorceress of the Naked people—he had come out alive. In fact, it was not possible for an infantryman or soldier to survive more than four weeks in that inhospitable jungle infested with beasts and Viet combatants. But Koyaga was not just any infantryman—he was the son of a Paleo man and woman, the son of Nadjuma and Tchao—and he had wandered for more than six weeks.

Corporal Koyaga, the hunter-hero, surprised everybody by emerging from the jungle eight weeks after the destruction of the post, at the head of a contingent, some fifty kilometers from Cao Bang. The contingent was returning with its equipment, its arms (the 36-millimeter weapons, the submachine gun, ammunition, and the bazooka), as well as with two guests of the military bordello (Commander Fatima and her assistant).

Dragging two fat, Moroccan whores through the jungle was an exploit that aroused great laughter in the mess tents. But when everybody found out that the corporal had accomplished that feat with a bullet in his shoulder blade, astonished, admiring cries of "shit!" replaced the insidious mockery.

The high command awarded you several medals and promoted you to sergeant as you shipped out on the SS *Pasteur* to return home with a medical discharge.

When veterans of Indochina meet, they recount to each other the feats of soldiers in the rice paddies. They always include the military exploit of the corporal who, despite his wounds and the burden of two accompanying prostitutes, led his unit for eight whole weeks in battle against the Viets and defied them. That was your exploit, Koyaga.

Thus it is that you will always be a legendary hero of the French army, as famous as your father. Your father's heroic deed was to have sprung all alone from his burrow at Verdun without any order from his corporal and, with his bayonet, to have speared five German soldiers in the facing trench. You will remain a hero to the end of the very universe for having saved two fat harlots in the jungle.

Even at the height of the harmattan, the sun occasionally pauses to request a veil of the clouds. Let us also interrupt for a brief repose, announces the *sèrè*. Bingo and his responder perform the second musical interlude. Tiekura dances. The *sèrè* ends the interlude with some thoughts and proverbs on respect for tradition.

Even in darkness, the calf does not lose his mother.
The elephant dies, but his tusks remain.
The baby centipede curls up like his mother.

3

Ah, Tiekura! We must respect our mothers. Our traditions in Africa demand that respect for our mothers go beyond that of our fathers. That which he inherits physically, the child owes to his father; to his mother, he owes what he acquires morally. The mountain Paleos—who are the bearers of the first authentic African civilization—always prefer their mothers to their fathers. Black traditions hold that all hardships endured by the mother in marriage are transformed into vital energy and merit—into success for the son. The son of a rich man is not necessarily rich. The son of a man who is exceptional in knowledge may be an idiot. While the child always becomes like his mother and always possesses what belongs to his mother. Among Whites, respect and love for the mother do not always surpass veneration for the father. The expeditionary force in the Far East did not know that Koyaga's mama, Nadjuma, had been the source of his exploit. In the mountains of Tchaotchi, everybody knew that and talked about it; nobody doubted it. Leading those who welcomed Koyaga when he stepped out of the postal truck in the mountains was his mother. People congratulated her more than Koyaga for the son's exploit. It was by the mother's magic, a part of the magic that had been willed by the mother to her son, that Koyaga had been able to save his unit and the Casablancan prostitutes.

When the Viets ran over Post PK 204, Koyaga had, by means of the magic taught by his mother, transformed himself into a powerful night owl. On his left wing, he bears the prostitutes. On his right wing, he takes some fifty mountain riflemen with their weapons. The Viets see nothing but smoke. Near the Hanoi airport, he unloads everybody where they only have to walk to the runway to be welcomed by the high command.

You have always admired and loved your mother, Koyaga. As long as she lives, the world will be at your command.

Ah, Tiekura, there are many women who believe that their maternal duty ends at childbirth.

No, the duty of a mother does not stop there, adds the accompanist. Others believe that their duty as a mother ends with nursing and carrying the baby on their backs for twenty-four months.

No, that is not enough.

Others believe that their obligation to a child ends with marriage.

No, no. For her entire life, a mother succors and teaches her child. The obligation of a true mother continues as long as she is alive, adds Tiekura.

Ah, Tiekura! A mother is everything in life; the misfortunes of our youth stem from the lack of veneration that youth consecrates to the mother. It is not easy to carry a child in the womb for nine whole moons!

Let us speak of Koyaga's mother. Let us glorify the woman who waited, at Ramaka in the mountains of the Republic of the Gulf, for the arrival of her son in the postal truck.

You have much good to say of your mother. You are right. Never will the mountains know another woman the equal of Nadjuma. She was beautiful—she is still beautiful. She was courageous—she is still courageous. She is intelligent. Speak, speak! The *sèrè* possesses only words, and no word can ever express the complete reality of Nadjuma. For all African women, she will remain a model, a perpetual source of inspiration. You, Koyaga, owe to your mother everything that you have, everything that you are. She was the champion of combat among the mountain girls, and she will die without any other woman managing to force her nape to the ground. The Naked people practice two types of marriage: engagement-marriage and abduction-marriage. Only scrawny or gawky women accept marriage by engagement. Koyaga, men and women with the stuff and blood of your parents accept marriage only by abduction.

From the fortified village of Sola at Tchaotchi, the unbeaten champion Tchao decided to kidnap Nadjuma, a girl from the village of Kaloa and the champion of the women. The two fiancés met beneath the baobab at the crossroad, some distance from the river. As required by convention, obviously, Tchao brought some ten archers from his clan, all armed with poisoned arrows. The archers from Nadjuma's clan had prepared an ambush. But there was no tribal war; the girl's parents had already accepted the dowry of two kola nuts and two goats. In order to witness the scene, each group of archers had hidden at some distance from the baobab. Nadjuma emerges from the bushes; Tchao gets rid of his arrows and quiver and, like a beast, rushes at his beloved, picks her up, and places her over his shoulders. The girl struggles and insults the young man—she launches the challenge. She is a virgin. So she has her honor to defend and cannot let herself be carried away like a dead doe. Her lover places her on the ground, and the man and woman immediately begin the combat, a real combat. A combat that lasts an entire afternoon. Tchao, the men's champion, against Nadjuma, unbeaten among women. It is not enough to flatten Nadjuma on the ground. He has to rape her—when the girl is a virgin, the abduction-marriage must be consummated with rape. The rape is generally limited to token resistance by the girl. Champion Nadjuma refuses to pretend. She defends herself with all her muscular strength, all her technique. Tchao, during the final days of his life in prison, was to recount once more that the combat in which he had engaged to possess Nadjuma was the roughest fight of his career. A combat of giants, a combat of professionals. Beneath the feet of champions, grass is uprooted and the earth is plowed deeply.

Since that day, that spot has been a clearing.

Never, until the last day of the world, will any blade of grass sprout in that circle where the rape by which you were engendered took place, Koyaga, Tiekura continues with a smile.

Tiekura! Proverbs are the steeds of speech; when speech fails, it is by the grace of proverbs that it is found again. One must rise early when one has a long path to cover in a day.

Koyaga's mama fought and suffered to conceive her son; she fought and suffered again to bring him into the world. The screams of pain that she emitted when she was in labor still continue to haunt the mountain peaks in the lands of the Naked people when the great winds blow from the east. Koyaga, you were a giant of a baby. Your mother swore that after having you she would never bear another child. In echo to her cries of pain, the sorcerers foretold that she would perish were she to bear another. There is no crest on the wave without wind. If we catch a dogfish in our land-animal traps, it is by great luck. One stops; there is no reason to continue hunting.

Nadjuma was blessed with Koyaga; she sought no more children; she had only one son.

You, Koyaga, were seven years old when your father, Tchao, was arrested, chained, and taken to be shut up in the prison at Ramaka, the seat of the mountain subdivision. Your mother went to see him. At Ramaka, she stored her meager belongings in a root hollow in the silk cotton tree next to the walls of the prison and began to organize the spot into a shelter of good fortune. Marriage is sacred. Whoever fulfills all the responsibilities imposed by marriage and hopes never waits in vain. In misfortune, the ancestral manes and Allah come to the aid of those who are united by the holy bond of matrimony.

An unknown woman approached and, to the surprise of the despair-

Waiting for the Vote of the Wild Animals

ing woman, greeted her in the pure language of mountain people from her land. Like Koyaga's mother, the unknown woman was from the Naked people, brought up in a fortified village an arrow's flight from the family house of Nadjuma. This woman belonged to the only mountain family in town. She was one of the five Paleo sisters married to a Mossi head nurse. This nurse answered to the good name of Kabore.

Ah, Tiekura! The mountain people are endogamous, and they remain the most closed and the most jealous people in the world. Their women do not go down from the mountains, and they do not marry a man outside of their ethnic group or region. So, we must interrupt this recital of your exploits a moment in order to explain how it happened that these mountain women became the wives of a Mossi, a man of the plains, an outsider living in Ramaka, the seat of the *cercle*.

Kabore was the first nurse the Whites posted at the clinic in the Tchaotchi mountains, where he was able, through several repeated miracles, to heal a number of sick and wounded people. The father of the five sisters, who would subsequently become the five wives of the nurse, had been beaten by the panther men and left for dead in a thicket.

The panther men! Panther men! Here in traditional Africa, what were these fearsome associations of panther men? The present-day Black inhabitants in cities are unaware that, on the roads to the bush country, there used to stand the panther men's huts.

As in many other African lands, the outlawed associations of panther men grew up along the routes to the mountains. In the beginning, the institution of the panther men was for the purpose of religious rites and human sacrifices intended to merit the goodwill of the gods and the ancestral manes. The murder of a clan brother was a frightful crime, and those who were charged with committing it (legally or not) surrendered in some way their membership in the clan, the tribe, even in the human race, and they were transformed into an animal. They arrived by covering themselves with panther skins and arming themselves with sharp claws. A murder committed in this garb thus became licit. With the coming of the colonial regime, the society of the panther men had lost its social function and began to act in an ambiguous and ambivalent manner, avenging hatreds and private grudges by killing for hire.

The panther men from the mountains had struck down the father of the five sisters for reasons that still remain unknown. Their wounded father was found dying in a thicket. Because of ritual and magic, and for fear of the panther men, no mountain healer dared help or care for him. The relatives of the wounded man had transported him to the Tchaotchi clinic in the mountains. The head nurse who directed that White establishment had been obliged to take him in and, through the use of both European and Mossi medications, had miraculously saved him. As a mark of gratitude, the healed man had proposed (in accordance with the rules of the mountains) to the nurse-healer a choice between a pig and his eldest daughter. The nurse preferred to marry the daughter. He behaved like a good husband, generously nourishing and dressing his wife and giving presents to his parents-in-law. Among the mountain people, when the parents-in-law are happy with their son-in-law, they are not content simply to bask in their good fortune. They demonstrate their feelings; they offered him another wife as a present. The parents-in-law of the nurse manifested their gratitude to the nurse four times. Each time that one of the married women returned to the family village for a vacation, she returned to the conjugal hearth with one of her sisters as a present for her husband. In this manner, the nurse acquired five sisters. The five co-wives made an agreement; the family did not experience the endless quarrels that plague everyone in polygamous households. The Mossi nurse was happy, but not proud. Kabore could not brag of the manner in which he had married five women. The Naked people of the mountains, the Paleos, have no respect for males who buy all their wives through engagement-marriages. Kabore was obliged and wanted to acquire a wife, at least one wife, through the trial of abduction-marriage. And it was in that manner that he was forced to leave Tchaotchi in the colony of the Gulf.

The nurse had set his heart on a chubby woman, a real turtledove, still sparkling because she was always coated with karite oil. Since she was a modern woman, she always wore the pagne of the elegant plains-women rather than the clusters of leaves worn by mountain women. The man and woman agreed on the spot for their meeting. The nurse should have been skeptical; he did not hire a team of archers to protect him, the wife thief. Everybody had found an excuse and ducked out. The pretext was slight—custom forbade protecting an abduction-marriage by someone from outside the clan.

So the nurse arrived at the chosen spot alone. He is the first and he waits. As soon as the woman jumps out of the grass, he rushes at her, picks her up, places her across his shoulders, makes his way through the brambles, and disappears with his conquest. Like a wildcat, the husband catches up with a leap and a few strides (he was a hunter and a fighter) and pulls his wife by one foot. The kidnapper lets go and takes off, but he is not able to get far; within the space of a few strides, he is caught by the jealous husband. The husband lifts him up, throws him to the ground, and overcomes the nurse, but stops short of jabbing him in the throat with a poisoned arrow because the man is in the service of the Whites (he is an employee of the colonial administration). Trembling with fear, the Mossi nurse breaks into tears and asks forgiveness in an abject manner that a mountain man would never use. The husband-hunter spits in the nurse's face, stands up, and commands the poor man to flee like a whipped puppy with his tail between his legs. The nurse obeys in a manner that no mountain man conscious of his dignity would ever do. He is dishonored and becomes an object of scorn throughout the mountain lands.

Among the mountain peoples, death is not the only killer—a certain type of dishonor is more fatal than loss of life. The status of dishonored man prevents the nurse from ever meeting the victor face to face, from attending ceremonies for men, and requires him to remain outdoors when certain masks are brought out. It is no longer possible for him to live in the Tchaotchi mountains. He requests and is granted an assignment at the seat of the subdivision in Ramaka.

He leaves Tchaotchi for Ramaka one stormy afternoon, leading his entire tribe: the five wives, who were sisters, and their twenty-two children, who were brothers, sisters, and cousins.

The five sisters greeted Nadjuma as a guest of honor. Like all the mountain peoples of the universe, they had admiration and respect for Tchao and his wife. Each wife, in turn, wanted to welcome Nadjuma into her own hut; they vied with each other in attentiveness to the great wife champion of the unbeatable combatant, Tchao. When Tchao succumbed under torture, in his own excrement and urine, the five sisters wept with his wife and that very evening initiated the funeral rites accorded to the champions of combat.

The customs of the Naked people require a bereaved widow to spend the night when her husband is buried in the arms of a consoling man. With great generosity, the five sisters lent their husband to their guest in order to comply with this obligation. This was also a way of giving to Nadjuma the greatest honor that mountain women can bestow on a great friend: placing her in their own husband's bed.

Never pour the juice of meat into the throat of a hyena expecting him to spit it out, objects the *koroduwa* responder. Getting a taste for Nadjuma, Kabore fell in love with her and did not want to leave her again.

In her youth, Koyaga, your mother was not only a great champion, she was also a veritable turtledove of a woman who was shorter than the poinsettia and appeared rooted in the earth like a palm tree. Her breasts and her buttocks were still as firm as rocks fallen from the mountain. She braided her hair like the tail of a varanus lizard and wore a length of white cloth wrapped around her head day and night. When they met, she appeared to the nurse (and indeed was) the very opposite of his five wives.

The five sisters resembled stalks of millet. They were all tall, thin, and slightly stooped like *wapiwapo* vines. Each season, they were either waiting for a child to be born or nursing a baby, so that, day and night, they always bore the persistent stench of baby vomit and urine. What the nurse was undergoing was the worst of the disagreeable consequences known to a polygamous husband: to experience each of his wives as if she were the same body, the same spice, the same millet beer in the same bed. From night to night, he never felt anything but boredom. That boredom against which polygamy had been instituted.

Your mother brought a different kind of health, a different energy, a fresh aroma, a new intoxication to the Mossi nurse. For the man who is in love, truly in love, nights never end before daybreak. Throughout the entire day, the nurse dreamed of the festive evenings as he whistled tunes from his distant land. On the sly, he lavished presents on each wife who voluntarily surrendered her periodic nocturnal rights and allowed herself to be replaced by Nadjuma.

After weeks of successive nights in that bed, the nurse retained his appetite. One morning, he gathered all his courage and forthrightly opened up to Nadjuma: "I want to marry you." Those were five words too many.

In the life of each person, there are words that one will always regret having uttered, words that should never have come out, words that one should have swallowed: words that change destiny.

The nurse's declaration of love unleashed a storm in the forest. The eyes of Koyaga's mother bulged from their sockets. As if stung by a crazy bee, she screamed, leapt up from the bed, and ran from the house into the night. She howled in the courtyard and threw herself onto the ground. From the neighboring huts, the neighbors came out with straw torches. They gathered around her. In the light, she was thrashing about the way a sacrificial chicken with slit throat beats its wings in the dust. The screams came out lower in tone and went down to a brief whimpering. Her looks were haggard and her body petrified; her swollen tongue bulged in her mouth, from which ran a sticky, milky slobber. She was possessed. Immediately, the nurse understood. No modern European medicine could help or awaken her. At dawn, Kabore had the unfortunate woman transported to the marabout healer Bokano Yakuba. Yakuba was also a maker of amulets and an inspired creator of prayers for protection.

There is no bird that sings for an entire day without pausing; let us also take another rest, announces Bingo. The *sèrè* and his responder go into a wild musical interlude that the master closes with a series of reflections on the veneration of tradition.

The old eye comes to an end, but never the old ear.
The monkey never throws away his tail, which he inherits either from his father or his mother.
The leopard is spotted; so is his tail.

4

Ah, Tiekura! As marabouts go, Bokano Yakuba was as whole as the trunk of a baobab and as full as the *djoliba* at the height of the rainy season. Music, dance, wisdom, and longevity are, like divination, special gifts, vocations, and charms. Present unemployment in our cities tempts many clever people and numerous mendacious individuals with honeyed tongues to practice divination without possessing the gift. A swift tongue is a semi-favor from Allah; but it is not divination. The gift of divination is a total privilege that the Ubiquitous One reserves for a few chosen individuals. Bokano Yakuba was one of the chosen. Allah had gratified him, endowed him with those great and full gifts of generosity that only He possesses. That is my first assertion, Tiekura. The second is this, Tiekura. When one does not wish to be whipped by the tails of monkeys, one avoids their bands. He who does not wish to be part of our many petty tricks should stay away from villages and all human communities. Bokano lived in a camp at a half day's ride on horseback from Ramaka, the seat of our circle.

Upon arrival at the camp of this healer of the possessed, the crazy, and the incurable, Nadjuma could be seen by the light of the torches stiff on the stretcher. "The Healer of the Possessed" and "Producer of Impossible Results" were among the names given to Bokano. Throughout the mountain country and far onto the plains, people spoke with awe of his knowledge in the arts of the marabout, the Qur'an, and arts of divination. With skill and success, he managed the prophecies of Muhammad taken from the Qur'an. The jinn and souls of the ancestors kept none of their secrets from him when his fingers interrogated them in the sands of geomancy.

So what were Bokano's origins?

The day before Saturday is called Friday. Friday is the holy day of the week. One Friday, some ten years earlier, the inhabitants of Ramaka were grouped on the square in front of the mosque, awaiting the call of their muezzin. Suddenly, from the tall grass of the bush, there appeared a marabout followed by his disciples. It was Bokano and his followers. By their dusty feet, bushy beards, and bramble-shredded attire, the inhabitants divined that the strangers had come a great distance and walked for a long time. Their *salamalekun* were swiftly answered by the pious greetings of the inhabitants. The strangers took their skimpy bundles down from their heads; they stacked them in a corner of the mosque. They asked permission from no one before taking over the washroom. After their ablutions, they came out, regrouped, and chanted their sura, all the while observing with condescension and a certain haughtiness the inhabitants crowding around them. They walked around the crowd and went into the mosque, traversed it from the door to the nave, approached the first rows, and took their places on the prayer carpets reserved for the noteworthy citizens of Ramaka. This was hardly the end of their arrogance; it went even further. Their leader took the liberty of emitting the call to prayer, a privilege that the Muslims of that region had given to their old muezzin, Bakary-courini, for fifty years, explains the responder. The marabout and his disciples turned their prayers in a different manner from local practice.

After the *juma,* the Muslims of Ramaka wanted to know the name of the marabout. He had no name. Anyone who found himself obliged to name him could call him Allama (by the will of Allah). It was only later that people gave him the name of Bokano (the fortunate one). Other inhabitants asked him where he came from and where he was headed. Bokano recited some sura and answered with a riddle. He came from nowhere, was going nowhere, was present nowhere. Because the land that he had left, that upon which he presently stood, and the one to which he would go constituted the same earth, and the earth is a gift from Allah. The Muslim community of Ramaka, the Jula of Ramaka, recognized the truth of these affirmations and offered him their hospitality. He rejected it with haughty scorn. Bokano and his companions had the same host everywhere they went: the Almighty.

Everywhere, their lodging was with the Almighty, in the confines of his house, which is the mosque, and never anywhere else.

The marabout no longer remembered the names of his father and mother; his sole inspiration came from one lone man, his master, a great ulama; he saw and followed only one light, the splendor of infinite goodness.

The interpreter and the cook of the white commander of the colonial administration were among the Muslims assembled. They reported to the authorities. The words of Bokano intrigued them, and their ears bristled like those of hounds on the lookout. That day they did not whimper or growl.

Bokano and his disciples were able to spend two nights on the grounds of the mosque. On the third day, after their third prayer, they stood up as one man. With his beads around his neck and his open Qur'an in his hand, the marabout first walked forward, then went away. With hatchets and picks lent to them by the inhabitants, his disciples followed in his footsteps. They walked to a hill past the river, and there they stopped and prayed for the rest of the day and the entire night. The next morning at dawn they began to fell trees, clearing the land, digging, and finally building. In less than a month the people of Ramaka saw a village with its own mosque, streets, and especially fields, spring forth from the land. Vast fields stretched around the hill and along the river. From all the villages in the area, the inhabitants came running to wonder at the model farm that had been created in so few days. The enterprise was named Hairaidougou (village of happiness) by its creator.

One of Bokano's dogmas, as tough as the rear end of an aging baboon, was that no entreaties from any individual could reach Allah. One could not rise and succeed in being heard by Allah without appearing with a minimum of corporeal cleanliness and moral probity. Reaching the Almighty with prayer came from profession of experience combined with intelligence. This professing had its exigencies. Bokano was perpetually involved in ablutions; he used and consumed only that which was clean and whole; he repudiated anything that might be tainted with a suspicion of sin, a shadow of vice, a hint of mendacity. As nourishment, he ate only that which he had sowed and harvested himself. He drank only water that he had himself drawn from the bowels of the earth. As cover—clothing and footwear—he used only what he himself had woven, crafted, tanned, and sewn.

The disciples of Bokano prayed more or less. They were reaching Allah (the light) through work; they were laboring for Allah. They were talented craftsmen, farmers, and breeders who received not the slightest grain or seed. The master fed them, dressed them, and took responsibility for all their material needs, along with those of the spirit. Yes, especially the spiritual needs! Bokano offered the prayers that his disciples owed to Allah. He was not satisfied merely to pray for his disciples; he prayed in their place. Praying was at the same time a task and a duty.

To address Allah for such an important number of Muslims with such important needs was an immense and exhausting undertaking. Bokano worked night and day attired in his prayer pelt and with his prayer beads. He intoned sura for his disciples, their relatives, and their friends. Free of their requirement of five prayers a day, the *talibaa* disciples could use all their time for work. They stopped only to accompany the master for prayer at four o'clock in the morning, the great prayers of the Muslim feast days, and for the great service on Friday.

It seemed—everybody noticed and said so from time to time—that Allah accorded to Bokano what he requested with his beads. Pilgrims came from all parts. Some of them came with armfuls of presents and money. The master listened to their entreaties, prayed for them, and allowed them to leave after a brief sojourn. Others arrived with empty hands, young people at odds with their tribes; fleeing from barbaric initiation rites, they placed themselves at Bokano's service and became *talibaa*. The master freed a *talibaa* when he wished. But he never did so unless the disciple was sufficiently open with God, learned in the Qur'an, divination, and the practice of a trade. During the prayer of separation, the master would bless the liberated disciple and offer what he was pleased to call a little viaticum: a Qur'an, a bit of money, and even a wife sometimes. The former *talibaa* remained a disciple who could never break with Bokano.

Bokano's fame rapidly spreads beyond the circle and the colony. The swell and the incessant going and coming of pilgrims finally made the white commander at Ramaka uneasy. The commander summons him in order to register his origins, his place and date of birth.

The marabout recites a history that the commander hears with the skepticism of a civilized man. Bokano claims and explains that he comes from a land squeezed between and lost in the immensity of a lake, the incommensurability of the desert, and the infinite blue of the sky. A very distant and beautiful country! He had as his master a holy ulama, one of Allah's elect, known and respected throughout Saharan

Africa. A man to whom Allah, in his infinite goodness, had given everything and who was able to accomplish everything. But he no longer remembers either the name of the country or that of the holy man. He
forgot them the day he was struck by revelation. In the course of pro-
longed sessions of nocturnal prayer that he had spent with the holy
ulama, Bokano had slept on his mat. He had been gripped by a dream
that any Muslim would want to experience. On a white steed, with
beads in hand, he had charged toward the east, climbing into the sky.
In the milky whiteness of the sun, the holy Kaba had appeared and he
had felt himself a light, winged creature. He bathed and sailed in a
world of delectation, a world of infinite enjoyment and pleasure. He
was brutally shaken and awakened by the ulama.

"Bokano, wake up! Wake up, Bokano! Repeat ten times after me,
'*Allahu akbar! Allahu akbar!*' (Allah is great!)"

Bokano repeats that ten times.

"You are one of the elect. You have been elected to succeed me. To
succeed me with my belongings, my fortune, my role, my dignity, my
presence, my friendships, my powers. Repeat ten times after me the
sura *Kouhouha.*"

Bokano had recited that sura ten times.

Bokano attempts to recount his dream to the holy man. The master
stops his explanation. He has already been informed of the dream. He
reveals the importance and the meaning of the dream to Bokano. It
means that Bokano has just died to be reborn. He is a new man. A new
man who was to free himself of the ulama, leave the country, and go
on, leave that very night, before daybreak. To walk in the same direction, never stopping, pursuing his course until the next manifestation
of the Almighty. His master, the ulama, awakened twenty of his pupils
and presented them to their new master. It was Bokano himself. They
had to follow him, follow him night and day. The only place on this
earth where Bokano could lead them was Mecca, the only place to
which he could take them beyond this world was paradise. The holy
man blessed Bokano and his disciples and offered Bokano two things
as a viaticum. Two treasures that were worth more than all the fortunes
of the universe. The two objects must always remain on Bokano's person, accompany him everywhere that he might live up to the moment
of his death.

The first was an ancient Holy Qur'an. The holy man had inherited
it from his paternal ancestors. His forebears had acquired it during
the Islamization of the Sahara and had always carried it with them.

Whoever has that Qur'an enjoys divine protection against invocations, evocations, and conspiracies. Whatever person the bearer places under the protection of that Qur'an acquires invincibility against all spells.

The second treasure was an aerolite inherited through his maternal ancestors. His mother came from a great line of holy fetishists of Wagadou (ancient Ghana). The chiefs of a line that has kept this aerolitic stone with them since the eras of the pharaohs.

Whoever bears that aerolite with him is protected against all sorts of sorcery, evil charms, and spells. Whomever the bearer places underneath the protection of the aerolite will be safe against all sorcery, all bewitching.

All the mystics and savants of the Sahara have known for centuries about the existence of the Qur'an and the aerolite. Everybody wishes to possess them.

But there was a mystery, an enigma, a difficulty. The Qur'an and the aerolite cannot be transferred by acquisition or as a gift. These objects themselves must indicate to the person who carries them the human being to whom they wish to be given. They make this known through a dream. The night when both decide to leave their owner—which they had just done—is above all the greatest happiness. In his infinite goodness, Allah has deemed that the bearer's ledger is complete and has found him worthy to come closer; the Almighty opens his garden to the faithful person.

We left the ulama in an atmosphere of sadness. Nobody had said it, but nobody was unaware of it, it was obvious: the holy man was living his final hours. Before the end of the day, he was to sleep the restful sleep of the elect.

At some distance from the village, the tree beneath which Bokano and his followers had fallen asleep was struck by lightning. The crash deafened them, and they fell into a deep sleep. They awoke with the break of day, all of them stricken by amnesia, all of them changed. Not one among them remembered where they had come from, where they were going, his own name or forebears. They began walking again in the only direction they could see: toward the rising sun. They avoided villages and hamlets as they walked, eating only roots and wild fruit, sleeping in the branches of trees in order not to be disturbed by wild animals.

One Friday, after their ablutions, they were about to line up to pray the *juma* when Bokano suddenly stood up and cried out ninety-nine times, *"Allahu akbar."* In the clouds, he had discerned, distinctly written, the name of the prophet. It was most assuredly a sign, the manifestation that they were awaiting. They understood: they had arrived, they did not hesitate an instant. They came out of nowhere and appeared at a mosque where all the inhabitants of a city were expecting them for prayer. It was the mosque of the city of Ramaka. Ramaka (the seat of the *cercle* where the Naked people of the mountains dwelled) was the place where they must wait for another sign from the Almighty.

Despite all the long explanations of all the black Muslim agents, the white commander was not convinced. He did not believe the story. He was not a Muslim but a Nazarene, and he did not believe that total amnesia had struck Bokano and his companions at daybreak. He ordered an inquiry. Confidentially, the commander learned that Bokano might belong to a sect of Islamic fundamentalists, the fundamentalists who had massacred Europeans in the French Sudan and in Upper Volta. The sect of Bobo Dioulasso in Upper Volta had been led by a marabout whom the colonial administration had arrested one night and shot at dawn, along with a certain number of his disciples. Might that executed agitator not be the one Bokano called the Holy Man? One group of the marabout's disciples had time to disappear and to escape the pursuit of the infantrymen; they had never been apprehended. Bokano and his disciples might be part of the fugitive group. The inquiry continued.

In the meanwhile, the commander informed Bokano that he was under house arrest at Ramaka. He could not leave without prior approval from the colonial authorities. Pilgrims and all visitors must request passes. Bokano was required to report to the commander's office each Friday and to give a full verbal report of his activities for the week.

The restrictions on Bokano's movements and the nuisance controls had no other effect than drawing more young and sick people to the camp. The marabout's reputation as an exorcist for mad and possessed people spread throughout West Africa.

That is why the nurse, at dawn, transported the possessed woman to the entrance of the inner courtyard of Bokano, the sole master of the site (after Allah).

This courtyard was at once a reading room, a school, a site for palaver, and a mosque. Remaining unconscious, Nadjuma was still possessed by the spirits.

The marabout exorcist's simple, rapid, and efficacious therapy varied little: a drubbing, a volley of blows, and a switching, regardless of who the patient was. He muttered verses from the Qur'an, stood up and was about to approach the patient, when he stopped. In the name of Allah, Koyaga's mother was beautiful. A very beautiful woman! She had kept the flesh of a maiden: her breasts stood out like raw mangoes in the first days of April; her muscles bulged solidly, and her buttocks had the round consistency of a cast-iron kettle. Her pagne was loosely draped; the marabout exorcist got lost in his sura, coughed, and started over several times with his series of *Allahu akbar* and getting the proper incantations in order. He finally succeeded and resolutely approached the stretcher to apply, with all his strength, four resounding blows to the patient. As if straightened by a silver pine, the woman sat up but remained half unconscious. The marabout signaled to one of his *talibaa,* who began reciting incantations, spit on a long rod he was carrying, approached, and with all his strength whipped the possessed woman. The patient yelped and took off. She ran so swiftly that her pagne dropped; once more, the marabout had the opportunity of observing appreciatively the young woman's body. In an instinctive gesture as unexpected as it was delayed, he had the cloth picked up and bade her to come back. She came to the entrance decently clad and as healthy in spirit as in body. Exorcised.

Usually, the marabout loses interest in the crazy and possessed people who have been exorcised by whipping. Everybody noted that, as an exception, he treated Nadjuma with great respect and a paternal manner. Three or four times he massaged the head of the patient, who kept writhing some time after the lashing given by the zealous *talibaa,* continues Tiekura. Confirming his exceptional interest in the patient, the marabout ordered one of the houses reserved for distinguished guests to be prepared for Nadjuma.

Returning to the courtyard, the marabout gave a justification for the unusual care and treatments. By certain signs, the marabout had perceived that the patient was one of the blessed, one of the elect. Born with the gift of divination, she had been possessed by Fa, the spirit of divination. The marabout was going to keep her several months at the farm in order to instruct her in the divination by geomancy. He listed the numerous prohibitions that the possessed woman, wife of the spirit of divination, must observe. She must remain chaste. Her partners would at any moment be under the threat of the spirit's vengeful anger and she herself might fall into a trance from which she would not recover if she did not abstain from all sexual relations.

The nurse trembled at the idea that he had fallen in love with the wife of the spirit Fa. He sacrificed a sheep and two chickens to assuage the spirit's anger.

After the marabout's revelations, Nadjuma felt relieved. Everything seemed to clear up; she understood and was happy. The fear that had gripped her since the death of her husband whenever men came close had been a form of possession. It was the spirit who had rendered her frigid following the difficult labor she had endured to bring Koyaga into the world. She decided to devote herself to clairvoyance and geomancy.

The marabout Bokano was learned in divination. He knew and used the ten divinatory arts: the Yi-king, geomancy, cartomancy, runes, qahwamancy, encaustomancy, acutomancy, grammatomancy, crystalomancy, and radiomancy. He treated geomancy as the knowledge of all things known and placed it above the other nine arts.

Geomancy had come from heaven soon after the creation of the universe. Allah, the Almighty, after shaping the world, decided to go away for a rest, far from the reach of human senses. The creator of everything here below was well deserving; the work accomplished was unique and incomparable. In one final gesture, Allah returned with the intention of perfecting that which was perfect. What was his surprise to discover that while he had been constructing the universe, liars, hypocrites, and the jealous had abused the freedom given to humans. They had taken over control of human society. The communities of animals were superior to those of humans. Beasts did not kill and destroy each other unless it was in the interest of survival or defense; human beings often annihilated each other for no reason, from viciousness or jealousy, continued the responder. Would it be necessary to remake the world, which in so many ways was so perfectly built, but which in other ways had turned out unjust, allowing the wicked to triumph? Allah hesitated for an entire night.

The successful making of another, totally just world would be arduous and success not guaranteed. He was in a hurry (he was expected elsewhere). But did he have to leave all human beings, even those who were wise, at the mercy of the wicked? The Merciful One could not do that. So he decided to put geomancy at the disposition of the elect, the prudent, and the sages in order that they might protect themselves against unjust fates and the wicked.

As a result, there were two types of blindness on this earth. First of all, there were those who had irremediably lost their sight and who traveled with a white cane in order to avoid obstacles. Those were the sightless blind. But those who did not believe and who did not use clairvoyance or sacrifices: they are the universally blind. They run headlong into all obstacles, all misfortunes that prevent their destiny from being fully realized. May Allah preserve us from remaining among or from continuing to dwell perpetually among the universally blind.

Several months after their separation, the marabout continued thinking of the young woman. She prevented him, against his will, from gaining access, body and soul, to Allah, the Almighty. Following the fervent prayers of *rhirib* and *icha,* between two and three o'clock in the morning, the marabout was accustomed to emerge from his house and to remain on the doorsill, scrutinizing the sky. Among the clouds hovering between the stars, he found signs of the undefinable and the ineffable. This quest had been perturbed several times by the inopportune and blasphemous irruption of visions of the young woman. In the heavens, he discovered the young woman's glance, her muscles, her half-undone pagne, and even . . . The marabout stopped his quest, repeated the *sarafulahi* (Allah's pardon) ninety-nine times, and prescribed for himself several supplementary days of extreme fasting by way of penance.

Upon awaking one morning, his glance, words, and sura were grave. He dispatched one of his pupils, who returned with Nadjuma and with you, Koyaga, her only son. He received you with piety and great pomp at the courtyard. He recited several verses of the Qur'an, and, allowing time for the griot to repeat after him each word, word for word, he announced the incredible news to you. The night before, the aerolite that his master's maternal lineage had possessed for millennia had appeared in a dream. The aerolite that had made Cissè's family one of the most powerful in the Sahara had addressed him in a dream. It had told him that he was moving. The aerolite had informed him that he had chosen Nadjuma as the bearer, the woman who would possess it. Let the will of the Almighty ever be done on earth and in heaven. Amen!

The master traced some symbols in the sand in order to reveal Koyaga's future and asked his mother to interpret what the geomantic figures told. His mother's face lit up. She was happy to learn that her son was going to be greater than his father. He was going to avenge his father. The master congratulated the geomancer for her talent. He finished the analyses.

There are two sorts of destiny in life. The destiny of those who blaze trails in the great lands of life and of those who follow existing trails. The former confront obstacles and the unknown. They are al-

Waiting for the Vote of the Wild Animals

ways wet with the morning dew because they are the first to push aside the grass entwined over the path.

The latter follow marked paths, they follow the well-established trails, they follow the explorers, the masters. They are unfamiliar with the soaking morning dew, the challenging obstacles, the unknown of the dead of night, the unknown of infinite spaces. Their problem in life is to find their own man of destiny. Their man of destiny is the one they must follow to develop themselves fully, to be definitively happy. It is never easy to find one's man of destiny; one is never sure of having found him.

The former, those who venture in the early morning into the bush, who blaze trails, the pioneers, also have their problem, their difficulty: that of knowing exactly when to stop, of knowing their limits; of not going beyond or stopping short of their point of perfect equilibrium. At their point of equilibrium, they are happy, they have exactly what they need—neither more nor less. They are totally fulfilled. If they stop short, they are sick with jealousy, miserable at having excess energy, miserable at being constantly underoccupied. Beyond that, they suffer from falling short, from their inability to perform, from being exhausted.

It is never easy to determine where to stop; one is never sure of having found that point.

Your son, added the marabout, is of the human race that explores, the men who lead others, the masters, those who know how to stop in time, those who neither stop short nor pass beyond.

Unfortunately, according to the diverse position of the geomantic figures, your son will go far, but will pass beyond the limits. He will finish too great, and therefore too small; too happy, therefore, unfortunate. He will be our pupil and our master, our wealth and our poverty, our happiness and our misfortune. Great! Everything that is sublime, beautiful, and good, along with the opposite of each, is in this child.

In order that Allah might gratify him with long life, we are going to protect him—you with the power of the aerolitic stone and I with that of the Qur'an.

Men of your son's race can never be just and humane, while neither the aerolitic stone nor the Qur'an can tolerate iniquity and ferocity. He could often be our perdition. Teach him that if perchance we were not there for him, he should not be thrown into panic. Let him quietly have his purificatory deeds, his cathartic *donsomana* recited by a *sèrè* (the singer of hunters) accompanied by a *koroduwa* responder. A *koro-*

duwa is an initiate of the sacred grove in his cathartic phase, a village jester. When he has confessed, recognized everything, when he is purified, when there no longer exists any shadow in his life, the aerolitic stone and the Qur'an will reveal where they are hidden. He will only need to seek them and to carry out his life as a guide and a chief.

Let us stop this *sumu* here; there is no long day that is not ended by a night. So announces Bingo. The *sèrè* takes up his *kora* and performs the musical finale for the *sumu*. The *koroduwa Tiekura accompanies* him at first. Abruptly, as if stung by a bee, he howls, emits obscenities, and gives himself up to dances of the hunt and lascivious gestures. The *sèrè* Bingo offers his final proverbs and adages about tradition and the veneration of tradition.

If the little mouse abandons the paths of his fathers, the prickles of the couch grass will put out his eyes.
Whatever tree your father may climb, if you cannot climb after him, at least place your hand on the trunk.
He who hides from people's eyes hugs his mother's pubis.

Second *Sumu*

The *sèrè* performs the musical prelude. The *koroduwa* gets carried away with outlandish and lewd gibes.

Tiekura, stop those shameful gestures and remember the theme I am going to develop in the pauses during this second *sumu* of the *donsomana*. It will center on death. Because:

When you see mice frolicking on the cat's back, you measure the challenge death can inflict on us.

Death is the older child, life its younger sibling. We humans are in error when we oppose death to life.

They say death is preferable to shame, but one must quickly add that shame bears fruit, while death has none.

5

Ah, master hunter Koyaga! You are of the race of the high born, from an egg laid by the sparrow hawk and hatched by the crow. You are of the race of those who forge over the bush in the morning, those who are always wet with dew.

Your mother, an expert in geomancy (she has a meteorite), has as her confidant, master, and friend a marabout with no father or mother and who possesses a venerable Qur'an. Not a day dawns or ends that she does not make live sacrifices for you in your name, in the name of her only son. Destiny has never surprised those who perpetually engage in blood sacrifices. Misfortune avoids them. On their road through life, they do not stumble on the pebbles of mischance but rather on those of advantageous fortune, continues the responder, Tiekura.

Upon your return as a wounded soldier, you were sent to the military hospital. They examined you. You were as sound as a carp at the end of the rainy season, as healthy as a baobab pod in the cemetery. You could reenlist if you wished, continue to climb in the ranks of the infantrymen. They explained to you that they were no longer seeking Paleos for the Far East, but for North Africa—for Algeria, where the French had opened a new zone of colonial war. In the captain's office, they explained the numerous advantages offered to reenlistees for Algeria and paid in cash your wages as a veteran of Indochina. More than 100,000 CFA francs. That was too much money for the young mountain man you were at the time, a bit more than you even dreamed of or needed. With those excessive riches, you immediately ran out of the office, bought a rifle, slung it over your shoulder, and went to catch the first bush taxi for the mountains, adds the responder.

We organized a welcome—as a *sèrè,* I was part of the group because Koyaga was already a master hunter. We put together a welcome befitting his glory, his fortune, and his good luck. Hunters lined up at the post office silk cotton tree on the little hill overlooking Ramaka. Their slave rifles thundered welcoming salvos as soon as the postal truck emerged from the cloud of dust. The vultures and giant bats flew up from the clusters of mango and tamarind trees and swirled in the dust of the fantasias.

It was under a leaden sky that you had the privilege of welcoming Koyaga. And you, Master, were at the side of the hero's mother, the seer Nadjuma. You had been invited to welcome an exceptional hunter. The hunter was a war hero. The hero, a rich man. This was your first encounter with Koyaga, explains Macledio.

Ah, Tiekura, the first encounter with a blessed person is always different from the contact with an unfortunate one. That first harmattan with the son of the Naked man and woman, our future Supreme Guide, was unlike any other harmattan in your life, continues the responder. The Paleo mountains have never engendered a more ferocious slayer of animals than you, Koyaga.

Beyond the mountains, at the edge of a river in the valley, was a solitary panther.

This panther lived on human flesh alone, adds the responder. In the night, his eyes glowed like beams from lighthouses and trucks. His fangs clattered like the branches of the silk cotton tree knocking against each other in the storm. His tongue licked his beard as the brushfire burns and cleanses the ground. For ages, all hunters worshiped fetishes and presented blood sacrifices to avoid meeting him along their paths.

Those who ran into him by bad luck in the great pitiless bush stole away on tiptoe with their slave rifle pointed at the ground. They recited ritual verses and used their best subterfuges to escape the powerful olfactory sense of the monster, adds Tiekura.

Waiting for the Vote of the Wild Animals

The panther no longer feared men, no longer avoided them, and, as a matter of pride, no longer protected himself with any of the numerous spells that he can use against hunters. "Boom!" went Koyaga's shot, and the panther fell to the ground. The blood-gorged monster had just passed from life to death.

To destroy, to extinguish all the powerful _nyama_ of the monster, Koyaga cut off his tail and crammed it in his maw, explains Tiekura.

By planting the end of the beast (his tail) in his beginning (his maw), all the _nyama_ are forced to remain whirling in a closed circuit within the remains of the beast, explains Macledio.

Thank you and thank you again! Ever our thanks, Koyaga, for having avenged the hundreds of humans whose throats have been mercilessly ripped open by the panther.

At the edge of a forest beyond the mountains, there was also a solitary black buffalo, the most ancient of all the buffalo in the universe. Between its horns there nested colonies of swallows and firebugs. Hundreds of sparrow hawks and other birds of prey continually whirled above the beast. Its presence could be noted kilometers away from the hordes and flocks of birds that darkened the horizon. This solitary buffalo feared neither men nor hunters. He respected neither plantations nor villages. Before going into the bush, hunters sacrificed white chickens in the hope of not encountering him on their path. As soon as they sensed his presence, entire villages lay low. For all the Paleo peoples and all the humans of the region, this buffalo was a veritable calamity.

Boom! The bullet from the carbine of the soothsayer's son thundered and sped away. The buffalo did not slump down. He knew of the misfortune that had transported the panther from life to death and he had prepared himself. He gathered terrible charms after the sparrow scouts informed him that Koyaga the hunter had arrived in the bush. Before the bullet reached him, the numerous nests perched between his horns were transmuted into so many tufts of flame, and the birds taking off from those nests became showers of sparks falling into the grass. Surrounded by a leaping brushfire, Koyaga escaped with his life thanks only to the charm that permitted him to liquefy himself, to transform himself into a torrent that smothered the flames. Boom! The second shot sped from the torrent and struck the monster, who knelt before falling down. The buffalo had just perished.

In order to stop and destroy the buffalo's terrible _nyama_, Koyaga cut his tail off and stuffed it into his steaming maw.

Thank you and thank you again, Koyaga! Ever our thanks!

In a forest on the mountains of Paleo country, there was also a solitary elephant. His tusks were as protruding and heavy as the trunk of a young silk cotton tree. His ears were as large as the roof of a village granary. In the mercilessly vast and towering forest, the transhumance of an elephant herd is a cataclysm. I shall pause and expand for a moment on the calamity of transhumance.

The transhumance of large creatures produces, first of all, a flow and ebb of beasts and birds of all species. Hundreds of pachyderms rip off and destroy the lianas, fell trees, and create a corridor with their advance. In the silence of the great tropical forest, the thundering is more deafening than storms in the month of April. Monkeys, antelope, serpents, and frightened birds abandon their lairs, scatter and run or fly toward more hospitable refuges. That is the ebb.

Beneath the feet of the pachyderms, however, the ground is covered with acorns, flowers, and fresh fruit, delicate and fresh from the treetops. This is the nourishment sought by the foragers who, faced with temptation, rush in whole colonies beneath the feet of the elephants. And by the thousands they are crushed. Their remains draw the carnivorous and predatory beasts. The steaming dung that covers the corridor created by the herd draws clouds of insects that are chased and eaten by thousands of sparrows. In turn, the sparrows are pursued by hundreds of birds of prey. So rushing herds of foragers and carnivores, clouds of insects, and swarms of birds, engulfed in the corridor opened by the pachyderms, fly over and follow the herd. That is the flow.

This solitary beast of the little forest in Paleo country could by himself create the ebb and flow of beasts and birds attracted by the great herds of pachyderms of the deep tropical forest. He destroyed crops and left behind mountains of dung on the plantations. On occasion, ever accompanied by his usual retinue of beasts and birds, he even traveled into the villages, removing the roofs of granaries and partaking of the harvests with impunity. For ages, hunters had lain low when they heard his approach. The solitary elephant knew of the mishap that had befallen his brothers, the panther and the buffalo, and he, the creature who roamed everywhere, he who prevents us from seeing the mountains, disappeared, adds the responder.

Still armed with your 350 Remington magnum carbine, Koyaga, you relentlessly set out in the forest to hunt him one Thursday morning at dawn. You walked for a day and a night. The day after Thursday is Friday. Friday at noon, bang! The shot sped forward. The solitary creature was not hit; he had changed into a needle, the smallest of human tools. Thanks to a charm inherited from your mother, you became thread. The thread raises the needle. Bang! A second shot resounded. The solitary one is still on his feet. He turned into fire and fire threatens the thread. You change into wind and wind extinguishes fire. Bang! For the third time, a shot from the 350 Remington magnum speeds off. Boom! A fourth shot rings out. The elephant did not have time to change into a mountain in order to resist the wind. The monster kneels. Boom! The rifle thunders for the fifth time. The elephant collapses. He perishes. Now you must simply counteract the *nyama* of the elephant by stuffing his tail in his maw—you sling your rifle over your shoulder and leave.

From all the mountains, villages, and fortified villages, the inhabitants come out or descend with long knives to replenish their supplies of meat. There is some for everybody: men, hyenas, and vultures.

Thank you, Koyaga, thank you again! Ever our thanks!

At the foot of the mountains in northern Paleo country, there flows a river. In one of the bends in the river, above the waterfall, there is a headrace of limpid water. In past times, among the trees hanging over the race, there were numerous sparrows surveying the limpidity of the flow, constantly removing the least twig or dead leaf that polluted it. In this way, these birds always paid homage to the water monster, the millenary saurian, the crocodile of Gbeglerini, who lived in the race. From head to tail, the beast measured more than ten paces, and an entire steer could stand on his shoulders.

This was the sacred crocodile who snatched a laundry maid every year as the waters rose unless he was offered a bull calf, a goat, and a sheep, explains Macledio. It was a terrible duty, an awesome tribute; the country needed to be rid of this homicidal beast.

As soon as you decided to undertake that public duty, the crocodile filled your sleep with dreams by which he attempted to alert you, to dissuade you from it. With great care, you reported all the dreams to your mother, to the marabout Bokano, and to other elders of the country. And, with just as great care, you slew and offered all the sacrifices recommended by those people.

Ah, Tiekura! The first morning Koyaga arose to engage battle against the sacred crocodile, he did not go far. The revered saurian, a killer and a sorcerer, had hidden his path. At some distance from the village, Koyaga became lost and no longer recognized the path leading to the race. The next morning, he headed south, although the river and the crocodile were in the north. Through this subterfuge, he managed to lull the monster's vigilance and, as the crocodile was preparing to take a sunbath on a hillock, he was surprised to see the hunter's reflection in the waters of his race. Face to face, the crocodile and the son of the Naked man and woman hurled challenges at each other.

I have come to kill you, announces Koyaga point-blank.

I am eternal, like this country; as impenetrable to bullets as the mountains and as immortal as the river in which you are reflected. You, the presumptuous hunter, are the one that I shall kill this morning. I shall make of you this morning's breakfast.

Koyaga does not wait for the beast to finish his pretentious speech before he aims and fires. The bullet ricochets on the surface of the water, metamorphoses into a ball of fire, and returns toward Koyaga, who barely dodges it by changing into a crab buried in the sand. The ball of fire lights a brushfire on the bank. Koyaga exits from his refuge and fires at the beast a second time. This time the ball emerges from the water as a flying serpent and descends on Koyaga, who dodges it by changing into an earthworm. The serpent follows its course and is annihilated by the brushfire raging on the bank. The beast, fully confident of its spells, comes out of the water, appears in its fearful monstrousness on the beach to defy Koyaga once more.

I shall eat you! roars the crocodile, gnashing its fangs.

That was a fatal mistake; the beast exposed its flank. The Paleo hunter emerges from his refuge, aims at the lower belly, which is not covered by carapace, and fires. The beast tries to return to the water. As it turns around, it exposes its throat, unprotected by the carapace, another soft part toward which the hunter, son of the Naked woman, discharges his rifle. Mortally wounded, the monster flutters and falls back in the water with its claws in the air. The hero of Indochina, that elite marksman, aims three more times and fires at the beast's side and breast. He slings his rifle back over his shoulder and kneels behind a tree to witness the giant's agony.

For a half day the monster thrashes about in the water, struggling against death. It lets out a terrifying bellow that is intensified by echoes and reaches the level of the hurricane's roar. All the animals that usually come to drink at the river before sundown witness the beast's death in silence. In the blood frothing on the lake, the crocodile gives up his spirit at the setting of the sun. Before night finally takes over the bush, Koyaga emerges from his hiding place, dives into the blood-reddened lake, and swims to the monster's remains, where he cuts off the tail and stuffs it into his maw.

Waiting for the Vote of the Wild Animals

The inhabitants of Tchaotchi were already in bed when you returned, Koyaga.

With your Remington magnum, Mister President and Supreme Guide, it was not enough to dispatch four monsters that had terrorized all the lands of the Paleos. You also killed, turned into orphans and widowers, a bunch of antelope, monkeys, and boars. It is impossible to list all the exploits of the born *sinbo* that you are, adds Macledio.

Every evening, we organized *sumu*, dances and hunters' feasts. Koyaga, you were the only hunter to provide wild game for the dances, feasts, and *sumu*. You were the only one who could manage because you were more skillful and you possessed a modern arm that no other hunter in the mountains had used before you. You not only furnished game for the feasts, *sumu*, and dances, you also financed them. You were the only person who could pay for the rice, millet, *dolo*, wine, and beer because they had given you part of your money as a combat veteran of Indochina. You were the richest Paleo in the mountains. You were rich, very rich for a Paleo. But no fortune is boundless. Seven successive nights make a week. Thirty successive nights make a moon. For many weeks, almost four moons, the feasting, dancing, and drinking continued uninterrupted. The harmattan does not last much more than four moons in our mountains. The rainy season set in.

No fortune can outlast four long moons of generosity and waste, of spending on feasts, dances, and drinking bouts: these festivities finally ruined you. Penniless and in debt, you stopped the feasting. One night, with your hands and pockets empty, you caught the first bush taxi leaving for the capital.

When poverty and debt assail, it is always at night and clandestinely that one leaves the country in which one has been received as a rich man, concludes the responder.

You needed money; money, urgently.

The hunter on the lookout for game stops to listen to the wind. Let us follow his example and take a breath. So announces the *sèrè* as he begins a musical interlude. The *koroduwa* Tiekura makes some lascivious gestures. Bingo delivers these proverbs on death.

It takes time to grow, but death comes without delay.
The place where one awaits death need not be vast.
If God takes the life of a rich man, he kills a friend; if he takes the life of a poor man, he kills scum.

6

Fortunately, Koyaga had reenlisted before going up to his native village of Tchaotchi. The numerous creditors who had been hounding him came by train from the North and arrived in the capital too late. Koyaga had already embarked for Algeria, where the French were beginning to get bogged down once more in a new zone of colonial warfare opened after Indochina. Koyaga was assigned to the Oran region in western Algeria, where he distinguished himself by his acts of bravery. Intrepid deeds that earned him a promotion to the rank of sergeant.

One morning, Sergeant Koyaga arrived happy and quite jovial. He was whistling and singing aloud the melody of an initiatory song from his village. At the mess hall, he bought a round for all the noncommissioned officers in the regiment. That was to toast an event. The Republic of the Gulf, his native country, had just gained its independence. After twenty years of struggle, President Fricassa Santos had grasped independence for the territory of the Gulf. Koyaga was celebrating the event because, at the end of his enlistment, in two years, he would leave the French army, get out of the colonial wars and operations distant from Africa, and join the young national army of his country. He would surely be able to reenlist in his country's army with the rank of an officer. In two years, he would put his experience at the service of his country. That was an event to celebrate, to toast. One is always better off at home. A man will never be seen or accepted as a great healer of leprosy if his mother is covered with sores.

His sojourn and the war in Algeria lasted less than two years. From his country place at Colombey-les-Deux-Églises, General de Gaulle, with eyes half open like an old crocodile, was following the events in Algeria. One morning, he became angry. Great soldier that he was, he could not stand the inefficacy of the French army in Algeria. Without the least hesitation, he took control of power in France. Once he was in the Élysée Palace, he stopped the war; he made the colonists in Algeria (the *pieds-noirs*) and the French soldiers embark for Marseilles. The African infantrymen, the Senegalese infantrymen were all sent home to be mustered out—France had just rejected colonial warfare for good. Koyaga found himself in the capital of the Republic of the Gulf.

Like his other African comrades from the Algerian conflict, Koyaga requested assignment to the young national army being constituted. He was surprised, very surprised, to discover that his request, the request of all of them, was not honored. The president of the republic did not want any Paleo mercenaries who had spent all their time as soldiers of fortune warring against the freedom of colonized peoples.

Koyaga and his comrades requested jobs reserved for veterans. These jobs were given to those who had participated in the resistance, who had fought against the colonialists, but not to the Paleo mercenaries. The returnees from Algeria had to go back to farming in their village or live unemployed in the city.

The French authorities were giving mustering-out pay and military pensions to those returning from Algeria. Koyaga and the Paleo infantrymen went to the French embassy to obtain their money. They were given the explanation that, upon the request of the president of the republic, father-of-the-nation-and-independence, the mustering-out pay and the military pensions had been deposited in the national treasury of the Republic of the Gulf. The national treasurer would, when he had time, call the beneficiaries one by one.

Faced with so many refusals and such intransigence, Koyaga returned to his village and consulted the geomancers, his mama, Nadjuma, and the marabout Bokano. They informed him about the character of Fricassa Santos. His totem was the boa constrictor, and his nickname was "the elegant gentleman," the *yovo*. The elegant gentleman of the boa totem was a grand initiate, a powerful sorcerer who feared the tragic end that seers had foreseen for him. He had been warned against the veterans. The president's seers had warned him never to accept or tolerate the veterans of Indochina in the national army. This was because there was, among the Paleo veterans, a man whose magic was very powerful and who might assassinate the president in spite of all his magic charms and the mystical ablutions protecting him.

Koyaga and the half-pay veterans had understood and found justified the ostracism that the president had imposed on them. They decided to give up their claim to service in the national army, but not the claim to their money. They continued to request a meeting with the chief of state and to claim their money.

They finally obtained an appointment with a minister of state, the minister for internal affairs, Thursday at three P.M. They arrived at the ministry at two P.M. At seven P.M., the minister was still unavailable. At seven-thirty, they were all angry to the point of insanity because of the long wait and the scorn with which they were being treated. That was the moment when they were invited into the office of the cabinet director.

The minister sent his excuses: he had been in an unexpected meeting with the president of the republic all afternoon. He was deeply regretful that he could not hear the delegation. He had charged his cabinet director with repeating and explaining the decision of the president of the republic to them. The decision was definitive; the dossier had been definitively dealt with and closed.

"We understand why he does not want us in the national army. Some sorcerers have lied to him and warned him against us. We have understood, we pardon him for his attitude, and we have decided to give up our request to serve. We are only requesting our pensions, our mustering-out pay, our money," said Koyaga.

"They will be disbursed to you later. For the moment, the funds are in the treasury; they are helping to sustain state coffers."

Koyaga became angry; in a wild gesture, he leapt from his chair, threw himself on the cabinet director, squeezed him. He was about to strangle the man. The other infantrymen intervened, separated the two men, and pulled Koyaga away. The cabinet director collapsed in his chair, half conscious. Koyaga, restrained by his comrades, was frothing with anger and kept on yelling.

"Let me go! Let me go! I'll kill him, I'm going to kill him. Then, I'll go to the presidential palace. I'll demand the president give us the money we earned with our blood."

The police came running in, overcame Koyaga, and arrested him. They locked him up in the central prison of the capital for several weeks. He was transported in chains to the prison at Ramaka. With instructions to sequester him in the cell, that sinister cell, in which his father had died.

President Fricassa Santos, who had refused to enlist the Paleo mercenaries in the young national army of the Republic of the Gulf, was different from other heads of state in the French-speaking countries. He was an exception. His career had been distinctive. The other fathers-of-the-nation-and-independence had been invented and manufactured by General de Gaulle. Fricassa Santos was a self-made father-of-the-nation-and-independence, the source of his own prosperity. He had fought for independence and had become chief of state by winning over General de Gaulle's candidate in a UN-supervised election. He was not a father-of-the-nation-and-independence invented and manufactured in France by General de Gaulle.

After the defeat in Indochina and the war in Algeria, General de Gaulle and France had decided to decolonize the French possessions in black Africa. For obvious reasons, it had seemed impossible to integrate into the French body politic a subcontinent inhabited by nearly fifty million Black savages, mostly primitive and sometimes cannibalistic, without running the risk of eventually allowing France to be colonized, in the long or short term, by its own colonies. It was equally impossible to leave these vast and rich territories and the considerable French investments and interest in the hands of African leaders, who were inexperienced, lying, and unconscious demagogues. General de Gaulle's political genius allowed him to find a satisfactory solution to the problem. De Gaulle managed to grant independence without decolonization. He succeeded in this by inventing and maintaining the presidents of the republic, who entitled themselves "fathers-of-the-nation-and-independence" in their respective countries although they had done absolutely nothing for the independence of their countries and were not even the true masters, the true leaders of their peoples.

General de Gaulle easily succeeded in completing his project because of the earlier measures of liberalization already accorded to the indigenous populations of the colonies by the France of Human Rights. France had outlawed the forced labor to which the autochthonous peoples had been subjected during the conquest. It had also granted equality without modifying by one cowrie shell the other regulations and practices of discrimination and racism. In a formal manner, France had accorded French citizenship to all Blacks, even to the Naked people, the Paleos. She had allocated seats in the assemblies to all the Black agitators who had graduated from the William Ponty School in Gorée and who, at the head of unions, had barricaded roads and set fire to a few houses. General de Gaulle's happy discovery had been the creation of the French Community with those Black leaders who, once acclimated to the banks of the Seine, feared an immediate and definitive return to their native bush. So concludes the responder.

And the Community succeeded everywhere, except in the Republic of the Mountains, where reigned the Man in White of the hare totem, who had not yet grown new feathers and turned into a bloodthirsty dictator. In the other territories, the Community had succeeded, through rigged legislative elections and referenda, in getting each colony to accept by plebiscite the man chosen by General de Gaulle and whose pronouncements did not counter too greatly the colonialist thesis of the inferiority of the thieving and slothful Black. The new head of the government chosen by the general had been forced, sometimes despite his own reticence—as in the Republic of the Ebony People, insinuates the responder—to proclaim the independence of the colony in interdependence and complete friendship with France. Once the solemn proclamation was made public, he presented the flag suggested to him as the emblem of the nation, had sung the national anthem composed for him, put on the Great Sash of the Order that he had just instituted, and proclaimed himself the president redeemer, father-of-the-nation-and-independence of the new republic.

De Gaulle had also dispatched a Caravelle to pick up the new chief of state: the latter along with his wives and servants. The Caravelle landed with them in Nice, where, for an entire week, masters of ceremony taught the new president, and more especially the new madame president, the indispensable rudiments and rules of etiquette that one must follow in order to advance in the Elysian court of General de Gaulle.

The Caravelle and the Mercedes took them aboard once more and transported them to Paris, to the square in front of the Élysée Palace. Before the hypnotized universe, General de Gaulle in person confirmed the plebiscite in his new charge to the supreme magistrate by addressing him as "His Excellency the President." He congratulated the president for his vigilant anticommunism. The queen of England and the president of the United States—as required by the cold war—received the new president with appropriate ceremony.

Before the General Assembly of the United Nations in New York, the new president read a speech prepared by the French ambassador to the UN. The representatives of the two worlds, the communist and the capitalist worlds, unanimously applauded and voted admission to the UN for the new state.

With the certificate for his country of a free and independent nation, endowed with rights equal to those of all the nations in the universe, the president returned to his country, settled down in the palace of the colonial governor and proclaimed the single political party.

The intellectuals of the new republic seeking posts as ambassadors busied themselves with creating historical legitimacy for the president. They composed hagiographies and poems to be sung by schoolchildren. Celebrities, the stars of the country, manufactured and recorded melodies on the thousand exploits of the father-of-the-nation-and-independence, the Promethean, the hero who had wrested the sovereignty of the land of the ancestors from the monstrous colonialists.

And from that day forth, there began the titanic struggle of the father-of-the-nation-and-independence against underdevelopment. A struggle with consequences known by all today, that is, the tragedies into which ineffable aberrations plunged the African continent. Concludes Tiekura.

No! President Fricassa Santos was different, very different from the other fathers-of-the-nation-and-independence in the French-speaking African republics.

In the first place, as his name suggests, he was the descendant of one of the slaves bought, freed, and repatriated by philanthropic organizations from America. As soon as his father set foot on ancestral soil, he rushed into the slave trade and rapidly made a fortune. With gold, he put together an arsenal for himself. With the arms, he carved out a little chiefdom for himself. In his chiefdom, he instituted a reign of terror. And he pillaged, extorted, and became a Christian prophet and friend respected by the westerners who frequented the coastal regions of slaves and male adults like vultures over carrion.

Little Fricassa Santos had a happy childhood. He did not go barefooted, did not wear a cache-sexe, did not sleep on a mat stretched out over the hard-packed ground in a hut, and no longer ran out to the *lugan* after age seven.

At first he lived like the son of an upper-middle-class European family. He mastered English and French when his father paid for courses in a European university, where he did brilliantly in economics. He rounded out his education with a license in international law and a series of short courses taken throughout pre–World War II Europe. This was a colonialist and racist Europe in which very few Blacks lived.

After his return from Europe, the young Fricassa Santos worked as a senior civil servant in a number of African countries: the Gold Coast, Côte d'Ivoire, Nigeria, Togo, Dahomey, and in his own country, the Colony of the Gulf. He earned a lot of money because he was a French citizen and had the salary of a White, not that of a native.

He used that money to educate himself in traditional knowledge, to combat colonialism, and to fight for his country's independence. In Nigeria he learned about Yoruba and Ibo magic, about that of the Fon people in Dahomey, that of the Ewe at Notsé in Togo, and the mysteries of the Akan in the Gold Coast.

During the war of 1939 to 1945, the Pétainists locked him up as a Gaullist. Of course, it was not Santos himself they had under lock and key, but one of his numerous avatars. While the governor of French West Africa thought that he had imprisoned the man, Fricassa Santos continued delving more deeply into traditional knowledge by acquainting himself with the sacred woods of the Senufo in Boundiali and the dances of the Dogon in the French Sudan. When the Gaullists overcame the Pétainists of Africa, they liberated Santos and decorated him with a medal as a Companion of the Liberation.

Companion of the Liberation Fricassa Santos did not cease his struggle against French colonialism, his fight for the independence of the Colony of the Gulf. The Gaullist colonial administration considered him to be a rebel, an agitator, and imprisoned him in turn. While he was rotting in prison, France decided to organize a referendum for or against independence in the Colony of the Gulf under the aegis of the UN. Fricassa Santos's party asked people to vote "yes" for independence. All of nationalist Fricassa Santos's followers in the territory were arrested, tortured, and thrown into prison on the day of the referendum. Once more, the French did not know that they had only avatars under lock and key. Fricassa Santos and his followers, who were invisible to non-initiates, were everywhere throughout the country and in each polling place. The partisans of independence were able to observe the colonial administrators stuffing the ballot boxes with "no" votes at their leisure.

In front of the international observers sent by the UN, the ballot boxes were opened and the votes counted. The colonial administrators could not believe their own eyes; their astonishment was like that of the husband who wishes to turn his wife over during the night only to find himself in the arms of a lioness. All the ballots, the entire group of "no" votes, had been changed into "yes" votes. This miracle had been worked by the great initiate Fricassa Santos, thanks to the magic the masters of the Notsé cult in Togo and the marabouts of Timbuktu had taught him during his initiation rites. And the independence of the Republic of the Gulf was proclaimed. This independence was recognized de facto by the UN, whose observers had been present at the counting of the votes. President Fricassa Santos was not required to make the pilgrimage to the Elysian court of General de Gaulle in order to gain international recognition for the sovereignty of the Republic of the Gulf.

He was a man who remained inflexible. He did not want any ignorant Paleo savages, trained by the colonial system to pillage and repress, belonging to the young national army of his country. Infantrymen who, according to the seers, might count among their number his assassin.

The hunter lying in wait must occasionally pause to take a chew of tobacco. We too may follow his example. Let us pause in our narrative. So announces the *sèrè*, and he takes up his *kora*. The *koroduwa* dances and blasphemes. Bingo recites as follows:

Death swallows man; it does not swallow his name and his reputation.
Death is an article of clothing that everyone will wear.
Sometimes death is falsely accused when it takes the life of old people who had, as a result of their age, already finished their life before it actually ended.

7

Ah, Tiekura! Here below, nobody escapes his own destiny; that destiny is the will of Allah and nobody can thwart it.

The cabinet director who put Koyaga in prison failed to inform his minister on that day; he did so only a week later. And the minister did not speak of the incident and the arrest of the sergeant to President Fricassa Santos until a week after that.

"What!?" yelled the president, "your cabinet director had a certain sergeant—a veteran of Indochina—put in prison two weeks ago and you come to inform me of it now?"

"Yes, Mr. President."

"That's serious, a serious error, criminal negligence. Haven't I told you several times to keep me informed of every little word and deed of the former combatants of Indochina?"

Worried, the president got up and went into a vestibule. He wanted to work some spells. Soon he returned even more worried and asked an abrupt question:

"What is his name?"

"Koyaga."

"Koyaga! Koyaga is the very soldier who has more powerful magic than my own. Koyaga is the soldier who has decided to assassinate me. My seers have just confirmed that."

"I'll hurry to mobilize all our means for finishing Koyaga in the capital."

"Bring Koyaga back to the central prison at once! I want him in irons in the central prison before sunset. Otherwise, Koyaga and his comrades will attempt a coup tonight. This is the fatal night. Either he will kill me or I will kill him before the end of the day. That is written in our respective destinies. Bring him back to the capital. Bring him to me here in the palace."

Ah, Tiekura! Alas, it was late, too late! The cabinet director's instructions were not followed. Koyaga's hands were not handcuffed and his feet were not in chains in that cell where his father had perished. Sama was the name of the director in the prison where Koyaga had been sent. Sama was a former combatant and a friend of Koyaga, and he had allowed Koyaga freedom of movement. For two weeks, Koyaga had been able to meet and plan with his mother, the sorceress, and with the marabout Bokano. Koyaga managed quietly to inform the marabout and the sorceress of his decision to assassinate the president. Koyaga had time to protect himself with every talisman. In short, Koyaga was able to get ready, to prepare himself magically.

For two whole weeks, Koyaga had also been able to travel about the capital, meeting with his former comrades from Indochina, talking and plotting with them, acquiring arms, getting accomplices, buying people's silence, preparing hiding places, and designating specific duties. In short, Koyaga had been able to make substantial preparations.

When the police from the ministry of the interior arrived at the prison where Koyaga was being held, they found the cell empty. Koyaga had already left; he was already on the road to the capital, en route toward his destiny. It was evening. Sergeant Koyaga and President Fricassa Santos, each in a different place and in his own way, were watching the Saturday sun going down toward the west in a splatter of red. Each knew that before Sunday daybreak in the east, one or the other would be dead. One of the two would no longer be on this earth.

Through his seers, President Fricassa Santos learns that Sergeant Koyaga will arrive this Saturday evening on the six o'clock train. Police in civilian clothes are called in; they are on the platforms and posted at all the station exits. From the train windows, Koyaga sees and easily recognizes them. He calmly looks around in the car and sees a Hausa poultry vendor sitting across from him with three baskets full of clucking chickens. Koyaga recites one of the magical prayers taught him by the marabout; he is transformed into a white rooster. The Hausa sees the rooster on the seat and thinks it has escaped from one of his baskets. The merchant grabs the rooster energetically, places him in the basket, and closes it. He steps down from the train with his baskets and leaves the station with all his fowl before the eyes of all the policemen in civilian clothes. The version of this story that recounts how Koyaga left the train disguised as a Hausa chicken vendor is not credible; there were too many vigilant policemen when the train arrived. The hunter could not have avoided them if he had been content with a simple disguise.

At eight o'clock, Koyaga begins to meet the other conspirators. At nine-thirty, all nineteen conspirators are present at the last meeting under the tree at the bottom of the hill where the barracks of the upper city are located. This is the tree beneath which the arms have been buried.

Before the meeting begins, the conspirators see two trucks with headlights lit, loaded with gendarmes, coming toward them. The gendarmes have been fully informed by the seers of the great initiate, Fricassa Santos. Heavily armed, they quickly jump from the trucks and bear down on the conspirators, who scatter and take off. The officers pursue them through the darkness to the lagoon, where the conspirators abandon their arms and dive into the brackish waters. Some of them disappear beneath the bridge or in hiding places that had been foreseen and prepared. Koyaga recites several magical prayers taught by the marabout; their effect is to blind the gendarmes, who can see nothing more. They cannot even see the conspirators hidden at their feet. Non-initiates will dispute this version and explain that, in order to get away from the gendarmes, the conspirators hid in the brackish waters of the lagoon, holding their breath as the Vietminh did in the rice paddies of Indochina. In all probability, that interpretation is false.

In any case, the total failure of the operation and the return of the empty-handed gendarmes surprise and worry Lyma, the minister of the interior. He was counting on the success of the operation without the least doubt and had not organized an alternate operation in case of failure. With great embarrassment he senses that the situation is slipping from his control, and he is seized with panic. He goes quickly to the headquarters of the gendarmes in the lower city, and despite the reticence of the head officers at the barracks, the French officers on the staff, he sounds the alarm. He goes to the presidential residence; the chief of state is dining. The minister's discomposure, feverishness, and quivering voice alarm the president, who receives him immediately in the small salon.

"Mr. President, I have to make all arrangements for your security at once. The situation is extremely serious. The armed attack by the colonial veterans will take place tonight. I thought that I could take all the conspirators prisoner during their last meeting. They got away from me; they are at large. Anything is possible at any moment!"

President Fricassa Santos begins calmly by reproaching the minister for his nervous state and lack of composure.

"Don't panic! Above all, don't panic! We will come out on top in the end; we will manage to put our hands on Koyaga tonight, along with his acolytes and all his cohorts. We are more skillful magicians. No initiate in all Africa has learned more than I have about the mysteries of the continent. I have been everywhere: with the Dogon in Bandiagara, the Senufo of Boundiali, the marabouts in Timbuktu, the great Vodu masters at Notsé and in Benin, etc. I've been everywhere, I tell you—even with the Pygmies. If an infantryman like Koyaga managed to kill me tonight, that would mean that everything I learned was false and that all of my masters lied to me. That would mean that all Africa is false, a lie, and that all the talismans and sacrifices are without effect. That is not possible; it's unthinkable. That cannot be true. Reinforce my guard, double, triple, quadruple the men. When the putschists get here, we will catch them just the way rats are caught in a rattrap. There's no use in informing the other ministers and officials of the country or in alerting the public or in creating useless panic in the capital. You can go home quietly; we shall win in the end. And I have the entire populace as a shield. As soon as the first shots are fired, the people will intervene and make it impossible for the mutineers to succeed. They will have to trample the bodies of all the citizens. This plot, like all the others that have been organized these last months, will be undone by the people.

The president sent his minister away and quietly went back to his meal.

The conspirators, who had dived into the brackish waters, were the first ones to be surprised by the rapid disengagement of the gendarmes. They regrouped at once after they left. They were about to recover from the scare and congratulate Koyaga on the success of his magic when the bugle sounded the alarm from the gendarmerie. That meant the grand initiate, Fricassa Santos, had just observed their regrouping from his palace. It also meant that not one of their movements escaped the great sorcerer's vigilance. That produced panic; a number of conspirators wanted to abandon their arms in the lagoon and suspend the operation without further ado. Koyaga made fun of the men who were backing out and reassured everybody by saying:

"On the hunt, the hunter discharges his weapon the minute he realizes he has been seen by his prey. We must carry out our operation right away—immediately and without losing a minute."

The commandos leave at once in the various directions assigned, and within less than half an hour, they have their hands on the weapons and munitions depots. The sergeants plotting with them had got the guard of the weapons depot drunk and were holding him at their place along with the keys to the storerooms.

The conspirators divide into two groups. With the assistance of certain individuals within the regiments and of magic, they simultaneously take over the two barracks in the capital—the military camp in the upper city and the gendarmerie in the lower city. All the loyalist African officers and noncommissioned officers are arrested and thrown in prison.

By their own volition or of necessity, the soldiers in the two barracks join the movement and put themselves at the disposition of the triumphant conspirators.

The plotters organize and take over the offices of the headquarters and the military camp in the upper city. Important persons are summoned by telephone from the headquarters to a presumed emergency meeting of the cabinet at the residence of the chief of state. Soldiers hide at the doors and in the vicinity of their residences. One after the other, the ministers fall into the trap as they leave their own homes. Platoons take them into custody and immediately transport them to the camp in the upper city.

The conspirators now have at their disposal noncoms and hundreds of soldiers, thanks to the rallying of various groups. They form commando teams and dispatch them to the main arteries and neighborhoods. The commando groups spread out through the city to arrest other government officials and other party leaders. During the night, the commando teams fire their weapons and sow terror through the city. The crackling of automatic weapons echoes in all the city's neighborhoods. Anxious, nervous inhabitants close themselves in their houses with doors double locked.

The military leaders, ministers, government officials, and political leaders are all arrested and detained in the offices of the barracks in the upper city.

Any resistance or counteroffensive seems impossible, and because they have understood what is happening, the few officials who are true initiates and still at large manage through magic to cross the borders and leave the country. For some of them, the departure is definitive.

Now it is one o'clock Sunday morning. The entire capital, which is to say the entire Republic of the Gulf, is under the authority and at the mercy of the noncom conspirators. Except . . . Except the presidency! All the political and military officials of the capital, that is, of the entire country, have been arrested. Except . . . Except the person of President Fricassa Santos! And as long as President Fricassa Santos is alive and free, nothing, absolutely nothing has been accomplished. The president is the essential element, and a plot for arresting everybody except the president is like the person who must eat a rat but has consumed only the tail, while the bigger part of the rat remains to be gobbled up.

The conspirators entrust the great mission of taking over the presidency and arresting President Fricassa Santos to that most intrepid and fearless, that most adroit and miracle-working noncom, the master hunter Koyaga. The intrepid soldier who distinguished himself in Indochina and Algeria accepts the honor of carrying out this mission. All his colleagues applaud and congratulate him noisily.

Koyaga summons his soldiers into formation and selects twenty Paleo infantrymen from among those he knows or who have distinguished themselves in Algeria or Indochina.

"You are my pack of twenty lycaons," he announces.

To one infantryman who asks what a pack of lycaons is and why a pack of lycaons, Koyaga replies with a smile. Also called wild dogs, the lycaons are the most vicious and the fiercest beasts on the face of the earth, so fierce and vicious that after dividing up a victim, each lycaon takes a great distance from the others in order to lick himself painstakingly and remove the least trace of blood from his coat.

"Thinking that they are wounded, the pack will devour on the spot any members of the band who have not cleaned themselves thoroughly," he explains. "And without the least hesitation we shall do away with anybody among us who seems to vacillate, doubt, or retreat," he concludes. Koyaga publicly hands out rifles and talismans to each lycaon. He places about his neck and in his pockets a bunch of powerful charms and spells. Curiously enough, he arms himself only with a bow and a quiver loaded with bamboo arrows.

Koyaga and his men are completely in control of the presidential compound. Leading six lycaons, the master hunter goes in through the gate. The other members of the commando team scale the walls. Everyone is in the garden and under the orders of Master Sergeant Koyaga and his aides. He assigns a post to each mutineer, just as they set up ambushes in Indochina and in the jebel. They run along stooped low to take their posts and camouflage themselves.

The yells of the chiefs, the clumping of boots, and the clatter of weapons awaken President Fricassa Santos and his wife.

With their rifle stocks, shots, and boots the rebels batter the main door of the ground floor and force it open. They go in. With their first steps into the vestibule, however, they must face a first and insurmountable trap. That great initiate Fricassa Santos paralyzes them by causing a general outage of electricity. The entire city finds itself plunged into opaque darkness such as you see during nights of great storms. Koyaga lets out a great "hmmm!" He was expecting magic spells from a president who had been washed and fortified by all the great masters of the coasts, forests, and savannas, but he had not anticipated that, from the very first moment of their confrontation, Fricassa Santos would make use of such powerful sorcery as a general electrical outage across the entire country. Koyaga remains silent and stunned at the door for a good ten minutes. His companions control their breathing and consider the reasons for the silence and immobility of their chief. They believe and whisper that the master hunter Koyaga has in the obscurity transformed himself into a nocturnal bird of prey and that he is busy hunting the sorcerer–head of state through the residence.

It is Koyaga who, with a martial voice, breaks the silence and the wait. He commands a corporal to run to the barracks and to return with a spell-proof lamp, a charmed lamp.

At the barracks in the upper city, the rebel in charge there summons the great Vodu master of the neighborhood and hands him a lamp. With a few gestures and incantations, the master renders the lamp proof against sorcery.

With that lamp, the rebels scour the residence room by room for over a half hour in search of the head of state. In vain. The presence of the president cannot be detected or discovered.

Koyaga himself posts the attackers about the residence, goes up to the camp, and gives the Vodu master an account of what has happened. The latter questions and calls upon the fetishes for ten minutes. He stands up once more with a smile on his lips and with great assurance declares:

"Fricassa Santos is in the residence all the same. He is there and nowhere else. He has been washed by too many masters. He knows too many magic formulas; he has too many powerful charms and talismans on him. That is why you cannot see him. Take this and this."

The master offers two charms of his own invention to Koyaga.

Back at the besieged villa, the master sergeant retreats into a room where he conducts a ceremony with incantations. Speechless, his men watch him with respect and admiration. They believe and whisper that their chief has metamorphosed into an ant by his first act of magic and that he is searching page by page through all the books in the library in order to find the president. With the second charm, he has changed into a needle and is going through every thread of all the garments in the closets in search of the president. All mystical searching and investigation prove to be in vain.

"This is not possible!" yells the angry Koyaga. "This hide-and-seek has gone on too long; it cannot continue!"

He gives orders. The soldiers run through the rooms and capture the president's wife and servants. They are roughly dragged to the living room, in great terror. Koyaga threatens them and points at the photograph of the president.

"Where is he?" he yells. "Where is he hiding? What form has he taken?"

Trembling, the president's wife keeps repeating, "I don't know; I don't know anything."

Koyaga fires at the photo hanging on the wall. The maids howl in fear. With their hands, soldiers close the maids' mouths to stifle their yelling. The soldiers fire at the bookshelf, overturn wardrobes, scatter books across the room, spraying them with bullets. The president's wife and her maids are roughed up and taken to the presidential bedroom. Wardrobes are peppered with bullets and overturned. Jackets and shirts are unwrapped, taken off hooks, and scattered over the floor. They too are sprayed with bullets.

All these operations are futile, without result.

Koyaga leaves the president's wife and the maids in the keeping of the soldiers and returns to the barracks where the insurrectionists' committee is meeting. He reports the futility and inefficacy of every means they have used. The members of the committee and the Vodu master are all uneasy, quite uneasy. It is five o'clock in the morning, the roosters have already crowed, and the president has not yet been apprehended. It is obvious that as long as the president is not under lock and key, the plot will not have succeeded. The committee chief says this to Koyaga in no uncertain terms and reproaches him for the futility of his operation. The Vodu master receives Koyaga and presides. He rises in a reassuring manner:

"The president is still there in his compound or in the vicinity. He

Waiting for the Vote of the Wild Animals

has metamorphosed into an object that one must recognize and touch in order to flush him out. But it will soon be daylight; he cannot remain in his assumed form for more than one day without running the risk of being trapped and being unable to reassume human form. So wait around the residence. Be alert—he will finally reappear at sunrise."

Koyaga returns to the residence, his heart beating. He is discouraged and demoralized despite the reassuring words of the Vodu master. Koyaga had been warned; through his sorcery, the president is invincible. The sun continues to rise over the sea. Soldiers are running to meet Koyaga. Fatigue and anxiety can be seen in their gestures and on their faces. Koyaga reassembles them and calms them with the predictions of the Vodu master.

"Be alert; we simply have to wait a few minutes. The president must reappear in human form in less than a half hour. Otherwise . . . , otherwise . . ."

He deploys them about the two adjoining complexes that constitute a square and an enclosure: the presidential palace and the embassy of the United States. The first counselor of the embassy arrives at that instant. He opens the gate. All the soldiers have their eyes fixed on the counselor, following his every movement.

Suddenly and mysteriously a whirlwind is unleashed, arising from the middle of the residential garden. The whirlwind ruffles the leaves and the dust, racing through the garden from west to east and following an erratic path through the neighboring courtyard in the enclosure of the U.S. Embassy. Koyaga instantly understands that the great initiate Fricassa Santos has changed into a wind in order to take refuge in the embassy. From the second-story balcony, Koyaga surveys the path of the whirlwind, which abruptly vanishes and dissipates near an old car parked in the garden. The great initiate Fricassa Santos emerges from the whirlwind, disguised as a gardener.

In their ignorance, the uninitiated doubt this version of the facts. They claim there was a passage between the president's residence and the embassy enclosure. Disguised as a gardener, the president presumably took that passage in the darkness and crouched down on the rear seat of the car all night long. Then he left the Buick when the embassy gates were opened. This is obviously the childish explanation of a White in need of a rational explanation.

As soon as the president appears completely in his own form, the soldiers run into the embassy enclosure in total disregard of diplomatic protocol, grab the president, rough him up, and shove him into the street.

The minute the president emerges from the gate of the embassy, a soldier fires and, curiously enough, misses him. He does not in fact miss him (you do not miss at point-blank), but metal objects cannot penetrate the flesh of a great initiate. The soldiers knew that; they had heard it many times. They are nonplussed, disoriented, terrified. They throw down their arms and take off. Alone in the street, the president calmly heads for the embassy. Koyaga runs up and, before the president reaches the gate, lets fly an arrow with poisoned rooster's spur on the tip. The seers had informed the hunter that nothing other than an arrow with a poisoned rooster's spur could annihilate the magical armor of the president, super-initiate that he was, allowing his flesh to be penetrated by metal. The arrow enters his right shoulder. The bleeding president staggers and sits down in the sand. Koyaga motions to the soldiers. They understand and come running back, grabbing their weapons and discharging them at the unfortunate president. The great initiate Fricassa Santos collapses and lets out a death rattle. A soldier finishes him off with a burst of fire. Two others bend over the body. They unbutton the president's trousers, emasculate him, and stuff the bloody penis into his mouth. This is the ritual emasculation. Every human life holds an immanent force, a force that avenges a murder by attacking the killer. The killer must neutralize that immanent force by emasculating the victim.

With a dagger, another soldier cuts the tendons and amputates the arms of the dead man. This is the mutilation ritual, which prevents a great initiate of President Fricassa Santos's caliber from resuscitating.

Praying and weeping, the president's wife hovers over a husband, a man horribly mutilated. This man, whose totem was the boa constrictor, this elegant gentleman, the *yovo,* lay dismembered and lifeless in the sand.

The sun had risen well above the first roofs. There was no wind, and nothing other than the sighs of the president's wife broke the heavy silence reigning over the city.

The hunter on the prowl stops motionless at times to determine where he is. Let us imitate him. Bingo does a little performance. Tiekura yells some crazy things and does an obscene little dance. His master stops him and speaks:

A pirogue is never too big to capsize.
Those who have few tears are quick to mourn the dead.
The dead nanny goat is a misfortune for her master; but the head of
the goat that is placed in the cauldron is a misfortune only for the goat
herself.

8

Ah! Macledio, a week after the assassination of Fricassa Santos, four chiefs shared power. Each had only part; each coveted all the power and believed in his own power to acquire it; each had been led by soothsayers and marabouts to believe that he was destined to become president-for-life of the republic.

First, there was Captain Koyaga (the sergeant had the rank of captain conferred on himself following the assassination). The master hunter and emasculator could claim to be first by his power. But everyone said he did not have the physique, the culture, and the aura to succeed President Fricassa Santos. Everyone thought the only thing the master hunter had learned and knew how to do, and to do well, was to kill. He was encumbered by arms that were too long. Struggling through life with arms that are too long produces shyness: he was shy. He did not speak much, and he spoke badly, stuttered. He was a poor, a very poor orator. His cheeks were marked by ritual, tribal scars. To go about with scars in modern Africa draws attention and leads to complexes. He was a bundle of complexes. He read hesitatingly and wrote with difficulty; he was a great simpleminded fellow. Simpleminded, full of complexes, poor speaker, shy: that cannot make a head of state. Koyaga knew and accepted that. What he was aiming for was to be the defense minister. With de Gaulle's France, the cold war, and the French Union, the other plotters and the heads of neighboring states agreed to give him that post. From this division of the spoils, Koyaga got the defense ministry.
And the vice presidency of the committee of public safety.

Second, there was Colonel Ledjo, the chief of the rebels. As soon as the adjutant learned of the assassination of Fricassa Santos, he had himself promoted to the rank of colonel, an infantry colonel. Colonel Ledjo, who was the most skillful speaker and schemer among the rebels, had naturally prevailed to become president of the insurgency committee. Ledjo was the best educated because he was a former seminary student. He had completed solid theological, philosophical, and literary studies and had just missed, because of a trivial matter of adultery, becoming the first priest from his people and region. On the night before his ordination, he had been discovered with a married woman in the choir loft of the church where the ceremony was to take place. The Catholic hierarchy, ever understanding where the colonized Black was concerned, was ready to forgive him, but the husband, who was chief of his village and an irascible hunter, came to the presbytery with his poisoned arrows that very night, and Ledjo escaped death only by crossing the border disguised as a woman. He took refuge in a neighboring colony where the French army was recruiting the very first Paleo infantrymen for the colonial wars. He enlisted under the name of Ledjo (his first and true name was Bodjo). He fought the Malagasy, Moroccan, Vietnamese (he was in Indochina twice), and Algerian nationalists. Every place he went, he proved to be a great leader of men and demonstrated cruelty toward the colonized peoples who were fighting for their freedom. In his peregrinations, he received the prestigious rank of adjutant and gained the conviction that, in this life, only treachery and scheming win out for sure and always pay off. He based his conduct on that credo, and upon returning to his country, he engaged in intrigue. He obtained his enlistment in the national army the very day he left the colonial troops. In the national army, he managed to become the counselor and provider of intelligence for the minister of the interior as well as one of the main instigators of the veterans' insurrection. He remained a double agent, played on both sides, and unabashedly avoided taking sides until it seemed clear that the veterans would be victorious. He organized all the operations of the insurgents and maneuvered to become the obvious choice as chair of the committee. Ultimately, this had a certain advantage.

To his credit, and unlike other unthinking colleagues in the colonial army, Ledjo's thinking was nationalist and a bit socialist. He held that the Black was not originally damned and that the domination of the Whites was not eternal. That gave a touch of coherence and elevation to his actions. In the name of the cold war and in keeping with the principle of respect for zones of influence, France did not want Ledjo as president of the republic. His fellow conspirators and the heads of the neighboring states did not want to confer supreme power on Ledjo. The insurgency committee, created as the plot developed, became the committee of public safety. The committee of public safety was above the government and the National Assembly. Ledjo was made president of the committee of public safety.

There was Tima. Who was this Tima? His father was a chief, a great chief in the North. But little Tima's agricultural studies in France were not paid from his father's fortune or by his power. The chief had bought or kidnapped too many wives who had given birth to too many children. The chief never had the time or interest to count the numbers of his progeny, and far less to concern himself with their education. At age seven, little Tima was cute like a smooth little agama, and the pedophile teacher who took him in made of him at once a son, a little servant, and a lover. The early colonial societies were too simplistic and virile to understand nuances, to accept peculiarities, or to tolerate vices such as that of the teacher. All complex things and peoples were excluded. The teacher was quickly forced to return to France with his little black boy.

In France, Tima was able to engage in all those studies that were forbidden for colonized Blacks in their status as natives. He came out an engineer, an agricultural engineer, the first from all the savage tribes of the North. His master and pedophile guardian was a communist. He was even a municipal councilman of his hometown in the suburbs of Grenoble, to which he retreated. He had continually asked young Tima to engage in politics, to fight against capitalism and colonialism, to free his home country. Tima ended up believing that he was endowed with a mission.

With the beginning of decolonization and the extension of voting rights to all Blacks, even to the Naked men of the mountains, Tima was able to return to Africa. He made a mistake in thinking everything would be easy, assured in advance. He believed that, once he disembarked on the wharf, it would be sufficient to pull his original diplomas out of the trunk in order to be recognized as one of the sons of the great chief of the Naked men, to gain the allegiance of all his compatriots in the North, and to be elected as a deputy of his own tribe and region. He ran into the ostracism of the Brazilian métis along with the suspicion and jealousy of the elder brother who had succeeded their father. Tima wanted to reorganize agricultural practices, to put his knowledge to the service of the Naked people and their lands; they refused to give him the means of doing that. He went into politics and organized the League of the North. The party was opposed by the local authorities and by the French colonial administration because he claimed to be a socialist and wanted to collectivize production equipment. When the Colony of the Gulf gained its independence, the government of President Fricassa Santos accused him of plotting and threw him into irons. He escaped and took refuge in a neighboring country, where, every evening on the radio, he vilified the dictator in power in his country and denounced the politics of the neocolonialist French Union, General de Gaulle, and the free West. The cold war West, France, and the French Union did not want Tima as chief of state—five times no! This was a definite and formal refusal. They could tolerate Tima as president of the interim National Assembly. Tima got the presidency of the assembly in the division of spoils.

Finally, there was the métis Crunet. Ah, Tiekura, when you meet a mulatto, you are face to face with a man unhappy not to be a White, but delighted not to be a Black. Life is always painful for those who adore the scornful haughty and scorn the amiable meek. J.-L. Crunet was a mulatto. He was, however, a lucky mulatto who experienced his prime youth in misfortune and the damnation of the colonized classes but the better part of his life in the opulence and arrogance of the white colonialists.

One day, an alert ranger of the *cercle* saw several rascals at the edge of the swamp. There were four of them. All four were barefoot and snot-nosed. They jumped into the water. The ranger was surprised to see that the fourth little fellow became white after he dove in and washed—whiter and whiter each time he went back underwater and washed more. He drew closer and noted that the rascal was not an albino, nor was he either a Moor or a Fula—he was a White, a real White. The conscientious ranger, unable to control himself, ran to the white commandant's residence, gave a precise military salute, and despite being breathless informed the chief of the circle about his discovery. The commander immediately summoned the chief of the village, the interpreter, the young woman, and her offspring. The mother was instructed to detail before all the village men of worth the name of the distant country in which she had strayed to the point of ending up with a little métis on her back.

Trembling with fear, the mother explained that she had never left the hills, but she recalled that, during the last rebellion by the Naked mountain men of the North, a passing detachment commanded by a white lieutenant had bivouacked several weeks in the region. Because of her beauty and her virginity, she had been charged with preparing hot water for the white lieutenant and for soaping the back of her White during his evening and morning baths. Day and night, she washed and rewashed the back of her White and did not limit herself to that sole task. What was her surprise just a few weeks after the departure of the detachment to discover that she was clearly in a state of pregnancy. Everybody agreed to the historical veracity of the presence of a company of infantrymen commanded by a white lieutenant in the area.

Becoming angry, the white administrator of the hill region reprimanded and threatened everyone: the interpreter, the chiefs of cantons, villages, and tribes, and the young mother. The people of the country did not have the right to hide and to raise a mulatto in their insalubrious shacks. He had explained that to them several times. A mulatto is a half-White, and therefore not a Black. The following morning, the child was taken from his mother and, with a good escort, was sent to an institute for métis in the colony's capital. There they soaped him several times, gave him shoes, dressed him, combed him, and sent him to a school bench. He was happy and immediately demonstrated that he was intelligent, hardworking, and even lucky. Very lucky.

One morning during recess, the entire school began calling and hunting for him. He went with a crowd of buddies to the office of the institute's director. The director congratulated him and announced his departure for metropolitan France on the next boat, Tiekura continued.

Reading through the travel diaries of her son, who had died of yellow fever, his old biddy of a French grandmother had discovered that she had a grandchild among the savages in the African bush. "I have to rescue him at once so the cannibals won't devour him," she exclaimed in tears. She was rich and had both financial and political power. Not losing a minute, she went in turn to see the minister of war and the minister of the colonies. The governors and all the colonial administrators were immediately called into action, and the machinery began to work; the little métis was located. Before she saw him, the old woman loved him; she loved him when she welcomed and became acquainted with him. He was a darling boy whose unpronounceable African names —Dahonton N'kongloberi—were immediately discarded, and he was baptized with the civilized, Catholic names Jean-Louis Crunet.

J.-L. Crunet turned out to be not only a faithful, practicing Catholic but also a genuine Crunet. A Crunet through whose veins had never flowed the least drop of colonized blood. He surmounted all those obstacles established for the purpose of testing the future leaders of eternal France. With brilliance he passed the common entrance examinations for the Grandes Écoles, and like every good Crunet, he chose from among them the Polytechnical School. And after he finished his course in the cavalry, he went to the School for Civil Engineering. In continental France, he behaved socially and morally like a Crunet until he was forty years old. After forty, there were periods when his African blood surged and dominated. The call of blood is certainly irresistible —a sheep is never made from a hyena. To the surprise of all the Crunets, Jean-Louis began to gamble and to cheat on his wife, whom he loved nonetheless. She obtained a legal separation. In order to drown his disappointment in love, he began hanging around Pigalle, where he became enamored of a black woman with all the sensuality, allure, and sex appeal of Josephine Baker. He lost himself in alcohol and drugs. In an instant, he squandered the great fortune his grandmother had left him. Rejected by his people and his milieu, he recalled his African ancestry and went to the minister of the colonies to proclaim, publicly and in a loud voice, that he fully recognized his blackness. The minister sent him to his home country. When he got off the boat, all the Blacks in the colony, proud to have a polytechnician from among them, welcomed him with tam-tam and lascivious dancing. The celebration was so spontaneous, colorful, enthusiastic, grandiose, and fine that it inspired the governor of the colony. For three months, the governor had been looking for an officer without any success—an officer who would have credibility among the black intellectuals and other worthies and who would be neither revolutionary nor anticolonialist. He needed this educated African for the next legislative elections. He wanted to make of this person a candidate by whom the colonial administration could rig the elections and bring about the defeat of the favorite nationalist, who was constantly bragging about his diplomas.

The governor received the métis and asked him to assume his responsibilities. J.-L. Crunet ceased getting drunk for two days, began to think, and hesitated. Ultimately, in order to keep his home country from falling into the throes of communism and colonial war, he accepted the proposal of the governor of the colony. He decided to don the protective shell of a political leader by definitively giving up drinking and taking drugs. He fell into line and even married Lucie, the most attractive métisse in the Gulf of Guinea.

In all sincerity, Crunet thought that there was some middle path between the East and the West and that his country should maintain its privileged ties with France in order to achieve its development in a harmonious manner. Through all the electoral consultations of fifteen years, the colonial administration systematically rigged the elections so that J.-L. Crunet's party would be victorious. Métis Crunet remained his country's deputy in the French national assembly for ten years and became the prime minister of the territory when the colony's autonomy was proclaimed. Up to the independence referendum, his party invariably enjoyed the favor of the voters. Unfortunately for him and his friends, the referendum for independence was supervised by UN observers, and the colonial administration was unable to establish and put back into place the misleading documents that would lead to his party's victory. The only choice left for J.-L. Crunet was exile. To flee from the authoritarian President Fricassa Santos, he took refuge in a neighboring country.

The French Union and the cold war West went hunting for him in exile to make him a head of state. The conspirators and the neighboring heads of state did not want him; they said no five times. After interminable discussions, the latter accepted his appointment as president of a temporary government with very limited powers. A government whose actions were supervised by a committee for public safety. In the maneuvering, he got the highest office, but the highest office devoid of the least substance.

Ah, Tiekura, I repeat that following the assassination of President Fricassa Santos, power in the Republic of the Gulf was divided among four leaders—J.-L. Crunet, Koyaga, Ledjo, and Tima. Power is a woman that cannot be shared. In one reach of the river, there can be only one male hippopotamus. What can be said, foreseen, or concluded about a government run by four leaders? With four, there is more than one; there are three leaders too many.

Alliances were formed; clans were created. Under pressure from France and the West of the cold war, Koyaga and J.-L. Crunet became allies and declared themselves, or pretended to be, conservatives and liberals. They constituted the liberal camp, the partisans of the Occident. On the other hand, Tima and Ledjo claimed to be nationalists and progressivists (under the probable guidance of agents from the East). They constituted the national clan, the progressivist camp, the partisans of international communism. The initial markers for each contestant were established. The race could commence; the merciless struggle for supreme power began.

More than the other three starters, the master hunter Koyaga was experienced in solitary combat and accustomed to merciless confrontations with the ferocious beasts of the distant, pitiless bush.

The clans accused each other of plots, prevarication, nepotism, and demagoguery.

During that winter season, not enough rain fell; the sun and the drought scorched the mountains and the plains: famine and distress reappeared in the mountains. This scourge afflicted the entire northern part of the country. The partisans of communism, the progressivist camp, made an investment in distributing gifts.

Unfortunately, if the sacks sent by the donors were abundant in the city markets, they did not reach the mountains, where the inhabitants continued to die of hunger. This aroused the international press, and they denounced those who benefited from the hijacked goods.

Demonstrations quietly encouraged by the liberal clan spread through the streets of the capital, and soldiers mutinied in the barracks. Demonstrators and mutineers went from the marketplace to the presidential palace with banners demanding the arrest, trial, and punishment of corrupt officials, thieves, and those starving the people. That is, they were demanding the arrest and condemnation of Tima and Ledjo.

The demonstrators and mutineers entered the gardens of the presidential palace, where President Crunet and Vice President Koyaga appeared on the balcony. They believed they had won and were ready to address the crowd when, abruptly, the demonstration went sour. Cries erupted and other banners were raised over the crowd; banners with very different inscriptions and slogans. Shouts and slogans demanded the resignation of President Crunet as well as the arrest and hanging of Fricassa Santos's assassins. There was confusion and a struggle between two groups of demonstrators and between two groups of mutineers. President Crunet quickly took refuge with Koyaga in the office. The movement that they had begun was turning against them; they had been betrayed.

Koyaga's followers, with the lycaons leading, ferociously repressed the demonstration by firing into the crowd, stabbing, and slitting throats. Seventeen demonstrators were killed, all of them brutally emasculated. All were emasculated to destroy the avenging forces that souls dispatch against their killers, the vital forces of people who have been brutally and unjustly assassinated.

After this slaughter, each camp withdrew to its territory. The country was split between four fierce animals, each keeping for himself, each controlling for himself the booty he had in his maw.

The administration of the country was blocked. Something had to be done.

In order to break the deadlock, it was decided to hold a roundtable conference of reconciliation and fraternity. This was decided at the joint initiative of Ledjo and President J.-L. Crunet, and it had the impact of reconciling the two camps. It was essential to reestablish confidence, to bring back fraternity, to stop the internal struggles and all together to forget the past, to turn toward the future, and to devote themselves to the development of the country.

It was a kind of council of ministers that was opened to officers and certain political personalities. It was the conference of hope; everybody was expecting an important change in the way affairs of state would be conducted.

The marabout Bokano and sorceress Nadjuma prepared the master hunter Koyaga in a serious manner for that meeting.

Koyaga arrived in the capital on the day and at the time prescribed by the marabout. He stopped at the edge of the city to carry out the sacrifices and magic that his mama, the sorceress Nadjuma, had recommended to him. He spent two nights in the capital before the opening of the conference, two nights totally devoted to consultations.

The opening of the conference was set for ten o'clock Saturday morning. Before the opening, two pieces of news erupted, spreading about the city the consternation that is provoked among a herd of goats by the hyena's cries on a dark night. The unions had declared a general one-day strike, and Tima, the president of the assembly, had decided not to participate in the meeting.

Let us imitate the expectant hunter, who sometimes interrupts his activity to swallow a mouthful of water. So proclaims the *sèrè* before he begins to play. His buffoon responder begins dancing. At a sign from the *sèrè*, the *koroduwa* calms down and recites the following proverbs:

Death grinds without boiling the water.
One does not place a sieve in front of death.
The cadaver of a bird does not rot in the air, but on the earth.

9

Ah, Tiekura! It is not always true that great events can be detected in the dawn of the days that bring them forth.

The morning of the roundtable conference of reconciliation was flat as the back of a wife one no longer loves, specifies the responder.

The conference took place under the presidency of the head of state, in the old party house that was partly occupied by the insurgency committee, after it had been the National Assembly. In a room next to the office of newly promoted General Ledjo, J.-L. Crunet, the head of state, insisted from his very first words on the importance of the meeting and explained why the vice president was not there. Tima would change his mind about resigning and reassume his place as soon as a bit of the road to the reconciliation of all the country's children had been illuminated. In order to mark the solemnity of the meeting and to ensure everyone's sincerity, the participants would take an oath. Some swore by the spirits of their ancestors while others swore by the Qur'an or the Bible. Koyaga swore by the spirits of his ancestors, the Qur'an, and the Bible. One is always more sincere when one calls on several gods instead of only one. So explains the disciple of the *sèrè*.

Koyaga went over to sit in a corner at the end of a row, far away from the other participants, and quiet as a boa warming himself beneath the first rays of the harmattan sun, he observed them. It is not through speech and gesticulation but by means of silence and seriousness that the wise man stands out in the assembly. The responder continues.

The proposals by the president of the republic were presented. They raised a storm equivalent to that in the great forest: howls, insults, and numerous hostile counterproposals. There were still the same splits: opposition between liberals and socialists, northerners and southerners, Catholics and Muslims.

Echoes of the cries of the unions parading in the capital's streets reached the room. They knew that similar movements were taking place in other cities of the country's interior.

When they had their fill of insults and threats, everyone grew tired and shut up. The doors of the meeting room remained closed, guarded by paratroopers. Each person knew that the doors would remain closed until the essential minimum of reconciliation had been achieved. Newly promoted General Ledjo, in control of the place, said that and repeated it, specifies Tiekura. There was nothing but silence, the silence of the deadend, the heavy silence that envelops village dwellings on a night when an old sorceress is buried. They stared at each other relentlessly and even smiled.

The sudden ringing of the telephone in the committee chair's office broke the silence. An orderly announced aloud that the general was wanted on the telephone. Ledjo politely excused himself (he was a former seminary student), asked the oldest member of the meeting to preside, and rose. Koyaga watched him leave. As a master hunter, you said to yourself, inwardly: only the idiot who is unfamiliar with the viper of the pyramids takes the little reptile by the tail.

As soon as the general disappeared, the doors and shutters of the room broke open as armed men leapt into the room shouting slogans such as "Our people are fed up! Death to the president! Death to the assassins!" They fired at all the participants. Submachine guns kept crackling for more than ten minutes. Howls, screams, blood; spurts of blood, pools of blood. Then there were final sighs, death rattles, and the silence of the dead.

The president of the insurgency committee returned and inspected the task performed by the commandos. He noted that all the participants—the president, ministers, officers, party leaders—all had been cut down, slaughtered. "Perfect!" he muttered in a very low voice to the head of the commando team. He checked in an offhanded way, sure of his plot, that Koyaga had been dispatched, slaughtered. The former noncom from Indochina was lying unconscious in the blood, half covered by two corpses. The little old lady who is careless picks up with her rags a live coal among the ashes, notes the responder. The president of the insurgency committee muttered a few thanks to the members of the commando team. He returned to his office and engaged in a long telephone conversation with Vice President Tima. He spoke loudly and did not close the door. His conversation could be heard in the meeting room. He hung up. When he inspected the cadavers, Ledjo had slightly soiled himself with blood. He must clean himself off. He unbuckled the belt, carelessly placed it with his pistol on the desk, and went into the toilet, shutting the door.

As if in a nightmare, he came out to find himself face to face with Koyaga. For an instant, he thought he was in the presence of a phantom, continues Tiekura. No, it was really the blood-spattered veteran of Indochina aiming a weapon at him, the very pistol of the general who had presided over the committee. The new general and former seminarist screamed like a trapped beast and swung around to retrace his steps. As if the nightmare were continuing, he found himself face to face with another Paleo, a lycaon who was blocking his escape. He let out another yell and headed toward the window on the left. A lycaon there was also targeting him. He leapt through the only opening that he thought was clear, the window on the left. Four Paleo infantrymen lycaons calmly greeted him, overwhelmed him, and took his clothes off. Koyaga phlegmatically leapt through the window with a dagger. Despite the new general's screams, the master hunter emasculated him—an uncircumcised man must be emasculated alive, adds the responder. Three of the soldiers pulled the jaws of the committee president open. You, Koyaga, veteran of Indochina, you crammed the penis and bloody scrotum into the gaping opening, and you left muttering, "Ledjo too was calling for the hanging of Fricassa Santos's assassin."

The committee chief was dead. He failed in his attempt to kill you, Koyaga, because he forgot a precept. One must never order Paleo infantrymen to execute a master hunter who is covered with charms, specifies the responder. The soldiers avoid aiming at him, fearing that the bullets will ricochet off the hunter's magic shell and come back to kill them.

A hunter pauses under certain trees. Let us follow his example; let us pause and repeat the following three truths:

A man arrives early in the morning at the place where he is fated to die.
When the vital nerve has been severed, the hen kills the wild cat.
If a kannari breaks on your head, wash with the water.

10

With fear in his guts, Tima, the president of the assembly, had been waiting since morning. The arrival of the presidential escort at the gates of the property relieved him. So everything had gone as planned and even more quickly than they had hoped. "What? Bravo! It's all finished, tied up, taken care of, successful," he cried out, free of his scare. He got up, went to the second floor, took out his speech, and looked through it quickly. It was perfect. Facing the mirror with a certain pride and newfound serenity, he adjusted his tie, put on his bowler hat, sprayed himself with cologne, and pulled on his gloves. As he went down the stairs, he took his ivory cane. The uniformed motorcyclists were surrounding the presidential Mercedes 600 in front of the entrance. They led him to the huge black car and opened the door; he settled back in the left rear seat. Outside the gate, there were two military patrols that joined the escort group, one in front and the other behind. The procession went up the main street leading from the palace to the congressional building. Armed paratroopers, placed every fifty meters along the avenue, held back the demonstrators waving banners with slogans hostile to the government: they demanded the resignation of J.-L. Crunet. Others were hostile to Koyaga, calling for the assassins to be hanged. Everybody was in the street. The general strike called by the central committee of the combined unions was being generally observed. . . . Anxiety could be seen in the looks of the demonstrators. Shots coming from near the congressional building created a mild panic and raised the crowd's perplexity. The most unlikely rumors were circulating.

At the congressional building, the presidential procession was directed toward the cafeteria located opposite the committee president's office. President Tima got out of the car and was directed to a seat. A noncommissioned officer came in with a tape recorder. He recorded the presidential declaration. Only after the journalist disappeared did Tima begin to feel uneasy, to feel a little doubt. He had not seen the bodies of the committee members, the ministers, or the president of the republic. He had called for the general who was presiding over the committee but did not see him appear. He would have liked to contact him by telephone, but there was a delay. He got up and went into the cafeteria manager's office, taking an armed soldier sitting at the telephone by surprise. What are you doing there? Give me the telephone! I am going to call the general myself. The soldier refused, and the astonished president started to return to summon the chief of protocol. He found himself facing two soldiers, two armed lycaons, real guard dogs who refused to allow him to pass. He ran toward the only other door, the one to the toilet, opened it, and found himself face to face with Koyaga. The Paleo, son of a Paleo and master hunter, was not dead. He was there with a dagger, facing the president, continues the responder. Tima erupted with a great "Help! Help!" A half-dozen soldiers ran in, surrounded him, and ordered him to shut his mouth. Weeping, he fell silent. His lips trembled like the ass of a nanny goat waiting for the male. The soldiers calmly undressed the president; he too was uncircumcised. All uncircumcised men must be treated alike. So Koyaga proceeded to sever the organs and introduced penis and bloody scrotum between the teeth as two smirking soldiers held the mouth open with arms of steel. "He was also demanding that the assassins be hanged," muttered Koyaga. An emasculated man ceases to be a male; he becomes a carcass, the prey of vultures. A master hunter never lowers himself to mess around with a carcass. Koyaga abandons the president of the assembly, howling with pain, to his lycaons and goes out.

Koyaga went back to the radio station on foot. He was in a frenzy, fuming, drunk with blood and rage, and he kept muttering, "They were all demanding that the assassins be hanged. For me to be hanged.

It was them or me." Koyaga had changed jackets, but the trousers and shoes he was wearing were stained with blood. So were his hands, which had only been hastily wiped. Also intoxicated with the scent of blood, a pack of lycaons were also milling around Koyaga. "Lycaon" means wild dog. They were as much assassins and criminals as their leader. Koyaga exhorted them:

"We'll go on without hesitation or pity. It was them or us."

The buildings and the studios had been occupied by a detachment of riflemen, lycaons equal in cruelty and savagery to those who were arriving, adds the responder. They greeted their leader Koyaga, and, just as they had done at their post in Tonkin or in the Algerian jebel, they gave him their report. They had meticulously followed orders, shooting nobody but permitting no one to enter the enclosure. No announcer or technician had come through the gateway. Not even sweepers or an orderly. But they had not found the station director at home and had not been able to get him there as they had been ordered. They mentioned that they had been forced to exercise a great deal of patience in order to bear Macledio.

In fact, it is that day and on that occasion, at 4 P.M. that your first meeting will take place, Koyaga—you and Macledio. The soldiers holding the radio station explained to you, Koyaga, who Macledio was: a famous announcer for the national radio station. With great passion, erudition, and an intense tone, he had done a weekly program that he called "Memorial of the Land of the Ancestors."

The soldiers told you that Macledio had gone to the station's gate three times. They had turned him back three times. Each time, he had only gone away after uttering insults and antimilitarist pronouncements in the Paleo language. The Paleo lycaons were waiting for him. They had saved a bullet for him. Despite orders, they would mow him down if he came back to the gate a fourth time. Macledio must not be far away. He must surely be grumbling somewhere close to the stadium where he was a referee for soccer matches every Sunday.

In the absence of the director, you proposed that Macledio be located. Both he and his technician were brought to you under escort. Right in front of you, Koyaga, Macledio expressed his hostility toward the army, soldiers, and war. And his scorn for the black infantrymen, those mercenaries used by French colonialism for vile and criminal tasks. Macledio's invectives simply served to amuse you, to make you smile. Now that you had your victory, you were relaxed; you had mellowed. Like all the other citizens of the republic, you knew Macledio without ever having met him. Macledio was a star. You cannot get angry with the famous lecturer, explains the responder. Koyaga, you waited quietly for Macledio to quiet down. You squeezed his face and, like a master hunter, calmly took your proclamation out of your pocket and held it out. You spoke out in a firm voice.

"Step in line and right now, or I'm going to cut your . . ."

At first Macledio did not take the threat seriously. He simply smiled, but when he wanted to take a step back, the fierce glares of the lycaons convinced him otherwise. He came back toward you with a tinge of haughtiness and grabbed the proclamation from your hand. He read through it with feigned goodwill, feverishly crossed out several lines, and with a smirk filled the margin with small handwriting. He spoke like a professor to a student. He judged that style is of the essence in a proclamation or a pronunciamento. The style must be constantly elegant, noble, and elevated. Such insipid phrases as "While we were busying ourselves with the people's famine, those men were filling their pockets" are trite and common: they have no place in a proclamation, he added. In an excellent pronunciamento, you assert nothing without proof. Unless there are ample, prior explanations, one cannot allege that "only three members of the committee were eating." Still sarcastic, Macledio kept picking out errors and blunders in substance and form. The paper finally took on the form and consistence of a real proclamation. Disdainfully, he handed the paper back to you.

"Don't count on me. I'll never assist you in taking power by recording such a criminal speech."

That is the way Macledio spoke to you, Koyaga. You decided that Macledio had gone beyond permissible limits. If you go too far in playing with a child, he will ultimately ask you to take off your pants so he can play with your penis and scrotum. Neither veterans nor their former leader could accept this outrageous affront, states the responder.

The armed soldiers abruptly fall on Macledio in great anger. The first man slaps him, the second goes after him with his bayonet, and without your quick intervention, he would have spilled out his guts. In an instant, Macledio runs to take refuge in the control room. He agrees to help in recording the speech, but he insists that you sign it, Koyaga.

"Sign what?" you asked.

"An affidavit that will absolve me in history. A certificate clearly stating I cooperated under threat of murderous riflemen's weapons," replied Macledio.

You looked at Macledio with condescension for quite a while. What kind of person could be so fanatic as to attach such importance to things as useless as the judgment of history? You smiled, showed your good humor once more, and you unflinchingly patted his shoulder and set your signature at the bottom of the page without even reading the paper he was holding out to you.

Koyaga, you read your proclamation with such candor, such good-will, and such concentration that Macledio was won over. Macledio the intellectual began to ask himself the sempiternal question.

"Yes, I, Macledio, asked myself the sempiternal question. What if this soldier who struck me as such a bumpkin were my man of destiny? Why couldn't he be the man that I had been seeking for some forty years? After my disappointing experience in the capital of the Republic of the Mountains, I had lost my illusions and despaired. The man I sought must not exist. I was telling myself that to continue my search would be folly. A folly that had almost cost me my life three times: I didn't want to start all over. And yet . . . ! I couldn't keep from examining the hick soldier you appeared to me from head to toe."

Ah, Koyaga! Since that day, Macledio has been your own louse, perpetually sticking to you, Koyaga. He is your shorts, striving wherever you go to hide your shameful parts. Hiding your shame and your dishonor. He has never left your side. You will never travel without him.

The *sumu* ends with these words, says the *sèrè*. He plays the *kora* while Tiekura howls, dances, and whirls in a thousand eccentric movements. Bingo calmly utters this string of proverbs:

Let no one be impatient to see the day when all his relatives and their families will praise him.

Condolences do not resuscitate the dead, but they maintain the confidence of those who remain.

If one sees the bearer of condolences crawling out of the sewer opening, it is because he was not content with the formula, "May God take pity on the dead."

Third *Sumu*

Accompanied by the responder, the *sèrè* executes a musical prelude. He announces that the theme to be developed during the refrains and pauses will have to do with predestination. Man cannot escape his own destiny.

A bird's feather may fly into the air, but it ends up on the ground.
Blood that must flow does not spend the night in the veins.
A man arrives early in the morning at the place where he is fated to die.

11

Ah, Tiekura! The journey, the life of Macledio before his meeting with Koyaga is not a short discourse. It is a mountain we must go around in order that the *donsomana* we are telling be free to continue. It is a river we must cross to find once again the route of the heroic narrative we are following. It is a storm to which we must be attentive before speaking our words and letting our song be heard. One may not recite the deeds of Koyaga without first dwelling during an entire *sumu* upon the path followed by Macledio.

Ah, Tiekura. *Nõrô* is a belief and a word from the Paleo and Malinke civilization that Africa and the world of today have forgotten and no longer recognize. That forgetfulness and ignorance are a source of many of today's misfortunes, many catastrophes that block our paths and delay us. *Nõrô* determines and explains the evolution and destiny of each individual. The person who is the bearer of an ill-fated *nõrô* is an unfortunate being who produces his own misfortune and that of those around him by his very presence, by his very existence. On the other hand, everything succeeds for the recipient of a fortunate *nõrô*, everything is easy for him, everything works with great facility about him, adds Tiekura. The bearer of an ill-fated *nõrô* will struggle in vain with his misery and his bad luck as long as he does not encounter the holder of the opposite *nõrô,* the neutralizing *nõrô.* Encountering, living with one who enjoys the opposite *nõrô* annihilates the condemnation and the ill luck of the person bearing the ill-fated *nõrô.* Every bearer of an ill- fated *nõrô* ought to seek the man or woman of his destiny and should never falter in that quest. That person is rarely in one's own neighborhood, but the man of destiny is not necessarily at the other end of the universe. Those bearing an ill-fated destiny who catch the man of their own destiny immediately become fortunate, concludes the responder.

Macledio, you were born with the malformations and the clear signs of the bearer of an ill-fated *nõrô.* Your parents hastened to the village geomancer-sorcerer, who informed them in no uncertain terms of the future of the unfortunate nursling you were and the misfortune that you would bring them. The accursed baby that you were loved neither father nor mother. In fact, your father was not your father and your mother was not your mother. They were birth parents both of whom ran the risk of perishing from an abrupt and violent death if they did not distance themselves from the child you were before you turned eight years old. Your parents, on the very day of your birth, had to promise the spirits of their ancestors that they would allow you to leave the village before your circumcision. Before the midwife could proceed to sever the umbilical cord, your dismayed father had to prostrate himself in front of the house where your mother was in labor and make a pathetic declaration to the little wildcat that was you.

"We are nothing," he said, "we are nothing but your genitors; we are not your parents. Upon the souls of our ancestors, we shall allow you to leave this village, this hearth, this family that you hate. We shall allow you to go in search of your man of destiny before you are circumcised."

Ah, Tiekura! The first steps of that child confirmed the prediction of the geomancer. The child proudly left his father and his mother but did not walk in the way of the ancestral fetishes nor through the family fields. Each time his mother let him go, he would head toward the East, without fail toward the East. The conclusion that Macledio's man of destiny lived in the East was easy to draw.

When the boy's seventh birthday came, his parents did not wait to be reminded of their oath. They made inquiries about members of their clan who lived in the East. There was only one native of the village living in that direction: Koro, the nurse Koro. He was surely Macledio's man of destiny. The child was sent off between a slave and a cousin, walking the 185 kilometers to join his uncle in Bindji.

His uncle Koro was the nurse, the "doctor," the sorcerer-healer of the white commandant and of all the subjects in the subdivision inhabited by some thirty-five thousand fearful, exploited Blacks, adds Tiekura.

One evening, as the supreme honor that could be paid to a little black boy in the colonial era, Macledio was introduced to the white administrator of Bindji, and the latter ordered the teacher to give him a seat in the local school the following day.

Macledio turned out to be more intelligent than the others. He had a phenomenal memory. It had been developed by the master of the Qur'anic school, who had been given the task of inculcating the suras of the Qur'an by means of the rod. Macledio quickly learned to read, and along with that talent . . . he noticed and recognized with regret that his uncle was not his man of destiny, adds Tiekura.

His uncle was handsome and as supple as a serpent, but, unfortunately, he was enthusiastically fond of millet beer, took snuff, worshiped the fetishes and spirits of the swamps, loved to hunt panthers, and beat his wives. Such a mixture of talents and faults could not be those of Macledio's man of destiny. A specific event was soon to confirm the need for and hasten separation from his uncle. From the moment of his birth, Macledio was not only the bearer of an ill-fated *nõrô*, he was also a sorcerer and an eater of souls. He was not only to be avoided, he was to be feared.

The uncle learned late that his nephew was pernicious, adds the responder.

Macledio's friend in combat and hunting was a young Senufo named Noncé. While on a rat hunt, a snake bit Noncé, who died that very evening. The illness or the accident that provokes the death of a child is always an obvious cause; the real cause and the person truly responsible is always to be sought elsewhere.

The afternoon of the burial, the entire school and village assembled about the balaphon and tam-tam on the square for the dance of the dead. This was located at the entrance to the teak plantation, between the sacred wood and the school yard. The balaphon were clinking and the tam-tam were thumping. Tearful women were chanting.

From between two thickets came the body, wrapped and tied in its shroud, on a stretcher made of branches and transported on the heads of two fellows adorned only in a cache-sexe with monkey tails attached: these were the dancers for the dead. They enter the circle with the remains. The rhythm changes. The drummers and balaphonists beat with greater fury. The soul of the dead man possesses the dancers, who no longer hear anything other than the voice of the dead or act except by his will. They are the deceased incarnate and he guides them. With erratic steps, the body and the bearers take two turns around the dance circle. Abruptly, they stop, and the body begins to vibrate and toss. The alternating movements signify that the soul of the dead man has been "eaten" by the brotherhood of malicious sorcerers and that the deceased, before reaching his final resting place, is determined to denounce the sorcerer who offered his soul to that brotherhood. The cadaver's griot chants incantations and praises. The body, with its bearers, swoops down on the group of women, who break and flee. The bearers and dead man return to the dance circle, turn, and stop a second time. A second time, the body vibrates and tosses. The griot cries out, the tam-tam and the balaphon change rhythm and tone. The body and bearers bear down directly on the groups of schoolchildren, who scatter. The cadaver pursues you, Macledio. Despite the numerous detours you take, it is you and you alone the cadaver is chasing and accusing. Running like mad with the cadaver on your heels, you cross through the teak plantation and come to the school principal's villa, run in the house, close the door, and run to take refuge beneath a bed in the most distant bedroom. The body, and its bearers stop on the terrace, at the door, and, still moved by anger, the cadaver begins to toss and vibrate once more. The principal goes out and offers two white kola nuts and a libation, asking the cadaver's pardon. The soul accepts the offerings, calms down, and goes quietly to its final resting place.

The denunciation was public.

Yes, Macledio, suspected since infancy of being a sorcerer, had just been recognized as the devourer of his dead friend's soul. He denied it and proclaimed his innocence with tears. He was not a sorcerer and had never eaten anybody's soul; he loved Noncé. Noncé had died from a viper's bite. But, in great detail, the fetishist described the forms assumed by Macledio in order to carry out his crime, the meetings he had attended, and the persons with whom he had shared the "flesh" of their unfortunate victim. Macledio continued his denial. All of that was grotesque and false. . . . But the facts, details, specificities followed one after another and finally became evident. At first, as if in a kind of dream, Macledio began to doubt himself, his own awareness, his memory. With the insistence and perseverance of the sorcerer, all the accusations took shape and the dream took on substance. The vague reality became experience. So it was true—he was, in fact, a sorcerer, a consumer of souls. It was true, that was really him, Macledio, who had given away his friend's soul. He accused himself before the public and accepted the fact with the attitude of a guilty man. He was responsible. It was terrible to recognize one's own malice and to be ashamed. Unhesitatingly, he made the decision never to see his uncle again and never to return to his house. What is more, his uncle no longer wanted such a malicious nephew.

When two individuals separate and neither feels any regrets, the separation has come too late. Macledio broke with his uncle too late and became a little servant boy for the director of the school, who had welcomed him in such a generous manner and protected him, adds Tiekura.

The director of the school was wonderful, and he seemed to have everything it would take to be a man of destiny. . . . Macledio's man of destiny, adds the responder. The director was the only Black in the country able to dress in a manner that was at once elegant and sober. His colonial helmet was khaki, his trousers were always impeccably pressed, and he wore suede shoes. He had a slightly ruddy complexion, marked by chicken pox, and his face was illumined by eyes that were incredibly fiery and tender at the same time. The director spoke little and read much. He expected people to call him Dymo Lodia, willingly allowed his wives to be unfaithful, never spit, and prayed very little.

These were not the trifles that led Macledio to break away from him. Because he did finally leave the director, announces Tiekura. The director had another unseemly habit.

At the end of each school year, following the awarding of certificates, he would invite one of the girls to his classroom at night, recite La Fontaine's fables to her, hum the chants of hunters, and rape her. Once the sin was consummated, remorse would torment his intestines and bring on diarrhea. He cried as copiously as his unfortunate victim, whom he would clean in a delicate fashion as he stuffed her with candy. He would proclaim his unworthiness and vomit all night long. Still tearful, he would sing and bellow out poetry the rest of the night. For two whole weeks, he would refuse to return to his villa, his wives, and his children, and would sleep out in the open on the school benches in order to observe the stars in the heaven and to interpret the howling of the hyenas at night after the moon had set. No doubt Director Dymo was a prophet, but he could not be my man of destiny; my man of destiny must be somewhere else, in my future, added Macledio.

Yes, Macledio understood that Director Dymo could not be his man of destiny. He left him and passed the competitive entrance examination for the colonial École Primaire Supérieure. At this boarding school, he had for a classmate and dormitory neighbor, and consequently for a friend, an exceptional fellow who he thought might be his man of destiny. The boy, called Bazon, had the heart of a puppy, was slightly cross-eyed, and dragged his left foot. Bazon said, and believed, that to love someone was to serve somebody other than oneself and to accept that person as a master. So he made you his master, Macledio. So specifies the responder.

At dawn, Bazon would do the chores that fell to Macledio by way of cleaning and maintaining the boarding school grounds and buildings before waking him up with a tumbler of hot coffee. During the day, he would wash Macledio's underwear and dirty shirts before taking care of his homework (especially the math assignments). All day long and everywhere they went, he would threaten with a knife any school comrades who were disrespectful to Macledio. It was at night in the dormitory, after lights-out, that things went awry between the two friends. Bazon would begin to cry like a little boy as he sought a bit of human warmth from Macledio. He could not stand sleeping alone. Each evening, Macledio would get angry again, insult him, and even slap him as he made him promise not to wet the sheets. Bazon would promise and begin to snore. The following morning when they woke up, the sheet was always wet.

One Sunday, before Mass, Macledio studied his friend; he was not handsome. A naughty fellow who, at age seventeen, was not clean could not be his man of destiny. In spite of tears and fake illnesses, Macledio dropped his school buddy Bazon. Despite the latter's jealousy, he turned his affection to the white French professor, Ricard.

This White had made a public pronouncement one morning.

"Macledio is the only Black who, in spite of his thick lips, is able to pronounce a mute *e*. He will be one of the first Africans who rises to the level of French civilization."

This praise touched Macledio. In gratitude, he was willing to spend Saturday evening and sometimes his siestas with French professor Ricard. Unfortunately, after several months, Macledio became sick of the White's touching and especially of his bad breath, which always reeked of onion, morning and night. He was unable and unwilling to put up with the man any longer.

One Monday morning, to flatter Macledio in front of the class, the White repeated that Macledio would be the first one of the group to assimilate civilization because he could pronounce a mute *e*. Instead of beaming with the usual pleasure and pride, Macledio publicly answered that he did not give a damn about the colonialist's mute *e* and French civilization. . . .

That was a challenge and an insult, explains the responder. The White slaps the pupil, who scornfully replies by spitting in the teacher's face. The insult was scandalous and subversive. Macledio is arrested, tortured, and assigned as a native to the regiments of Senegalese riflemen in the colonial army at Bouaké. . . .

The regulations of the colonial army distinguished between two races: the French soldiers and the native riflemen, adds Macledio.

French soldiers were superior, and a thousand rules had been established in order to maintain the natives as inferiors. The native infantryman must wear the chechia, the red flannel sash, during all seasons, a jacket of Gonfreville cloth, and go barefoot. He must salute his Black superiors and every White man, military or civilian. . . . That was what French colonization held in store for the smiling native infantrymen, those big children who had fought in France during the last two wars. Nothing other than a persnickety and petty form of racism! Adds Macledio.

They sent your regiment, Macledio, to the forest in the colony of the Ebony people in order to repress the Blacks of the Rassemblement Démocratique Africain, who were proclaiming communist slogans and revolting against forced labor. Around Gagnoa, you killed two Bétés armed with arrows. Beyond Daloa, the captain ordered you to burn houses in the villages. You burned hundreds of them as you ran, going farther and farther away from the regiment until you reached that enormous, hundred-year-old silk cotton tree with its roots plunging into the earth. You coiled up in the hollows of its roots and waited for the shots to fade into the distance and fall silent and . . . you disappeared into the forest.

You had just deserted, deserted the colonial army, explains the responder.

For two weeks, Macledio wandered through the uninhabited forest, living on wild roots and pillaging as he avoided villages and roads. Exhausted, he came into a clearing and saw the sky once more. Armed men took him prisoner. Macledio, you had just stumbled on one of the lumber camps of the colonist Reste.

Colonist Reste was the owner of sky, earth, water, and the trees of the vast region of the impenetrable forest of Côte d'Ivoire and he held the power of life and death over some two hundred slave laborers, who were scrawny, stinking, and covered with sores. The poor devils cut and dragged the enormous blocks of wood to the wharf. The guards dragged Macledio to Monsieur Reste himself when they found out their prisoner wrote and spoke French.

Macledio explained his situation as a deserter. He asked the master of this place to have him taken back to the captain of his regiment in Bouaké. He preferred life in the military prisons to that of a Black hauling logs in Reste's lumber camps.

But Reste had other ideas; he liked renegade Blacks and had been seeking an assistant for a lumber camp in Cameroon. So Macledio was welcomed. Because of the purity with which you spoke French, the White shared a calabash of palm wine with you and hired you for his camp in the Cameroonian forest, adds the responder.

Ready to go to work in Cameroon, Macledio needed to choose a young servant boy from among the forced laborers (he was a time-keeper, and the timekeepers at Reste's camps were allocated, along with a pencil and notebook, a boy to do their laundry and cooking). Macledio's preference was for the young Gaston, who was a Bamileke.

Gaston was more faithful than a puppy and more silent than a vir-gin's cache-sexe. He opened his mouth only to praise and venerate one lone being in this vast world: the king of his people, the *fe'eh*, adds the responder. He spoke of him, pronounced his name, described him as the "rain that falls suddenly," as the "father with fine clothing," as the "one whose eyes are planted at the crossroads," as the "one who dis-tributes without favoring either hand," and even as the "one who does not become nauseous at the sight of excrement." When Gaston, the servant boy, added to all those qualities the distinction that the king, his *fe'eh*, was also the "father of orphans," Macledio's doubts van-ished. The Bamileke king was his man of destiny. The servant boy was only a means, the way chosen by the Almighty to show him the road to his man of destiny. Macledio deserted the camp during the night and the next morning was in the service of the *fe'eh*, the Bamileke king Fundoing.

The Bamileke are Bantu. The Bantu are one of the most important ethnic groups among the forest peoples of Central Africa who attacked the world of the Naked people from the south. Explains Macledio.

Your first days at the court of the Bamileke king corroborated your premonition, Macledio. The king was surely the man of destiny whom you had been seeking across the earth.

He was an exceptional being, the sole possessor of 212 wives, 403 pigs, 64 servants, a great palace, more than 60,000 subjects, 36,082 of the female sex, over whom he held seignorial rights. Explains Macledio. This was incontestably an onerous duty, which, in addition to his numerous other obligations, exhausted King Fundoing. The king was always exhausted.

Like many of the *fe'eh*'s servants, Macledio was kindly disposed to assist his master and even to replace him in his nocturnal obligations. He tenderly consoled and paid court to Hélène, the only young wife in the harem able to read the Bible and write her master's name in French. He applied himself to this task with his characteristic conscientiousness and passion so that in barely seven months Hélène managed to give birth to a boy with Macledio's exact nose. The king noticed and congratulated Macledio, but all the subjects congratulated the king, the *fe'eh,* on the occasion of his 231st heir, who was baptized by the priest with the fine and impressive name of Augustin.

Macledio loved Augustin and swore never to separate from his first son. He would never leave the kingdom: the *fe'eh* was and remained his man of destiny. He even decided that he, Macledio, had been created by Allah to serve the king and swore to remain at the court for the rest of his days.

This good resolution was thwarted by two mistakes committed by Macledio. The servant was expected to stay away from any wife who became the object of the *fe'eh*'s attention. Yet, for a period of two weeks, the *fe'eh* required the presence of the charming Hélène as part of his nighttime contingent without Macledio understanding that he should desist from Bible commentaries and French lessons with the young woman. And then, a servant must never become attached to a child of whom he is the mere biological father.

Macledio spent the better part of his days bouncing little Augustin on his knees, kissing him, and even whispering words from the dialects of his distant country in the baby's ears.

Macledio's case was presented one Friday morning at the king's council, and it was unanimously decided to assassinate the culprit on Saturday at the first crow of the cock. Nobody will ever know who broke secrecy. Who was the traitor? That night, as the moon set, Macledio eluded the vigilance of the guards, slipped out unnoticed, went into the hut sanctuary, and grabbed the holy baskets, the *bieri* containing the skulls of the king's ancestors.

The Bamileke are Bantu. Like every Bantu king, the Bamileke Fundoing received his political, social, and mystical powers from the skulls of his ancestors, which the *gnwala'a* worshiped once every week with libations of wine and anointments of palm oil. Explains Macledio.

You disappeared into the night with one lone piece of baggage on your shoulder, a sack loaded with the most venerable skulls of the Bamileke king's ancestors.

At dawn, the sicarii slipped into the house of the condemned man: nothing was there except the mat, with no trace or effluvia of Macledio. They looked toward the sanctuary and saw the damage! The profanation, the sacrilege! No Bantu or Bamileke would ever have dared do such a thing. Macledio had desecrated the sanctuary and carried off the skulls of the ancients! Relics that a foreigner would not have dared touch. This was the worst possible catastrophe for the king, for his entire dynasty, for the entire country! The *fe'eh* and his prime minister initiated the *tse'eh*, which was both the name for the dance of the king and for a secret society. The master of the *kèn* called all the young men to the sacred wood; those affiliated with the *lali* gathered on the plateau with their arms for the war dance; the members of the *mwuop* gathered at the marketplace, and the women of the *masoh* trooped to the various gates of the city. The entire country danced and had to keep dancing in mourning for the skulls until the relics returned to their sanctuary.

Eighty-eight stalwarts from among the fiercest warriors and hunters were armed and sent after the fugitive. They quickly caught him, encircled him, challenged him, and threatened him. And you, Macledio, you kept right on walking calmly, as if you did not see the pack of killers waving their hatchets, rifles, arrows, and spears, howling and jumping on the forest path behind, in front, to your right, and to your left. You knew that as long as you held firmly onto the macabre sack, no Bamileke in this world would dare attack. From time to time, you would provoke cries of horror among the crowd with your impious pretense at breaking the skulls against a tree trunk. For nearly 150 kilometers, over one night and two days, you continued your journey surrounded by the killers chasing you.

Ah, Tiekura! The passing of the horde through the thick of the forest created a hubbub among the great orangutans, and the birds flew off to better skies. Your arrival in villages made people believe that tribal warfare had begun once more, and by instinct, they fled to take refuge in the forest.

When you arrived in Douala, rich Bamileke businessmen came to meet you with a thousand proposals. Macledio was only willing to consider them and discuss them once he was quite ensconced among shipments on the deck of a boat. He exchanged his macabre packet for a briefcase filled with banknotes.

It was not so much the money (I have never tried to get rich). It was so I would not seem to be an idiot. I knew and admired the Bamileke for their cupidity and their business sense. The rich businessmen would have taken me for the most naive person in the universe had I not traded the skulls of the ancestors for solid cash. Explains Macledio. But in Yaounde, whatever their Beti compatriots who hate their guts may think, the Bamileke are the kindest and most easygoing people in the world. Those armed killers and rich businessmen spontaneously bade me farewell with the broadest smiles and friendliest of gestures as the boat weighed anchor.

As soon as Cameroonian territory disappeared from the horizon and nothing was visible except the sea and gray sky, Macledio was gripped by remorse and seasickness. He was angry with himself and blamed himself for the stupidity of his behavior. He would remain a coward and weakling all his life! A man who could abandon his first son, who could exchange his first son for a briefcase full of banknotes! He was ashamed! Every father, every Paleo would have shown a bit of dignity in such a situation, would have quietly accepted being assassinated! For his son! Because of his son! In order to be buried in that earth which would be trampled by his son's first steps! He was an unworthy father, and he would remain so all his life. Staggering, he went to vomit from the afterdeck. He opened the briefcase and hurled the bundles of bills into the wind. But, lacking physical courage, he did not leap from the deck into the foaming waves to be devoured by the sharks and remain in the guts of the dogfish, close to his first son, Augustin! That cowardice remains, and shall always remain one of the great regrets of your life, Macledio. Concludes the responder.

Macledio disembarked with his attaché case at Takoradi in the Gold Coast. This was the time when African countries were better known by the name of their dictator than by their real name. And the dictator of the Gold Coast was Kwame Nkrumah, adds the responder.

Macledio had to avoid French territory on the Slave Coast, the Coast of the Virile People, the Republic of the Ebony People (of which the dictator was Tiekoroni, the man with the fedora), and the Republic of the Mountains (Nkutigi Fondio was the dictator), all francophone states in which he was wanted as a renegade and a deserter.

On the west side of the port of Takoradi, it is not at all difficult to corrupt the customs and police officials (fortunately, a few banknotes had stuck to the bottom of the briefcase), to leave the port, and to disappear into the impenetrable forest. Macledio walked for three days in a straight path toward the northwest. The fourth morning, he came upon Kouassikro, an Anyi village lost in the forest.

The Anyi are Akan. The Akan are one of the most important ethnic groups in the forest of the Ebony people and the Gold Coast. Adds Macledio.

All the inhabitants of Kouassikro were dancing, singing, and awaiting you, Macledio, as if you were the Messiah. As soon as you emerged from the forest, the warriors took you, undressed you, washed you with herb potions, covered you with new clothing, gold, and kaolin. And the royal welcome that had been prepared for you ensued at once: a chicken was sacrificed, and there were libations of palm wine.

Ah, Tiekura! While all the inhabitants are busying themselves with his person, Macledio is looking right and left between the huts for the way that will let him escape the warriors and return to the forest. All of a sudden, he understood everything. He was going to have his throat slit, to be sacrificed and buried with a dead person. Among the Anyi, who belong to the Akan group, a king never enters his tomb alone. He is always inhumed with those who will serve him in the hereafter. Before European colonization, the king was inhumed with his prisoners. Since the suppression of slavery, the Anyi kidnap lone travelers. Many travelers who had ventured into the forests inhabited by the Anyi, the Baule, and other peoples of the Akan group have never been seen again. Macledio was living his final minutes; he understood and told himself that. He could read it in the eyes of all the inhabitants, who were closely following his every movement. They brought him before the tallest and largest house in the village and seated him on a throne. This was the final confirmation of his suspicions. People related that the Anyi never slit the throat of a stranger without first having consecrated him king. In tears, Macledio recited his final prayers. The village patriarch approached him and spoke.

He wishes you welcome, Macledio, you a stranger. He tells you that you are fortunate. Very fortunate. You are a truly blessed man. You have just been crowned as the prince consort of the village and are destined to be the companion of their queen. You will be the sire of the future king or the future queen of the country. The entire village congratulates you; all the inhabitants are at your disposition. Your ears are worthless; you are unable to comprehend the honorable old man. The patriarch patiently stops and begins once more.

Several weeks earlier, their princess was taken with a desire to know a man and to become a mother. As required by Akan custom, the princess had been washed. That is to say that she was initiated first of all. Then, during a public ceremony, she was deflowered by a matron using her fingers and was given a warm bath in a special preparation.

The deflowering was requisite. Any baby that the princess might have conceived before this initiation would have been impure and would have been strangled at his first cries.

The old man added that they, the people of Kouassikro, practiced a radical form of matriarchy. In order to avoid any paternal acknowledgment or claims (which were always a source of conflict in a community), they always led their princess, when she was of age to procreate, to be loved by a passing stranger. Macledio happened in at the right time.

Since the princess had been deflowered, the inhabitants had been dancing, waiting, and hoping for the providential man. Many travelers had arrived and left; Macledio was the first one the princess wished to possess. Upon seeing him emerge from the forest, she had cried out: "There is the man whom I desire to have in me!" Adjua was not only the princess of the village, she was also the priestess and seer, and Macledio, as prince consort, would automatically become her coadjutor.

Finally, the princess comes out of the house and draws close. She is charming. From the belts of pearls enhancing her buttocks falls a cache-sexe that half reveals the generous folds of flesh. Between her breasts, true green March mangos, run many cowrie necklaces, stretching from her neck to her navel. With a honeyed smile, she wishes the stranger welcome.

"I desire you, I desire you, I desire you," you cry out with all your being, Macledio, as you make an intensely respectful bow.

The princess draws near, takes you by the hand, and you both disappear into the sanctuary dwelling and palace of the princess. The ceremony is over. And, without delay, you engage in your appointed task, Macledio.

Being a priestess, Adjua officiated all day long. People came to consult from all the surrounding villages. As coadjutor and prince consort, Macledio rang bells and recited incantations in his costume of a great fetishist. Obeying Macledio's supplications, the princess first moaned and finally went into a trance. In the trance, she made many lascivious gestures that excited and psychologically prepared the prince consort for his demanding and essential nocturnal duties.

All day long, your agama danced beneath your trousers, adds the responder laughing.

Macledio was physically sustained and conditioned by baths in preparations of aphrodisiacal roots and by eating fresh meat prepared with aphrodisiacal leaves. The princess slept very little during the night;

he had to respond to her entreaties at each moment. Macledio proved himself worthy of the task. Better yet, the more he gave of himself, the more he loved the princess. This life was far too exceptional not to be the end and the crowning of an entire existence.

Ah, Tiekura! Surely his man of destiny was not a man. . . .

Yes, I began by thinking that my man of destiny was not a man but a woman. My man of destiny was the Princess Adjua. Explains Macledio. It is in the force of that conviction that I yield to the princess with such insistent energy that, in less than eight moons, I endow her with not two but three twins. Three adorable boys!

Boys that even malice and jealousy would have loved, adds Tiekura.

With the birth of the twins, Macledio's siring function was at an end. That was the beginning of his woes. Since one of the twins would become king, the subjects were forced not only to forget the king's biological father, but even to be ignorant of the very place where that father might be found. Among the Akan, a true king has no father, adds the responder. Macledio must leave and never return to the village of Kouassikro. Really, never again!

Before colonization, the sire had his throat slit and was sacrificed, adds Tiekura.

Macledio unhesitatingly begged to have his throat slit, to be killed, to be sacrificed. He preferred death to departure, banishment. He loved the twins; he loved the princess; she was his woman of destiny. The twins were his second, third, and fourth children; the princess was the first wife he had ever received, who belonged to him, and the first woman he had freely loved with all his soul, with all his body. He wanted to die for them, to remain ever beneath the ground that their feet would tread. He could not imagine living anywhere else, adds Tiekura. The great fetishist answers that, since the arrival of the English in the Gold Coast, the sire has no longer had his throat slit. He is castrated, has his tongue cut out, loses his two eyes, has his eardrums pierced. Macledio was ready to die, to die at once, but not to undergo barbaric torture. He did not want to live the rest of his life deaf, dumb, blind, and impotent. Adds the responder.

During the night, Macledio quietly slips out, enters the sacred dwelling, takes his bell ringer's costume, and steals one of the purses filled with gold from among all those placed at the feet of the ancestors. Dressed as a fetishist's bell ringer, he has no difficulty in passing through the forest villages. The fetishists' bell ringers are always feared and respected among the Anyi. Specifies the responder.

As he walks on, Macledio notes that the farther he goes, the thinner is the forest, and after a certain distance he notices among the vegetation the first karite trees. He has crossed the forest and reached the savanna, and he remembers that griots say that all the territory where the karite tree grows belongs to the Mandinka savanna.

On the Sudanese savanna, Macledio sits down to reflect for a moment. The ease with which he had been able to leave Kouassikro seemed amazing to him. That could not have been by chance. The sanctuary that was always guarded day and night had no lookouts. His escape had been desired, prepared, and organized. Surely by the princess in order to save him from torture. Macledio, you concluded that the princess loved you as much as you continued to cherish her. The princess whom you had not seen since she had given birth and whom you were not supposed to see again was thinking of you and suffering. She was suffering atrociously. Macledio was ashamed for such a charming woman to be afflicted because of his cowardice. Adds the responder.

Why had he not remained there courageously to undergo mutilation and to remain for the rest of his life at the side of his children and a wife who loved him so much? Far from his children and the princess from that point onward, his life would evolve uselessly, with neither pleasure nor dignity. His fate would remain misery and bad luck.

I, Macledio, must revolt against such a destiny, and I am decided to retrace my steps in order to yield to the torturers and to ask them to fulfill their duty, to carry out their barbaric custom. I look around: I am at the edge of the Sudanese savanna, and the beginning of the Sahel is before me. I walked for days and nights without any point of reference. It is impossible for me to turn back and find the village of Kouassikro. Tearful, demoralized, and discouraged, I continue on my route toward the north.

Those who, like Macledio, have never had any fate other than bad luck and who still look forward to happiness walk relentlessly northward. Continues the responder.

Let us imitate the traveler who stops from time to time to take a breath, announces the *sèrè* to signal a break. The *koroduwa* lapses into the usual suggestive quips. Everyone breaks out laughing. The *sèrè* recites a few proverbs.

When the vital nerve has been cut, the chicken kills the wildcat.
The eye does not see the object that jabs it.
When fate cuts all ties, no parent can hide the child.

12

Ah, Tiekura! The pensive Macledio continues his solitary journey on the road northward. Suddenly, from thickets on the right and the left, five *koroduwa* emerge. Real *koroduwa*. They have the same costume as you and they are playing flutes, dancing, and uttering crazy things just as you do, Tiekura.

Each *koroduwa* was in a frightening costume. On their heads was a cap with an old vulture's beak as a visor; a vulture's beak to signify that every man is a greedy scavenger like the repulsive vulture. And nothing else. Around their necks were a calabash for begging, a cup for drinking, a spoon for eating, and a large bone. The large bone was to signify that man is also a wandering dog in perpetual search of food. And nothing else. Slung across their shoulders was a pouch with a flute for making music and a bag of antidote against poisons. A bag of antidote against poisons so that they might never eat what somebody gave them without being sure they would not be poisoned. And nothing else. At each *koroduwa*'s waist there was a monkey skin with its tail beating against their buttocks. The monkey tail on their buttocks was to show that every man is a maker of farts. And nothing else. When he is not playing his flute, he is saying crazy things and making jokes. Crazy things and jokes in order to signify that man is a liar, falsehood tree, a tree of lies and stupidities. And nothing, absolutely nothing else.

Macledio recognized that he was in Senufo country and somewhere close to a village from which the young men were undergoing a period of purification before entering the sacred grove for their initiation. After playing their flutes, singing, and dancing for Macledio, the *koroduwa* held out their calabashes: they were begging for food. Macledio generously took several pieces of gold out of his purse and tried to offer one to each *koroduwa*. In unison, the five young men let out cries of horror, threw down the pieces of gold, and ran for cover in the thickets. Macledio quietly picked up the coins, stood up, and continued on his route toward the village. He had only taken a few steps when the *koroduwa* came out of the thickets again, ran after him, and barred his path, forbidding his entry into the village.

"You have a purse full of gold. So you are either a great bandit or a rich man. In either case, we shall not allow you to go into our village."

They surrounded Macledio, still playing, singing, and dancing, and forced him to go around the village. They accompanied him quite a way past the village, and, before leaving, they warned him.

"Do not come back, and do not approach our village again. We want neither thieves nor rich men. We assassinate them. We will kill you if we see you in these parts again."

Saddened, still pensive, and ever lonely, Macledio continued his journey toward the north. At the edge of a village, two individuals resembling sleepwalkers attacked him. They were dressed in tatters and were as strong as bulls. Red eyes popped out of their heads; trembling lips were white with slobber; noisy, irregular breathing. Macledio struggled with all his strength, but in vain. They overcame him and dragged him without ceremony in front of the *nzima* priest's dwelling, where a crowd was gathered about a dance of possession.

The aggressors were not maniacs but were possessed, explains Tiekura.

In the middle of the circle, some ten possessed individuals were rolling and crawling in the dust, digging into the laterite soil with their fingers and teeth like robots to the rhythm of the resounding drums.

Abruptly, the tam-tam change rhythm: the crowd draws back. Two of the possessed come in with a puppy, place it on the ground, and slit its throat. All the possessed throw themselves on the remains with incredible violence, pulling it to pieces and taking parts of it. The weaker people get only the intestines, paws, head, or tail. Staggering, each of them displays the piece won in the scramble and eats it raw. Every last part of the dog is consumed—including the skin, bones, and even the excrement. The ground soiled with blood is licked and then raked with steel teeth. Nothing from the dog remains on the ground: neither a hair or the least drop of blood. Adds the responder.

As if in choreographed movement, the possessed turn around. They stare fixedly at you, Macledio. You tremble with fear like a girl faced with rapists, and you take refuge behind the priest of the ceremony. Two possessed men go around the priest, push you to the middle of the circle, undress you, grab your purse, and throw it on the ground. The purse bursts open and the pieces of gold are scattered. Exclamations burst from the crowd. In stupefaction, everyone—priests, spectators, drummers—stops the ritual. Everybody shoves to get a closer look at you. Meanwhile, two possessed men have swallowed several gold coins, and the *nzima* points at them. Several other possessed people jump on the unfortunate pair, pummel them to death, and drag them by the feet to the middle of the circle, where they drop them on the ground at Macledio's feet.

The people where you have just arrived are the Songhai. They live in Niger. This was at the time when African states were known by the name of their dictators rather than by their own names. The dictators of Niger, one after the other, were called Hamani Diori and Kountché.

The Songhai were one of the first Black peoples to convert to Islam. But they were no more given to the great mysticism than hyenas are to ritual ablutions. Explains Tiekura. They took up Muhammadanism in the eleventh century but were never willing to abandon their ancient beliefs or to give up their dances of possession. From among Muslim myths, they derived some new beliefs, new elements, the *malaka,* and added them to the cult of the ancestors and the traditional Black African spirits of water, sky, wind, lightning, and the bush, thus constituting a coherent pantheon and a complex mythology called the *Holle.* The essential principle of the *Holle* cult lies in the dances of possession, during which the spirit is embodied in the dancer, mounts him as a rider mounts his horse, and speaks through his mouth. Adds Macledio.

The *Holle* ceremonies bring the entire village before the dwelling of the *nzima.* Dancers are chosen among the inhabitants possessed by the spirit. The musicians and the auxiliary "quiet women" watch over the proper organization of the ceremony.

For eight centuries, the Songhai were happy with this mythology and the spirits. The *Holle* cult remained unchanged. Upon the onslaught of colonization that befell them, repressed them, and scattered them across all West Africa, the Songhai discovered that one category was missing from their universe—malice—and one category of spirits —the malicious spirits. They created the *Hauka.* The *Hauka* are the malicious spirits. The administrative hierarchy of the evil spirits is based on the organization of the colonial administration. It is thus that the malicious spirit Gomno (the governor), the Zeneral Malia (the general of the soldiers), King Zuzi (the king of the judges), the Sekter (the secretary of the administration), and the Kapral Gardi (the corporal of the guard) are found in that hierarchy.

The colonial administrator Croccichia, who finally became governor of the colonies, wanted to outlaw the dances of possession. He did not succeed and ended up being deified himself in the form of the most malicious of malicious spirits, the Krosisya or Komando Magu (the evil commander). A half century after the colonization, Croccichia continues to be reincarnated among the Songhai, to mount them, and to speak through their mouths. Adds Macledio.

Following the independences, after 1960, Diori's single party, and the military dictatorship of General Kountché in Niamey (the capital of Niger), the Songhai invented the lying spirits. The lying spirits resemble their compatriots, those city politicians who come out to the villages every Sunday and make promises that are never kept. Like other spirits, the lying spirits are embodied in a Songhai dancer, mounting and lying through the mouth of the possessed man.

But never in the existence of Africa and the Songhai, never during the dance of possession, had a man covered with kaolin and wearing a many-colored pagne emerged from the bush with a purse of gold. Macledio was, he could only be, a spirit, the spirit of gold. The new spirit was named Maklesani, specifies Tiekura.

The possessed who had pilfered pieces of gold were treated with such ferociousness as would have killed a donkey, but it did not manage to destroy them or even make them bleed. They were made to ingest powerful laxatives that made them yield their booty, which was cleaned and returned to Macledio.

A jinni must never be attacked or robbed (the guilty possessed learned this in the grips of pain, adds the responder). The jinni must be taken care of, respected. Staying in the house of the priest, Macledio lived like a prince. He was able to maintain his status and his spiritual aura by gratifying one citizen, chosen at random each day, with a piece of gold. So he was a jinni who performed a miracle every day. Macledio's purse was growing visibly lighter.

A circumstance as fortunate as it was unexpected kept me from exhausting every piece of my gold, explains Macledio. One morning, I was awakened by people fighting around my house. In the hubbub, the Songhai were muttering some incredible news. The village divine had predicted during the night that I would perform my final and ultimate miracle during that day (the first Friday of the moon of Sorghum) before I disappeared to return to a jinni dwelling in the river like other jinn. People were fighting and shoving to get close to the door and be part of the group from which would be chosen the last beneficiary of the final extraordinary prodigality of the good jinni of gold, Maklesani. . . . My last liberality went to my host, the *nzima,* and the crowd dispersed. That night, as soon as the moon had set, I left his house. The village was silent, the doors were barricaded: it was dangerous to witness the immaterialization of a jinni. Quietly, I slipped between the stalls and disappeared in the bush, despite the barking of the dogs. No one followed me, no one looked for me.

The least of a jinni's talents is to dissolve, to evaporate, to vanish. Adds the responder.

It was at Niamey (the capital of the state of Niger, whose dictator is called Hamani Diori), on the bank of the Niger River, where I went to meditate every morning, that I understood that neither money nor greatness yields happiness. I was a jinni who, to the very end of all worlds, would be embodied, would mount, and would predict through the mouths of possessed Songhai . . . and I remained perpetually desperate. I was stumbling beneath the weight of gold and I was still poverty-stricken. Squatting on a stone in a little thicket near the municipal slaughterhouse, I wept and pondered. What damnation had made me leave the *nzima* who was perhaps my man of destiny? What fate and indignity had led me to abandon my first son to the Bamileke and my twins to the Anyi? I kept weeping every morning on the very same stone and on the same riverbank. The Niger River was drying up and yet there was a possibility that I would make it overflow with my tears, when a Tuareg as poor as I came up, greeted me, and began talking. I kept reciting my litany of misfortune. The blue man's reply was spontaneous, clear, and without digressions. He knew what ill was gnawing away at me, he was quite familiar with that sorrow and its remedies. As a Tuareg, he too had suffered from it.

After the great drought that had stricken the Sahara and the Sahel, he had come south, like many of his compatriots, the blue men. He had wandered from city to city with his wife and three children: Cotonou, Lomé, Accra, Abidjan, seeking charity. But everywhere the "slaves" (he asked pardon for using the word *slaves* to designate Blacks and explained that in the Tuareg language, the same word means Black and slave). So, everywhere in the coastal cities, the Blacks (slaves) offered to them, people of the desert, the means to sleep, eat, and travel. But they never gave them money. To offer hospitality and to give money are two different acts. Giving money is done with the heart, while offering hospitality is done through a sense of duty in order to get rid of a beggar who hangs on. Through having survived by what was dutifully given and because he had never found in the action of the donors a heart that went out to another heart, he had been eaten by the same ill from which I was suffering—despair, "Afro-pessimism."

He had gone back to the Sahel and the Sahara, his native land, and had once more begun the great tribal wandering. And he had been completely cured. There is no place but the desert to cure despair. That's because the desert is infinite space, the silence of the dunes, a nocturnal sky enameled with thousands of stars. An environment that saves people in great despair, without fail. In the desert, one could cry without fear of making a river overflow. No other form of nature is as propitious to meditation. That is why all the great prophets were born in the desert.

The blue man who had spoken with me and comforted me was called Ould (and several other names similar to Ould). Ould was preparing a caravan to cross the desert, from Niamey to Algiers. He asked me why I wouldn't join the caravan. Why shouldn't I go to Algiers? Algiers is the door of the world, he stated. From Algiers, one can easily go to Mecca, Cairo, Tunis, Casablanca, Paris, Rome. The Tuareg fell silent for a moment so he could listen to the wind playing in the leaves and the Niger flowing along its bed—and, especially, to look at me. I was disconcerted by his reasoning and was reflecting on a thousand things.

In fact, why shouldn't I go to Algiers? Go on up to Paris from Algiers. In Paris, I could make one of my old dreams come true: take up my studies once more. Loaded down with diplomas, I could return to the Bamileke country in Cameroon, to the Gold Coast, and even to the village of Kouassikro. With slangy Parisian French and Oxonian English on my lips, I could certainly win my children back. With my omniscience in psychoanalysis, psychology, sociology, ethnology, and phraseology, I could embody a spirit other than the jinni of gold. . . . Most assuredly, I should join the caravan. I decided at once to pay cash for a camel so I could try my luck.

All day long, the caravan stretched out over the immensity of the desert. It stopped only for salaams. In order not to draw the attention of thieves and greedy Tuareg to his gold, Macledio had metamorphosed into a pious Muslim, like the explorer René Caillié. The vertigo of the desert's barrenness intoxicated him and made him call out long sura. He understood why the Sahara attracted great men and transformed them into mystics. In the evening, they drank tea around the fire before sleeping beneath the stars.

On the fifth morning, Macledio felt happy . . . very happy. His four sons had joined him; he was a great mystic doubling with a true jinni and had finally found his man of destiny. His man of destiny was a blue man of the desert who, by his dress, reminded him of his friend Ould. Abruptly, a painful emptiness came over him: his man of destiny was going away, fleeing him. He flew in pursuit of him on horseback, camel, and by swimming. He swallowed a mouthful of the muddy water from the Niger River; the liquid was bitter, stifling, deadly—he cried out . . . and woke up. Adds the responder.

He felt bad, beaten, overcome with cramps from his toes to his neck —heavy head, dry mouth. With his eyes still closed, he tried to rediscover himself, to understand. He remembered that they had tea together the previous night, as every evening, and he scolded himself for having had too much. But why hadn't his companions awakened him at dawn for salaams, like every other morning? Why? He cracked his eyelids, gave a start, yelled, and stood up! He was alone, alone! About him was only sand, dunes, the desert, the immensity of the desert. The entire caravan had disappeared. His companions had vanished with his gold and his camel. By way of provisions, they had left him only a few cookies and a goatskin of water. Macledio recalled the advice the blue men had given him the previous evening, the elementary precautions and customs that a man lost in the desert should never forget: to huddle in the shadow of a dune while the sun is high and walk at night with the stars as his guide, not the responder.

I walked for many night One moonlit night—I shall never remember whether it was a dream or a mirage—I smelled that I was drawing close to an oasis. I woke up and tried to move. It was impossible. . . . because he was in irons inside a tent. What had he done? Where was he? They answered that he should be respectful like all slaves. They had found him, wallowing in the mud of the oasis, near the camels' watering trough. They had chained him: from that moment on, he belonged to the master of the region, Sheikh Mahomet Karami Ould Mayaba, king of the Tuareg. He was the sheikh's sixth black slave. They were beginning to make him swallow the decoction that breaks the will of a Black and gives him the soul of a slave: camel milk mixed with a marabout's elixirs. In less than six weeks, Macledio gave in and appeared submissive. They took off his irons and placed him in the service of the queen, Princess Sali, only wife of the sheikh.

The princess was elephantine! The upbringing of a Tuareg princess is most assuredly the most careful and the most exacting of any in the world. She is taught to recite the Qur'an and to play the harp. But not much. The main part of this education is taken care of by a grandmother who is a torturer.

The grandmother takes charge of her granddaughter at age seven. As she wakes up each morning, her index, middle, and ring fingers are inserted between two wooden logs. With all her strength and the greatest cruelty, the torturer-grandmother presses the logs, crushing the fingers. The little girl wails and weeps with all her child's heart. She is given some milk curds along with some food high in caloric value. She gobbles it all up so her grandmother will release the pressure and stop the torture. She is force-fed like a goose. She is stuffed and has no taste for food. She vomits the milk mixture. Grandmother gets angry, beats her, and starts the torture again. The little martyr begins to eat once more, to swallow, to stuff herself. She bloats, swells each day. She quickly takes on the volume of two baby elephants. She can no longer bathe or move without a slave, her own slave. Then she is ripe for marriage when she is no more than thirteen years old, adds Tiekura.

They wait for a moonlit night to slip a blue man, skinny as a rail, into her tent. She plays the harp for him. A real prince will not snuggle up to his dulcinea unless her corporeal volume is ten times his own.

Madame Sali Karami was a true princess; she had four slaves in her service—two eunuchs and two women. Macledio completed her staff. The eunuchs and the black slave women kept busy with the princess all day long. They fed her, turned her over, and washed her. Rarely her entire body; the princess only took a full bath once a year. Macledio guarded the entrance to the tent and only worked occasionally to hoist or lower, not an easy task, the princess into her cage on the back of a camel during the interminable wanderings of the tribe through the desert.

The princess was admired as the most beautiful woman in the desert. But one had to be a blue man, thin and dry as a stalk of rice three months after the harvest, to fall into an ecstasy before the giant mollusk she had become. Adds the responder.

Moussa (this is invariably the name given by the Tuareg to the first eunuch serving a princess), Moussa himself told me (Macledio) that a week before my arrival the princess smelled to high heaven. For three days, everybody had looked in vain for whatever was putrid in the tent or about the princess. Prince Karim in person came to our assistance, to help us black captives. Together, we raised the rolls of fat on the princess and cleansed them one by one. What a surprise! We found the decomposing cadaver of a little viper of the pyramids, a streamlined little serpent that had ventured between the folds. It had been suffocated before it could prepare its powerful fangs and inject her with its deadly venom.

People admired the princess as the most talented musician in the desert. But one had to be a man of the desert, a man of the silence and the infinite spaces, to appreciate her sonatas that were as monotonous as the dunes. She plucked her harp all day long for her husband, and especially for all her lovers. For the princess was much courted. As soon as her husband left the tent, one of her lovers would slip in and claim the entryway by leaving his shoes there. Nobody else dare expel him or bother them, not even the husband. Tuareg etiquette forbids any male, including the husband, from entering a tent where the lady has company.

When the prince was absent, it was not unusual for the princess to receive as many as three lovers, one after the other, in one day. Macledio, an unrepentant voyeur, finally learned by spying through all the openings of the tent the technique of the skinny little Tuareg for turning the princess over.

One afternoon (the prince was away of course and no pair of shoes barred the entrance to the tent), the princess sends for me, Macledio. I block the entrance to the tent by placing my *sambara* at the entrance. What do I see? Indescribable, unique! The most bloated legs in the world raised in the air. The roundest buttocks on a rug and, in the middle, the positively galactic female genitalia. The black slave woman is busy washing it. Flies are hovering around. In the dark, I hear a feeble voice, that of the princess, ordering me to get to work and to do it instantly, to perform quickly.

This was not a task that I had foreseen; I was not prepared; I take time to understand, and I stammer. Since I have no choice as a slave, I comply and begin to move in, to crawl (like an agama on the cupola of the basilica in Yamoussoukro) onto the biggest belly in the world, the galactic one. My prick goes in no farther than a comma.

When I get off and set my feet on the ground, I am embarrassed, ashamed, and frustrated for not having gone beyond the surface, for having barely tickled her. To my surprise, the princess congratulates me and announces that she enjoyed it, that she tingled. And so, from that day on, she gets the habit of having me climb on each time the prince leaves on one of his numerous trips across the desert. And I too, I begin to delight in chasing away the flies and in my climbing duties.

Out of jealousy, the slave woman with whom you made merry at night behind the tent told the husband. Karim, who was a good prince, did not say a thing to his wife. Tuareg etiquette forbids a husband to reproach his wife for her little infidelities with a slave. The slave woman had surely told the master during one of their little romps. Among the tents in the sand, any man in the tribe (the Tuareg practice polyandry) could take his pleasure with any woman.

Macledio kept playing the agama on the cupola and even took a liking to this pleasure. One night, he asked himself whether the person he was seeking (his man or woman of destiny) might not be this mollusk who gave him such a thrill. He was beginning to believe it, even to admit it, when the princess in one of her rare moments of confiding in a slave, announced that she was expecting a child. Macledio gave a start and leapt down to the ground. This was disturbing, very serious! While the Tuareg remains discreet when his wife cheats on him, he slits the throat of the baby and the black slave if she gives birth to a mulatto. Macledio decided to stay and let his throat be slit, not to desert. He loved the belly and the child that it held. He wanted to see that child, his fifth, and die in the desert.

I felt that I was so predestined and thought that no individual can escape destiny, adds Macledio.

The oasis over which Prince Karim was the sheikh was located at the juncture of Algeria, Niger, and Libya. (On the African continent at that time, countries were better known by the titles of their dictators than by their own names. Let us hasten to recall that Algeria had Boumedienne as its dictator, Niger had Kountché or Hamani Diori, and Libya had Qaddafi.) Each of these three dictatorships claimed the oasis and sent in patrols from time to time.

Since heaven created the desert, the only operation the Tuareg have managed to make profitable has been the razzia, in which they invade black Sahelian villages, setting fire, letting blood on all sides, and kidnapping women, children, men, cattle, along with other goods, before they disappear in the immensity of the desert. Since independence and the departure of the colonial army, the razzias have multiplied—the Tuaregs have been unwilling to accept the authority of the Blacks of Niger and Mali. Niger patrols, ever more nervous, have become increasingly frequent in the oasis. As soon as they loomed on the horizon, Sheikh Karim hid Macledio. One morning, they appeared unexpectedly in the sheikh's absence. Without discussion, they burst into the tents and discovered Macledio busy chasing the flies away from the womb he admired and adored. Unceremoniously, the soldiers wrested Macledio away from his vice, made him leave the tent, and announced that he was liberated.

I did not want to be free; I did not intend to abandon that great belly sheltering my child. I believed that my man of destiny was a woman, that Moorish woman. My destiny was to be a slave all my life, and I wanted to fulfill it. Explains Macledio.

The soldiers were deaf to your reasoning, your laments, your jeremiads, your entreaties. They understood that you had been kidnapped; thieves had been captured with your effects and, in particular, with your fetish. Your effects were returned to you, and you were forceably handed over to a patrol leaving for the north, for white Algiers. (The dictator of the Democratic Republic of Algeria was called Boumedienne.)

What the soldiers had called a fetish—because it was covered with coagulated blood and feathers—was the sack, Macledio's purse with the gold. They had handled it with great precautions, without daring to open it, and had given it back with all its contents, all the pieces of gold filched from Kouassikro.

Macledio rich in Paris. Rich as he had been in Niamey. Just as had happened in Niamey, he had a fortune but was depressed. He tried for his *baccalauréat* four times and failed four times because of English and mathematics. Since he could not return to Africa without a university diploma, he showed up at the École des Langues Orientales, managed to see the director, and immediately announced that he spoke Kabye, Konkomba, Daka, Kanga, Bamileke, Malinke, Hausa, Ashanti, Kirdi, Tuareg, Berber, Bobo, Senufo, Tiokossi, and ten other Paleonegritic languages that are not listed on any register of human languages in his school. The director unhesitatingly gave him the school's diploma and authorized him to prepare a thesis on Paleonegritic civilization.

I spent very long days in the filthy French libraries and made important discoveries. "The Paleonegritic civilization is not only the most ancient African civilization, it is absolutely the best civilization. It has left traces everywhere, but it is preserved only in pockets in the mountains, in the hilly regions of Senegal, on the cliffs of the bend of the Niger River, in the northern ranges of the Ebony Coast, in Ghana, Togo, Benin, in the Bauchi region of Nigeria, in the Kordofan in the Sudan, and in the regions of the Great Lakes. The Paleos took refuge in these retreats in order to escape the ascendancy of the warrior states. The Paleos in these regions all have common traits, identifiable vestiges of one homogeneous civilization, a civilization that once covered the better part of Africa. The mountain pockets and refuges have been asylums. Although they are quite diverse, each of these peoples claims to be descended from a common ancestor. There existed and still exist resemblances between these peoples. In their style of dress, up to the wave of independences, they were all naked. It was not for reasons of prudery but for two magical purposes that the women covered themselves with leaves and the men wore wicker or calabash penile sheaths. With effective techniques, they engaged in intensive agriculture. They also had in common a remarkably ingenious architecture. This civilization was destroyed by the warring hordes of Berbers, Mandinga, Bantu, Hamites, Nilotes, and Zulus."

Macledio's thesis director did not hide his disappointment when he looked at the first results of his investigation. He accused you of having done nothing more than plagiarize entire pages. All the ideas expressed in the thesis had been known since the beginning of the century. Explains the responder. The professor asked you to continue your writing, nevertheless: you were the first researcher capable of establishing links between the multiple dialects of the Paleonegritic peoples.

Macledio—who since leaving the oasis had disciplined himself to an unusual period of abstention, broken only by occasional sorties in the Pigalle neighborhood—was busy writing his thesis when he noticed that a serving woman in the Cité Universitaire had eyes only for him. She filled his plates more often and much better than those of other African students. Out of digestive gratitude, Macledio decided to pay a call on the serving woman.

She lived in a three-room apartment in an HLM close to the Charlety Stadium. Macledio wanted to elicit pity, and he poured out an endless tale of woe. Children abandoned in Cameroon, the Gold Coast, the dunes of the Sahara, and his unconsolable nostalgia for the elephantine thighs of the Moorish woman. He cried; she consoled him. He continued crying; tears formed pearls on the serving woman's face. Such abundant tears that Macledio began consoling her. She was truly generous and her tears were too copious. She went to her bedroom and continued crying in her bed. Macledio joined her beneath the sheets. They cried together and hugged each other so vigorously that a fourth pregnancy and a sixth child were the inevitable result. What a handsome boy!

Let us imitate the traveler who upon arriving beneath the shade of a tree stops to take his breath, says the *sèrè*. And he plays the *kora*. The *koroduwa* dances for a few minutes. Bingo recites the following proverbs:

If a fly dies in a wound, it has died at the appointed place.
A lone sorrow does not rend the womb on one occasion.
The female camel has long retained her skinny rump, ever since the time when she was a virgin.

13

Ah, Tiekura! Macledio was busy changing his child's diaper in their three-room apartment and wondering whether the mother of his sixth son or his thesis director might be his man of destiny when a close-up of Nkutigi flailing about in his boubou appeared on the TV screen in a historical retrospective. Nkutigi Fondio, still called the "Man in

White," had the hare as his totem and was the dictator of the Republic of the Mountains. The Man in White was brilliantly expounding on the dignity of Africa and the dignity of the black man, and, in the face of the universe and before the chief, General de Gaulle, he uttered a categorical No! No to the French Community! No to France! No to neocolonialism! For the Republic of the Mountains, the Man in White preferred poverty in freedom to opulence in slavery. He shouted the same thing several times.

Without a doubt, Nkutigi, the Man in White, had the tone, the style, the size, the passion, the boubou's whiteness, and the garrison cap of a man of destiny. The Man in White ended his speech with a grave and pathetic appeal to all black intellectuals. They were all invited to come to the capital of the Republic of the Mountains to build the first truly independent state of West Africa and to avenge Emperor Samory.

Ah, Tiekura! A man sometimes makes a mistake in life on the plate of food that is reserved for him, but never on the words that are destined to be his. Nkutigi was certainly speaking directly to Macledio. Macledio understood that immediately. He was moved and began to cry. He could not fail to answer.

Macledio was not making any progress in writing his thesis. Nkutigi Fondio's appeal was a windfall. It allowed him to return to Africa without completing and presenting the thesis. He could arrive at the airport in the capital of the Republic of the Mountains with nothing but his drafts, without losing face. If you like your couscous, eat it while it is hot. Concludes the responder.

Macledio, Marie-Christine (that was the name of the serving woman from the university restaurant), and their child arrived one Monday morning at the airport in the capital of the Republic of the Mountains. That very evening, Nkutigi sent for Macledio, and, to the great surprise of the invitee, before even responding to his greetings, he began to criticize certain ideas in the thesis on the original black civilization. So he knew everything!

You went into raptures in the presence of the dictator. Both in his physical and moral nature, what a man! What eloquence! What culture! What intransigence! You believed and stated that Nkutigi was your man of destiny. You affirmed and believed that your man of destiny could be none other than Nkutigi.

Courageously, Macledio openly stated how certain he was that Nkutigi was his man of destiny. The Man in White did not seem to be impressed by Macledio's declaration. The despot received such testimonies of admiration, sympathy, and allegiance every day. Says the responder.

Waiting for the Vote of the Wild Animals

The dictator announced to Macledio that he was appointed deputy director general of Capital Radio in the Republic of the Mountains. Macledio thanked the president for his kindness and swore allegiance even if it required the supreme sacrifice. After his third radio editorial, he had the honor of being summoned to the presidential palace. He was gratified by the laudatory assessment of the president, who nonetheless discreetly remarked that his nationalist faith as a Black and an ex-subject of colonialism did not quite fit with his marriage to a European woman.

For the sake of Africa and his dignity as a black man, Macledio instantly decided on separation from his wife. Marie-Christine did not wait for him to repeat his words a second time. Without regrets or hesitation, she left the little black boy with his father and, that very evening, took the plane back to Paris. She preferred by far to remain a server in the Cité Universitaire in Paris rather than to be the wife of a black high official in the capital of the Republic of the Mountains. She did not like Africa, the Republic of the Mountains, Nkutigi, the heat, or, when all was said and done, the Blacks, and she was sorry that, out of pity, she had had a child with Macledio.

The Man in White was a passionate and fascinating man whom Macledio discovered anew each day and to whom he wanted to belong fully. He converted to Islam at the request of Nkutigi, who gave him one of his own mistresses as a wife. Macledio did not love the woman, but he considered it an honor to have under his own roof a mistress of his man of destiny. By the intermediary of his wife, he become a person close to, well-known to, and even related to Nkutigi, who gave him charge of ideology for the radio. This was an important position, which, in fact, placed him above the minister of information. His task was difficult. No six-month period went by without some plot being hatched in the socialist regime of the Republic of the Mountains. Some of these plots were organized by the dictator to get rid of potential opponents, who were often denounced by seers and marabouts. Nkutigi's faith in Islam and in socialism had not excluded his daily practice of traditional African customs (sorcery, sacrifices, charms). Macledio's principal task consisted in inventing the words, the lies, the cynicism, and the eloquence that would supply an element of rational justification to acts that had none, since they came from the various prognostications of marabout-fetishists.

With a great deal of imagination and talent, Macledio was successful in this endeavor. Whatever he dreamed up out of whole cloth became fact, the true phases of a veritable plot, for the police, the judicial system, the party, and the international press. Says the responder. Subjected to instruments of torture, victims repeated Macledio's phrases, adorning them with many details, and finally made them sound accurate, logical, and irrefutable.

Ah, Tiekura! Truth and lie are never distant, one from the other, and rarely does truth win out. Macledio's lies became solid truths, even for their originator, who always ended up believing that he had discovered the threads of plots rather than having created them.

The Man in White was not happy with simply killing the plotters: he slept with the widows of men condemned to death the very night of the execution or the hanging of the husbands. The very night while the wives were still burning from the death of their husbands, not always for pleasure or through sadism, but by simple necessity, a sense of duty. This sacred rite (of occupying the bed of a woman at the very instant her husband was being shot) allowed the Man in White with the hare totem to assimilate all the vital energy of the victims. So it is simply not true that he invented many plots in order to assassinate the husbands of women with whom he wanted to make love. No! The truth is that, for magical reasons, he wanted those women on the night when their husband plotters were executed in order to fully enjoy their death. Explains Tiekura.

Macledio shared with the Supreme Leader (that is the nickname that the dictator of the Republic of the Mountains liked best of all) the same wife and often the same roof and meal. He was one of the close associates who believed he was sufficiently protected against the potentate's paranoia. That error cost him dearly. One evening, when Macledio was particularly verbal . . .

One evening, when I was inveighing against the traitors, the henchmen of imperialism, and predicting the depths of Allah's hell for all those who had no plan other than overthrowing the only authentically African regime, which had been constituted by the Supreme Leader, I saw the door of the studio open. It was the brother of the dictator himself, Minister Fondio, who swept into the studio. The minister pushed me aside and took my place. He began reading a long list of new plotters involved in a new plot! There were seventy-two names. And I, Macledio, had a prominent spot. Fifth!

Camp Kabako was a gendarme post east of the capital of the Republic of the Mountains. Except for the torture room, everything was as dilapidated as a leper's hut. Called the "technical booth" by the torturers, the torture room had the advantage of an installation of ultramodern equipment.

Like all political prisoners, Macledio went to the technical booth first. There he underwent whipping, the slow burning of the soles of his feet, fingernail extraction, and other trials such as torture by water and electricity. He did not weaken. . . . Did not confess.

He resolutely continued to love Nkutigi. Nkutigi remained his man of destiny. One does not confess to participating in a plot against one's own man of destiny! He refused to confess the least involvement in an imaginary plot against Nkutigi. The torturers use all their cruel measures in their ultimate refinement. Finally, Macledio, you slip into unconsciousness without admitting to any of their accusations. They untie you and hurl you into a cell. A doctor and several nurses hover over you and finally manage to bring you back to life. In less than a week, with lots of attention, intensive care, and good food, you are back in shape and ready for a new interrogation, for more torture.

They send you back to the technical booth, put you in place, strap you down, and plug you in. For two days and nights they torment you. . . . In vain. You keep refusing to talk or to admit any bad intentions toward Nkutigi, against the Man in White. You would rather die under the Supreme Leader's torture than to declare publicly that you are guilty of disloyalty toward him. They persist until you lose consciousness a second time. A second time you receive the care by doctors and nurses to get you back on your feet and in shape for a third interrogation, new torture.

They install you in the booth for the third time. The torturers are ready to turn on the current when the telephone rings. It is Nkutigi himself on the phone. In unison, the torturers yell "ready for the revolution" and snap to attention when they recognize the voice of the dictator. The Supreme Leader wants to speak with Macledio. The conversation between the absolute master of the country and the torture victim is carried out in an intimate, friendly, affectionate, and even matter-of-fact tone. The dictator expresses his renewed confidence in you, encourages you. He calls on you. "Each to his post to accomplish all his duties, all his duties to Africa, to Blacks, and to socialism," he states. He finishes by reciting a line from Senghor's poetry:

Black savanna like me, fire of death that prepares the re-birth.

Without seeking an explanation, you break down, you begin crying like a child for almost a quarter of an hour. You ask the torturers to stop. You request a tape recorder. They record your declarations. Without pausing, you piece together a story that the national radio, the police, and the international press take, embroider on, and finally make as solid as the behind of a baboon. The great revolutionary people's tribunal uses the completed story as undeniable fact to sentence you, Macledio, along with your ninety-two fellow conspirators, to death.

You never explained to anyone the reasons why hearing that line by Senghor made you break down. You have always simply revealed in what circumstances the line became a password between you and the dictator.

In his socialist republic, Nkutigi was called the greatest soccer player, the first among doctors, the best farmer, the best husband, the most pious and greatest Muslim, etc. Among all this praise, he preferred that which treated him as a talented writer, the greatest poet in his country. Says the responder.

Before each edition of the three daily newscasts, the Capital Radio announcer of the Republic of the Mountains would read a few lines by the Supreme Leader. It was uninspired poetry. The Man in White was an insomniac and a poor versifier who, in order to relax between dossiers, would scribble some lines on pages of a schoolchild's notebook that were treated as poetry and thoughts, collected by the presidential services, and published in handsomely bound books. These books were the only ones that were read, studied, and subjected to commentary in schools, institutes, and universities of the Republic of the Mountains. When they first met, the dictator had interrogated Macledio about his favorite poetry. Without hesitating, Macledio had recited that line from Senghor:

Black savanna like me, fire of death that prepares the re-birth.

That was a mistake. Macledio failed to quote one of the dictator's thoughts. Nkutigi, the Man in White, without blinking, had declared that he did not care for poetry by the reactionary Senegalese. Macledio thought the incident was closed and had forgotten it. What a surprise when, one year after their meeting, the dictator had called him in one night and recited the line, expressing his gratitude that Macledio had introduced him to the most beautiful poem written by a Black man on the condition of his race. The two interlocutors turned out the lights and, in the dark, had a conversation that neither of them ever revealed. You, Macledio, swore fidelity to the dictator. It was the memory of that meeting and the words exchanged that made you break down and led you to invent the story that would allow the tribunal to sentence you (you and your fellow prisoners) to death.

That was the only sentence known in that jurisdiction, moreover. But the sentence was rarely carried out. Nkutigi preferred to let the political prisoners croak from hunger and thirst in their own excrement and urine in the depths of some cell. Adds Tiekura. That is why Macledio and his fellow detainees, who had survived the torture and the horrendous conditions of detention during the first months, continued to hope and wait for a possible pardon from the dictator. That hope fled one Monday morning.

They awaken us at 4 A.M., explains Macledio. They serve us an ample breakfast, tie us to one another, and load us into military trucks. We are headed for the firing range. At the firing range, we get out. We are quickly attached to the seventy-three poles that are waiting. The order to fire is about to be given to the firing squad. Suddenly, an officer jumps out of a jeep. He is breathless and sweating. He shouts out, asks for me, and calls me. "Untie Macledio. He is wanted on the telephone," orders the officer. I take the receiver. It is Nkutigi, the dictator, the Man in White, in person on the other end of the line. He chats with me calmly, me with a beating heart, waiting for death. In his serene voice and without the least urgency, he tells me that, in spite of my betrayal, he still considers me a friend, a revolutionary, and an African patriot. All his life, he will continue to have confidence in me, he states without any irony. He does not let me get one word in, but recites Senghor's beautiful line:

Black savanna like me, fire of death . . .

I can't even hear the whole line—a salvo resounds. My seventy-two codetainees have just been shot. I grab the phone, shout, and insult the dictator.

Bastard! *Fa fòrò!* Mother of a bitch! I challenge you, you godless liar! Order your men to assassinate me with the others. Assassin! Yes, you're an assassin!

I calm down to listen to his reaction. The telephone emits a busy signal. He didn't hear me—the connection is cut off because he hung up after reciting the line. Miserable and in tears, I return to Camp Kabako in one of the trucks.

Ah, Tiekura! Why such a massacre that Monday morning? Tell us, master, replies the *koroduwa.*

On all the vast African continent, Nkutigi Fondio knew only one worthy enemy: Tiekoroni, the crafty little old man with the fedora. His totem was the crocodile, and he was the dictator of the Republic of the Ebony People, the Sage of Africa. In fact, in that Africa of a thousand dictatorships, Nkutigi and Tiekoroni, the crafty little old man, were the only two potentates who, although they had a different stature, resembled each other in their manner of acting.

The Man in White had the tall stature of the Malinke of the savanna, while Tiekoroni, the man with the fedora, was a dwarf of the build of the forest people. That difference in height was not connected with distinctness of character. Both men were proud and unrepentant dictators, adds the *koroduwa*.

The Man in White wore the traditional garb of West Africa in all seasons, a white garrison cap and boubou; Tiekoroni always had his fedora, tie, and three-piece European suit. Their different style of dress meant nothing, absolutely nothing. Each of them always hid under his respective disguise the protective charms from the marabout-fetishists. Explains the responder.

The Man in White was a pious, practicing Muslim who transformed his country into an Islamic country; Tiekoroni was a Catholic who built on his ancestral land the most lavish site outside of Rome for the Catholic faith. That opposition of religious beliefs was a pure matter of form.

Both were deeply animistic. Adds the responder.

The Man in White was a socialist who was cultivated by and had the support of the East; Tiekoroni, the capitalist, was supported by the West. This opposition of thought had no impact on the political organization of the two regimes.

The people of the two countries were under the thumbs of the corrupt heads of lying, single-party slayers of freedom. Adds Tiekura.

In the final analysis, what distinguished these two fathers-of-the-nation and presidents of one-party systems? What distinguished and separated the two dictators was faith. Not religious faith (we already said that in spite of appearances they were both fetishists), but faith in the word and in man, in the Black man in particular. The Man in White believed in words, in men, and in the Black man. Managing independence meant, to Nkutigi, replacing at each level every White man (technician or not) by any available Black man.

The crafty and aristocratic Tiekoroni did not believe in words, in man, and certainly not in any Black man. Managing an independent African republic consisted, for him, in giving responsibilities to the Whites, keeping the Blacks in check, and striking blows once in a while at any compatriot who looked up.

Ah, Tiekura! Do you know who, in the final analysis, was right and won? It was Tiekoroni, the crafty little old man with the fedora. When you have to choose between two men in life, always turn to the one who does not believe in man, the one who has no faith. All the greedy people in the Republic of the Mountains and all the greedy people of West Africa turned toward the Republic of the Ebony People of Tiekoroni, the land of peace that welcomed refugees.

Not a single person could be found who wanted to follow the Republic of the Mountains, the land of the Black man's dignity. Adds the responder.

In fact, Tiekura, it is always falsehood that wins out. With his game-playing, Tiekoroni managed to appear exactly the opposite of what he really was: a sage, an incorruptible man, someone who would never shed a drop of human blood, etc. The Man in White stood out in all his nakedness as a cruel dictator, a megalomaniac, a fanatic, a tribalist, a sadist, the man who left his country lifeless.

The Man in White and Tiekoroni fought with each other on all fronts and by all means: insults, arms, secret services, soccer. And by all visible and imaginable material means. They did not manage to destroy each other—there was no loser or winner. So they decided to confront each other in a higher realm, that of invisible things—sorcery, magic, sacrifices. Still, there was no loser or winner.

Then it was that one of the marabout-fetishists in Tiekoroni's camp deserted the capitalist side in the heat of the fray. His name was Boukari, and he went to the side of scientific socialism in the interests of the Black man. He instructed Nkutigi in the secrets, research, and works that he, Boukari, had done successfully for Tiekoroni and capitalism.

Socialism's chances were annihilated in Africa and the future of Nkutigi was locked up. Tiekoroni's performance had succeeded because of abundant sacrifices of different species of animals that he had shown to the public. In order to preserve Africa from a capitalist future, to save it from the exploitation of man by man, Nkutigi had to do better than Tiekoroni, had to make human sacrifice. Boukari recommended to the leader of scientific socialism that he wait for daybreak on the seventy-first anniversary of the Ram of Fasso to sacrifice seventy-one people. On October 18, at dawn, the Man in White had Macledio's seventy-one codetainees shot. . . . This was for the triumph of rationalist socialism, adds the responder.

As for me, I was so obsessed by Nkutigi's words that day that I was a bit angry with him for not having assassinated me for the noble cause along with my seventy-one codetainees, says Macledio.

You never found out, nobody has every verified whether, in order to assimilate the vital energy of the seventy-one executees, the dictator of the Republic of the Mountains slept with the seventy-one tearful widows on the night of October 18.

That is how you found yourself alone in Camp Kabako, Macledio. Upon awakening each morning, you ran through the camp from one end to the other; you prostrated yourself at each empty cot, spoke the name of each dead man, cried, and prayed. You had an uneasy conscience, you still have an uneasy conscience, and you continue berating yourself for inventing the stories that the prosecution used to condemn innocent men. You deem that you are as guilty as the megalomaniacal fetishist of the massacre. You thought the dictator left you alive so that you could atone for your lies. You did not want such an unworthy life. You wanted to commit suicide: you were waiting for news from your sons before ending your life. You were waiting for news, especially from the last born, the little mulatto. But nothing came through to the prisons of Nkutigi. The condemned man had no news from his family and the family had no information about the detainee. Each day was alike. The absence of a calendar and of any contact with the outside world finally made the prisoner of Camp Kabako lose all sense of time. Eventually, the prisoner no longer knew the number of days, months, years that he had been waiting, hoping for clemency from the megalomaniacal dictator.

One morning, you summoned up courage and asked your guard to take you to the adjutant-chief in charge of the section. The latter welcomed you with unusual friendliness and, without your asking, handed you the telephone. You did not believe your ears! You had Nkutigi himself, the Man in White, on the telephone. In his personal way, the dictator says, "How are you, old friend?" Surprised, you drop the receiver, and without waiting for the guard, you go running back into prison like a crazy man. Back within the four walls, you were sorry you did not yell:

Black savanna like me, fire of death that prepares the re-birth.

A few days later, the guard came to get me. The commanding officer of the camp had summoned me. I go in. The commander orders me to kneel in order to praise the Supreme Leader for his humanity, his generosity, his faith in Allah and in the socialist revolution, his wisdom, and his nationalism. . . . And he raises his tone in order to declaim: "Nkutigi is setting you free!"

Waiting for the Vote of the Wild Animals

The president of the Republic of the Gulf, President Fricassa Santos, had come to the Republic of the Mountains to study revolution, wisdom, and African nationalism. President Nkutigi presented his guest, along with his complete works, with the liberation of Macledio.

Shaven and dressed in new clothes, I arrive by military vehicle at the bottom of the air stairs of a waiting airplane. I board, and the airplane takes off. In accordance with an order from the control tower, the craft does not climb through the clouds but circles above the capital of the Republic of the Mountains several times. In the pilot's conversation with the tower, my name is mentioned three times. The airplane returns, lands, and waits at the end of the runway. I am afraid, and my heart is beating. I know Nkutigi's cruelty. I imagine he is sadistically making me wait in order to kill me, assassinate me. But here is the president's chief of protocol, accompanied by a gendarme, climbing up to the cabin. They come toward my seat and hand me a large packet. Feverishly, I open the envelope attached to the packet: it is the complete works of Nkutigi, autographed by the author. In his dedication, Nkutigi thanks me for my contribution to the realization of scientific socialism in Africa and ends with:

Black savanna like me, fire of death that prepares the re-birth.

And the Man in White humbly asks me to turn to the last paragraph of page 100 in the fourth volume of his works. I open the package impatiently, open the volume to that page, and read the paragraph. Like all the dictator's work, the style of the paragraph is convoluted and bloated. I read and reread the paragraph. The word FREEDOM is there four times. I play around by replacing that beloved word, used so abusively, with "Savanna," "Fire," "Death," and "Re-birth." The message appears, and everything becomes clear. Because of his religious and totemic beliefs, the Man in White was not and could not be the holder of my contrary *nõrô,* the neutralizing *nõrô.* The dictator was not my man of destiny. I had to continue my quest. This was the sense of the message from the chief of state of the Republic of the Mountains. I was relieved to get this confirmation. I was able to leave the capital of the Republic of the Mountains without the least regret, without any intention of ever returning. The roofs of Nkutigi's capital city were so squalid that no person has ever been known to leave the city with any desire to return.

That is how you returned home, Macledio, after so many peregrinations. And without having located your man of destiny in this vast and varied Africa. With no wealth other than your shorts and the complete works of Nkutigi Fondio, the Man in White, the bloodthirsty dictator of the Republic of the Mountains.

Knowing the forty volumes of the works of the Man in White by heart was not considered as knowledge anywhere outside the Republic of the Mountains. For the minister of public works in the Republic of the Gulf, the works of the dictator were not worth a single one of the diplomas required to be hired. After endless maneuvering and much pressure, you were hired as a temporary replacement at the radio station. Twice a week you gave a report on great African leaders. The program was quite successful.

Koyaga, that was the man you and your putschist cohorts, the lycaons, found at the station, concludes Tiekura, the responder.

There is no journey that does not finish one day: this is the end of this *sumu*. Announces the *sèrè* before he performs the final musical part. Tiekura plays the flute and dances. Bingo recites the final proverbs on destiny.

He who is fated to live must survive, even if you crush him in a mortar.

For every arrow that is fated to hit you, simply stick out your belly so the mark will be hit in the center.

When a man with a rope about his neck passes close to a dead man, he changes step and gives thanks to Allah for the fate that the Almighty has reserved for him.

Fourth *Sumu*

The *sèrè* performs the musical prelude. The *koroduwa* breaks into grotesque and salacious jokes.

Stop, Tiekura, and remember that I shall recite proverbs on power during this fourth *sumu*. Because:

> *Only the person who has never tasted power finds it unpleasant.*
> *When might blocks the road, the weak man has a right to head into the bush.*
> *One lone subject's cry of distress is not heard over the drum.*

14

Ah, Tiekura, we are back at the day after the assassination and emasculation of J.-L. Crunet (the president of the republic), of Ledjo (chief of the Committee of Public Safety), Tima (president of the National Assembly), five ministers, and four party secretaries-general by the lycaons—intoxicated with the effluvia of blood and alcohol. The lycaons are still breathing heavily and are rowdy, still avid for blood and more alcohol. They are running through the streets with their fingers on the triggers. Ready to assassinate and emasculate anybody who might try to oppose their law. And you, Koyaga, with excellent foresight, order them to return to the barracks and to calm down before you talk to the parties. One does not receive guests in the house with the guard dogs chained in the courtyard, adds the *koroduwa*.

Then with Macledio on your right, you talked to the leaders of all parties, you invited everybody. You set up a government of national unity. Calm and silence returned, or fear made silence and peace return to the country. You won, and, with victory, you behaved like a hunter.

You are a master hunter of the boa race that never eats the slaughtered victim warm. Of the eagle race that feasts on the cockerel stolen from the barnyard only once it has returned to its nest at the top of the silk cotton tree.

You returned to the North, the mountains of Paleo country that had witnessed your birth, to eat your victim—power—once it was cold. You had just acquired supreme power in the Republic of the Gulf, adds Tiekura.

In the mountains of Paleo country you were in your sanctuary. In the sanctuary with your mama the sorceress, Bokano the marabout, and your advisor Macledio. All four of you were in council, squatting before the altar upon which were smoking generous sacrifices made in gratitude to the souls of the ancestors. You were offering reverent prayers, intense entreaties in which you begged the souls of the ancestors to better inspire you, help you, protect you, and guide your steps toward a good administration of citizens and the country. Your prayers were answered and your sacrifices accepted.

Yes, accepted, resumes the *koroduwa*. For suddenly someone pushes the door of the sanctuary open. An old sorceress comes in, kneels, and introduces herself. Skipping the usual salutations and verbiage, she begins to recount the strange dream that interrupted her night's sleep. A dream in which you, Koyaga, appeared in all your hunting clothes and equipment, mounted on a steed decked out with all the accoutrements of power. Beginning with your first steps into the bush, the sorceress saw you surrounded, intercepted by predators of the most fearsome and pitiless species. In turn, each carnivorous animal told you about the tactics and location for taking game by surprise. The dreamer could clearly distinguish a desert jackal, the hyena of the savanna, a vulture, and a panther. In addition, dancing and singing in a mocking round some fifty paces from you, there were other dangerous species that she had difficulty in identifying.

The marabout, knowledgeable in the meanings of dreams, that oneiromancer Bokano, traces lines in the sand in which his interpretation of the old woman's nocturnal dream becomes clear.

Politics is like the hunt, and you engage in political activity as you would join an association of hunters. The great bush where hunters go is vast, inhuman, and merciless just as is the arena of the political world. Before going into the bush, the novice hunter goes to the school of master hunters in order to listen, to admire, and to be initiated. You must not risk any political act as head of state before you have taken an initiatory journey and studied the perilous arts of dictatorial science in the traditions of autocracy. You must first travel, meet, and listen to the masters of absolutism and one-party governing, the most prestigious heads of state in the four cardinal directions of this liberticidal Africa.

The desert jackal that appeared in the dream means you must visit a sovereign of the jebel, a dictator having the jackal as a totem or who is as much a rogue as the jackal, adds Tiekura. The panther that appeared signifies that you must meet the master of a single-party state in the Gulf of Guinea, in West Africa. A West African potentate whose totem is the panther or who is as fierce as a panther, adds the responder. The vulture, a dictator of the Central African forest. Of the vulture totem or who is as gluttonous as a vulture. The hyena is the master of a single-party state in East Africa. His totem is the hyena or he is as stupid and lawless as a hyena, adds the *koroduwa*. And the leopard: a dictator of the great, impenetrable forest floating along a great river. His totem is the leopard or he is as bloodthirsty as a leopard, adds Tiekura.

Koyaga, you decide unhesitatingly to begin your rule, your power, by an initiatory journey. You go down from the mountains to the capital, where you order your command airplane to be equipped.

After reviewing the guard of honor, you are heading for the air stairs when an ambassador cuts you off and introduces himself. It is the plenipotentiary minister of the dictator with the crocodile totem. He informs you, the novice head of state, of the rules and procedures that have been established for decades among the dictators and masters of single-party states in old Africa. Since the crocodile is called and recognized as the oldest of terrestrial beasts, all visits by an apprentice head of state to his African peers begin with a visit to the dictator of the crocodile totem. Yes, that was a rule you could not fail to obey, adds Tiekura.

You are ready to leave for your first visit, with the dictator of the crocodile totem, but you have not taken two steps when another ambassador steps out from the guard of honor. He comes up to you and presents himself diplomatically. He is the plenipotentiary minister from the chief of the boa totem. You cannot take your tour of Africa without quenching your thirst with the experience of the Redeemer of Africa.

You are finally in the seat of the head of state in your state airplane when a cable is handed to you from the Horn of Africa, from the dictator with the lion totem. This autocrat reminds you that he is ruddy and weighted down by age but has not ceased being the king of continental dictators. A king who must not be forgotten or left to the side in this initiatory journey.

The interventions of these three ambassadors sweep away the concerns of the seers accompanying you, the seers of the presidential delegation. They hover about you and explain everything. The predators the dreamer was not able to identify in her premonitory dream were the crocodile, the boa, and the lion. The dream has been fully elucidated. You can begin. You know with which country and which government you must begin; with which country and which dictatorship you must finish your initiatory journey. The airplane takes off.

Tiekoroni, the master of the Republic of the Ebony People, had the crocodile as his totem. He was a crafty little old man who was referred to as the man with the fedora and who wanted to be called in his own realm the Ram of Fasso and the Sage of Africa.

It is not difficult from the air to recognize the capital city of the dictator with the crocodile totem, the capital of the Republic of the Ebony People. It is at the bottom of a rosary of lagoons. When you arrive, the airport is teeming with noisy, smiling Black men and women. In order to impress you and to show you that he is sole master of his country—the only hippopotamus in the channel—that he can do whatever he wishes and can do anything . . . He decreed a two-day holiday throughout the territory and brought in dancers, schoolchildren, youth organizations, and women from the twenty-four regions of his republic. The crowd was lined along the edges of the road in the villages, at the entrance and exit of each village all along the three hundred kilometers that separate the capital from the hometown of the dictator. By that route, lined in each village with two uninterrupted rows of smiling dancers and applauding people, your convoy of three hundred huge Mercedes reaches Fasso, the native city of the dictator.

Fasso is a curious city.

They say that one day the dictator dragged in from France the scientist who had been most whitened by his science, his knowledge, and his defense of the environment.

"Tell me, at our rhythm of development," asked the dictator, "how many decades will it take for my native village, Fasso, to resemble a Swiss village, and will it have the comfort and cleanliness of a European town?"

"At least a century," answered the economist.

"That is, long after I'm gone."

"Yes," affirmed the economist.

"No! I cannot die without seeing my native village as beautiful as any European village and without seeing my relatives and close associates as rich as the richest Europeans."

The man with the crocodile totem rejected the pessimistic reading of development and decided to go against destiny. He was the master of the country and could manufacture fortunate people. He recalled the precept of an old proverb from home. The proverb advises the person who enriches a stranger with one finger to turn his ten fingers at once to cover himself with gold. He must run and point five fingers toward his relatives and children, three fingers toward the people in his village and tribe, before going out into the world to create happiness for the other people in the universe.

With the state's money, the dictator had made each of his relatives, close associates, and servants as rich as the princes of a state in the Persian Gulf. He had raised all the members of his tribe to the happiness and material comfort known to the citizens of the richest developed countries in the world. For every inhabitant of the villages around his ancestral house, he had the state donate a villa. He personally directed the construction sites of the broad avenues that go from one end of his native city to the other and continue on into the forest and the bush. In the bush and forest, far from all human activity, where the avenues are used only as clearings by serpents partaking of the sun's first rays and monkeys depositing their excrements and making love. On weekends and at night, he had taken delight in the construction of splendid and immense projects, financed by the state budget, among the inhabitants' poor little huts with their corrugated iron roofs. There were palaces with gilded facades, magnificent marble hotels, and even a basilica. These splendors stretched to the horizons of the village, splendors used and frequented only by flights of swallows, gendarmes, and the croaking of bats.

In his desire to shower his native region's animals with such splendors, he was particularly generous to the crocodiles, as is fitting for one's own totem. He had all the reptiles in the entire region's surrounding rivers caught. He constructed a marble lake for them. In that lake, they receive the three daily meals that many citizens of the republic will never get through the next century.

There, right in front of the crocodile lake built at the foot of his residence, your host awaits you. The dictator of the crocodile totem is sitting quietly, right on one of the marble steps of the immense perron before his palace. A short-sleeved brocatelle shirt molds his frail body, his fedora is poised on his head, and he is wearing large black sunglasses with gold frames. His white flannel trousers and his sport socks complete the elegantly conceived casual attire in which the dictator wishes to welcome you.

Ah, Tiekura! Let us relate the career, the *donsomana,* the epic of the potentate who is welcoming Koyaga.

The story of the man with the crocodile totem, the man with the fedora, begins with the arrival of the Whites.

A tribal chief named Sika Kourou betrays the African nationalists who are fighting with poisoned arrows and blocking the way against the conquerors. The nationalist combatants assassinate Chief Sika Kourou and vow to kill all members of his family. The French conquerors detail a detachment of Senegalese riflemen to protect the family of the treacherous tribal chief. That detachment is commanded by a corporal named Samba Cissé.

Samba Cissé is from the very old Cissé family of the Sahel. The very old Cissé family to whom it was announced that it would produce an illustrious man and which has been awaiting that man for centuries. For centuries, all the branches of the family have engaged in rich and costly ceremonies with blood sacrifices in an attempt to hasten the birth, the advent of their illustrious man. Corporal Samba Cissé, chief of the detachment given the mission of protection, has a little adventure with the sister of the traitor, Sika Kourou. By chance, a son arrives. After fifteen years of loyal service, Samba Cissé leaves the army and returns to his native village in the Sahel. The seers of the Sahel report to Samba Cissé that the son he abandoned in the South is the man all the branches of the Cissé family have been awaiting for centuries. Samba Cissé hurriedly returns to the South and demands his son, tries to get him back no matter what the conditions.

Among the people of the treacherous chief, matriarchy is dominant; a son does not belong to his father, who is nothing but a common genitor; the child belongs to his mother, to the family of the mother. The father cannot have his son; they will never yield the son to him. Corporal Samba Cissé returns to his native Sahel in tears, sorrowing for the son he abandoned in the hands of forest Kaffirs.

That son will be called Tiekoroni, the man of the crocodile totem, the man with the fedora, who is to become the dictator of the Republic of the Ebony People.

The child was able to go to school. In class, he proved to be gifted and went on to the William Ponty School on the island of Gorée, where future high officials of the colonial administration were trained. Nothing is more deceptive than the good nature of youth.

Waiting for the Vote of the Wild Animals

Young Tiekoroni's good nature misled the high official and induced him to denounce and fight against forced labor. This was a youthful error that led him—the man of the crocodile totem—to believe, write, and state that there was something better and more humane than the whip and forced labor to better the lot of the Blacks and bring about development in Africa. That was an error that needlessly broke up the friendship between the family of Sika Kourou and the French colonial administration. It was an error recalled by the colonizers when the crocodile man, as a young colonial official, asked for their support in his campaign to be elected as a deputy. On all his posters and in all his electoral campaign speeches, he proclaimed to no avail that he was Sika Kourou's nephew, the heir of the chief who had collaborated with the French conquerors and, thus, "a man of good blood who could not lie": nothing worked. These reminders did not make the colonial governor yield an inch. The governor continued to insult him in all his own writings. The man of the crocodile totem had lost, definitively lost, any support from the administration because of his sensibilities. He had lost the attributes of the good colonial subject. The entire apparatus of the colonial administration had to, and in fact did, come together to fight the man of the crocodile totem. In the bush, his supporters were thrown in prison. He did not change: he declared himself a nationalist, an anticolonialist, a Marxist, and lashed out in demagogical speeches. The peasants believed him, unfortunately, voted for him, and rose up to demand other freedoms besides the suppression of forced labor. This became a veritable jacquerie that inflamed the entire territory.

The mercenaries of the French army were sent chasing the tribune, the new deputy. They just missed him at Gouroflé, where they assassinated his follower, Bika Dabo. This was a red alert and the deputy flees. With the spirit and manner of the monkey who has escaped a pack leaving behind a good piece of his tail in the mouth of a dog. This is a mad flight that leads him to Bamako, Dakar, Bordeaux, Paris. He can find neither refuge nor a lawyer to defend him. Once more Bordeaux, Bamako; then Dakar and Paris, where his pursuers corner him in the bath of a hotel room. He is out of breath. He does not wait for questions. On his own initiative and in his excellent French, he announces his renunciation of all illusions and recalls the eternal friendship between his family and France, the colonizing country. Loudly and strongly, he proclaims his choice of liberalism, the camp of freedom.

As a token of good faith, he immediately returns to his country hand in hand with his pursuers. In the capital and in the major cities, he organizes great demonstrations during which he publicly speaks of his conversion to liberal ideology, his gratitude to the colonizers, his visceral anticommunism, his horror of liberation wars, and of the right of nations to determine their own destiny. His oratory and his tone ring out so sincerely that France, America, and the entire Occident proclaim him the spearhead of the cold war and the leader of the anticommunist struggle in West Africa. Caught between two countries seen as progressive, his country occupied a strategic place in the struggle against envelopment by totalitarian international communism.

His country became the only one in the region to be able to feed its people, to build roads, to accept those who were driven by drought from the savanna and the Sahel. What a success! A miracle! The West decided to make a showcase of this country and helped the man with the crocodile totem to acquire an image and respectability. The West lent him significant financial means to organize and pay at home for the forces that would fight to defend the positions of the liberal camp. It financed forces favorable to the West in all conflicts: Biafra, Angola, Mozambique, Guinea, the Republic of the Great River, etc.

To your surprise, Koyaga, he announced that he had been informed in advance about your intention to organize a coup d'état. You were successful because the West, which is to say Tiekoroni himself, had not judged that it would be against western interests. The man with the crocodile totem was considered, in fact, a general in the struggle of the West against Red imperialism. A battle leader on the front must not be sullied. All criticism that was formulated about him appeared to be partisan; all those who denounced his system were fiercely defended by the western media.

"To begin with, you are a brother, a friend. We shall be on familiar terms. I invite you to go with me on my usual evening walk," he states by way of greeting.

Before you can overcome your astonishment, he continues calmly:

"I challenge you. I challenge you despite the fact that you are a colossus, a hunter, and a veteran while I am a peaceful peasant, a brother, and a little old man. This is a challenge for you to accept. We are going walking to visit my plantations on foot. I shall certainly not be the first to tire and ask to take a breather."

With a condescending smile, you scrutinize this minuscule ant of a pretentious old man from head to toes. You greet him politely, thank him for his welcome and for the attention you have been given, before answering:

"I accept your challenge. Right now without going to the hotel to change clothes or shoes. Old man (that is one of the nicknames used by the dictator with the crocodile totem), I'll go with you on your walk."

And without proverbs, you take off on the road leading up to the pineapple plantations.

The dictator with the crocodile totem had been diagnosed with prostatitis. He refused to undergo an operation—his marabout seers had predicted with great pomp certain death within the year that he accepted being cut open. Many assurances from surgeons had not managed to get his approval for a procedure that contradicted the prophecies, and his urologist had limited his prescriptions to taking long walks. The dictator had come to enjoy this healthful daily exercise. Since, in his republic, his every gesture was interpreted as being the result of charismatic gifts, the flatterers had been quick to call him "the great walker of Africa." The dictator believed them and made a great effort to demonstrate to each of his visitors that the title was deserved, fully deserved. He never failed to drag his friends along on extended walks, during which he made confidential revelations and shared the judicious advice of an old dictator aged by deceitfulness and corruption.

Starting with their first steps, the dictator gave orders. The men in charge of security must be limited to what was strictly necessary and made to follow the two heads of state discreetly and at a good distance.

You lengthen your cranelike strides, obliging the little old man to increase the speed of his little puppy trot in order to keep up with his master. You quickly find yourselves alone. The vast pineapple fields extend from one slope to the next, clear to the horizon. The dictator with the crocodile totem politely begs your pardon and explains. The walk and the challenge are only pretexts to have an intimate conversation far from all indiscreet ears. He declares his love as if he were speaking to a woman. He loves you with all his soul and body, and he is going to reveal confidential matters that have never been uttered to anybody else. You must keep these confidential revelations as you did the first drops of milk on the day of your birth. These are words that will be more beneficial for your career as a dictator than are white canes for nonsighted people.

"The first vicious beast that threatens a head of state and president of a single party in the independent Africa of the cold war," he says (and he informs you that you will become, whether you like it or not, a father-of-the-nation), "the first vicious beast who threatens at the summit of the state and at the head of the single party is the awkward tendency in the early career to separate the state coffers from those of the individual. The personal needs of a head of state and president of the single party always serve the country, and they mingle directly or indirectly with the interests of his republic and his country. There is no future or authority in independent Africa for the person who exercises supreme power if he fails to present himself as the richest and most generous man in his country. A true and great African chief is always, endlessly and every day, giving. Giving to those who love him, to those who hate him, to those who are poor and deprived, and to those who are rich and opulent. On the occasion of all funerals, marriages, and feasts, those gifts must have the most expensive price tag, and no one in the republic can be authorized to appear more generous than the head of state."

He advises you to direct the economy and to have the totality of all income received from the products of investment deposited in the state coffers before they reach the rough hands of the good peasants. The Agricultural Marketing Boards have proven themselves to be excellent tools for such a stratagem. They offer control at the source of the intake of currency in a republic. The resources of these establishments go to the public treasury. And the dictator with the crocodile totem specifies, with a crafty smile, that he does not need to tell you that the resources of the treasury are one with the receipts of the single party and thus can be commingled with the private coffers of the president of the single party and supreme head of the state and its armies. Raising his voice, he adds that this is simply the right way of seeing things.

"In Africa today, everybody knows that and admits it. Never will any African be so petty as to try to establish what can be imputed to the accounts of the chief designated by universal suffrage. With us, you do not look into the mouth of the person you have told to shell the peanuts or into the mouth of the person in charge of smoking the agoutis brought in by the village hunt. In Africa, we trust our chiefs."

The walk has continued for over an hour. The dictator with the crocodile totem is taking three steps for each of Koyaga's steps. He continues walking without giving the least sign or gesture of fatigue. He continues talking nasally in his own rhythm, stringing his words one after the other as if his time were, like his plantations, without limit. His advice on the governing of human society and the management of a state are occasionally interrupted by learned technical lessons about the cultivation of pineapples.

The man in the fedora likes to be called a peasant; he really was one. He had the shortcomings of a wily villager, petty, vindictive, and yet sometimes simple and generous. He had remained a peasant in the love he bore toward the land and in the knowledge he had of plants and seasons. He had never forgotten that he had acquired his supreme office and the responsibility of the single party through his association with farmers. Of course, the family plantation with which he had begun did not resemble the modern enterprise he was showing you. An enterprise apparently without limits.

As soon as he had reached the highest office, the man with the crocodile totem decreed numerous advantages for the members of his union of large-scale farmers—advantages that accrued first of all to the peasant-president himself. For any enterprise larger than one thousand hectares, the cultivator had a right to agronomists, tractors, fertilizers, insecticides—all free. The dictator's plantations were plowed, planted, maintained, and harvested at state expense. His harvests were marketed by his personal enterprise rather than by the Agricultural Marketing Board—only he had the right, in this republic, to use a channel other than the marketing board for exporting his harvests. And yet that bank had the duty of daily delivery sacks of banknotes for the small expenses of the president of the republic and the single party. All peasants in the republic were exempted from income tax. And the man with the reptilian totem, by far holder of the greatest fortune in the republic, paid not a single penny to the state treasury.

About two years ago, the president tires of pernicious criticism by the foreign press and decides to eliminate all misunderstanding. He organizes one of those great palavers for which only he holds the secret, and during the course of the gigantic ceremonies, gives his agricultural enterprises to his country and his people. But the festivities are so beautiful and the praises so sycophantic that one may forget the essential purpose of the ceremonies: the transfer of property is never completed and signed. The plantations, after having been given to the people, become the public and political property of the state even as they remain the private property of the president, who alone pockets the entire profit, exempted of the least tax. The ceremonies do nothing more than compound the misunderstandings, transforming the misunderstandings into ambiguities.

The sun was setting. The man with the reptilian totem was not sweating in spite of his serious efforts to keep up with you. He seemed as fresh as someone who has just stepped out of an air-conditioned house. He maintained his rapid little pace, the same rhythm since the beginning of the walk. Without weakening. From the grove of trees that seems insignificant to us comes the liana that can be used to tie us down. Koyaga, you were beginning to regret undertaking this walk without changing shoes. Your toes are burning in the sharp-toed shoes, and you are hobbling along. The crafty little old man did not let on that he had noticed your pain. He even tried to demoralize you. Between the proverbs with which he adorned his conversation, he noted that you had hardly reached the midpoint of the walk. And he continued.

The second great vicious beast that threatens a novice chief of state, he said, is to create a distinction between truth and lie. Truth is often only another way of repeating a lie, he added. A president of the republic and the founding president of a single party—and Koyaga will necessarily be the founding president of a single party—does not allow himself to be encumbered with respect for such Jesuitical distinctions. He states or utters those words that will support a certain cause or realize a goal. Besides, it is rare—as rare as hair on the behind of a chimpanzee—that a citizen of an independent African republic will stand up to utter blasphemies that might contradict what the chief of state has said. People listen to what they are told, to what they are ordered to do. They do not have time to examine, weigh, and compare the acts of a president. What believer evaluates the aims of the divinities before executing their will? Who are the individuals we call great men? They are without any doubt those who are the greatest fabricators. What are the most beautiful birds? Those birds who have the most beautiful songs. The greatest human literary works, in every civilization, will always be tales, legends. After all, what are the Bible, the Qur'an, and all the other fundamental texts of literate civilizations, the great civilizations, those everlasting civilizations? What are they? Well, what do those great religious and literary stories teach us? Just one truth, and it is ever the same truth. A man has reached his fullest measure and become a thaumaturge when he has freed himself from the distinction between truth and lie. Koyaga, your host is teaching you that he has never cared much about any discrepancy between his words and deeds. And that is the habit, the behavior that has been the basis of his universally recognized image and wisdom.

The sun was falling behind the domes of the religious monuments. The horizon was blurring; brusque flights of night birds followed one another. Your feet were killing you, and even your knees and your calves; you were limping. The curious, frail, and sententious little old man summoned his aide as he kept trotting at his own pace. You thought it was to end the walk and your torments. To your great despair, he ordered him to have the headlights of the automobiles lit: the light was essential in order to continue the walk under optimum conditions. He announced in passing that you had another hour or so to walk. You were about to stop, to stop and admit that you were suffering, without false modesty, when some security officers arrived and approached the man with the crocodile totem. There was a certain danger for heads of state to walk around at night on the plantations. He should stop. The chief of protocol had prepared an official dinner. There was just enough time to get ready.

The Mercedes pulled up to where you were.

The next morning, at five o'clock, the tireless little old man was seated in the vast sitting room of the guest palace, that luxurious guest palace, and you heard him speak to the sentinel.

I have come to awaken my friend and younger brother, Koyaga, for our morning walk.

You went down. To get rid of him politely, you claimed you hated morning walks. He smiled and explained that you were not going to undertake another walk through the plantation but to visit the garden of his residence. With a smile, you went back upstairs, dressed, and went with him.

The guest palace was located on the private property of the man with the crocodile totem, the ancestral property of his native village. Along with the presidential palace and the family villas, it constituted a vast property surrounded by a wall two meters high. Gateways in the wall opened to the four cardinal directions, gateways that were closed by heavy iron gates with handles of solid gold—the little old man loved to make a show of his wealth.

Once you were on the broad paths of the guest palace garden, the man with the crocodile totem began the conversation again exactly where you left off the night before. That was just at the end of the second rule a novice president must know, apply, and remember not to be swept away by a coup d'état.

The third vicious beast that threatens the one at the head of the state and the single party is for the president to take the men and women surrounding him, and those he encounters and with whom he converses, exactly as they present themselves to him culturally. A chief of state takes people as they exist in reality. He must know, as the charmer knows the anatomy of his serpents, the feelings and the means for cajoling human beings:

Every man is an impersonator. The finer feelings are only stratagems. The cockroach devours us by breathing on our wounds.

You continue your visit to the garden on the side where the crocodile lake is located. Suddenly, you found yourselves before an unusual architectural development—as unusual as an enormous dog mounted by a monkey in the middle of a band of red monkeys. This unusual development was made up of sheet-metal houses surrounded by a high wall topped by a tangle of barbed wire. At the four corners, watchtowers rose above the wall. These watchtowers reminded you, Koyaga, of the posts in Indochina. You stopped and wanted to ask questions. The wily little old man beat you to the draw with his explanations.

You certainly want to know what this enclosure represents in the middle of the park. Well, it is the Saoubas Prison, the prison where my friends, supporters, relatives, and close associates are in detention, he announced.

You stopped, mouth agape. You did not understand. You thought he was joking.

No, I am not joking. I really said the prison for my true friends and my close relatives. I said that with all the seriousness of the man digging a grave for his mother-in-law.

A president, chief of the single party, father-of-the-nation, has many political adversaries and few sincere friends. The political adversaries are enemies. Things are clear and simple with them. They are the individuals who get in a president's way, the individuals who aspire to supreme power—two male hippopotamuses cannot be in one race of the river. You treat them as they deserve. You torture, exile, or assassinate them. But how do you behave with sincere friends and close relatives? How do you treat them? More clearly, how do you distinguish true from false friends? It is a universally recognized rule that one can only be betrayed by a friend or a close associate. One must forestall treachery, flush out the false friend, the jealous relative, the traitor, before he can inject his venom. That is an operation as complex as cleaning the hyena's anus.

The man with the crocodile totem has given you his recipe, his method. He begins by narrating an edifying anecdote.

During a siesta, he has a dream. His fetishists, marabouts, and sorcerers interpret the dream. Without giving precise descriptions, they reveal to him that certain friends are preparing a plot. What friends should he arrest? In his doubt, he has his most dependable and oldest friend arrested and tortured. This man pours out contradictory stories day after day. Without being discouraged or remorseful, the dictator with the crocodile totem checks and compares the details of the prisoner's wild fictions and discovers to his astonishment the existence of a real plot under way. From that experience, he concludes that he must periodically verify the sincerity of the fidelity of the friends and close associates who surround him, just as an automobile that is working perfectly well goes for a checkup after a certain number of kilometers. He organizes a procedure for and a team of men to take care of periodic checks and maintenance.

A sorcerer, fetishist, marabout, or seer makes vague predictions and reveals that a relative or friend is about to betray the chief or participate in preparations for a plot. The friend or relative falls under accusation and is immediately arrested and imprisoned by the director of security, Head Commissioner Garbio. Garbio invents the outline, the facts, and creates the evidence. The accused person is sent in chains to Saoubas Prison and placed under the care of Deputy Sambio, the cruel torturer who manages to elicit through torture an admission of the facts and evidence established by the director of security. It is not unusual for the president, sweating after his morning outing, to enter the torture chamber and supervise the interrogation himself. The confession is submitted to him. The president with the crocodile totem analyses, compares, and verifies the details with the care of a husband mending his wife's bloomers, and decides whether or not to refer the accused to the state security tribunal.

During a trial behind closed doors, the secretary general of the single party, Deputy Philippio Yaco, attorney general of the republic and a great specialist in criminal law, sentences the accused to death or to perpetual detention.

The private prison was reserved for such condemned or accused prisoners. A prison adjoining the palace of the man with the crocodile totem. The president could visit it night or day. He himself controlled internment or release from the prison.

You accompanied the man with the crocodile totem into Saoubas Prison, the prison for his friends and close associates. He took you to visit a number of cells. One was that of his real nephew Abynn. Then those of his first fighting comrade, Yekom, and of the mother of that patriot. Those of his first confidant and go-between, Djibé Lasidi, and of that individual's wife. Then there were the cells of the former ministers of health, of education, of labor . . .

You went to the torture chamber, where he showed you the seat where he presided during sessions of torture. He showed you the different instruments employed. Then he had a real leper brought in. An awful, libidinous leper. When he could not manage to wrest a confession from a prisoner by means of physical torture, he threatened him. He threatened to have the leper make love to the mother or wife of the prisoner. He also threatened to have the accused thrown to the sacred crocodiles, who were visible through the gates of the prison. They were always ravenous for human flesh. The man with the crocodile totem informed you that his very own sister prepared the food served to those detained in Saoubas Prison, the prison of his friends. His sister was in command of a team of sorcerers and marabouts, who constantly invented potions. She had the detainees consume these potions to cleanse their mind of any will to gain power or to cleanse their heart of any hatred toward the man with the crocodile totem.

Following the visit to the prison, you went toward the park. The sun was beginning to appear. You inquired how the man with the crocodile totem managed to hide and make people forget all these practices —torture, corruption, arbitrary imprisonment. How had he succeeded in passing as the Sage of Africa? How had he managed to preserve such respectability? Such respectability that important international organizations awarded him prizes and had even created a prize in his name. He added that this was because he was an African chief of state. You did not understand right away. So he continued:

During a beauty contest, when the sheep is not admired, it is because the steer is not present. My practices might be blameworthy in other situations, beneath other skies, in other contexts; but not in Africa. During your initiatory journey, you will be led to compare me with other chiefs of state, and you will quickly conclude that I am an angel, a wise man who deserves humanity's gratitude.

Then he explained to you what he called the fourth savage beast that threatens the head of a single party: making a poor choice. During the cold war that controlled the universe, the choosing of a side was essential, but it was a risky act, as risky as choosing a woman as wife. In his own case, the man with the crocodile totem, the man with the fedora, had not been forced to make a choice. History had imposed on him the liberal camp, the best choice. And in a curious manner.

As a young man entering politics, he had believed, like every adolescent, in nonsense such as the dignity of the Black man, solidarity among nations, between colonized peoples and communism, the right of nations to determine their own course, the struggle against colonialism, etc. He intoned these stupid things to his compatriots who were subjected to forced labor, exploitation, and who suffered from hunger, scorn, and racism. Naturally, they revolted and subjected the still colonized country to fire and sword. We know what happened.

The days, nights, and moments spent with Tiekoroni, the little old man, taught you much about the science of governing a people and a country. These were moments, words, thoughts that you would never forget.

The dictator with the crocodile totem was a whole man. He was a man who possessed all qualities and all faults of a human being, but carried to extremes. A man who was extreme in his virtues and his vices, a bag of contradictions. A man who was at once as generous as a she-goat's rump and as vindictive, petty, and vicious as lice or the yaws; as much a liar and a fabricator as an adulterous wife and as trustworthy and loyal as a hunter of wild beasts; as cruel as a stuffed cat holding a wounded mouse in its claws and as tender as a hen with the chicks she has hatched.

Let us demonstrate first that he was generous. He adopted the children of all African chiefs of state who were assassinated or overthrown and took their widows and mistresses under his wing. He built churches and mosques. Yes, he was very generous, but was he not equally vindictive and petty? He was petty to the point of stealing the white cane of a blind man, the brother-in-law of the nephew of an individual he had condemned. He was vicious to the point of inventing as a type of torture the submission of the seventy-year-old mother of an accused prisoner to rape by the repulsive and libidinous leper.

Let us speak of his lies. He was more than a liar. In fact, he was a tree of lies or, rather, a wholesaler of lies. Yes, he was deceitful; but was he not equally truthful when, with courage and without demagoguery, he was the only chief of state to tell his compatriots that they were liars, sloths, and savages?

Let us add that he was cruel. He tortured in a horrendous manner friends and relatives whom he continued to love and know were perfectly innocent. Yes, he was ferocious, but was he not equally humane when he had residences constructed for beggars and disabled people and showed himself more hospitable than other African dictators?

The dictator with the crocodile totem believed in God, fetishes, and sorcery, but not in man, honor, faith, or unselfishness. He always had a bag of banknotes at hand, and no visitor left without an envelope. It was by the subterfuge of those envelopes that he managed to neutralize the tongues and pens of all the journalists who had to speak of him and his country.

Koyaga, you were curious as to who among his collaborators was his aide and possible successor. He smiled and replied that he would never choose a successor willingly and freely, and he counseled you never to do that. That is because a successor, whether you wish it or not, is a competitor, and people draw away from a guide whose disappearance will no longer be a catastrophe for the country. However, should circumstances oblige you to designate a successor one day, he indicated some rules to follow.

The successor must resemble you, be another you in character and behavior, but be publicly recognized as inferior to you in virtue and superior in vice. That is the precaution that takes from your successor the weapons for criticizing you after you are gone. If people say you are too tall, your successor must be a giant. If they think you are short, he must be a real dwarf. If you are a thief and a liar, he must be a kleptomaniac and a shameless fabricator.

Gossips claim that toward the end of his life the dictator with the crocodile totem was stricken with kleptomania. Like a thieving rat or a louse, he filched his own money, hid banknotes in dossiers, shoes, and jacket pockets in his closets, and then forgot them. His valets, guards, and the aides in charge of protocol—everyone around him—picked up, used, saved, and invested those bills. After his disappearance, they were the ones who became rich and the masters of the Republic of the Ebony People.

It is probably true that such a mania took hold of him. It is a sign of great men ever to be stricken with such little follies toward the end of their life. And, incontestably, the man with the crocodile totem was great among the great.

At the edge of the forest, he had a Catholic religious monument built to halt the spread of fanatical Muslim hordes coming from the Sahel and the savannas of the North.

When he died, his funeral was conducted by a nephew he had slandered, imprisoned, tortured, and condemned to death. Then pardoned and covered with wealth and honor. Politicians like the nephew the dictator had slandered, imprisoned, tortured horribly, condemned to death, and pardoned were declared to be the ones most affected when he disappeared, and, more than other citizens of the republic, they gathered around the president of the National Assembly to bemoan his loss and weep for him.

An important international organization created a foundation and a humanitarian prize in his honor. All we who believe, like the man with the crocodile totem, in fetishes, decisions, and condemnations based on the divination of sorcerers, take that consecration to have been deserved. But everybody else, all the rationalists who refuse to accept magic as truth, consider that honor as incongruous as the beads of a Muslim pilgrim knotted about the neck of a hyena.

Ah, Koyaga! You did not leave the Republic of the Ebony People from the airport at the capital, but from the one at Fasso, the native village of the president with the crocodile totem. As when you arrived, the dancers and tam-tam were brought from all parts of the country to honor your departure. The airport was vibrant with tam-tam, festivals, half-naked Blacks, smiling—fools who were becoming breathless with the dangerous acrobatic dances of monkeys. Women, schoolchildren, and old people in traditional costume shoved each other like herds along the road between the guest palace and the airport. They kept applauding like fools, shouting and howling the stupid slogans like deaf people. Slogans celebrating the friendship between the Republic of the Gulf and that of the Ebony People. Foolish gestures celebrating fraternity between you, the man with the hawk totem, and the man with the crocodile totem. Concludes the *koroduwa*.

In the seats of the hall of honor at the airport, you were side by side, Koyaga, you and your host, the man with the fedora. You were waiting for his arrival. He was supposed to debark at any moment. You were talking. The roar of an airplane landing interrupted your conversation. Your host got up and went toward the runway, accompanied by all his ministers.

It was too late. Bosuma, the man of the hyena totem, also called "Red Table Wine," the emperor of the Land of the Two Rivers, was already on the terrace of the hall of honor. He had not waited for all the steps of welcoming a head of state to be carried out. With his marshal's kepi and the smile of a scoundrel, chest bedecked with decorations, Emperor Bosuma was already in the hall. He did not have the patience to wait for the protocol services to greet him at the foot of the air stairs. He was there facing your host, whom he politely called his true father. The marshal snapped to rigid attention like a real rifleman. Even when he is rich, the dog does not stop eating excrement, explains the responder.

The emperor took off his kepi and humbly kissed the hand of the dictator with the crocodile totem. After this silliness, he rushed to kiss you warmly and noisily on the mouth. His tongue and lips were spicy —they stunk like the putrid aroma of a hyena's ass. He truly deserved the name of Bosuma (*bosuma* means "essence of fart" in Malinke).

You did not have time to offer a salute or a proverb. He drew away with the medals clinking on his chest.

Grabbing his penis with both hands, the emperor headed toward the toilet and disappeared. You and your host broke out laughing and could not stop. It did not last long. He came back, pulling by the hand one of the young women in charge of cleaning the toilet.

He found that she was beautiful, nice, and asked your host for her hand. The young woman was yelling but seemed to be putting up weak resistance. Your host thought so too; she was defending herself out of modesty. Your host asked if she were married. No, she did not even have a fiancé, she answered. With frank humor, the dictator with the crocodile totem ordered his chief of protocol to go to town with the young woman. She would have to inform her parents of her engagement and voyage. In less than five minutes, Emperor Bosuma had just entered into one of the thirty marriages he celebrated each year.

The man of the hyena totem told you that, in any case, he had come to pick you up and would not leave without you. All the people in his empire had been dancing, singing, and awaiting you for a week—ever since the day you left the capital of the Republic of the Gulf. You could not disappoint an entire nation that loved you. You could not prolong the wait of an entire country that had, henceforth, adopted you and considered you like a father-of-the-nation. A people that had ceased all activities to scrutinize the heavens. A people that were waiting night and day for your airplane to pierce through the clouds and were preparing for you the most fantastic welcome of your life.

He had come to welcome you and to take you with him, and you could not do otherwise because he, the emperor, was your true, your true big brother by blood.

Regardless of the enthusiasm of the dancers, the tam-tam drummer stops the feast from time to time in order to warm up his instrument. Let us follow his example.

The *sèrè* stops his narrative, performs a musical interlude, and recites three proverbs on power:

The frogs croaking do not prevent the elephant from drinking.
If the mighty eats a chameleon, they say that it is for his health—it is a medicine. If the poor man eats one, he is accused of gluttony.
If a small tree sprouts through the ground beneath a baobab, it dies still a sapling.

15

Ah, Koyaga! It must have been toward four o'clock in the afternoon when your airplane pierced through the clouds above the airport in the capital of the Land of the Two Rivers. You will always remember the revulsion that made you start. You did not believe your eyes: the airport was deserted, without even a starved dog looking for a pittance. A successful coup d'état against the emperor seemed the only explanation. Only a coup d'état could have scared away the crowd that was supposed to be there to welcome you. You threw yourself onto the emperor and shook him unceremoniously. He was sleeping—noisily snoring. During the flight, he had emptied a bottle of whiskey and two bottles of table Bordeaux. He was heavy and deaf as a rock. You slapped him, yelling, "The coup d'état!" The emperor jumps, howls "oh!" and looks out the window. His tranquility surprises you and reassures you. He explains one of the ruses you must remember if you want to reach the rank of emperor one day. Never let anybody know the time and date of your return to your country because attacks on an airplane that has just landed cannot be parried.

You landed and went to the palace without fanfare. That afternoon, the dancers, tam-tam drummers, and military delegations appeared in the streets and invaded the airport and its surroundings. You returned to the airport—you, your host, and all your followers, surrounded by an armed escort. You embarked once more in the imperial airplane and circled around the city twice. Landed in the middle of a festive crowd with delegations and parades. You received one of those welcomes that only an African emperor like the man with the decorated chest can offer to a guest.

In the splitting up of Africa decreed by the Christian states at the Conference of Berlin in 1885, the territory of the Two Rivers was bled dry by the razzias of slave-trading Arab sultans. The French conquered it and decided to stress forced labor, requisitioning, and the use of indigenous labor. The colonialists began their operation with means and methods that finally reduced by half the population, which was already scattered about. The few inhabitants walking about the country were dumb with fear and sleeping sickness. They were, as a consequence, inhabitants from whom it was difficult to ask much effort. The longer the French colonization (the improvement of the country) lasted, the more the country's population was thinned and impoverished.

Disappointed, the French concluded it was impossible to make the territory productive and decided to let it go. They made proposals to the English and the Germans. The negotiations were about to be concluded when the First World War broke out.

After the armistice of 1918, the international context had changed and the transfer could no longer be carried out. The French government decreed a new policy for managing the territory. The colony was divided among the colonists. The colonists held a monopoly of selling and buying over the cantons that were ceded to them and, along with that, the control of transportation. The development of Lobaye was given to the powerful Sangha-Oubangi Lumber Company. That company, the only one to continue the laborious collection of rubber, severely repressed the workers' revolts against levies and forced labor. In Bobangi, the father of the man of the hyena totem rebelled three times. The first time, his right ear was cut off; the second time, the left ear. The third time, he was executed by the firing squad.

The grandfather of the future emperor sent his orphaned grandson to the missionary school in the territorial capital and then to the Petit Séminaire of the Federation of French Equatorial Africa. The man of the hyena totem was called to be a priest, like his uncle. But the seminarian turned out to be undisciplined. He left at night to engage in orgies and came back drunk on Sunday mornings in time for the Holy Sacrifice. The priests dismissed him from their school.

It is 1940, and French Equatorial Africa has just rallied to General de Gaulle's partisans. Free France is recruiting in order to organize the military force that will go up through the Libyan desert. The man of the hyena totem goes to the enlistment office. He is welcomed with open arms, enrolled, and given a uniform. The eighteen-year-old orphan finds a family and fraternity in the army. He fights in campaigns in France and Germany and heaps up his promotions: corporal, sergeant. He is sent to Indochina, where he works as a noncommissioned officer in broadcasting operations. He goes back to his own country with the rank of lieutenant. His cousin, the president of the republic, makes him first a captain, then colonel and chief of staff. He makes him chief of staff because he thinks Bosuma is too stupid and has too little education to attempt and succeed in a pronunciamento. The chief of staff gets picked up dead drunk in the streets on Saturday evenings.

One officer, Captain Zaban, is quite intelligent and wants to pull a coup d'état. He engages in a blood pact with the man of the hyena totem who is chief of staff. On New Year's Eve, Captain Zaban organizes, leads, and succeeds with all the operations of the coup. The man of the hyena totem beats him to the radio in the wee hours of the morning, reads the declaration, proclaims himself head of state, arrests the president of the republic, assassinates all his accomplices, including even, several months later, the initiator and executor of the coup d'état.

Each of us has personal preoccupations, and among them the two principal ones are usually death and God. Bosuma, the man of the hyena totem, had only one preoccupation here below: that of always remaining the highest ranked soldier of the multilateral Africa of the cold war.

He attained power one Monday with the rank of colonel. Tuesday morning, he awarded himself the stars of a general. When people mentioned to him that four other dictators already had that rank on the continent, he proclaimed himself marshal on Thursday evening. When two other generals joined him in the marshalcy, he asked France, his own army, and his people to crown him emperor. France, the army, and the people of the Land of the Two Rivers invited guests and journalists from the entire world to attend the coronation. Since that time, no other dictator has been recognized as emperor. Bosuma (essence of fart), the man with the bedecked chest, has remained incontestably the highest-ranking soldier on the continent of multiple dictators.

It was already approaching dawn. Everyone had been drinking. The emperor was drunk. Everyone had eaten, sung, and danced quite a bit. Everyone was dead tired. The emperor alone kept dancing, singing, drinking, and eating. The soiree organized in your honor, Koyaga, kept going. Diplomats, civil personalities, and even high-ranking officers with wives had quietly slipped out, disappeared like cats. The emperor had noticed because of the increasing number of empty chairs. He had a fit and ordered the gates of the palace closed. He locked them in person and stuffed the keys in his pocket. Nobody else could leave. Dead tired, the wives of the ambassadors and civil personalities had stretched out on the grass of the lawns. The military band kept beating time. The musicians, who were as drunk as the guests, drummed, played, and sang like a bunch of crazy people. The emperor continued dancing. From time to time, he left the dance floor, went into the palace garden to shake and awaken some ambassador's wife, and then dragged her back to the dance floor to waltz, twist, and jerk. The few officers, officials, and ambassadors still awake applauded and let out admiring cries. Koyaga, he asked you several times to join him on the dance floor. Several times he shoved the empress or some ambassador's wife into your arms, and from sheer politeness, you were obliged to do a cha-cha, java, tango, or twist.

But when you saw the sun rising over the tops of the first trees in the forest, you asked to go. Against all the fine rules of etiquette, you asked to go. The man of the hyena totem reminded you of the African precept by which a guest must ask to go three times.

I ask to go once; I ask to go twice; I ask to go three times. I am tired and I ask to go, you said in a clearly irritated tone.

The emperor stopped the drums, trumpets, guitars, and chanting, but only to launch into an interminable speech on your fraternity. You were his true brother, his brother through blood and arms. A speech on the time-honored friendship between your countries. A speech that put you so sound asleep that you snored. Two of you—you and the French ambassador—were snoring at the table of honor. You were awakened by the applause and hurrahs at the end of the speech. The gates were finally wide open.

The guest palace where you stayed was not far. In less than five minutes, you were there. But it was only to encounter another surprise. The eight girls from the Zende people who had been waiting for you since eleven o'clock at the orders of the minister of protocol leapt from their seats, began to dance, and engaged in obscene wiggling and hand-clapping as they sang shameless songs.

The Zende are a people from the northeast of the Land of the Two Rivers. They are one of the most intelligent and wisest peoples in the world because they are alone in considering love to be at once a great art and a sport. They teach love to children at an age when, in other countries, girls are learning music. In the Zende villages, during the warm season, they have love bouts when, among the neighboring peoples, the championships of combat are beginning.

Women fought over any stranger who wandered into a Zende village. And the woman who succeeded in winning him for herself would immediately drag him into bed to wrestle him, play with him until he was exhausted, detumescent, and in a state of anerection. She would tease him until he admitted defeat out loud, "with his whole mouth." Then the Zende woman would abandon the man, exhausted and useless; she would hurriedly knot her pagne, go out into the street, running from house to house, from neighbor to neighbor, with his underwear in hand, bragging about her exploit.

For three weeks, since the moment your journey had been announced, competition had opened in all the Zende villages to select the women most expert in lovemaking. The best girls and women had first been judged by their public mime to the beat of the tam-tam. Then they were judged by practical trials in bed. Those who managed to obtain the apology, out loud and "with the whole mouth," from the most stalwart and insatiable riflemen were selected. From among the thirty worthy contestants, the eight most beautiful women were reserved for you and the others for the members of your delegation.

The eight victorious women were the ones dancing and singing in your living room. Their lascivious mimes and chanting could not lessen or sweep away the simple desire that had come over you to sleep alone, to sprawl alone in a bed.

You took the hand of the first woman, the one closest to you, and went to the bedroom with her. The chief of protocol rudely dismissed the others who, with untied pagnes, wanted to rape you. In bed, you surrendered with the first skirmishes. You made your excuses, as a Zende woman always requires of a defeated man, out loud and with your whole mouth.

The stench—a mixture of death, infections, urine, excrement—was unbearable. A tremulous voice, the voice of a man at death's doorstep, came from the back of the cell.

"Kill me. For once in your life, be humane. Hang me. Shoot me. Kill me right now."

"Shut your trap, filthy communist," answered the fuming emperor.

"For Christ's sake, kill me. For the sake of your mother and father, kill me," the prisoner continued to chant.

"Koyaga!" (now the voice was addressed to you). "Koyaga! You who are humane and a believer, pardon; ask him to finish me off."

"Colonel Otto Sacher, make this plotter, this communist criminal shut up," commanded the emperor.

Colonel Otto, the absolute master of the institution, dove into the shadows and gave the dying prisoner several slaps. The voice did not stop, despite the deserved punishment.

The angry emperor took you by the hand, and you continued your visit to Ngaragla Prison. Emperor Bosuma kept grumbling, and his anger did not diminish. He had his own reasons. He did not even like to terminate the torments of common-law criminals by executing them. So why should he accord that favor to a political prisoner, a communist plotter, and a man from the Gbaya nation who had confessed? From the emperor's angry oaths, you gathered that Colonel Zaban was the prisoner chained to a hook at the back of the cell. You knew Colonel Zaban quite well.

According to custom, the emperor wanted the colonel to drink his own urine and eat his own excrement before he died. Zaban was the officer who, at the head of the student officers of the École Nationale d'Administration, had engineered the success of the putsch and had made the man with the hyena totem head of state. So he was a great friend and the primary comrade of the emperor. . . . Thus, it was humane for the emperor to torture him and condemn him to death.

Even in the case of two blind chicken thieves, each one knows that following a successful operation, you are never at ease, nothing is certain as long as the comrade is also alive here below. Adds Tiekura the *koroduwa*.

Because the man of the hyena totem was the only dictator to have himself proclaimed emperor, he was less of a liar and a hypocrite than the heads of state in the other republics.

"It's from treachery and hypocrisy that the other African presidents begin the presentation of their republics with the national assembly or a school. The main institution in any single-party government is the prison. So I am having you begin your visit of the empire with the prison," stated the man of the hyena totem.

The emperor loved France and the French—or at least, he liked to say so. They were proper people who must not be criticized publicly. The French had left many important achievements in the Land of the Two Rivers, but they had clearly failed to construct enough prisons. In the capital, they had left only one prison, Ngaragla. This was a minuscule prison, squeezed between the river and the forest, cramped in an enclosure of one hundred meters square and having only five usable parts: solitary cells, the Birao cells, the safari or anteroom of death, the white house, and the red doors. The isolation ward and Birao had only fourteen cells each, and safari only two. That made a total of only thirty cells, two of which were for prisoners condemned to death.

The French had not understood anything about the Blacks; they did not know that when you condemn a Black man to death, you have to make his entire clan disappear in order to maintain peace in the country. Blacks are always vindictive and have a sense of family. The close relatives of a condemned man never pardon the hanging of a relative. In order to be effective, a good prison in Africa must have twelve, not two, cells for its death row. In Africa, it is necessary to have prisons throughout the country or recruit experienced prison wardens. The recruitment of prison wardens is an important task, and the choice of the director of the central prison where all the political detainees are held should be made only by the head of state.

The director of Ngaragla Prison was Colonel Otto Sacher. He was a Czech who believed the emperor to be his man of destiny. In Prague, the young Otto had unsuccessfully sought his man of destiny in his own family, in the schools, and in six different careers. He had pursued his quest in the Czechoslovakian army, where he had fought his way to the rank of lieutenant without encountering that man of destiny.

He left for France and enlisted in the foreign legion. After the armistice, he joined General de Gaulle in London, fought with General Leclerc in Egypt, in Libya (particularly at Abyar al'Hakim), and in Syria. He realized, after so many campaigns in the service of the French, that neither de Gaulle nor General Leclerc, who had nonetheless decorated him, was his man of destiny.

At age thirty, he left the French army and participated in the liberation of his country as a lieutenant-colonel in the Russian army. Disappointed at not having found his man of destiny in the Russian army or among the communists in power in Czechoslovakia, he drew his revolver and, instead of blowing his brains out, fired at a globe. The bullet went clear through and came out just at the spot where Loko was located—the city of Loko in the Lobaye, at the heart of the tropical forest.

Otto arrived in Africa, plunged into the deepest part of the forest, settled down as a planter and lumberman in Loko, where, for five long years, he failed to meet his man of destiny among the savages and Pygmies.

One Sunday, in revolt against an unjust fate, he decked himself out with all his many medals—medals awarded by many nations on the battlefields of Europe, Russia, Asia, the Sahara, the rice paddies of Indochina, etc. He plunged into the forest, determined to locate his man of destiny or to be eaten by giant ants. Relentlessly, for six nights and days, he walked. The seventh morning, he came out of the forest to find himself in front of a cathedral. The cathedral was brimful of the faithful. Gawkers spilled off the square and lined the two sides of the avenue leading up to the house of God in the city. Colonel Otto assumed a place at the head of the line and quietly waited for the end of the Mass.

The emperor and empress came out of the cathedral first and got into their carriage. Coming abreast with the former colonel covered with all his decorations, the emperor with the hyena totem gave a cry of admiration, jumped from the imperial carriage, rushed to the officer, and kissed him on the lips. The former officer of the Czech, French, Russian legions, the former locomotive engineer, truck driver, airplane pilot, procurer, picador, butcher, woodsman, poultryman, coffee planter . . . had just found, at age fifty, his man of destiny. The two men congratulated each other and drank toasts. The emperor immediately gave Otto the highest office that can be given to a White, the office that, according to the hierarchy—after the emperor, the empress, and the heir to the throne—was the fourth highest in the country. This was an office that surpassed the responsibilities of prime minister: the prodigious post as director of Ngaragla Prison.

With a trusted man like Otto as director, the emperor worried no more. He sent to prison, and to death, everybody who fell into his hands. His former enemies, the members of their families, and the friends of those enemies. All those he did not like along with their associates and friends. Former and future plotters. Former and future communists. What always happens in such a situation took place quite rapidly: the inevitable overpopulation.

Ngaragla Prison had an overpopulation. In order to reduce that overpopulation, the emperor and the director resorted to the same technique that everybody else—even the blind poultry farmer of the village—uses. Suppress, kill. Adds the responder.

For purposes of assassination, the emperor and the prison director resorted to the kidnapping of prisoners. These were generally prisoners who had not been declared or introduced before the tribunals— the associates and distant friends of condemned personal prisoners of the emperor. During the night, a truck covered with tarpaulins slipped into the prison, and men with hoods jumped out, opened the cells, grabbed prisoners, and drove them to the riverbank, where they executed the prisoners, buried them in the reeds, or threw them to the crocodiles.

Even the increased number of disappearances of prisoners on moonless nights could not take care of the overpopulation because the emperor had new personal prisoners brought in for housing each morning. Worse still: an additional problem of the overpopulation loomed. The budget, which was already insufficient for feeding the prisoners, ran out. "Prisoners eat too much and don't do a damned bit of work!" exclaimed the emperor in anger.

He decided that the prisoners should earn their own upkeep. At kilometer 26 on the road to Mbaiki, he confiscated the plantations of former ministers who were in prison. He took twenty-five detainees from the teams of prisoners working in the fields of the Imperial Court and sent them to the stolen plantations. What always happens in such cases happened—people are never trustworthy: the worker prisoners and their guards consumed the entire fruit of their labor on the spot.

Waiting for the Vote of the Wild Animals

Without thinking about their codetainees or the prisoners chained to hooks deep in the cells, without commiseration for the weaker ones dragging balls chained to their feet. Not getting the least bit of cassava to nibble on, the forgotten prisoners began to die one by one, and then by whole teams, on an average of twelve per day. Adds the *koroduwa*.

Since there were ever more cadavers, Colonel Otto was forced to enlarge the team of prisoner gravediggers. The team had to be enlarged at the expense of the prisoner laborer team. Finally, there was not one single prisoner in the fields to plant cassava. All able prisoners were assigned to the burial of dead detainees. There was no longer any manioc farming or any manioc harvest. No prisoner had anything to eat. There was no way out.

Good father of all the citizens of the empire that he was, the emperor intervened. He had cassava roots dug from his own farms, sold them to the state, and offered them to the prisoners, who stopped dying.

You, Koyaga, and the emperor were still following Colonel Otto on the visit of the prison. You were accompanied by the corteges that escort heads of state. At the entrance to the buildings referred to as the red doors, Otto turned around, went over to the emperor, and muttered a few words as he pointed to some prisoners standing in the middle of the central courtyard. You saw the right ear of the emperor twitch, vibrate, and tremble. His lips and his limbs all trembled. He was insanely angry. The prisoners at whom Colonel Otto had pointed, the ones assembled in the middle of the courtyard, had been captured stealing in the fields of corn and cassava of the Imperial Court. Yes, on the very property of the Imperial Court.

What the man of the hyena totem called the Imperial Court was a vast clutter of agricultural fields, sewing workshops, photographic studios, and buildings for storage of fabrics and building materials, factories, silos, mills, stables, movie houses, slaughterhouses, ranches, scaffolds for executions, sports fields, studios, brick and tile factories, etc.—all grouped around a rectangular courtyard. This constituted a heterogeneous clutter that resembled the property of an illiterate and miserly Malinke who had become enormously rich in diamond traffic, taking advantage of a thousand and one ways for maintaining a harem of twenty wives with some hundred children.

To keep the country's money from going to the Lebanese, Hindus, West Africans, and Hausa, the emperor had been obliged to engage in all enterprises and to appropriate all monopolies for himself. The monopoly for ceremonial photography in the empire, the management of hotels for prostitution and bars in the red-light districts, the production of peanut butter and that of supplying meat, rice, and cassava to the army, the procurement of toilet paper, school supplies, and uniforms for schoolchildren, parachutists, and sailors, etc. The emperor did everything for the country, and instead of helping, the inhabitants went out plundering his fields.

So it was understandable that the emperor was trembling with anger at the sight of communist plotters who, jealous of the successes of his liberal undertakings, sabotaged his work. At his order, all the prisoners arrested for stealing were chained, made to lie on the ground, lined up. Recalling the precepts of the Qur'an, the emperor ordered the regiment to beat the chained prisoners to death before cutting off their hands, as the Belgians used to do in the Congo, and their ears, as the French did in Ubangi-Chari.

The emperor taught you that the priority for an African head of state is the fight against thieving and pilfering. Africans are born thieves. You thanked him for his judicious advice.

"You understand, my true brother, why you must have no pity for poachers, saboteurs of an undertaking so essential for Africa first of all and, beyond that, the entire universe. This will be the end of all wars on earth, the end of all injustice, the end of all misunderstandings between peoples. By my initiative, Africa will transform the world into a paradise, Africa will save mankind, all animal species, all plants, the entire Earth, the whole Universe."

The enthusiastic emperor could talk on and on about the advantages of what he called the project of his life. Both of you were in hunting uniform, seated side by side in a Jeep. You were driving through the Imperial Park of Awakaba. Since morning, the emperor had been giving you details about this gigantic project.

His intention was to make of the Imperial Park of Awakaba an informal meeting place for all the heads of state in the world. A project he conceived as bringing the transfer of the UN to Awakaba, to Africa. Since Awakaba was the largest hunting park in the world, and the richest in game, the emperor wanted to assign to each head of state his own hunting reserve. Each head of state would have his own private hotel. The financing of some hundred private hotels had already been promised by South Africa. Each private hotel would be splendidly equipped with furniture and even with a team of Zende women who would take charge of getting the heads of state in form after the interminable meetings of the UN. Because of the performance of the Zende women, the heads of state would become fond of Awakaba and want to spend their vacations in the park. And then, one day, there would be a unanimous vote to consecrate the transfer of the UN to Awakaba.

The emperor showed you, you Kogaya, the hunting reserve he had chosen for you. Thanks to Awakaba, all the important problems that currently divide the world would become nothing but the trivialities of neighborhood quarrels.

You are touring your own hunting reserve, Koyaga. In the distance, you see some vultures making arabesques and circles in the sky with their infernal cawing. The emperor asks you to be silent. He wanted to take you on a lion hunt, so he is happy to have the occasion. He is sure that the vultures are whirling above a couple of wild animals that have just downed some large game. You get out of the Jeep silently. You file quietly through the thorny scrub trees of the bush. Stupefaction! It is not lions you discover, but a gang of poachers with assegai, surrounding a dead elephant. In panic, the poachers hurl their assegai, and an Imperial Park ranger is mortally wounded. Unfortunately, not all the poachers manage to flee into the thickets, and the emperor has time to aim at the last one, to bring him down. The emperor leans over the poacher's body. It is one of the inhabitants of the village of Demi II. He gives orders to the soldiers to raze the village and to take all the inhabitants to the death house, Ngaragla Prison.

Suddenly, there is the drone of an airplane, then two . . . it is a flight of about ten planes in the serene skies of the Empire. Koyaga, you are intrigued. Very intrigued because you knew that the emperor, the man of the hyena totem, personally owns the only airplane in the entire empire, a Caravelle. He rents it occasionally to his air force and to the National Company for Air Transport. He holds the monopoly for renting airliners in this country.

Your host, the emperor, understands your uneasiness and reassures you. The comings and goings of airplanes in the sky signaled the arrival of the man of the leopard totem. The man of the leopard totem was coming to spend the weekend in his chalet at Awakaba. He was suspicious and prudent, the man of the leopard totem. He never left his country without taking the entire treasury and all the high officials of his republic. That is a ruse that has proven itself and brought about the failure of three plots. Three times, plotters have wanted to take advantage of a trip by the kleptomaniacal Dinosaur (one of the nicknames of the dictator of the leopard totem) to try their luck. The prospect of finding themselves with empty coffers has discouraged them. This was a lesson for you, Koyaga, a lesson that you thought about all afternoon.

Whatever may be the enthusiasm of the drummer beating the tam-tam, the dancer must interrupt once in a while to take a breath. Let us follow his example and consider the following three proverbs on power. The *sèrè* plays, the responder dances, and these proverbs are recited:

In a despotic regime, the hand binds the foot; in a democracy, the foot binds the hand.
For the king, one changes the rhythm of the tam-tam but not the firewood that heats the skin on the tam-tam.
The fly attending the king is king.

16

Ah, Tiekura! The man of the leopard totem was a potentate. Of the worst criminal species. When one has to speak in a tale about a dictator of such strangeness and with such rough edges, it is better to begin with his deeds, the *donsomana* of the country, and the people who have engendered such a dictator. Adds the responder.

The country of the dictator with the leopard totem is the basin of one of the greatest rivers in the world. The territory is called the Republic of the Great River.

The *donsomana* of the basin of the Great River began in 1870 with the second king of a minuscule country in western Europe. His name was Paul II. Paul II was too great for his kingdom of thirty thousand square kilometers, too ambitious, too complex and wily for eight million petty bourgeois Europeans who were Christian and pacific. Not everything that Allah accomplishes is just and perfect: sometimes, he gives you a big head without giving you the means to acquire a long turban. This was the case of Paul II. He was too big for his pants, his ideas, his religions, his country: he always slept poorly. At night, after the compline, he did not kneel before the Holy Virgin but rather before a map of Africa; he did not read the Bible but rather adventure stories, and he dreamed of space. One evening, something obvious struck him in his books, a real discovery! No, it could not be true, it was not claimed! No, the French, English, Portuguese, those great experts in the colonization of savages had not set their hearts on every vacant territory in Black Africa! Those nations so expert in colonization had limited themselves to locking up the African coastline. The ferocity of the cannibals had dissuaded them from venturing into the interior of the continent. There remained vacant lands in the interior. That clear evidence, that discovery made Paul II weep. It was going to change his destiny, the fortune of his people, and the future of central Africa. Yes, there remained possibilities in Africa, possibilities for him! Chances for Christianity! Chances for his kingdom! Chances for the anthropophagous savages and the great equatorial forest! Paul II went into his chapel and asked his confessor to pray to Saint Mary for a mission. He was going to devote the rest of his life to a great Christian mission: he was going to save the Blacks of the vast basin of the Great River from slavery, ignorance, and paganism. Amen! And everything hurtled onward, like the falls of the great river.

Under the aegis of Paul II, the International Geographical Conference opened in the kingdom's capital on 12 September 1876. That conference formed the African International Association. The association made the definitive decision to plant the standard of civilization in the heart of the forest.

After the conference, Paul II summoned the explorer Stanley to his palace. Stanley had just returned from a journey of twelve thousand kilometers through the Africa of cannibals and malaria. On that journey, he had lost all of his European companions. The civilized world had celebrated him; governments and kings had congratulated him; academies and learned societies had honored him. But . . . but Stanley had not become rich—the essential thing was missing. He was popular without ceasing to be poor. Adds Tiekura. Stanley was suffering because of that; the king consoled him. The king made of him a friend and a confidant; he offered him a heavy purse of louis d'or. Paul II confided to his new friend his secret projects.

Paul II wanted to take the lands of central Africa without awakening the suspicions of those powers so expert in the conquest of Africa. Without those powers that boast of their natural right, of divine right over all African lands, suspecting. In the framework of the African International Association, the king and the explorer, as friends, created the International Association of the Great River. Under an altruistic, scientific, and humanitarian banner, Stanley undertook a new exploration financed by the king. He was not content merely to establish cultural and scientific relations with the people, he also made treaties with village chiefs and set up trading posts. He was to make over five hundred treaties and was able to sign a trade treaty one year later giving to Paul II's International Association of the Great River an absolute monopoly over the peoples, the natural wealth, the savannas, and the forests of the basin of the Great River, a territory eighty times more vast than his little kingdom.

During the conference on the partition of Africa, held at Berlin in 1884, the king maliciously, and to general surprise, exhibited the treaties signed with the peoples of the Republic of the Great River in the name of his scientific and humanitarian association. The game had been played. The French and the British, who considered themselves to be naturally endowed with the right to colonize savages, found that they had been taken in, and they protested. They could not leave such a big piece of land to an association directed by the king of such a little country, even if the association were scientific, Christian, humanitarian, and antislave. The crafty king, with his hand on the Bible, insisted on the sole Christian, humanitarian, and scientific concerns of his association.

He allayed the fury of the two powers by making a few false concessions. The territory would become the independent state of the Republic of the Great River. Commerce would be open to the commercial traffic of all nations, and any European could settle without prior authorization on any vacant land. These details were demanded by the English. In case of the failure of the mission of the king's association, the Gallic Cockerel (France) would have a right to preempt the basin of the Republic of the Great River. That was the goal of the French.

Recognized as sole proprietor of the basin of the Republic of the Great River, the wily and enormously voracious king wanted to make his conquest profitable at once. He allocated 10 percent of the land to the crown foundation, that is, to himself. He required contributions and income taxes in the name of the benefits of civilization brought by the king. As a contribution, the villages furnished men for the posts and missions. Each bush family paid a tax in kind, which was a certain quantity of ivory and red rubber per inhabitant. Woe to the people who could not manage to furnish the weight of rubber or the volume of ivory required. Rebellious or recalcitrant inhabitants had their right hands dipped in boiling pitch and then cut off. This punishment, inherited from the Muslims, was applied by the ascarids (the indigenous soldiers).

The able inhabitants deserted en masse, fled into the deepest brush. Increasingly, the villages became camps for communities of one-armed men. The British, the missionaries, and especially the French journalists (the French still hoped to exercise their right of preemption and were afraid of inheriting a nation of one-armed people) denounced the scandal of cutting off hands and the cupidity of King Paul II. At the point of being dispossessed of his property by the great powers, the king swiftly gave up his own initiative in the independent state of the Republic of the Great River and offered it to the kingdom in 1908.

As soon as it took over, the kingdom put an end to the abuses and entrusted the social evolution of the country to religious missionaries. The missions set a term of one and one-half centuries to make proper human beings of the natives: individuals who would cease being indolent and preoccupied with sex, who would stop stealing, and who would become pious Catholics. The good fathers said that from that date to the year 2050, the natives of the Great River would become people capable of abstract thought, with intellectuals who could run their country.

On the occasion of the Brussels World's Fair in the fifties, the imperturbable missionaries, who still thought they had a century to go, finally permitted a group of natives from the Great River to travel to Europe. These natives lived in a pavilion in which the fathers had reproduced the entire traditional habitat of the savages, with forest and huts, instead of simply reserving a hotel for them. The good fathers believed, in a humane and Christian manner, that they had housed their Blacks according to their customs. They were expecting warm gratitude when the incredible news burst. These ungrateful, savage natives from the Great River were demanding independence, total independence—at once, and immediately! Truly crazy people!

The *donsomana* for the dictator of the leopard totem, properly speaking, begins following the era of the very Catholic King Paul II. The king had undertaken to aggravate the curse that the Negroes of the Republic of the Great River already bore from being black with the additional infirmity of being a people with only one arm.

In a certain year, the grandfather of the dictator did not have the required weight of red rubber and he only escaped the hand-cutters by a hair, thanks to the solid arms of a paddler, which allowed him to reach the other bank and disappear deep into the forest.

It was deep in that forest that the mother of the future dictator, the beautiful Momo, was born. Momo, who was generous of heart, generous with her smiles, generous with her body, to which the customary chief of the Ngaka took a liking, just as he appropriated everything that was exceptional and well put together in his forest. When the era of direct government by the religious began in the Republic of the Great River, the marvelous Momo judged the old customary chief to be unworthy of her body and her great soul, so, one Sunday morning, she became angry. She left her two legitimate children to the old chief, took her two bastards (one of them was to become the man of the leopard totem) by the hand, went out of the forest, crossed the river, and walked straight, determined to reach the mission and the good fathers. She was never to arrive.

The first person who saw her arriving at the door of the mission stopped her, welcomed her, and married her at once, in a Christian manner, recognizing the bastards both religiously and civilly. The man who, in that fortunate act, had taken the inspiring Momo and had kept her for some ten years was the excellent cook of the good fathers, Bermani. Alberic Bermani he was called. The good fathers did not appreciate their cook's astuteness (abduction) and reproached him. Bermani left his employers with his little family and offered his services to the nearest neighbor of the mission, the colonial judge, Monsieur Delcourt. Madame Delcourt taught French to the little boy (the future dictator) who hung around the pantry every day. When the Delcourts went home, the priests, who still had not found a cook with talent equal to that of Bermani, rehired him and accepted his adopted son in the mission school.

One year during school vacation, the boy (future master of the country) returned to the riverbank to undergo the initiation rites. These rites prepare a boy for the tasks deemed necessary by the tribe.

The Ngandi, the future dictator's tribe and one branch of the Bangala people—pirogue pilots and fishermen—give priority to theft, lying, and courage. During his initiation, the boy stole two steers, kidnapped two girls, killed a leopard with his assegai, and, with a mere little stick sharpened on both ends in his bare hands, conquered and pulled from the water the fiercest killer crocodile in the river. All the Ngandi sorcerers predicted that the young initiate would be the greatest of their race. They gave him many talismans and fetishes and taught him secret verbal charms and many prayers for protection against evil spells.

As for Mama Momo, age finally made the beautiful Momo wiser. After the death of her husband, she wanted to keep her son in religious schools at all costs, and, to that end, she offered her services from one convent to another. Momo's greatest dream was to see her son, whose professors thought him intelligent, a voracious reader, and undisciplined, become a priest, a good father. He was never to reach the seminary.

Waiting for the Vote of the Wild Animals

One morning at dawn, at the foot of the wall that he often climbed to return to the boarding school after roaming the unsavory neighborhoods of the city, he found a noncommissioned officer and two men from the colonial public forces. They were waiting for him and enrolled him immediately. This was the ingenious way the good fathers had found to get rid of an undisciplined student: send him to the service. Explains Macledio.

But when one tries to throw the toad too far, one may accidently cast him into a swamp for his greater good fortune. The man of the leopard totem was born for the *Force publique,* and the *Force publique* was made for him. There, he learned accounting, typing, and especially journalism. He learned enough to pass a *certificat d'évolué* (certificate of civilization).

It is necessary to understand that the missions and the colonial administration thought they had succeeded well beyond their own expectations in their educational program. Without realizing, they had managed to educate five university students in fifty years. They were well ahead of the schedule they had foreseen. The education of intellectuals had not been foreseen before the year 2000! They were also ahead of schedule, too far ahead, in what was to be found in the cities of the Great River. The streets were full of Blacks who imitated to perfection the walk and the accent of the Whites, wearing jackets, ties, and even bow ties. They had seen and heard the natives of French colonies speaking. The natives of the opposite bank of the river had gotten their independence. The French had gotten rid of their possessions and had bungled matters by leaving them to Black demagogues. In the Republic of the Great River, it would be necessary to manage the new order of things. The good fathers and the colonial administration did this by creating the *certificat d'évolué,* the certificate of civilization (or becoming civilized!), for their natives. This certificate would allow them to distinguish the Europeanized natives of the Republic of the Great River (such as the man of the leopard totem) from their compatriots who were still in the savage state.

The examination was quite meticulous. They had to learn a number of things from White culture. Drinking from a glass without sucking the liquid through the nose. Eating with forks and not dropping crumbs from the corners of the mouth. Blowing their noses and spitting in a handkerchief. Aiming a good solid turd, perfectly formed, at the hole in the floor of the toilet. Kissing his wife with no obscene gestures before making love and making love to nobody else for the whole year. Proclaiming one's faith in the Bible, which relates the blessedness of the Whites (Shem and Japhet) and the curse on the Blacks (Ham and Canaan). And recognizing as a natural and irreversible law the predominance of the light (incarnate in the Whites) over the dark (the Blacks). Adds the *koroduwa.*

One does not teach the young crocodile about the water nor how to swim. The man of the leopard totem, who had learned French from the wife of a white judge, religion with the theologians of the seminary, law with officers in the *Force publique,* could not fail such an examination. He got twenty out of twenty on his certificate.

Because of his excellent grades on the examination for his *certificat d'évoluant* (for it was indeed a certificate of an "evolving" student he had passed, since the good fathers had not foreseen awarding a certificate for the "evolved" graduate before the year 2000—it was the boasting, pretentious natives of the Great River who called their lowly *certificat d'évoluant* a *certificat d'évolué*), because of the prodigious grades he received on the examination, *L'Avenir,* the most important daily in the country, hired the evolving evolved young man as a journalist. And they were able to send him for further study in the kingdom's capital (evolving or evolved natives had, among other rights, that of traveling to Europe).

In the kingdom's capital, the scholarship turned out to be derisory. He had to supplement his income by continuing his nocturnal visits to nightclubs. The man of the leopard totem supplemented his income by contacting the kingdom's secret service, which was looking for agents who could penetrate the circles of nationalist natives from the Great River. And when Pace Humba, the great nationalist of the Republic of the Great River, came to the kingdom's capital, the man of the leopard totem accompanied him day and night wherever he went in order to inform the colonizers of every word and deed of the talkative patriot. Pace Humba, who was generous and trusting, mistook this attachment for friendship and confided in the handsome young journalist. The Americans of the CIA made him an "honored correspondent" when they saw that he was an excellent mole for the colonizers and close to Humba. With the goodwill of Humba, the kingdom's secret service, and the CIA, everything worked marvelously for the man of the leopard totem.

When the *Force publique* was disbanded and the African gendarmes were hunting down its colonial officers, they had to manufacture a native chief of staff at once. The kingdom's secret service and the CIA guided the enlightened ideas of Pace Humba and his kindly hands, which awarded the rank of general to the man of the leopard totem—

he had only been a noncommissioned officer in the *Force publique*— and they appointed him the supreme chief of staff in the largest country of central Africa, the country with the richest mineral deposits.

After this promotion and appointment, it is no longer possible to distinguish falsehood from truth in the life of the dictator or the excrement of the red monkey from that of the black monkey. The man of the leopard totem is a Ngandi, and the cardinal virtues prized by the people of that tribe are lies, theft, and courage. With great courage, the man of the leopard totem was to show marvelous talent for stealing and killing.

That is the man with whom you, Koyaga, took your hour flight. In the airport, you received the welcome reserved by the dictator for heads of state.

"I picked you up outside of my country. I will take leave of you outside my country," said the dictator of the hyena totem.

"Thank you for the great honor, for the great generosity with which you have treated me. Thank you for the exceptional and enormous lessons you have taught me during my stay. But it would be too much for you to go to the trouble of forcing yourself to take an extra journey."

"I insist on accompanying you because that is part of my etiquette and my habits," the man of the hyena totem replied at once.

You continued begging him to spare himself, to remain and take care of his high duties, and not to abandon his people. You were to travel with the man of the leopard totem. You did not have to worry about traveling in solitude. What he had already done was more than enough.

The man of the hyena totem leaned over and spluttered a few words in your ear. You smiled and immediately asked the man of the leopard totem to allow your host to travel along.

What he had whispered was a state secret that was revealed only later. He had given you his real motivation. He had no appointments. He had only one duty on his calendar. But he did not have the tranquility demanded by that appointment. His Zende mistress had not been satisfied; she was angry and was waiting naked in the bed of the bachelor quarters of the Imperial Court. He did not have the strength to finish her off, to quench her thirst, to satisfy her. Explains the responder.

That was the sufficient reason for which there were three of you disembarking from the airplane, three chiefs of state in the capital of the Republic of the Great River. The men of the leopard totem, the hyena totem, and yourself, the hawk totem.

Thousands of girls draped in pagnes imprinted with the effigies of the three heads of state are dancing and singing. The dances are salacious, and the songs proclaim the glory of the heads of state.

"Oh shit! Shit! Each one is more beautiful than the others! I have never seen so many beauties gathered together."

Thus the man of the hyena totem howls in admiration as he leers at the girls. He leaves the other heads of state to review honor guard. He heads right for the dance circles. Acclamations, howls, hooting blend together. The tam-tam change rhythm. The emperor's anthem rings out. In front of him, as the girls approach, the half untied pagnes are lost in the dancing! Those buttocks are really lascivious and immodest! It is impossible to restrain oneself, to resist their provocation, their appeal! The man of the leopard totem barges into the dance circle: he jerks, swings, and twists. He is not just a cruel dictator, he knows how to dance. The latter talent is ample justification of the former. He is an artist, a talented person, a great and hefty choreographer. He waves his cane. His numerous, heavy decorations—all acquired during the colonial wars—are beating on his chest. His other attributes, all the other attributes of a great emperor, are billowing on his shoulders and buttocks. He goes around the dance circle twice—alone, quite alone. The third time he engages goatlike in the pursuit of a young dancer. She is certainly lascivious. Five little steps, then she stops and makes an obscene gesture, a gesture to bring on an erection. She is inviting the emperor. The man of the hyena totem imitates her. On a live broadcast before all the world's television stations, he demonstrates. He makes a show of his talent. He has it to spare.

His shame, his shame—the man of the leopard totem is mastering it poorly. The emperor continues wiggling. Your host takes you by the arm, Koyaga, and you go to the hall of honor. You are face to face with him—and something must have been bothering him—he begins to justify himself, to confess. You must not believe what the imperialists (that is what he calls the international press) published about him, his people, and his country. There were economic difficulties, they really existed. But the imperialists knew they were temporary, and he was worried about that. With the dancing and the songs, the imperialists knew that the citizens would soon have the knowledge and awareness to develop the country. The whole Republic of the Great River would become rich. The country's citizens had failed in management and industrialization, but not in dancing, singing, and show business. They would transform and develop the country through show business. Through show business they would reach their objectives. That would happen more quickly than the pessimists believed. The music of the Republic of the Great River was already one of the most important rhythms in the contemporary world. The singers of his country were already the most popular in the world. From this conversation, Koyaga was to remember that in the struggle against underdevelopment and famine, song and dance, singing and dancing the greater glory of the head of state, are also instruments for development.

The emperor had stopped wiggling for lack of breath. There were great drops of sweat on his forehead. He took the girl by the hand and dragged her to the hall of honor. Before the other two chiefs, the girl bowed and did some suggestive movements to cries of delight from the crowd. The emperor introduced the girl and explained. She was the most beautiful and talented of the performers, and he bent over to whisper in your ear, "and certainly the most licentious." That was why he had two requests to make of his brother and friend, the man of the leopard totem. First, he asked for the hand of the dancer, and second, he asked to take leave.

At the airport, the airplane bearing the emperor's coat of arms took off and disappeared into the clouds. Whew! To general relief! Everyone took a breath, and the man of the leopard totem was about to start besmirching the emperor when the airplane reappeared out of the clouds and requested permission to land. The emperor came out and reassured everybody: he had not returned because of technical trouble. It was not until they were in the clouds that he remembered he had left behind the young dancer his brother and friend had given him in marriage.

In a festival, the dancer and the tam-tam drummer are not alone— there is also the singer. The dancer stops from time to time to listen to the singer. Let us listen also to the following reflections on power:

The drum that fails to punish the crime is a cracked jug.
One king sits on his throne while another is having his carved.
There is no bad king, only bad courtiers.

17

Ah, Tiekura! The man of the leopard totem had been living on his boat for some time. As soon as the helicopter deposited you on the deck of the M.S. *Balola,* the man of the leopard totem began spitting out all his scorn for the dictator of the hyena totem. The bile in his heart was eating away at him.

"Emperor! Emperor! The real shame of all Africa! A ruffian! His foolishness undermines the honor of an African head of state. A bastard who claims to be the highest-ranking head of state because he proclaimed himself emperor! He is a simpleton!"

And he explained: the empire was a European creation. The emperor had far fewer prerogatives than an African chief of authenticity. It was the manes of the ancestors that had named him, the leopard-man, the chief of authenticity, the father-of-the-nation. The emperor's decisions had to be confirmed by the voters; not those of an African chief. The African chief consults the advisors he has named but is not forced to follow their advice. The expenses of an emperor are limited by a budget; a true and authentic African chief has at his control all the money in his treasury and the central bank, and nobody counts or controls what he spends. An emperor is hemmed in by laws; a true African chief exercises clemency, and that is all. A true African chief is clearly superior to an emperor, concluded the man of the leopard totem, and he advised you to put such a government, a government of authenticity, into operation. That was the form of government that suited Africans.

With authenticity, there is a perpetual feast wherever the true chief is. The presidential yacht was a veritable beehive, the branches of a silk cotton tree inhabited by a colony of gendarmes. The rotations of helicopters were always in the sky above. There was rhythmic chanting of hostesses on the bridge night and day. They kept howling the same dithyrambs about the leopard-man to encourage him in his deeds. They performed belly dances and twirled their behinds. There were perpetual erotic movements to excite him. A true and authentic African chief has at all times the courage of a lion and the sexual prowess of a bull.

The leopard-man summoned his four closest helpers and presented them to you one after the other.

The advisor with whom the dictator began the presentations held, in the hierarchy, the rank of fourth counselor and was called Sakombi, citizen Sakombi Inongo. He was the minister of propaganda and national orientation. Sakombi had been childhood friends with the man of the leopard totem. Like the dictator, he had passed his diploma as an *évoluant*. He thoroughly knew and was acquainted with the dictator. He had understood that the leopard-man had been propelled from too humble a level to be so high. The dictator was always in a daze.

He had a permanent need for people to howl where he was in order for him to see himself, believe himself, and believe others.

During his trips to China and North Korea, Mao Tse-tung and Kim Il Sung had planned extraordinary welcomes for the man of the leopard totem. Minister Sakombi Inongo had been very attentive and had carefully observed and reflected on the events. Back home, Sakombi knew that he was fated to disappear and be replaced by a young university graduate for the sole reason that he, Sakombi, was a simpleminded person.

Very early one morning, before the official confirmation of the ministerial reorganization, Sakombi went to the dictator and announced that he had lived the destiny of his country during the night and received messages. The manes of the ancestors had come during the night to take him, half asleep and half dreaming, to the foot of a hundred-year-old silk cotton tree in a cemetery on the bank of the river. He cited witnesses: his wife, who had heard the wind whistling through the window and noticed the disappearance of her husband from their bed during the remainder of the night, and their guard, who at midnight had seen a specter go out by the gate and come back before dawn through the leaves of the filao tree in the garden. In the cemetery, an assembly of manes had charged him to deliver a message for the nation. The manes had asked him to say that the man of the leopard totem had been sent to save the people of the Republic of the Great River. They had designated the leopard totem as chief, only chief, and sole intermediary between the living and the manes. They had revealed his names: *fouilli tè kèrèmassa mi lalo* (the great warrior who triumphs over all obstacles). They had revealed his powers: the sole chief who gives orders and must be obeyed; the chief who, through his orders, brings the vital juices that vivify the republic. It is because the orders emanating from the chief had not been scrupulously respected in the past that such a weakening of the vital force of the collective whole had been noted. The inhabitants of the country had become impotent peoples, thieves, liars, and slothful, unconscious individuals. That was the source of the country's ills. The manes charged the chief with leading his people on the path that the ancients had traced, the way of authenticity.

Sakombi had come dressed in a white Mao suit (he had put away his own suit and tie): this was the garment recommended by the manes. He had renounced his Christian name (he would henceforth be known only as Inongo). The man of the leopard totem was never to go out without his accoutrements as chief: the leopard skin and the ivory cane with its solid gold knob. He announced the various names by which the inhabitants of the Republic of the Great River were authorized to call their chief: the Sun-President, the Genius of the Great River, the Strategist, the Father of the Nation, the Unifier, the Pacifier . . .

The reorganization took place. Minister Sakombi was allowed to keep his post in order to continue tending to the instructions of the ancestral manes.

The minister could dispose of part of the presidential yacht to house the performers, journalists, and propaganda personnel.

"Good morning, Mister Counselor. Good morning, Mister Minister Sakombi."

"My respects, Your Excellency Koyaga. We are very happy to welcome you and wish you a pleasant stay among us in the Republic of the Great River."

The second personage presented to you by the man of the leopard totem was the Senegalese architect Tapa Gaby. The architect was third in the ranked order of advisors.

Through their long association with Whites, the Senegalese had, as seen by the man of the leopard totem, lost some of the congenital defects of Blacks. So it was with a certain respect that the architect Gaby had been introduced for the first time to the president's office. The architect was a Senegalese and a Senegalese who had in his hand a letter of recommendation from the president of Senegal. The president of Senegal had been obliged to intervene so that his compatriot might have direct access to the man of the leopard totem. To have access in order to present directly to the dictator a project for the construction of the radio and television building. In spite of the number of beards that had been copiously watered in the dictator's entourage, the architect had never succeeded in obtaining any business in the country. His rivals had always been more generous in their manner of "speaking French," in their "national gesture." Explains the responder.

During the first meeting, the architect's project does not arouse any enthusiasm in the man of the leopard totem. The architect believes in marabouts, in fetishists, and knows that the dictator frequents them and follows them even more than he. Before leaving empty-handed, his plans under his arms, Gaby stops, mutters something, and invents a lie. A marabout had met him the evening before his trip and had entrusted him with a message. It is an important prediction. A plot is being woven against the man of the leopard totem. The conspirators have bound him, enchanted him, and may well succeed. The marabout recommends that, before Friday, he sacrifice to the manes of the ancestors two bulls by darkest night on a new grave in a cemetery and a black chicken at the bottom of a well. The dictator's rule is always to make all sacrifices he is counseled to make. Out of habit, he sacrifices the two steers and the black chicken, then forgets about it.

But it happens that, five days after the meeting and on a Friday, in fact, the dictator barely escapes an attempt on his life. An attempt carried out under the conditions described by the marabout.

An airplane takes off that evening from the capital and comes back the same night with the architect Gaby and the marabout Kaba on board. Rewarded with money, Kaba is hired immediately as the chief of the dictator's marabouts. And Gaby becomes the official supplier of marabouts, sorcerers, and other experts in occult matters to the chief of state. And incidentally, his project is accepted.

From that event came a profound friendship and a trusting collaboration between the dictator of the Republic of the Great River and the astute Senegalese. The architect excels in his duties, so well so that the man of the leopard totem recommends him to other dictators on the continent. He also acquires the title of supplier of expert marabouts to potentates and chiefs of single parties in Cameroon, Gabon, the Land of the Two Rivers, and other great men of our multiple and liberticidal Africa. And in all those countries, incidentally, he always has orders. Overloaded and fatigued by technical studies, solicitations, and the exhaustive search for competent marabouts, the architect no longer puts in frequent appearances at the court where the man of the leopard totem rules.

One day, the dictator needs him: he summons him and expects him within forty-eight hours. An airplane takes off to bring him back.

"How much do you estimate that you earn from the services you perform for other chiefs of state? What is your total income?"

"I cannot say offhand, Mr. President."

"No matter. From now on, you are in my service. In my service alone. You are hired as a counselor. Your salary is double the amount that you declare to the secretary of my cabinet," announces the dictator in a reproachful tone.

He is the advisor in charge of occult affairs for the president. A counselor who has at his disposal a dozen cabins on the yacht and multiple responsibilities. As a talented architect, the Senegalese is successful in the performances he stages. From time to time, he brings by helicopter to the yacht some marabouts floating in their embroidered, starched boubous. He organizes seances with comforting incantations.

The marabouts surround the dictator and slip rings and bracelets on his fingers and wrists.

The dictator never travels without a suitcase full of fetishes. Each marabout adds to his collection of lucky charms.

Before each of the dictator's trips, the sacred tortoise is consulted. The architect seats the president on the shell. The tortoise moves: the trip begins immediately. Otherwise, the marabouts practice other incantations.

"Good morning, Mr. Counselor of Occult Affairs. Good morning, Mr. Gaby."

"My respects, Your Excellency Koyaga. We are very happy to welcome you and wish you a pleasant stay among us in the Republic of the Great River."

A large part of the yacht is reserved for finance and the treasury. This was the fief of the financial advisor, the mulatto Konga. A mulatto, a half-caste, a hybrid. Konga is a métis. For the colonizers, a métis is an improved Bantu but an imperfect White. A Black who is half-liar, half-idiot, but a White who is half-thieving and half-intelligent. For a Black, a métis is at once a compatriot, a stranger, and a traitor. That is a universal natural law. In the South Africa of apartheid and in numerous other countries where many métis have been born, the duties and role as intermediary or bridge have been recognized by law and stipulated in the constitution. In the Republic of the Great River, before independence, the white colonialists who feared the bitter effluvia of the Bantu were able, through the intermediary of the métis, to limit occasions for contact between Whites and natives. The great colonial enterprises always had métis as cashiers. That was something that the young native and future dictator had noticed immediately when he came from the bush. He appreciated that fact while he was living in his status as an évoluant. Konga, the mulatto cashier of an important company, helped the noncommissioned officer and future dictator to make ends meet at the end of difficult months. Those are matters that cannot be forgotten and that are rewarded when one becomes absolute master of a country eighty times larger than the colonizing state.

The dictator entrusted the management of all his financial institutions to the métis. Konga was his financial advisor on the yacht. Four cabins were filled to the ceiling with banknotes. The value of currency in the Republic of the Great River was less than that of the paper on which it was printed. That had a worthwhile advantage. One did not need a safe to keep that money. It no longer tempted thieves. The quantity of bills that could be purloined would always have less value than the means necessary to carry them away.

"Good morning, Mr. Minister Konga."

"My respects, Your Excellency Koyaga. We are very happy to welcome you and wish you a very, very happy stay among us in the Republic of the Great River."

The fourth gray eminence attending the man of the leopard totem had responsibility even greater than that of the métis. That is why he was a White, a white American and a former CIA agent, the honorable Robert Maheu. He had to his credit as an FBI spy during the Second World War a number of affairs, numerous murders. Murders that, forty years later, had not been solved and still could not be. He was a very experienced killer.

"But why would an African, chief of a poor state and in the Third World like yours, wear himself out participating in the planetary combat of the West?"

The man of the leopard totem looked at you with a frightened glance.

"Quiet! Don't repeat such stupidities, especially in front of Mr. Maheu. Democrats only help and protect anticommunists. Even if the struggle between communists and westerners is only a brotherly quarrel among Whites, among the rich, it is necessary to participate in it. We Africans participate in order to profit from it!"

Maheu had set up the most sophisticated system in the world for protecting the man of the leopard totem.

"Anybody who wants my skin will pay dearly," the man of the leopard totem told you by way of conclusion.

That was surely true.

"Good morning, Mr. Counselor Maheu."

"My respects, Your Excellency Koyaga. We are very, very, and very happy to welcome you and to wish you a very, very, and very happy stay among us in the Republic of the Great River."

Five airplanes took you to Labodite, the native city of the man with the leopard totem. The security airplane of Counselor Maheu with his killers, his men, and their equipment. The airplane for propaganda and dithyrambs of Minister Sakombi, with the performers and presidential mistresses. Following them came the command airplane, the presidential craft in which you traveled with your host. It preceded the plane moving the banknotes and the other carting the marabouts. Just two hours following the welcome at the airport, everything was set up and everyone was at his post. The Pygmies in the trees in the surrounding area, the frogmen in the water, the marabouts at their sacrifices, and the supermoneyman of the country at the financial branch in the villa filled to the ceiling with banknotes.

At the airport, the persistent rotors of the helicopters began, the landing and takeoffs of airplanes loaded with banknotes, visitors, and prebendaries.

Labodite is a whim of the dictator. A tragic and sinister farce.

The dictator of the leopard totem is a big sentimental fool, a sentimental fellow who is kindly with certain polite gestures. He loves women and he loves his first wife, Annette, very much; he said so and he showed it. In official ceremonies—and he was the only dictator in our multiple Africa to allow such precedence to his wife—he followed Annette.

Like many dictators of our eternal Africa, he suffered because he had been born, come from the womb, of an illiterate Negress. He never said as much. He was content to deny it through images. Images that flashed on the country's television screens eight times each day. In these images, the dictator did not flow from his mother Momo: he descended directly from heaven; he broke through the milky clouds against a blue background. Annette was not forgotten in the images. No, she was not forgotten! She did not come from the empty empyrean, but, like Christ, she atoned largely by distributing on earth much good and many fine things to children and miracles for the unfortunate.

The dictator is violent; he was born with a violent nature. At times he manages to hide his temperament behind a burlesque act. But on moonlit nights, his behavior takes over and he becomes as fierce as a wild beast, as fierce as his totem. One of those nights, he penetrated Annette furiously and violently. For no reason, just a hint of marital disagreement. He strikes her with his fists and his cane. He fractures her arm. She cries out.

"I'm expecting a baby."

"That's just it, I'm going to get rid of it," answers her husband.

He knocks the fetus out with a blow from his shoe. When he sees her unconscious, half dead, lying in a pool of blood, he stops hitting her and begins to howl.

"I'm an idiot, a real idiot. A bastard, a criminal, truly! What to do now? What can I do?"

He sits down and holds his head; he is crying, crying hot tears. He bends over her. He takes her in his arms, as it happens, and sees himself in the American soap operas; he takes her to an airplane. The airplane evacuates her to the most expensive clinic in the world. There, in Switzerland, the most skillful surgeons operate on her. Without success. She never rises again. She dies and leaves the man of the leopard totem inconsolable.

He brings the body back to the Republic of the Great River and organizes a great funeral ceremony for Annette—a funeral that will become the great event of the year in his country and in the former colonial kingdom. He decides to have her inhumed in the forest, far from all civilization. He orders the Senegalese architect Gaby (his supplier of marabouts) to design a crypt. Around the crypt a basilica is built. Around the basilica, a palace. Surrounding the palace, the villas of the dignitaries of his kingdom. Then roads, movie houses, banks, schools, supermarkets, an airport, a dam, ranches, plantations. Everything needed for a city. A city, a capital with buildings five stories high. All this was conceived by the fetishist architect. That is Labodite. Labodite will become the official capital of the country when Pope John Paul XII has the time to come to Labodite to beatify Annette and bless the basilica.

Before the pope's visit, Labodite is a phantom city. A city that does not exist, that is not seen when the dictator of the leopard totem is not in residence. In his absence, everything, except the crypt, which is guarded by a Spanish penitent dressed in red, is closed in the city of Labodite. Absolutely everything. The schools, hospitals, movie houses, dam, airport, supermarkets are not open, do not exist.

When the dictator appears, everything takes off again, begins anew, starts working. The superhighways, which start nowhere and go nowhere, are busy once more. The airport opens its runway and its doors. The German nuns come back with their patients—their lepers in the hospitals. French teachers and their pupils come to the schools. The children's choir with Gregorian chants on its lips is back in the pews of the basilica. All the dignitaries, ministers, former ministers, generals, ambassadors, and traditional chiefs peek out, appear—they all return to occupy their space, their villas in Labodite. Their place and rank in the decor.

Obviously, all visits to Labodite begin with the crypt of the dictator's Annette. That is as it should be. That is the only permanent institution in the city. It is customary for the dictator to introduce the members of his family and of his clan to visitors as they leave the tomb.

They were all there, lined up. They were all making an effort to mourn the regretted Annette. All the happy beneficiaries of the confiscation, the nationalization of prosperous foreign companies.

You, Koyaga, you saluted them.

"Good day. . . . Good day. . . . Good day, rich people. Good day, monopolists."

Ah, Tiekura. It was in the gold and diamond mines of the Republic of the Great River. The gold and diamond mines of the north, south, east, and west in the vast Republic of the Great River. Handicapped people transported able people in their little carriages. Blind people guided the sighted, sifted the mud, scrutinized the brown water, set up compartments to stop the stones. The lepers with the stumps of their arms dug and pierced the ground for the able people with hands and arms. . . . These were the miracles worked by the man of the leopard totem in his vast Republic of the Great River.

Ah, Tiekura! Let us begin at the beginning.

One morning, the man of the leopard totem thinks and counts. He has exercised power for twenty years, and the ledger sheet is negative, completely negative.

The country has no roads, hospitals, telephones, airplanes, or . . . or . . . Doctors do not practice for lack of medicine and because they have not received salaries for months. The young people no longer dance or make love because the entire country is infected with AIDS.

The man of the leopard totem can hold his head up, look beyond in the distance to no avail—he cannot see the least glimmer of hope.

The members of his family and his closest collaborators are all a bunch of slothful, pleasure-loving individuals. They have been unable to engineer development, the resurgence of the country, the nation of the Great River.

The soldiers and police are all ransomers and pilferers. They have been unable to ensure order or the security of the country.

Those who run the party, the chiefs and high officials, are all prevaricators and corrupt individuals. They have not managed to mobilize and administer the country.

There is only one way left for development, one last thing to try: the people. The man of the leopard totem decides to leave the development of the country to the people, to the informal sector—he will let the people manage themselves. In a sovereign manner and quite consciously, he decides on the total liberalization of mining development in the country with the richest mineral deposits in the world. Each citizen can dig wherever he or she wants with all available means.

This is folly. Everywhere across the vast Republic of the Great River, everywhere in the precious stone mines, the workers are the first to desert the enterprises that house and care for them. They begin digging, working for themselves, trying their luck. Miraculously, a few brilliant specks and even a few pebbles appear at the bottom of their sieves.

Nothing spreads faster than the echo of happiness. The rumor runs from north to south, from west to east in the vast Republic of the Great River. Chance, hope (people no longer believed in it) still exist, still exist somewhere in the Republic of the Great River, the vast country of three time zones. By tens of thousands, teachers and officials abandon their classrooms and offices to become "rock breakers."

The potentate takes advantage of the occasion to conform to the recommendations of the IMF and proceeds to a massive firing of publication workers. Entire classes of schoolchildren follow their teachers to the field. Patients, lepers, and those ill with the sleeping sickness follow their nurses and doctors to the mines. Coffee and cotton growers and fishermen by the entire village desert their plantations or pirogues to become "rock breakers." By the class, the village, the hospital, the whole family, everybody attacks the hills like ants. Lepers with stumps and the blind are sifting.

Some meters away from the diggers, women assemble stones, build shelters, cook beans and cassava porridge. For some gold powder, the diggers can have a repast. Further off, the *nganda* (canteens), called "maquis" elsewhere, and the *supernganda* (supermaquis) are set up, and they blare out their thunderous music. In exchange for diamonds, the diggers can have a drink. Cattlemen bring entire herds toward the mining cities and they are butchered within a few hours.

All the adventure seekers on the face of the Earth rush toward the mining cities of the Republic of the Great River. Marabouts, seers, sorcerers. Prostitutes from Europe and Kenya; West African merchants with their bric-a-brac. The Lebanese, who are usually Chiites, set up exchange offices in competition with people from the republic. The Lebanese are the most prosperous. In fact, these are simply establishments for laundering all the dirty money in the world—drug money, arms-trafficking money. These establishments need protection, security guards. All the strongmen, muscle men, and marksmen of the country come to the mining cities.

The flood of trucks transporting passengers to the mining cities turns upside-down the lives of the villages and communities they traverse. The people who, for some recompense, wash cars during the rainy season must get out their hoes and their picks night and day. The excess work does not bring the excess rewards expected (the adventurers headed for the mining cities are stingy). The good villagers let the trucks get stuck and even worse, for enraged or vengeful acts create deeper ditches by the roads. Highways are cut off and totally useless. There is no more transportation to take people to the gold and diamond mines in the Republic of the Great River.

In times of crisis, strikes, disorder, penury, or short supply of fuel, there are always three corporations in the capital of the Republic of the Great River that supplement the usual modes of transport for people and merchandise. There are the noisy associations of ricksha men, the associations of the handicapped who manage to transport merchandise with their little carts, and groups of women with a strap around their forehead that holds a basket taller than the bearer.

The echo of the total absence of transportation to the mining cities resounds in the capital, and the three associations for difficult times (the ricksha men, the handicapped, and the women with baskets) come running to take care of transporting people and merchandise over the roads to the mining villages, where the entire Republic of the Great River has a rendezvous.

Soldiers and policemen, who have not received their salaries for many moons, take leave and set off in civilian clothes for the mining villages. They arrive in units and want to get their part of the booty. They attack the diggers, who defend their fortunes energetically. Shots are fired, battles are squared away, and there are fatalities. The government intervenes to maintain order. Uniformed soldiers and policemen on active duty disembark from helicopters, intervene, and ask the diggers to pay the badge-wearers, the single party, and the effigy of the man with the leopard totem.

This is the new world that your host, the man of the leopard totem, wanted to show you before bidding you farewell, Koyaga. He believed in it, in this new Country of the Great River, the Great River of the informal sector. He called his new policies liberalism.

Yes! The handicapped carried and transported able people in their carts. The blind led the sighted, sifted the mud, scrutinized the brown water, constructed boxes to stop rocks. The lepers with stumps dug and pierced the land for the healthy people with hands and fingers.

This was in the gold and diamond mines of the Republic of the Great River. The gold and diamond mines of the north, south, east, and west of the vast Republic of the Great River.

The master of the Republic of the Great River is one of the richest men in the universe.

Sometimes the tam-tam drummer stops to request a calabash of water. Let us follow his example. A glass of water is served to the *sèrè*, who quenches his thirst and plays while the *koroduwa* dances. The *sèrè* recites three proverbs on power:

One does not catch the hippopotamus with a hook.
If you see a goat in the lion's den, be afraid.
If the rat puts on a pair of shorts, the cats will take them off.

18

Ah, Koyaga. You ended your initiatory journey with a Muslim country in North Africa, the country of the potentate of the desert, the man of the jackal totem. That is the Land of Jebels and Sand. This autocrat had the duty during the cold war of quelling all rebellions that took place in Africa through the use of paratroops that he dispatched in Transalls (troop transport airplanes) generously placed at his disposition by the great Republic of the Northern Mediterranean. The potentate had been chosen, for the entire cold war, as the coordinator of the anticommunist struggle in Africa, as an emblematic representative of liberalism against envelopment by the Red dictatorship in Africa. This was for two reasons. First, he was a white Muslim and not an unpredictable and surly black fetishist. Then, he appeared to be a modern head of state belonging to a dynasty that had been in power for centuries in a kingdom several centuries old. He was not one of those noncommissioned officers who, after assassinating an innocent and kindly head of state somewhat tolerant of communism, promoted himself general and chief of state. With this choice, the West believed its combat in Africa would gain in honorability because its cold war would be conducted by a respectable regime ensconced on a centuries-old base.

This was not true. The dictator of the jackal totem was as medieval, barbarian, cruel, lying, and criminal as all the other African fathers-of-the-nation during the cold war.

He knew he was perpetually threatened and reprieved; he was always uneasy, anxious, tormented. He had the wariness of a monkey who has lost a piece of his tail to a dog and the viciousness of the jaws of a beast with one foot caught in the teeth of a wolf trap. This potentate was governing a people of warriors who, heroically and repeatedly for centuries, had been trying to assassinate their leader and striving to achieve their freedom.

Until the end of the nineteenth century and the division of Africa at the Berlin Conference, the people of the Jebels and Sand had prevented a hegemonic power from being established and had managed to limit the power of their chief to the spiritual realm, strictly to the spiritual.

The westerners from the northern Mediterranean disembarked on the coasts of the Jebels and Sand; they invaded and conquered the plains without passion or firing a shot. It was only when they tried to continue their triumphal march through the mountains that the westerners discovered what the Berber mountaineers were.

The warriors of the Jebels and Sand came to meet them. They fell on the Spaniards, conquered them, and took away their arms. They turned the arms of the Spaniards against the other westerners and put them to flight. With their chief, they set up a modern and independent republic. For the entire Occident, this was a humiliation, and for France, with the aureole of its 1918 victory, it was a challenge that they could not fail to take up and severely punish. It was inadmissible to allow a modern Arab republic to exist freely at the doorstep of the Occident. "It must be crushed," the French general in charge of occupying the Land of Jebels had said.

France recalled its most prestigious marshal from retirement and put under his command sixty generals, seven hundred thousand men from continental France and from all the colonies of the empire: Senegalese riflemen, Moroccans, Algerians, Vietnamese. It was an army equipped with all modern arms (artillery, tanks, machine guns) and supported by forty-four squadrons of airplanes. The Spanish, not to be left behind, complemented the French forces with a force of one hundred thousand men. One hundred thousand Spaniards commanded by General Franco, the most talented Iberian general.

In all, there were eight hundred thousand westerners, heavily equipped, who were ordered to subjugate the twenty-five thousand warriors of the Jebels and Sand, armed with their rifles.

Before engaging in final combat, the French marshal, the generalissimo of the occupation forces, paid a visit to the king reigning over the Land of Jebels and Sand and informed him of the means he had at his disposal to undo the nationalist chief. The sultan wished him great success in the war and said to him, "Get rid of that rebel (quickly)."

And the westerners launched into combat with the certainty of crushing the warriors of the Jebels and Sand in a few weeks. The war against the rebel chief and the warriors of the Jebels lasted for a year. The combatants of the Land of Jebels and Sand heroically resisted for twelve moons. And the capture of their prestigious chief did not put an end to the fighting: the war of conquest of the Jebels and Sand was only ended at the price of a long war of five years that cost the French army more than thirty-seven thousand dead, much more than the war of independence in Algeria.

The conquest of the South continued for ten years after the arrest of the nationalist chief of the Jebels and was led by General Mangin, the famous butcher of 1914–1918, who took recourse to massive reprisals, taking women and children hostage, and to abominable war tactics such as the sugarloaves filled with explosives and distributed in rebel zones.

When, in 1934, the resident general of the Jebels went up to the palace to proclaim the complete pacification of the country, the young sultan reigning at that time welcomed him warmly and expressed "his gratitude for the excellent pacificatory action."

He had reason to congratulate the general. This was the first time in thirteen centuries that the political regime in the palace was accepted by all regions of the Jebels. But he rejoiced too early, congratulated the French too soon. France imposed a protectorate on him, and the representative of France, called the resident, held the real political power of the entire kingdom. The palace was reduced to exercising religious power, reduced to the status of a symbol, a jewel.

The French were not content with simple political power. They took over all the good land and expelled the peasants, who became itinerants, agricultural workers, or laborers who crowded into horrendous slums in the ports and cities.

For the first time in thirteen centuries, the lands of the Jebels existed under foreign occupation. For the first time in thirteen centuries, the people of the Jebels and their sovereign had something in common—they had the same interest, the same enemy, the same goal. They had to drive the arrogant, racist, and exploiting colonialist out of their country. The combat the people of the Land of Jebels traditionally waged against their sovereign was turned against the French invader. Opposition and anticolonial unrest began in the cities and ports of the plains. To slow them down, the colonialists divided the country into two different entities through a *dahir,* a Berber *dahir:* the Arabs and the Berbers, the plains and the mountains. All the country's inhabitants, who were behind their sovereign, saw in this decree a challenge to their unity, the amputation of their nation. They all vigorously launched into an anticolonial struggle, and the combat spread throughout the country and intensified. At first the French replied with brutal repressive measures: torture, lynching, deportations. To no avail: without daunting the determination of the inhabitants of the Jebels.

So the French decided to depose the reigning king and to exile him on one of the islands of the Indian Ocean. That was a mistake, a great error. The inhabitants of the Jebels, by a phenomenon of collective hallucination, saw their king exiled in heaven on moonlit nights and in a cemetery on dark nights. They heard him in the wind and the muezzin's calls to prayer. Everywhere and at all times, the spirit of their king called on them to fight the colonialist and the unbelievers, to engage in a jihad. In the Qur'an, Allah stated that those who die in the jihad are saved.

The peasants who had been expropriated in the plains and mountains of the Jebels and the workers, overexploited in the cities, rose up. In a massive movement, they joined the religious and the nationalists in attacking the colonist and recovering freedom. The entire country took part in the resistance against the protectorate.

It was at a time when the French, already conquered and chased out of Indochina, were hanging onto another country in North Africa. They had not completely forgotten the war of the Jebels after the war of 1914–1918. They recalled the legendary bravery of the Jebel warriors. They could not have the luxury of maintaining another front in North Africa. They had no choice. They sent for the exiled king so that the inhabitants would cease looking for his effigy in the sky and hearing his voice in the cemeteries during the dark nights. The French dropped the Land of Jebels, restored its independence with the same urgency of the animal spitting out a burning ball it has carelessly snatched.

So here are the king and his people, after a half century of colonization, still facing off, beginning ever again the combat that has set them in opposition for centuries.

The perpetual struggle between a rebellious people and their king has been reengaged. The reigning king is the man of the jackal totem. The sovereign of the jackal totem was striving to extend his despotic power through repression, corruption, and ruse. The subjects of the Jebels were trying to regain the freedom they had enjoyed from the chief of believers before the European conquest. They were demanding something more. They were demanding, like all other peoples of the Maghreb, a democratic state.

The blackest, the worst of insults an Arab can hurl at another Arab is to treat him as a Black, to call him the Black. The subjects of the Jebels who do not like their king, the sovereign of the jackal totem, call him the Black. He was born of a Black woman given to his father by a pasha from the South.

Knowing he was detested, the king had the intelligence to make use of the Jebel Arabs' resentment toward him as a stratagem. He twice turned it back against the inhabitants of the Jebels with success. Twice, the stratagem allowed him to get out of a desperate situation.

The first time, in a resort city on the Mediterranean coast, army cadets of the Jebels, shocked by the luxury and waste with which the sovereign was living, massacre his guests, arrest the king, and hold him prisoner. The radio announces: "The king is dead, long live the republic!" Against a background of military marches, a recorded communiqué is broadcast:

"The army has just taken power. The monarchical system has been swept away. The people's army has taken power. The people and its army are in power. A new era has just dawned."

The inhabitants of the Jebels begin dancing and feasting the ouster of their king. The feast is so beautiful, the joy is so great and so contagious, that the mutineers neglect to finish their work. They forget the king sequestered in an office. The sovereign of the jackal totem, as in a bad cowboy film, manages to charm the jailers, to escape, and to reassume power.

The repression was terrible. The king declared that Allah had "placed him on the throne to safeguard the monarchy" and reminded them that "to accomplish this task, the Malakite rite, which is my own, specifies that one must not hesitate when necessary to doom the third of the population swayed by nefarious ideas in order to preserve the healthy two-thirds of the population." He had all the conspirators shot and, without trial, had their wives, children, brothers, and sisters confined in secret in a fort for the rest of their lives.

A second time, still in the seventies, the Boeing 727 in which the king is returning to the Land of Jebels is attacked by six F-5 fighters. The Boeing flaps its wings, considerably damaged. The cabin, pierced by bullets, is filled with thick smoke. The F-5s leave to refuel and come back for the coup de grâce. The crafty king has a mechanic announce,

"The king has been killed and my copilot too. I am trying to keep the airplane going. Think of my wife and children. Spare my life."

Instead of firing the fatal bursts, the fighters go crazy and begin festive acrobatics in the clear sky over the Jebels: nosedives, flips, sideslips, the falling leaf, the reverse falling leaf, hedgehopping. On the ground, the radio broadcasts military marches and the celebrations are organized.

The royal Boeing, seriously damaged, lands without any problem. Surprise! The attacking pilots see the man of the jackal totem exit the airplane. They stop the celebration, bombard the airport and the palace. Too late! The king has been able to get away, to hide, and to reassume power.

The repression was inhuman. Once more, the king repeated that Allah had "placed him on the throne to safeguard the monarchy and that "to accomplish this task, one must not hesitate when necessary to doom a third of the population." He had all the conspirators shot and, without trial, had their wives, children, brothers, and sisters confined in secret in a fort for the rest of their lives. . . .

After that event, the monarch understood that wile, the use of the people's resentment toward him, and playing dead could not be used in case of a third plot. He had to invent another stratagem. He remembered the proverb that advises throwing a large bone to the vicious dog (the people of the Jebels is surely a vicious dog) in order to prevent him from biting you.

One Friday, after the juma, the monarch grabbed a green flag, raised it, and began haranguing his people of believers as he pointed to the South.

"You are deaf, blind, and cowardly. You do not see that we are still colonized, that a large part of our country, the most important part of our nation, is occupied by Christians, infidels, and arrogant racist colonialists. You do not hear their insults or the cries of our compatriots who are slaughtered by them. Follow me—I am going to open your eyes, ears, heart, and spirit."

All the people of the Land of Jebels took green books and flags and, as one man, like a herd, followed their king into the desert.

He was the chief of believers, and he continued to harangue them with religious fervor. He was the king and incarnated the nation; he continued to harangue the subjects of the Jebels with chauvinistic exaltation:

"You are wrong when you simply try to assassinate me to gain your freedom. You are mistaken when you reproach me for your poverty.

You are wrong when you detest me as if I were not an Arab, a Muslim, a believer."

At his country's border, the king addressed the Spaniards and the inhabitants of the Sahara:

"I arrive before your gates with all my people. We have in hand only the green flag and the Qur'an. We are men of peace who hate war. Let us enter upon your deserts, let us occupy your country. Join us. Accept to be among our subjects. We shall treat you as Muslims, believers, as our own children."

The people of the Sahara, despite these supplications, refused to open the border gates, refused to join the subjects of His Majesty. Disappointed, the king anathematized them:

"Inhabitants of the Sahara, you have rejected our entreaties, our fraternity, our peaceful act, when you are our compatriots and followers of the same religion. We shall bring you to resipiscence, contrition, and compunction through arms and war. We shall combat you as we kill infidels."

The king turned toward his people in a movement of magnanimity and spoke:

"The entire world has seen your peaceful act, heard your supplications and your prayers. The entire world will be witness before Allah. Now, let us make war against them, a war without mercy, total war."

And all the Land of Jebels engaged in a great war with modern arms, a deadly war, an economically disastrous war, an impoverishing war. All the Land of Jebels, in one movement, began to commune with their king as in the time of the colonization.

Only the monarch can stop the killing. And he will never throw away this war because he knows that the day he stops it, the subjects of the Jebels will begin once more to hate him, will try to assassinate him again.

That is the monarch chosen by the West to lead the cold war against the African states. He fulfilled his task conscientiously and intelligently. Each time a nation in Africa rebelled against its oppressor, the king sent a detachment of his combat forces against the resistance fighters in the Sahara and sent it to check the revolution.

The sovereign of the jackal totem received you, Koyaga, and gave you the reasons for which the West had preferred you to President Fricassa Santos, that Fricassa Santos whom you and your lycaons assassinated and emasculated.

To your surprise, he informed you that a plot was under way in your capital. He recommended that you not announce the date of your return, that you land at a small airport in the north rather than at the international airport. To fool the conspirators waiting for you at the end of the runway.

The drummer stops the feast when the night has grown too long. Let us interrupt this *sumu*. The *sèrè* performs the final part. The *koroduwa* engages in febrile dancing and movements. The *sèrè* asks his responder to calm down and recites four maxims:

An acacia does not fall at the will of a skinny goat salivating over its fruit.
The sky does not have two suns; the people do not have two sovereigns.
The chief needs men and men a chief.
Slippery ground does not make the chicken stumble.

Fifth *Sumu*

The *sèrè* plucks the *kora*; the *koroduwa* goes into a wild dance. Calm down a bit, Tiekura—the president and the master hunters have not come together to see you dance and blaspheme, but to listen to us. I can tell you that treachery is the theme to which the proverbs of the pauses will pertain during this fifth *sumu*. Because:

The fire that burns you is the same as that at which you warm yourself.
An enormous elephant does not always have enormous tusks.
The civet deposits his offal at the spring from which he has drunk.

19

Ah, Macledio! Remember your welcome. In the distance, at the other end of the runway, you saw a silhouette come out of the grass as an animal appears on the plains. It was a man, a rifleman. In the name of all the ancestors' souls, a real rifleman! He runs, first to the right, then to the left, hesitates, drops down, disappears, reappears. Like a tracked beast. And there is a second rifleman who appears, takes off, in just as hesitant a manner, as searching and lost as a horse antelope imprisoned within an enclosure. Then a third and a fourth emerge from the earth and scatter in all directions at full speed like a band of red monkeys pursued by a pack of dogs. The fleeing men are followed by an entire platoon of riflemen in combat uniform. There are cries everywhere. Everybody is murmuring, everybody who is on the field, everybody who has come to welcome you is moving about nervously. People are pointing at the deserters. The deserters are disappearing into the grass, reappearing, and leaving again. Every one of them is seeking his own line of flight. The presidential guard, your own guard, has quickly run up and makes a circle around you. Certain members of the presidential guard throw down their arms (the traitors) and disappear through hidden doors.

You have just landed, arriving from your long journey. After reviewing the troops at the foot of the air stairs, you have gone to the hall of honor, where you are shaking hands with the ministers and ambassadors when the commotion breaks out. Your personal guard draws close to protect you. You have just escaped an attempt on your life, a military plot. You were warned but did not believe it.

An entire platoon was camouflaged in a trench at the end of the runway, right in line with the landing trajectory. The submachine gun was oriented to rake the airplane. The aircraft stopped opposite, right in the line of fire. The sergeant, an elite marksman who had been ordered to fire, was not in his normal state.

"He was drunk and drugged—he was sleeping. Like a real Paleo."

"He acted awkwardly and sluggishly."

Realizing somewhat late his foolishness, he loses his head, gets muddled, and the machine gun jams.

"That is lucky. The shots are not fired. The riflemen in the platoon, the commando members, do not understand what has happened to their leader, and they too lose their heads. They yell out helplessly, 'He's a fetishist! We're under a spell—we're lost and bewitched!' And they scatter."

Around the hall of honor, there is total confusion. The guards around you push you into an armored car and surround it with tanks. With sirens screaming, the convoy heads toward the presidential palace at full speed. All the populace and dancers who had gathered along the route to welcome and applaud you scatter, fleeing in commotion, disorder, and complete craziness. The entire city is in turmoil, everyone is excited. And yet, there is not a single shot. Not one shot was heard.

The following Sunday, you invited the ambassadors of France and the United States to a diplomatic hunting party.

"Your Excellency, Mister Ambassador of France, I come back to the latest plot. As your intelligence services determined, that plot smacks of Moscow's hand. It is a carefully woven communist plot, well organized. Our Black people would be incapable of putting together such a conspiracy."

"Your Excellency, Mister President, my thanks for this hunting party, first of all. . . . That was certainly a communist assassination attempt —that is the information my cipher office obtained in Paris. You are a young anticommunist president, and Moscow wants to get rid of you. That is what has been said and understood in Paris," replies the ambassador of France.

"Your Excellency, Mister Ambassador of the United States, you have the CIA, and you know all the machinations of international communism. Our intelligence services have communicated to your advisors all of the irrefutable evidence."

"Thank you, Mister President, and my dear friend, for this pleasant hunting party. We are very grateful. My country's entire press is unanimous that what happened here is a communist plot. We are engaged in a cold war and Moscow wants to get rid of you. Everybody knows that, everybody is fully aware of it. That is why Moral Rearmament for the struggle against international communism is sending you a delegation," replies the ambassador of the United States.

The delegation arrives and decorates you with the medal of the Great Cross. Accompanying the delegation, there is the rector of an American university who awards you a doctorate *honoris causa*.

The plotters see that the medals and congratulations addressed to you and the condemnations intended for them come from the entire free world of Europe, the Americas, and Africa. They grasp the extent of their misfortune, their woes. They understand that nowhere on this earth, nowhere in the world can they hope or count on the least compassion or justice. Some of them commit suicide in desperation.

Nobody believed the suicide theory, nobody believed the official version. The official version that suggested the desperate men, seized with remorse and in a bloody fit, emasculated themselves before ending their lives by hanging themselves. So notes the responder.

Whether the living believed that or not is unimportant. The dead were dead and already happy in heaven, very happy in the company of God. Does the Qur'an not announce and repeat that the brave who die arms in hand defending their conviction perish in the jihad and go directly to paradise? So explains Macledio.

"An official inquiry was carried out to determine the actual causes of their suicide."

"An inquiry from which the results were never published."

All the radios in the universe announced the news that Koyaga had just escaped an assassination attempt.

This was the first assassination attempt of your regime. Every despot of the vast African continent, a land as rich in potentates as in pachyderms, sent a plenipotentiary delegate to the capital of the Republic of the Gulf. Airplanes cluttered the small airport. The envoys of brothers and friends—it is thus that African autocrats call their peers—remained for an entire day.

They came to congratulate Koyaga, to repeat to him their fraternal,

African support and their condemnation of the villainous assassination attempt. That was, officially, the mission of the plenipotentiary envoys. But in fact, each tyrant wanted to assure himself of the reality, the truth of the attempt. Each dictator wanted to verify that events had taken place as reported. To know whether in fact real plotters had actually hidden in trenches at the end of the runway, with a real submachine gun, loaded with real bullets.

The envoy from each autocrat engaged in his own intense inquiry for a day and a night. Their respective masters let out cries of astonishment when, after returning to their respective countries, the plenipotentiary envoys confirmed the events. All the potentates remained perplexed and skeptical. They were convinced their diplomatic dolts had been taken in easily. They too were despots, and they readily knew what an African dictator is capable of inventing in order to bamboozle his own people and the entire universe.

Ah, Koyaga! You escaped, survived thanks to the occult powers of your mama and the blood sacrifices and benedictions of the marabout Bokano. This news would be learned abroad later. In the Republic of the Gulf, everyone already knew that and everyone was saying so. Throughout the country they were looking for your mama and the marabout to congratulate them, to get acquainted.

Your mother and the marabout Bokano were in the North, praying and worshiping for you. Koyaga and Macledio, you joined them. The four of you were hidden in a sanctuary—your mama, the marabout, Macledio, and yourself. Sacrifices of thanksgiving to the souls of the ancestors were smoking.

Your mama and the marabout engaged in various divinatory practices. And in long and fruitful meditations. They told you that the members of the presidential guard must come from your own clan. They must not enter that corps until they had made a blood pact with you in the sacred wood.

That is the way in which the airport plot was useful. That plot allowed you to ensure that you had a trustworthy personal guard.

You do not remember anything, or almost nothing. You were sleeping, that is for sure.

"Stupefied, the pilot and copilot yell out for you to fasten your seatbelt. You wake up with a start. You feel the airplane losing altitude, sense that the landing gear is not going down and that the pilot has lost control. A flash and an infernal noise. You have the impression that you have bounced on the ground, split it open, and been swallowed

Waiting for the Vote of the Wild Animals

up. Then, silence, dreams, relaxation, nothingness, the ineffable. Even today, you still cannot remember what happened and what became of you."

"No, you will never know."

Help arrived from the city an hour after the accident. The accident took place on landing, less than five kilometers from the airport. The little airport near your birthplace, an airport with no emergency crew. The gendarmes and the hunters got there first. Then came the army. None of them had equipment or means for assisting.

"The carcass of the airplane is entangled in the trees and half consumed by a growing fire."

There were five of you on board. They remove four bodies and identify them. You are not among the dead. Without losing any time, they attack the cabin with axes, picks, and blowtorches, ripping it apart. They poke around and search through the hidden recesses: your body is not there.

"Everybody thinks, everybody believes that you were ejected in the crash, the forced landing. The gendarmes, hunters, and soldiers scatter, search, and comb the adjoining bush. Thicket by thicket, every blade of grass—they check everything. To no avail."

"It is at that moment that I, Macledio, arrive from the capital. I take command of the search operation. I have them start over and continue the searching until nightfall. I, Macledio. The searching goes on by the light of straw torches. Until . . ."

Until they come to inform you, Macledio, you and the other searchers, that a foreign radio station has announced the accident and the death of the president. You lose your temper. Macledio, you angrily take charge of a delegation. You did not want to see old Nadjuma, the mother, before you had found the body of your man of destiny. The delegation includes the minister of the interior, the prefect, officers, hunters, religious men, and fetishists.

"We arrive at Nadjuma's villa. The door is closed. Your old mama has been waiting for the results of the search for twelve hours. Certainly in anguish, in prayer. We get them to open the door, go in with our hearts in our throats, unable to breathe. What can we say? What words can we find to console her? We want nothing more than to assure her of our determination to locate the body of her son. . . . What a surprise!"

Your stupefaction is overwhelming. You cannot believe your own eyes. . . .

I, Koyaga, was already there, seated with my head on my mother's knees.

The dictator with a thousand nicknames was there in his mother's arms—quite alive, in one piece, and a smile on his lips. Weeds never die, the *koroduwa* adds with a devilish smile.

The man of a thousand forms had only a few minor bruises, a band around his head, and another on his knee. Koyaga the master hunter was not dead.

I, Macledio, cannot resist the pleasure of throwing myself on you and hugging you. Crying with joy. While the other members of the delegation are struggling to believe their own eyes, I go out, I run. I catch a team of reporters from the national radio. The national radio immediately corrects the misinformation announcing your death. The radio announces, shouts, proclaims the miracle.

When the tam-tam beat resounds, one does not proclaim himself to be the best dancer. One proves it. We had to reassure your friends and discourage your enemies immediately. You make a declaration on the radio. Everybody hears your voice. You make a calm proclamation in an intelligible and eloquent voice:

"I am indeed alive. With a few minor, very minor bruises. I am a hunter, a hunter of a thousand shapes. Neither this soon nor for such a minor incident will I give up the fight. The airplane was sabotaged. I discovered that. It was my phantom that boarded it. It will take more, a great deal more for me to stop defending the interests and development of the country. The enemies of the Republic of the Gulf and of Africa will never manage to assassinate me; they will never attain their goal as long as my mother Nadjuma is alive. And in any case, my death is worth nothing. The death of one lone combatant has never stopped the battle. I know the perpetrators, I know the hands that sabotaged the airplane. They are the same ones. The colonialists, the colonialists took advantage of the communists for this assassination attempt. The manes of the ancestors were there to validate my mother's charms. I am and I hold myself to be a combatant in the service of my country. A combatant who is ever prepared to die for the country and for the people."

And then . . . and then you shouted, "Long live the Republic of the Gulf! Long live the people's struggle, the struggle against international communism, the struggle for freedom!" And then . . . and then there followed all the words, all the declarations that a head of state in the cold war can utter to justify the torture and assassination of members of the opposition. Adds the responder.

That speech resounds, it has an incredible echo throughout all Africa. In all the African republics, the news is rebroadcast several times. It is repeated time and time again.

This was the second assassination attempt. Every tyrant on the vast continent of Africa, a land that abounds in violators of human rights as much as in hyenas, sent two envoys—a diplomat and a military officer. For the second time, the airplanes cluttered the small airport. The envoys of brothers and friends—it is thus that African dictators call their peers—remained for two entire days.

They came to congratulate Koyaga, to repeat to him their fraternal, African support and their condemnation of the criminal assassination attempt. That was, officially, the mission of the delegations. But in fact, each despot wanted to assure himself of the reality, the truth of the attempt. Each tyrant wanted to verify that the events had occurred as reported. To know that Koyaga had, in fact, boarded the airplane and that, in fact, there had been a crash. To know that all his associates had died (that real cadavers had been removed), and that he alone was the sole survivor.

The two envoys from each despot engaged in a minute inquiry for two days and nights. They learned that Koyaga had two protectors: a mother who was a sorceress along with a great magician—a marabout who never closed his eyes at night.

Upon the envoys' return to their respective countries, their respective masters uttered cries of astonishment when the envoys presented their discoveries, confirming those facts. The dictators appeared interested, perplexed, and skeptical. They decided they were insufficiently informed and rather believed that their envoys—both the diplomats and the soldiers—had been manipulated. They were dictators, and they knew everything an African dictator is capable of doing in order to fool people.

In the Republic of the Gulf, everybody knew, everybody admitted to himself that you were capable of the unbelievable. First, in the villages, they had believed, admitted, and reported that you were dead—definitely dead and buried. The Koyaga who spoke, the one they heard on the radio, had been raised from the dead. You were considered to be a man returned from the dead, a man resuscitated by his sorceress mother.

Feasts are spontaneously organized in the villages. Everybody wants to see and touch the man who has returned to life, the hunter, the president.

Delegations come spontaneously from all regions of the country. They converge on your native village to congratulate you. By night, by day, they arrive from all the villages. They take over, they invade your village, the streets, the squares, and the surrounding country. It is necessary to stop the flood, the crowd. You declare you have decided to visit the entire country, village by village. You will travel through the country from border to border, from the northern mountains to the ocean.

And that was what, in your saga, in your saint's life, has been called the "Triumphal March." The Triumphal March was a myth, a lie that reinforced your prestige and thus your license to kill, emasculate, and steal with impunity.

To descend from the Kakolo and Paleo mountains to the capital on the coast of the Republic of the Gulf, it is necessary to travel some four hundred kilometers, to go through hundreds of cities, villages, communities, meeting many different peoples. Peoples who, by their customs and practices, can be grouped into two races, two societies, two civilizations. In the North, there are communities of the Kakolo and Paleo civilizations and, in the South, the civilizations of the forest, the Vodu peoples.

At the first stop, the hunters welcome your cortege five kilometers in advance of the village. The cortege proceeds surrounded by hunters. It advances in a cloud of dust and a wealth of rifle shots, in the middle of a gigantic fantasia. At the edge of the village, you get out of your automobile. The sacrificial priest of the village slits the throats of a goat and two chickens at your feet. He intones his prayers, the sacramental words. He observes the vermilion blood and the death throes of the victims: they die with their feet in the air. The priest interprets this and concludes that the manes of the village have accepted the libations. The manes are happy to welcome you to their land; they bless you with warm benedictions.

When the solemnities and silence of the libations have ended, the association of women takes you with them. Screeching and chanting, groups of women surround you and take hold of you. Others cleanse you and fan you, they spread their pagnes before your feet. They do not want your feet to touch the ground. They pick you up, remove your shoes, wash your feet, and drink the water with which your hooves have been rinsed. You finally arrive at the foot of the sacred tree, the *sumu* tree in the center of the village square, carted along on the shoulders and backs of the women with bare torsos. Words of welcome are proffered. The chief of the village requests things that you cannot give and will never give.

Waiting for the Vote of the Wild Animals

Politics is an illusion for the people, for those subject to the regime. They see in it the things about which they dream. You can satisfy dreams only through lies and tricks. Politics is successful only through duplicity.

Amid thunderous applause, you answer the inhabitants with deceitful promises from the president-founder of the single party. You justify the coup d'état and the assassination of the democratically elected president. The army intervened and you assumed power to save the country from the catastrophe that was threatening, to wrest it from the hands of racists, thieves, nepotisms.

The same speech, ever the same nonsense. You finish your oratory with other false promises; the promise to restore, through free elections, power to the people to whom it belongs. Explains the responder.

The villagers present gifts for the brother and father that you are. In the first village, these gifts are only a steer and a sheep. You continued on your journey.

But at the second and third villages, the welcome ceremony becomes more complex. Each village wants to be original, to offer a different and warmer welcome. By adding too many condiments, the cook often spoils the best sauces. Too many ghosts ruin the best of dreams.

The hunters keep meeting you farther and farther in advance of their village and accompany you farther and farther beyond. Up to the lands of the adjoining communities. Territorial conflicts result. Hunters from two neighboring villages finally engage in a veritable battle with their slave rifles. There are fatalities. The order is given that hunters are not to go beyond the territorial limits of their community. Territorial disputes are resolved.

Because you are a *sinbo*, a *donsoba* (master hunter), hunters at the edge of a distant village take the initiative of presenting you with a bubal shoulder. At the edge of the next village, they give you shoulders, hindquarters, and heads. At the next village, the third one, you receive a stinking heap of animal carcasses of all species: does, monkeys, and even elephants. Above the pile, the tree branches are black with vultures. In the sky, vultures fight with terrifying screeching. Bands of hyenas, lycaons, and lions hover and threaten.

The order is given to hunters to offer no more gifts, not to present their master hunter guest with any more shoulders of game taken by the hunters during the week as is normally required by societal code.

In another village, to distinguish itself, the sacrificial priest is not content with two chickens and the goat—he offers four chickens, two goats, and a steer to the manes of the ancestors. This practice reaches the level of some twenty steers, as many goats, and around forty chickens. The libations become interminable—a veritable hecatomb. An appeal is sent out to limit the number of sacrifices for the libations.

The women of the first villages had been satisfied with abandoning their scarves, camisoles, and various overgarments. To be different and surpass them, the women of the next village appear naked, except for their briefs. At the following stop, the briefs fall. You found yourself handled by groups of completely unclad women. They wear only the strings of pearls around their waists.

Because the women of independent nations cannot have their pubic area exposed to the flies, the Paleo women, who had found themselves obliged to cover their behinds, accepted the pagne only grudgingly. They wanted to take advantage of the situation to reassume their original nudity. Says the responder.

They are quickly reminded that the wearing of the pagne is still required. There are foreign journalists. The female citizens of an independent republic must not allow themselves to be photographed with their behinds exposed.

In villages following Vodu traditions, the welcome is different. At each stop, the village elders have you coiffed with a cap decorated with motifs of gold, coral, and ancient glass beads. They drape you in a multicolored pagne, slip rings on your arms and forearms, and place gilded *sambara* on your feet. They slit the throats of sacrificial animals for the manes of the ancestors and seat you as chief of the tribe.

In one village, the chief makes an innovation by offering you one of his daughters in marriage. In the following village, three daughters are offered to you, then five, and even seven. That is too many! You thank the donors of women for their generosity. But you are obliged to request that they keep their daughters in the villages until further instruction.

At a stop in another village, a woman takes the initiative of asking you to adopt her son, to make of him your own son. At the next village, they propose three boys, then four, and then seven are offered. You put a stop to this escalation by asking the parents to keep their sons, and you promise assistance. This was a veritable Triumphal March!

A true Triumphal March, which became one of the important watchwords of the Paleo master hunter, that dictator and great emasculator of men and beasts. Concludes the *koroduwa*.

The Triumphal March can allow visiting only a handful of privileged villages, those located along the central axis of the republic. All the other villages in the east and west of the country, all the innumerable small and inaccessible hamlets, lost in the mountains, in the distant bush, and in the forest, lost in misery, ignorance, disease, and obscurantism, consider themselves frustrated and forgotten. They proclaim their indignation. They too wanted to see and touch the resuscitated president, and they had their own congratulations to present in person to the miraculous leader, they too had their requests to present to the powerful man of good fortune. Each village sent a delegation.

It took many days to receive all those delegations in strict respect of the rules of good and interminable African *sumu*. Much patience, saliva, and many lies to accept the gifts, reply to the benedictions, and conduct all the libations. During his normal hours of audience and his usual office hours, the president could not give all the time necessary without renouncing all his other obligations as chief of state, dictator, and father of the nation.

And as the great seducer of other men's wives, wives of citizens. The responder adds maliciously.

You could not renounce that which was imperative and indispensable for so many long weeks. This was neither conceivable nor possible. As a former rifleman, hunter, and man of duty, you decided to take the time to welcome the delegations during your leisure hours and your sleeping hours. You made arrangements to receive them mornings, very early, beginning at four o'clock.

These morning audiences lasted for three moons. Those three months of meeting and consulting with your people created a habit, a need . . . and gave you ideas.

You could not begin your daily tasks without being immersed in those pointless daily palavers of underdevelopment, without the endless trial from four to six o'clock in the morning.

You noticed that those early morning encounters were beneficial and useful. You made of them an original method of direct government. You discovered great advantages in that method. One sometimes finds a magnificent doe caught in the trap set for agouti.

You, Macledio, minister of the interior and of national orientation, immediately understood the demagogical advantages that the regime could derive from this method. The rules for audiences were codified, and the morning audiences became an institution. All the people were informed of the procedure to be followed. The citizen who had claims or requests appeared at the audiences, the public palaver of the presidency, at four o'clock in the morning. The president heard the petitioners with the patience of a master hunter. The president immediately, that very night, summoned the minister or high official involved. The discussion was held, the case was heard and judged right on the spot.

Unfortunately, every underdeveloped Black villager is born for the palaver, and offering him the chance to plead, to defend his case whenever he wishes, is to offer a plain to the flooding river. The Black peoples invaded and occupied the presidential estate just as the river spreads and takes over the plain.

Beginning at three o'clock in the morning, the courtyard of the presidential palace is swarming with petitioners. A procedure is codified. All petitioners are heard by bailiffs in advance and then are selected and placed on a list. The bailiffs class them by date of arrival, theme, and minister or official implicated. The bailiffs choose according to the looks of the petitioner and, often enough, according to the extent to which the latter manages to dampen their beards with libations.

Beginning at three in the morning, the chosen are called in order. They enter the presidential palace—but never alone: they are accompanied by relatives or witnesses, two or three people. Petitioners and those accompanying them wait in the presidential office.

At the stroke of four o'clock (you frequently wait one or two minutes in the stairway in order not to arrive early), you make your entrance as you raise your arms and salute.

Standing, those present applaud. Without further ado, the public palaver begins. The petitioners present their suits in turn.

An underdeveloped Black man can complain about anything and everything. . . . The most crying abuses, thefts of chickens, women, the casting of evil spells.

All the cases are heard and judged on the spot and to everyone's satisfaction. Everyone smiles and laughs when you begin to speak. The people applaud your judgments, your comments, your wit.

At six o'clock, the palavers are followed by ecumenical public prayer. Muslims, Catholics, Protestants, and fetishists together, each according to his own liturgy addresses a warm prayer of thanks to God. All finish with benedictions for the country and for you, Koyaga, for your perennial power, for your health and long life.

Once the prayers are over, everyone goes back up to the palace reception hall. Everyone partakes of a warm breakfast with their president. Before leaving and returning to their respective villages, the petitioners and those accompanying them attend the raising of the flag on the terreplein of the presidential palace.

The petitioners came from all throughout the country, sometimes traveling over eight hundred kilometers. They sometimes remained in the capital for nearly three months: three months during which they went each morning at three o'clock to the presidential palace. The underdeveloped Black man is a veritable sinew, a misery of patience.

Those public audiences constituted, in the final analysis, one of the truly original elements of your dictatorial and bloody regime. They softened it, in a certain manner, and made it popular. Not everything is negative, not completely negative, even in an emasculatory tyranny. White spots can be found even in the asshole of a hyena. Concludes the *koroduwa*.

That morning, ten cases were presented that you heard and judged to the satisfaction of all. Like every morning except Sunday, you shared your coffee and hot croissants with the ministers, officials, petitioners, and those accompanying them. On that morning, you went down to the garden and ordered the supreme chief of the army to conduct the ceremony for raising the colors on the terreplein of the presidential estate. This was exceptional: you usually watched the ceremony of raising the colors from the palace balcony. There were three ministers, two prefects, and five heads of state societies or ministries along with some fifty petitioners and those accompanying gathered about you. You piously listened to the national anthem, which glorifies you and your single party.

It was as you began to review the platoon in charge of raising the colors that the shot rang out. It was fired at about ten meters away from you. Nine meters and seventy centimeters would later be determined officially. The soldier Bedio fired at you. Almost at point-blank he fired at you . . . and missed you.

Really missed you, at less than ten meters!

The members of your personal guard disarm him. They do not give him a chance to fire a second time. They master him and bring him to you. Your first inclination is to be generous, chivalrous. You take your time, quite calmly take your time. Calmly, you give him a vigorous slap. Your face beams in a sinister, ironic smile, and you hurl insults in the soldier's face.

"You idiotic, bumbling dogface! A really incompetent marksman! I am not slapping you or punishing you for having fired at me. That will be the job of the judicial system. As supreme chief of the army, I'm giving you two weeks of official detention because you are a poor marksman, the worst in the regiment. You cannot miss a target of my importance and size at a distance of ten meters!"

With composure, the composure of a master hunter, you retrace your steps. Your bodyguards press against you, surround you. Before the bewildered assembly, you leave in silence for the presidential offices. You arrive at the stairway and go up. You are at the landing. At that moment and only at that moment there is a spontaneous burst of hurrahs and noisy applause.

You continue climbing the stairs.

Even the river that is inexorably going down to the sea stops to rest when it arrives on the plain. Let us interrupt this *sumu* in the same fashion, says the *sèrè*. He orders his dancing and gesticulating responder to stop and reflect on the following proverbs:

The man whose impotence you have healed is the one who steals your wife.

If those beating the millet mutually hide the hair of their armpits, the millet will not be clean.

Often it is the man for whom you brought water from the river who provokes the leopard to attack you.

20

Ah, Koyaga! We are in a cold war, and your first preoccupation is naturally to prove to the free world, to the West, that this is another communist conspiracy, a plot organized by international communism. The well-known thief pays for the chicken he has not pilfered.

You quickly and easily organized and published the proof. The West is quick and does not examine too closely the method or reasoning.

That soldier Bedio, the poor marksman, is only an agent. The poor, awkward agent of a plot woven by communist politicians who are jealous and cowardly. Arrests are made on all sides. Under torture, many of the detainees come to the table. There are multiple supporting confessions. The truth breaks forth like the noon sun.

That soldier Bedio has a cousin studying in France. The friend of that cousin, also a student, is the cousin of a veterinarian who is among the people arrested. That veterinarian owns an agropastural enterprise ten miles from the capital. There is a straw hut in the middle of that land. A straw hut just ten meters from the gigantic roots of a silk cotton tree. They get busy at the roots of the tree, digging with great effort and patience before the press, cameras, and radios. What is found exceeds all expectations. There is a footlocker full of Marxist books. By

Marx, obviously, but also some treatises by Lenin, Stalin, and Mao. Inside one of the books, there is a pistol, a real pistol loaded with five bullets capable of downing any living creature. Farther down, there are some books with plans for a constitution, the text of a proclamation, the names of some potential ministers, the list of a cabinet—a complete government. There are letters from Conakry and Moscow. This is incontestably the arsenal and equipment of communist subversives. Everything is corroborated, organized, and baptized with declarations and testimonies from prisoners chained up in torture chambers. Declarations that disturb even the most incredulous people.

A real and credible communist plot!

The West, the free world, and all the anticommunist organizations of the cold war are in agreement. They check the balance sheet, the summary, and draw conclusions.

In less than three years, three assassination attempts perpetrated by international communism, aiming at the physical suppression of Koyaga have been organized. What perseverance! A real persistence, which only one good motive could justify. Koyaga is a kingpin, an important one, for stopping the spread of international communism in Africa. Koyaga is a master player in the struggle against liberticidal communism. The West must know this, recognize it, help, succor, and sustain its shield much more and much better.

Two American universities confer doctorates *honoris causa* on you. Three organizations, two of them European, come to award you, in your own palace and before your people, the highest decorations given to the most meritorious people. And that is not all! In supreme witness to the understanding of the West, the French minister of defense comes in person, accompanied by his military chief of staff and the chief of his counterespionage unit, to pay you a visit of three whole days.

You are considered the rock on which that wave of rising international communism will break. The media and public opinion of the free world have no more right to criticize you. A soldier at the front must not be demoralized by criticism of his methods and techniques for handling his weapon.

This was the third assassination attempt. Every dictator on the vast continent of Africa, as rich in brazen liars as in vultures, sent three envoys this time—a diplomat, a soldier, and a policeman. For the third time, airplanes cluttered the small airport. The envoys of brothers and friends—it is thus that African dictators call each other when they kiss on the mouth—remained for three entire days. They came to congratulate Koyaga, to repeat to him their fraternal, African support and their condemnation of the criminal assassination attempt. That was, officially, the mission of the delegations. But in fact, each dictator wanted to assure himself of the reality, the truth of the attempt. Each dictator wanted to verify that the events had occurred as reported. To know that, in fact, the soldier had really fired on Koyaga, with real bullets and at close range. To know that, in fact, the bullets had not been able to pierce his body. To hear that, in fact, their fellow dictator was not wearing a bullet-proof vest. The three envoys from each African potentate engaged in three days and three nights of minute inquiries. They went so far as Koyaga's native village. They paid a courtesy call on his old mother and offered her presents sent by their masters. In return, the old woman gave her benedictions, prayers, and sacramental words for the autocrats. The envoys also went to the camp of the marabout Bokano. They offered the marabout sumptuous presents that only potentates can offer. The marabout recited some sura for each dictator, some benedictions, and recommended to each tyrant the appropriate sacrifice for self-protection.

Upon the envoys' return to their respective countries, their respective masters uttered cries of astonishment when the envoys confirmed that the soldier had, with a real bullet, fired at a distance of less than ten meters. The bullet had ricocheted off the medals. The dictators prayed in turn that the benedictions and sacramental words of the old woman and the marabout might be accepted by Allah and the manes of the ancestors. They made sacrifices. But they felt themselves insufficiently informed and remained both skeptical and perplexed. They were rather tempted to think that their envoys—the soldier, the diplomat, and the policeman—had been manipulated. They were despots and knew everything that the peers of their kind know how to arrange in order to fool people.

In villages of the Republic of the Gulf, in all the villages . . . in the capitals of multiple Africa, in all the palaces of impenitent dictators, everybody observed and followed events. Everybody counted and reviewed. In less than three years, sorcery had produced three veritable miracles.

Koyaga's airplane, returning from the Maghreb, heads into the line of fire of the antiaircraft defense. At the moment of pressing the triggers, the operators of the submachine guns find themselves suddenly stricken with inertia. Their fingers are paralyzed, their sight is cloudy, their breath is short. They flee.

Waiting for the Vote of the Wild Animals

That was the first thing that had never been seen or reported in any other country.

The aircraft in which Koyaga was returning to his village had been sabotaged. Expertly sabotaged. The inevitable accident takes place. Koyaga cannot be found in the cabin.

That was the second thing that had never been seen or reported in any other country.

At point-blank range, a rifleman fires on Koyaga. The bullet does not even damage your uniform.

In what country has anybody reported or seen such a thing?

The sorcery of Nadjuma, Koyaga's mama, is the most powerful magic on the continent. She is the most inspired of sorceresses of our times. Her son is invulnerable.

In all the villages of the Republic of the Gulf, people say and repeat that phrase. It is sung in the evening by moonlight.

People also think the same and whisper it in the air-conditioned offices of the dictators' palaces of our vast continent.

Numerous arrests were made during and following the three plots. Many politicians are behind barbed wire or under house arrest. They are in an uncomfortable situation; in their prisons, they too count and draw conclusions. They do not see how they can get out of their situation.

Nothing is to be heard or expected from the established defenders of human rights in the West from the moment they are identified as communists. During the cold war, communists are denied any commiseration, pity, or treatment as fellow human beings by the West.

Nothing can be expected either from sorcerers, sacrifices, the ancestors. Koyaga has protection, the favor of the African gods; they have made him invulnerable.

Nothing can be expected either from African *sumu*. Koyaga's mama possesses the most powerful sorcery on the continent, and all Africa fears it.

The political prisoners understand that they have been abandoned by men, gods, and religions. They panic and commit suicide.

In their bloody and suicidal madness, they amputate their own penises before acting, says the responder ironically.

In any case, suicide is not the best solution for the country. Macledio tells the politicians that and suggests other paths of action.

You, Macledio, counsel them rather to satisfy Koyaga's secret desire . . . and death will cease roaming among them. You suggest that they sabotage all their parties and join the Rally of the Gulf People. That is the single party Koyaga secretly wants to found.

Spontaneously, they all unite, and together, they speak strong, sincere words. With tears in their eyes and trembling lips, they approve petitions. Those petitions demand nothing other than Koyaga's clemency, his pity, his humanity. They renounce the cache-sexe of the *bilakoro*—that uncircumcised rascal—renounce their ideas, their friends, their beliefs, and their parties. They understand and they act. They betray their parties, bury them, forget them as they would the nightmare of a stormy night. One by one, they swear on their honor, by great Allah in heaven, and on the manes of their ancestors in their tombs. Solemnly, they enter the sacred wood of the single party, where they become initiates, children, and adepts of that party: they, their wives, their progeny, their relatives, their friends, and their acquaintances—along with their dogs and chickens.

The sun begins to shine in the heaven of our republic, and smiles appear between Koyaga's cheeks when he hears the numerous tremulous voices, sees the tearful eyes of the detained and other tortured people glorifying him.

In the name of Allah, I say that death is the most frightful of phenomena. Fear of death makes prisoners say and carry out foolish things and the most abject of renunciations.

The date for the constituent assembly of the single party was set.

The creation of the single party and his nomination as president-founder and president-for-life brought only an ephemeral moment of joy to Koyaga. These events cannot bring back his joviality of before the accident. He continues to grumble, to complain about the ingratitude of men and the nature of the soldier who fired at him. Something must be done, he must not be discouraged. It is you, Macledio, who intervene and find the solution. You delve into that rich experience acquired during your unforgettable journey to the Republic of the Great River. You decide to create shock groups who will repeat the saga and sing praise for Koyaga everywhere and all day long. They will unceasingly remind him of what he is doing for the country, unceasingly recall that his existence is the good fortune of the country, fortune equal to what the Nile is for Egypt. Without him, the country would fall back into its misery, Africa would return to the colonial period, to slavery, to its congenital savagery.

Girls and boys in all the villages enroll in the League for Revolutionary Youth and organize the shock groups. These groups hold evening dances during which they rival with each other in praises and hymns of honor for their Supreme Guide. That does you good.

The shock groups raise your morale, Koyaga; they help you regain your joviality. You like to hear them singing and dancing for you. Each morning, after the public audiences and the raising of the colors, the shock groups in the gardens of the presidential estate dance and sing your praises, they intone your praises. Their poems, their speeches, their music, and their chants give you strength and fire for the entire day. You are becoming happy. Radiant at all times.

In the republican dictatorship of Koyaga, two people play very important roles: your mama and the marabout.

The last time we recalled them and sang about them—the marabout Bokano and Nadjuma, Koyaga's mama—was during the first *sumu*. They are then at Hairaidougou, the camp and agricultural enterprise of the marabout, about ten kilometers from Ramaka. The marabout Bokano has just exorcised Nadjuma and freed her from enchantment through his own particular and infallible methods: slaps and flagellation. He has just discovered that she has gifts for magic, divination, and geomancy. He has just discovered that, from her womb, there had sprung a boy who was the terror of the bush. The terror of the social bush among men; the terror of the natural bush in the land. A great name. He has an inclination, more than a tender feeling for Nadjuma. Her physical beauty disturbs him when he wants to recall the sura of the Qur'an. He asks the young woman to remain by his side during his ministry so she might know the will of Allah, might learn the word of Allah, might convert to Islam. He pronounces no words of love or proposal of marriage. But Nadjuma is not misled about his unexpressed intentions. She refuses outright. She wants to return to the hamlet of Tchaotchi. She wants to continue planting and devoting herself to the manes of her late husband in order to protect and build the future of her son. Tchaotchi is located beyond the mountains and not more than fifteen kilometers from Ramaka. So it is about twenty-five kilometers from Hairaidougou, the camp and agricultural enterprise of the marabout. The young woman and the marabout continue to see each other. They continue to watch over the future of the rifleman Koyaga.

At night, she often thinks about her son, calls on her husband's double, and her sleep is often filled with maleficent dreams. She continues practicing geomancy, and occasionally, evil portents emerge from the sand beneath her fingers. Each time, she walks to Hairaidougou and reveals the dreams and vaticinations. The marabout interprets them, evaluates them. He seeks and reveals the sacrifices that may ward off the evil happenings. Seeking the sacrifices to annihilate and ward off the great evils can take several days and nights. Combining several practices, Bokano engages in *achura,* expiatory fasting, retreating and closing himself in a locked hut. He prays night and day while about the hut his *talibaa,* disciples, chant the *sama,* the spiritual concert of the brotherhood, and engage in the *djadb,* the ecstatic dance.

Twice, the marabout sends for Nadjuma on stormy nights for urgent sacrifices. This is to keep away the two ill fortunes that Koyaga escapes miraculously.

As soon as you become uncontested master of the Republic of the Gulf, your first concern is to construct in your native village in the mountains, in Tchaotchi, a vast estate, an estate as vast as the one you visited in the Republic of the Ebony People. Construct as sumptuous an estate as the one that the dictator of the crocodile totem built in his native village.

A person does not change character. You are a combat veteran of Indochina. You are not interested in palaces, villas, and luxurious bourgeois gardens. Your first concern is security.

You can only construct a fortified camp. The former rifleman's security concerns undermine the project and take precedence over all other considerations. At the foot of a hill, you have a terrain of about four hundred hectares enclosed by a wall as high as that of the residence at Fasso.

But it is an enclosure bristling with chevaux-de-frise and dominated by unaesthetic watchtowers, flanked by searchlights, every hundred meters around the entire perimeter. It is really an entrenched camp. A camp that resembles many of the advance posts in the rice paddies of Indochina, or the imperial court of the man with the hyena totem, or the secondary residence of the dictator with the crocodile totem, which serve as models.

In the middle of this construction, there is a traffic circle around a tall bronze statue set on a monumental pedestal. It is a statue of Koyaga as general of the army, facing east and pointing the way with his finger. The traffic circle is located at the intersection of two crossing boulevards. Thus, four roads head off from the circle. They are all bordered on both sides with monuments to Koyaga or his mama. The first road, to the north, leads to the residence of the Supreme Guide. It is a three-story building in the depressing style of an HLM. The southern road leads to his mama's court, a real family compound, a family courtyard like those in the suburbs of all African capitals. An agglomeration of villas, depots, worker's huts, kennels, chicken houses, goat yards, and latrines, one after the other and filling all the extra space. The ways to the east and west are dominated by great arches of triumph from which fly banners with slogans glorifying Koyaga and his mama.

In the capital also, what is pompously referred to as the private residence of Koyaga is in fact a fortified bourgeois house with his mama's villa next door.

Nadjuma is respectfully referred to throughout the country as the "Old Woman" or "Mama." When the dictator and his mama are both in Tchaotchi or in the capital, Koyaga visits her twice every day: before lunch and before bedtime in the evening. One of those little Paleo dishes simmered in Paleo style waits for him on a table in his mother's apartment every night. Koyaga loves them and delights in them, even after copious official dinners at the palace.

When he is away in another city, Koyaga telephones his mama at least twice a day: at the end of the morning and at bedtime.

Your relations with your mama are too close, Koyaga. People accuse you of an incestuous love. This is an accusation to which you never reply. It is an accusation that the master hunter finds undeserving of a reply. But the accusation is justified by your behavior. She often sits on your lap, or you sit on her lap. Often, you sleep in the same bed with your mother. Every time significant worries torture you, you go into your mother's bedroom, take off your general's cap and your heavy jacket with its twenty decorations, your tie, your shoes, and dive into your mother's bed. In order to think things out.

"And I never leave my mama's bedroom without the solutions for my problems."

When Mama is not preparing meals for her son—she alone and no one else cooks for Koyaga—or is not presenting sacrifices, is not praying for her son, is not geomancing for her son, she is receiving. Yes, she receives. There is always a long list of women and men who wish to meet her. Priority is given to foreign heads of state. African dictators, impressed by the miracles that have allowed Koyaga to escape several assassination attempts, seek vaticinations about their own future.

She also receives candidates for ministerial posts, all of them seeking positions of responsibility in the Republic of the Gulf. She predicts their future and informs her son of the results of these consultations. Countless petitioners for prebends fill Mama's waiting room.

Nadjuma is the root that pumps the sap to nourish the regime of the master hunter Koyaga.

Koyaga also has daily contact with the marabout Bokano. Bokano has a compound in the capital. A compound constructed on the edge of the city, about five kilometers to the north. As in Ramaka, the buildings themselves are surrounded by a very high enclosure with one lone entry gate. The courtyard is the heart, the center of agricultural enterprise, a model farm. The farm is cultivated and run by the *talibaa,* the marabout's disciples. They are excellent, competent farmers and do not ask for pay. The marabout provides them with food, clothing, lodging, women, and, in particular, with prayers. In the brotherhood, prayer is not an individual act. It is the domain of the marabout, who prays for his disciples, washes away the sins of all the disciples, saves all his disciples through the intensity of his prayers. According to the credo of the brotherhood, the ability to reach God through prayer is given only to certain, chosen individuals. Bokano is one of those individuals.

And yet Bokano is no longer the ascetic he was when he arrived in Ramaka. Since his protégé attained supreme power, he is much changed. There is more luxury than asceticism in his life. The marabout lives in blatant luxury. He is the richest, or one of the richest, men in the country. People say he is the business director or the straw man for Koyaga and his mother. He travels in a large Mercedes, often travels by air, and always first class. He likes large palaces. He is the owner of a hundred or so compounds and villas in the capital, of apartments in Paris, New York, and Brussels. He also has mistresses in all those cities. He goes to Mecca twice a year for the hajj and the *umrah.*

He claims, people say, that he fasts all year long and spends his nights in prayer.

The marabout's relations with Mama are quite ambiguous. When they are in the same city, he visits her every morning at ten o'clock. He enters her private bedroom; Mama closes her door. The two of them remain alone in the bedroom, behind closed doors, for more than an hour sometimes. What can they possibly be doing or saying for an hour?

In all the capitals of the African dictators, the marabout is considered Mama's source of inspiration. People come from far away to consult him. They offer him automobiles—generally Mercedes models —apartments, and above all lots of money.

He practices geomancy and characterology. After visiting Mama, the ministerial candidate, designate for office, or person chosen for a responsible position goes to see the marabout. Marabout Bokano's welcome is always warm. He shakes the visitor's hand. He serves tea that the visitor must drink. He begs pardon because he cannot drink with his guest on account of the perpetual fasting he must observe. The short visit is sufficient. His expertise in characterology is such that he needs no more than a few minutes to discover all the hidden faults of the visitor.

It is particularly from the visitor's walk that he derives the greatest insights. He hides, finds a place behind a judas hole, in order to observe the visitor approaching through a maze of paths, taking time to study the walk and the general posture of the person arriving. When the person leaves, Bokano goes to the steps with him, shakes his hand, and blesses him with long benedictions. A disciple takes the person in hand and leads him through the maze of paths, allowing the marabout to observe him clear to the parking lot. It is recognized that, following this visit, contact, conversation, observation of the walk and gait of the visitor, nothing about the character, the future, the hidden intentions escape the master's knowledge.

What can be thought, said, chanted, danced concerning Koyaga's relationships and dealings with women during his regime?

First of all, it must be said that he consorts with many women and enjoys them enormously.

He is of the Paleo race, a people for whom companionship does not imply fidelity.

So Koyaga loves, frequents, uses women in the Paleo manner. Infatuations and passing affairs—nothing more in general. The hunter, the veteran rifleman thinks that the function, the main function of women is for reproduction. He considers himself dishonored, and publicly reproaches himself, when he sleeps with a woman several weeks without managing to impregnate her. He recruits his lovers among the girls of the shock groups. The shock groups are the brigades of girls who welcome him, chant and dance his praise and his saga. They are everywhere he goes or resides. These girls fight for the favor of the president, and the more resourceful ones make provocative faces and engage in lascivious gestures during the parties.

When one of the girls manages to stand out, to draw his attention, to please him, a blink, a twinkle in the eyes, the imperceptible movement of a finger are quickly noted and interpreted by a guard, a pimp. Without fail, the girl who has been noticed finds herself in your bed that evening, Koyaga. You do her honor, you feast on her as you would the flesh of the game taken during the day. She then becomes one of the president's wives. Even in the midst of unbridled debauchery, the preoccupations of higher politics are not absent. You consider that in order to manage the republic properly, you have to belong to an extent to all the ethnic groups in the country, to be allied to all of them. You take at least one wife from each of the forty-three ethnic groups of the republic.

A wife of the president has everything material. But she is closely watched. Like every master hunter, Koyaga has the jealousy of a lion. The girl is watched during her gestation and up to bearing her child. Then Koyaga does not summon her any more, or spaces out his visits. He always recognizes the children. Nadjuma, Koyaga's mama, takes care of the baby and the mother, organizes and pays for the baptism, and Koyaga provides lodging and nourishment for the mothers and children until such time as they find a husband able to maintain them decently. He pays for and presides at the remarriage ceremonies of his former mistresses. When the groom does not strike him as being serious enough, Koyaga challenges him. Former mistresses have easy access to bank credit; they become "Benz mamas." That is what the buxom women of rich businessmen riding around on the backseats of a Mercedes are called. Koyaga never abandons a former mistress. The management, the allocation of subsidies, and the payment of rent for the houses inhabited by the former mistresses is one of the most difficult and ruinous affairs of the republic. It was through this enterprise that computer systems first made their way into the Republic of the Gulf. It is handled through a network of five powerful microcomputers. To the satisfaction of everybody, and Koyaga first of all.

Koyaga's progeny never run loose. His child is taken and sent to the Children's Academy of the Presidential Palace. This is the title of an organization placed in the private residence of the president and that of his mama, Nadjuma. It is an organization that includes a center for infant care, a kindergarten, a boarding school, and a primary school. The secondary school originally foreseen is not in operation: there are not enough children for the sixth, ninth, and final years. A full schoolbus leaves the president's private residence each morning to take the president's children to the secondary schools in the capital. All the president's children are prepared for the military. The girls marry officers. There is no headquarters or regiment that does not have at least one son or son-in-law of Koyaga. It is those blood ties, family ties, that ensure the cohesion of the country's army.

What more can we say, chant, or dance concerning Koyaga's dealings, relations with women?

Waiting for the Vote of the Wild Animals

As with all Paleos, all hunters, his mama is an unusual woman, a holy woman, esteemed as a prophetess, a female guru.

As with all Paleos, he won his first wife by rape-marriage. She too has a place apart. She is respected, and she has produced nine children. These children live just like the little bastards at the Children's Academy of the Presidential Palace. There is no difference in treatment between Koyaga's legitimate children and his bastards. He neither sees nor feels the difference.

You do not have much to do with married women. Once, a married woman manages to seduce you. The indulgent husband gets a post in an embassy abroad. Another time, you are seduced by a married woman. The jealous, vindictive husband is forced into exile. . . .

Under Koyaga's rule, it is difficult for the citizen to utter a sigh, to mutter something indistinct, to whistle a tune in private, even at home, without the president being informed of it. It is very difficult to go out in the evening, to change clothes, to eat and drink with friends or relatives without your knowing about it. You alone, only you know the number of intelligence networks that teem and swarm in this land of fifty-six thousand square kilometers and less than four million inhabitants.

There are the police, the military intelligence services, and those of the presidential office. They have their means conferred on them by dictatorships, and they operate by the peculiar methods common among all African fathers-of-the-nation. There is the Association of Divines, Seers, and Geomancers. Mama is the president of this association, and all the members come running to report their clients' confidential revelations to the president.

Bokano presides over the Union of Marabouts, and each marabout visits him in order to be rewarded for the least bit of unusual information. There are your former mistresses, the mothers of your children, who continually have access to the presidency. There are the combat veterans of Indochina and the hunters. Every citizen can be remunerated for an important piece of information by reporting it directly to somebody close to the president at four o'clock in the morning outside of the public audiences. It is not a rare happening for an official or politician to receive a morning call from the president repeating some imprudent statement made the previous evening at the private home of some trustworthy friend. The president usually ends those calls with a sarcastic laugh followed by weighty silence. It is a threat: the official panics. He feels they are on his trail, and he no longer has confidence in anyone around him, in any of his friends. In your re-public, everybody spies and everybody is spied upon. The hyena says that it remains ever on the alert because it has very few sincere friends on the face of the earth.

So it is certain that something was going around concerning prepara-tions for a plot by parents-in-law. How can one explain or understand in any other way what happened last Friday at 1:35 in the afternoon, less than two kilometers from the private residence of the Supreme Guide?

How did he manage to come out of such a carefully prepared as-sassination attempt unscathed? How can we believe that he was pulled alive from the Mercedes riddled with thirty-two bullets at close range? Pulled unscathed from that heap of iron lying in the ditch?

On the avenue that bears your name, you arrive from the headquar-ters of your armed forces at one o'clock as you do every Friday. You are headed for your private residence. You have not been traveling for more than three minutes when the firing first breaks out. The motor-cycle guards around your car are sprayed with bullets, swept away. They fly off their saddles, the motorcycles swerve and end up in the ditch with their wheels in the air. Your cortege—your own car along with the one ahead and the one following—is hit by rockets. This is an ambush such as the ones the Viets carried out in the rice paddies of Indochina! And it is a hecatomb! Thirteen dead, six seriously wounded. You alone escaped—you are picked up unscathed, without the least scratch. Another miracle. A miracle attributed to the Old Woman and the marabout.

The assassination attempt was organized and carried out by two officers: Captain Sama, your son-in-law, and Commander Tacho, your brother-in-law. The attempt is called the "plot of the in-laws."

Misfortune, an evil spell, strikes down both traitors on the same day. Officially, Commander Tacho got into a traffic accident as he fled after the assassination attempt. He is seriously wounded. He is taken unconscious to a clinic. Surgeons operate. There is a telephone call—the operator maintains that it came from the presidential office—ask-ing for news of the wounded man. The surgeon replies that everything went well and that Commander Tacho's chances of survival are good. But then, less than a half hour later, just as in a third-rate police film, men in white smocks invade the clinic. They pull submachine guns out from under their smocks and subdue the surgeons and nurses before they finish off the wounded officer and emasculate him. You deplore this assassination and promise an inquiry.

That inquiry is still going on. The results of the inquiry into the assassination of Commander Tacho, your brother-in-law, will never be published.

Your son-in-law, Captain Sama, was pulled out of the lagoon: dead from drowning. He had a heavy stone tied to his knees. According to official reports, he weighted himself down with the stone before jumping into the water and committing suicide from shame.

But he emasculated himself first. Of his own free will, he emasculated himself. Nobody caught him in the process of that amputation on the dock before the suicide.

This was the fourth assassination attempt. Every autocrat on the vast continent of Africa, as rich in kleptomaniacal dictators as in catastrophes, sent, on this fourth occasion, four officials: a diplomat, a soldier, a policeman, and a professor. For the fourth time, airplanes cluttered the small airport. The emissaries of brothers and friends—it is thus that the African fathers-of-the-nation call themselves when slapping each other on the back during their frequent encounters—spent four entire days with their hosts.

They came to congratulate Koyaga, to repeat to him their fraternal, African support and their condemnation of the villainous assassination attempt. That was, officially, the mission given to the emissaries. But in fact, each tyrant wanted to assure himself of the reality, the truth of the attempt. Every autocrat wanted to know that events had transpired as reported. To verify that in fact an ambush had been organized by real officers, the actual in-laws of their brother and friend. That real rockets had been fired at the escort. That a true hecatomb had taken place and that real corpses had been picked up. To hear that in fact their brother, Supreme Guide, had been the sole survivor.

The four messengers from each dictator engaged in four days and four nights of intense activity. They went so far as Koyaga's native village. They paid a courtesy call to the Old Woman and offered her sumptuous gifts that only rich despots could offer. The emissaries learned that Nadjuma was the possessor of a meteorite. An aerolite that she worshiped and that protected her son. The emissaries also went to the marabout Bokano's camp. They overwhelmed the marabout with sumptuous presents that only despots can afford to give. The plenipotentiary ministers learned that the marabout was the possessor of a sacred Qur'an that also protected Koyaga.

Upon the envoys' return to their respective countries, their respective masters uttered cries of astonishment when the envoys confirmed that the ambush had really been planned and executed by real officers. Rockets had really been fired at the armored Mercedes of their brother and friend. That the dead were real cadavers. They were interested, very interested in finding out whether anything had been hidden. Mysteries, esoteric matters, magic, sorcery. They too wanted the protection of the aerolite and the Qur'an. But they were afraid that their emissaries— the soldier, the diplomat, the policeman, and the professor—might have been manipulated. They were mendacious despots and knew everything persons of their species can invent in order to fool the people and international opinion.

In the Republic of the Gulf, the Supreme Guide was everywhere, omnipresent at all times. All active officials in the party, all those who held a shred of authority in the republic, wore a medal with his effigy on it. The most insignificant hamlets, however isolated, had a Koyaga Square and House. In each community, however important, a statue of Koyaga was enthroned on Koyaga Square.

A monument had been erected in memorial at all the places where he had escaped assassination attempts.

Before creating the waterfall, the river becomes calm and creates a little lake. Let us follow its example. So announces Bingo the *sèrè*. He stops speaking and plucks his *kora*. The responder plays the flute and dances. The *sèrè* offers three proverbs on treachery:

If a person bites you, it is a reminder that you have teeth.

If you have been carrying an old man since dawn but are dragging him at eventide, he remembers only that you have dragged him.

He who is often at the court of the king always ends up by betraying his friends.

21

The assassination, or the liquidation, of Commander Tacho and Captain Sama, the conspirators who carried out an armed assassination attempt, is a unique case, an exception. Koyaga usually has perpetrators of assassination attempts brought before the judicial system. They have the right to proper public trials and to well-deserved death sentences. And then, in magnanimity, the father-of-the-nation commutes their sentence. Koyaga, you have always held that the conspirator who has the audacity to confront you with weapon in hand deserves the consideration of boys, of males who fully assume responsibility for their actions, the respect of the grave, of trustworthy men, and deserves the fate and status of a combatant and warrior. The conspirators you kill without remission, without consideration, without pity, are the accomplices and silent partners of assassination attempts. They wanted to be the big winners, the profit-takers who would not be publicly exposed and would not risk their lives. They are cockroaches. Cockroaches that one squashes with one's feet. You do not arrest them or bring them to justice: you liquidate them directly, emasculate them right away. They do not deserve arrest, interrogation, pretrial investigation, or public trial. They acted in the shadows—you have them done in clandestinely. So you did not assassinate Commander Tacho and Captain Sama because they shot at you. No. You assassinated them because they were close to you, allies. Allies and friends who had betrayed the clan.

Perpetrators of assassination attempts against your person who are not relatives or friends have always come out alive. You keep them for festivities. They become active participants in your numerous and endless national feast days.

In your republic, people are always on the ramparts. Children must be kept busy with games to keep them from doing foolish things. To prevent her cubs from wandering away and getting lost in the bush, the lioness plays with them all day long. The people of your republic are ever feasting or preparing commemorative events. Your subjects never have time for reflection. During your reign, they lose themselves, become intoxicated in public rejoicing.

The country celebrates the dates of your initiation, along with those of your father and mother. The dates of initiations instead of birthdays because nobody knows the date of your birth. The commemoration of the anniversary of your father's death is called the Feast of Victims of Colonialism, one of the most important holidays in the year. You actively participate in all the fetishist, Catholic, Muslim, and Jewish holidays—you preside over all of them. They are all paid holidays. Schoolchildren, officials, and shock groups are mobilized for the numerous visits by your peers, those dictators and fathers-of-the-nation. These events are all paid holidays and provoke rejoicing.

Commemorations of conspiracies and assassination attempts are important holidays and are characteristic of your regime. These holidays have names with a biblical or Qur'anic resonance: the Feast of Divine Goodness, of Sanctification, of the Third Miracle, of the Night of Destiny. These feasts are carried out according to consecrated ritual and ceremonial pomp.

They begin at four o'clock in the morning at the party office with collective prayers—Muslim, Protestant, Catholic, and ecumenical—over which you personally preside. They continue at the memorial monument. There is a monument at each spot where you escaped death.

All of the regime's dignitaries gather before the monument in white boubous. A wreath of flowers is laid at the feet of your statue. The call for the dead is religiously sounded and heard by those attending. It is followed by the broadcast and recording of one of your speeches.

These feasts continue at the presidential palace with a breakfast to which figures of the regime, diplomats, and, in particular, prisoners are invited. You drink public toasts with the prisoners. With the prisoners who have been sentenced specifically for those assassination attempts that you are commemorating. You give your speech. A speech in which you explain the meaning of the feast. You explain directly and at great length the significance and the import of the day to your assassins. A memorable day, a day of pomp between you and them. Your common fate, theirs and yours, has resulted from their ineptitude, an ineptitude willed by the manes, a clumsiness brought on through sorcery and sacrifices. Their success—your assassination—would have brought the immediate return fire of bodyguards, who would have gunned them down and emasculated them at once. The condemned prisoners hug you and join in dance circles, twisting and jerking.

The feast continues outside the palace with a military parade, ballets by the shock groups, and, very late into the night, with celebration in the popular neighborhoods of the city. By moonlight, the dances are organized in the villages, and the echoes of the tam-tam resound through the mountains and the bush.

Before everything else, Koyaga, you are a Paleo and a master hunter; after everything else, you will remain a hunter and Paleo. Now, there is no hunter worthy of his tribe who does not participate every year in the initiatory combats of the mountains. There is no rifle bearer worthy of the name hunter who does not participate each year in the feast of his brotherhood. Because the chief of state is a Paleo and a hunter, the initiatory combats and the feast of hunters are each year the two most important national celebrations in the Republic of the Gulf.

They take place in Tchaotchi, the president's native village, in the mountains and territory of the Naked people. These feasts take place one after the other for four weeks. For a month, the capital of the Republic of the Gulf has become depopulated and moved to your native village of Tchaotchi. The council of ministers meets in the offices of your residence; the ceremonies of accreditation of ambassadors take place in your salon, and official receptions are given in your garden. At four o'clock in the morning, you receive beneath your apatam the petitioners, favor seekers, and prebendaries. Those four weeks of feasting and rejoicing turn out to be your only time of leisure, the only vacation you take during the year. You wear leisure clothing during those weeks. And everyone—ministers, ambassadors, high officials, high-ranking officers—follows your example. They appear in shirtsleeves.

The months of feasting begin with the meeting of the hunters, the *dankun*. The *dankun* brings everyone together (you hunters and we, the hunters' griots), every year, with the first shiver of the good season.

Koyaga had undergone his hunter's training at Kati when he was in the school for military children in Kati. His roommate—he was called Birahima Niare and soon became Koyaga's inseparable friend—was a native of Kati. His father, Sakuna Niare, was a master hunter and the chief of the hunters in that city—the *donsoba* of the hunters in Kati, one of the most prestigious *donsoba* in the Niger Valley and the great land of the Mandingo. He was called the "father of orphans and the poor." He generously distributed the better part of game from the hunt to the needy. Sakuna was, like all great hunters, a divine, a characterologist, and a magician. When he was not hunting in the distant and merciless bush, he remained silent at the door of his hut all day long.

He watches Koyaga come in and go out of his courtyard twice, and he observes him. He counts his steps, studies his pace and his walk. In a flash, everything about the future of his son's young friend is revealed. His character, his destiny as a future hunter and exceptional dictator. He at once decides to make of him a neophyte hunter, one of his hunter apprentices.

Sakuna gave lessons on the terrain, the trails through the valleys, and on the mountains. He hunted far from Kati in the Niger Valley and in the hills of Koulouba. Koyaga and four other neophytes accompanied him on hunting parties, day and night on weekends. Through practice, Sakuna taught them the technique of the hunt, the rites, the myths, the ideology and the organization of the Mandingo and Senufo hunters' brotherhood, the *donsoton*.

The *donsoton* is, in fact, a freemasonry, a religion.

It was created in the time of the pharaohs by a mother, Saane, and her hunter son, Kontoron. Saane and Kontoron were Paleos. The brotherhood was established to resist oppression by rulers and to combat slavery. It preached equality and fraternity among all men of every race, social origin, caste, belief, and duty. For fifty centuries it had remained the way to rally all those who, under all regimes, said no two times: no to oppression and no to renunciation in the face of adversity.

The great myths of the brotherhood, the manes of Saane and Kontoron, the manes of some of the great hunters are always invoked, always present, always brought into meetings and rites. The members of the brotherhood are called the "children of Saane and Kontoron." They group into communities.

At the head of each community of hunters, there is a *donsokuntigi,* a chief who guarantees the observance of the laws and ethics of the brotherhood. He rules, surrounded by a council of old hunters, of former great hunters who have ceased all activity. The master hunters, or simple masters, have hunters assigned to them, *donsodenw,* who continue to be initiated into the technique of the hunter and the cult of Saane and Kontoron. Future postulants such as you were, Koyaga, are called *donsodege,* children who imitate the hunters. Certain members of the community, we who sing of the hunters' exploits, the bards, the griots of the hunters, are called *sèrè.* We are hierarchically associated with the great hunters, we are considered as great hunters, we are great hunters. We are the musicians and historians of the brotherhood. We organize the meetings, recount the deeds of those great hunters, both the living and the dead, during the gatherings. During these festivities, we sing of the deeds and the exploits of the hunter who enters into the dance circle; we sing and play, on the harp, the *kora,* the hymn of his rank and his category in the brotherhood.

For the younger hunters, the *Nyama tutu* is intoned, the song for the cocks of the pagoda. Sakuna taught Koyaga the tune and the words of the verses to this hymn:

> *Great cocks of the pagodas!*
> *Clear out, free the floor, the dance circle,*
> *Maleficent forces, evil people!*
> *Here are the young hunters who are gamboling and dancing.*

For the initiated hunters, members of the association, the *Bibi mansa,* the hymn of the royal eagle, is sung and played. Koyaga, you know the tune and the verses of this hymn:

> *Oh, eagle!*
> *Oh, royal eagle!*

You swoop down on your prey and never rise up
With empty claws.

For the great hunters, the *Don so baw ka dunun Kan* is intoned and played—the voice of the drum for the great hunters:

Oh, people of the area!
Do you hear this hymn?
Do you hear this hymn of the master of buffaloes?
Do you hear this hymn of the master of elephants?
Do you hear this hymn of the master of great hunters?

The *dyandyon,* which means strength of soul, sangfroid, is the hymn of valor, courage, bravery, temerity. It is sung and played for the hunter who has black game on his hunting tablet. That means he has killed at least one of the six large game animals that are called "black": the elephant, the hippopotamus, the buffalo, the lion, the horse antelope, or the hunter python.

Over time, the *dyandyon* has become the hymn of heroism in all circumstances for the Mandingo and Senufo peoples. It is sung for the heroes of all the epics. But it can only be danced by heroes whose exploits are well-known. Woe, woe to him who breaks that rule! It is danced with the steps of wild creatures. Every Paleo, Mandingo, and Senufo hunter knows the song of bravery:

Dance, listen to the dyandyon,
The hymn of heroes,
The hymn of misfortune.
It resounds when the hunter strikes ill,
Or when misfortune strikes the hunter.
It is the hymn of Kontoron and Saane.
It is not played for somebody
Because he may have a great fortune.
It is not played for somebody
Because he might be an all-powerful monarch.
It is danced by the killers of untamed wild creatures. It is danced
*   by the killers of those untamed wild creatures.*

The *dyandyon,* the hymn of courage, is not just a tune for hunters. It has been the hymn of great empires because the great emperors were heroic hunters. In our time, it still remains the hymn of great events, fortunate or unfortunate. It rings out to salute the exploits of heroes, their death, the arrival of catastrophes. The *dyandyon* is never a hymn of mere indulgence.

The initiation ritual made of Koyaga a member of the brotherhood, a child of Saane and Kontoron. His master insisted on the importance of the brotherhood for the peoples of the savanna in West Africa. Everything great and noble in the cultures of the Mandingo, Bambara, Mossi, Senegalese, Hausa, Songhai, and Senufo has been deposited by the brotherhood of hunters. Mandingo music, the divine music of the Mandingo, has its origins in the hunters' tunes. The art of the Mandingo and the Senufo, Dogon, Bambara is animal imagery—art that comes from the hunters. All the revolutions, the struggles for freedom in the world of the Bambara, Mandingo, and Senufo peoples of the savanna were initiated by the hunters.

Sakuna recommended that you organize and attend a celebration of the *dankun* at least once a year. And that is a recommendation you intend to respect all your life, Koyaga.

Koyaga, you have faults, great faults. You were, and you still are, authoritarian like a wild animal, as mendacious as an echo, as brutal as the lightning, as bloodthirsty as a lycaon, as much of an emasculator as the castrating priest, as much of a demagogue as a griot, as prevaricating as a louse, as libidinous as two ducks. You are . . . You are . . . You have so many other faults that to try to present them all, to lay them out one by one, even in great haste, would doubtless split my lips. So recites the responder *koroduwa* as he indulges in other gibes, bringing a smile to the lips of the person they appear to insult.

Koyaga, you have some great qualities, very great. You are generous like a she-goat's behind, a good son like a root, an early riser like the cock, as faithful as the fingers to the hand. You are . . . You are . . . You have so many other qualities and merits that to attempt to proclaim them would destroy the vocal cords. So replies Macledio, who smiles also.

But there is one thing constant, one truth about the character of master Koyaga, one thing in his bag of faults and qualities—and he proclaims this truth often, brags about it. If, on the day of the Resurrection, Allah, in his infinite mercy, orders him to define himself by one trait and to join one lone rank, he will unhesitatingly say he belongs to the brotherhood of hunters. You consider yourself first of all to be a hunter. Second, you are the son of your beloved mother, Nadjuma.

We have said that the code of the brotherhood of hunters confers the title of master hunter, with the right to dance the *dyandyon* (the music of bravery), to those hunters whose tablet marks at least one of the six black game animals. Koyaga's tablet shows 33 elephants, 21 hippopotamuses, 27 buffaloes, 17 lions, 38 black or solitary horse antelope, and 19 hunter pythons. So Koyaga has killed more than 155 black game animals. He has killed pilgrim sharks, bull sharks, and all the whales that have ventured into the waters of the Republic of the Gulf for thirty years. For thirty years, each time the wild animals of a certain canton in the inhospitable bush become killers or man-eaters, or impenitent ravagers of crops, the inhabitants do not hesitate. They immediately call upon Koyaga, the master hunter. You undoubtedly have the fullest and most diversified hunting tablet in Africa after the pharaoh Ramses II.

You are more than a *sinbo* (master hunter), you are a *donsoba* (mother and father of hunters). You have given to your native village a sacred wood and a *dankun* for hunters.

You have made a paradise and a refuge for animals in your village. A Mecca for hunters. You built an entire hotel to receive needy hunters. You have given your country the greatest hunting preserve in West Africa, the greatest animal park in the region.

It is true that you achieved this by your own methods, in your own way.

Brutally, inhumanly, and with great cruelty.

Over thousands of hectares, along the river, villages were razed. The farmers were expelled from their lands and forced to abandon the tombs of their ancestors, their sacred woods, and holy places. Without being moved by the least sigh of pity and without giving the least verbal sign of a possible compensation for the unfortunate people.

You protected the animals and instituted the management of the park and its animals. By the same drastic and inhumane methods, continues the *koroduwa*. Without warning, brigades of soldiers fired on and killed poachers. At dinnertime, patrols ran through the villages bordering the reserve. They rifled through their bags, their gourds, and examined the teeth of people eating. Those who were eating game animals were arrested, judged, and heavily sentenced on the spot. That is how your hunting ground and your reserve became one of the richest in game of the entire African savanna.

Hunters celebrate three ceremonies, of which the most important is the *dankun son* (sacrifices and offerings at the ritual crossroad), also called "offerings to the termitarium or to Kontoron." The ceremony simply repeats symbolically the rites of the construction of the first hunting altar and commemorates the birth of the brotherhood thanks to the mythical ancestors of the association. We repeat that the *dankun,* in the Republic of the Gulf, ranks as an official feast day. An important feast with festivities that extend over seven entire days throughout the mountains.

For three days, from daybreak to sunset, Koyaga's native village is shaken by salvos of rifle shots. They resound at the gates of the little city and announce the entrance of groups of hunters who have come to celebrate Koyaga's *dankun.*

The hunters come from neighboring villages, distant provinces, and from foreign countries. They come by all modes of transportation. On foot, on horseback, on bicycle, in public transport—buses and trucks —and by air. They arrive at any hour of the night and day, but they wait at the gates of the city patiently until daybreak or sunset to fire the salvos signaling their arrival and to enter the town. They are taken in hand and guided toward encampments of tents, toward the barracks or the schools. They take up very little room: they hang their slave rifles and belongings on stakes and spread their mats on the ground, in a space as narrow as a fly skin.

The meeting, the feast itself, properly speaking, goes on for three days, from Saturday to Monday. The real ceremonies take place on Sunday.

Saturday morning, beginning at ten o'clock, we *sèrè* take our places at the back of the stands on the square, and we sing and play the harp. The hunters parade by, dance and don the *duga kaman,* the wings of the vulture.

The wings of the vulture are barbecued or dried shoulders of all the game killed by the hunters during the month before the celebration of the *dankun* of grand master Koyaga. The hunters have brought their game bags. It is for that reason that groups of hunters stink like ten cadavers ten days old and are surrounded by swarms of huge black flies.

While the vulture's wings are distributed to various stands, we *sèrè* play and declaim the initiatory narratives of the hunt and the saga of master hunter Koyaga. The hunters dance and continue dancing the rest of the morning, all afternoon, and even until late at night.

Sunday morning, the members of the brotherhood swarm toward Koyaga's residence, all in costume and armed. Suits and headdresses of hunters, hunters' whistles, rifles, powder horns, flyswatters, knives, and sometimes great cutlasses on the belt or axes for hurling slung over the shoulder. Some have their dog on a leash. They fill the paths in the gardens of Koyaga's residence and spill out onto the terraces. We *sèrè* continue reciting our initiatory narratives and the saga of

Waiting for the Vote of the Wild Animals

Koyaga. We gather around our master *sèrè*, Djigiba Djire, the oldest and most talented of the hunters' bards of modern times. Upon his signal, we stop our music and the dancers stop. The short silence is broken by a solid salvo of more than seven hundred slave rifles. A great cloud of smoke rises and envelops the town as if all the huts were being consumed by fire at one time. The salvo salutes your appearance, the appearance of grand master Koyaga.

You come out of your villa and stand on the terrace. You are in your hunter's uniform, not the traditional hunter's uniform like those of the other men but a European hunter's uniform. The little plumed hat, the jacket, the telescopic rifle, the binoculars, the riding breeches and gaiters. You descend the stairway. Master *sèrè* Djire stands before you. You review the long honor guard of hunters who present arms as do soldiers.

At the garden gate, you wait for the great hunters, the great hunters who, like you, have the right to dance the *dyandyon,* the hymn of bravery. They welcome you and line up behind you. A very long procession is organized. A procession that stretches in a line into the heart of the immense crowd that has assembled from the entire country. At the head of the procession are you and Djire. You are followed by the dignitaries of the brotherhood, closely followed by their *sèrè,* and then by the columns of hunters. The hunters dance and swing their rifles. Long columns of hunters are broken here and there by squads of *sèrè.* The procession takes the hunters to the forest, the sacred wood of the hunters. Only hunters and their dogs can go in. When all have entered the wood, some long minutes of silence are observed before the singing and dancing begin again, more lively than ever.

At noon when the sun is at its zenith, the hunters line up. You and master Djire take your places at the head of the column and lead the hunters to the *dankun.* We *sèrè* chant and play until all the hunters have assembled around the sacred place, until each hunter has collected leafy tree branches and offered them to his master as a seat. That is because at the *dankun,* the sacred site, the code of the brotherhood requires every hunter to offer as a gesture of recognition a seat to his leader. We *sèrè* observe a moment of silence as everything falls into place. Koyaga alone advances toward the *dankun,* the sacred site, the termitarium at the crossroad. He advances because he is the sacrificial priest. After him come we *sèrè* and then the master hunters, their apprentices and former pupils. The members of the brotherhood are assembled in the forest. Around the sacred wood, on the plain, there is an immense crowd of curious onlookers.

Djire, the master *sèrè,* intones the *dyandyon* that is taken up in chorus. A young hunter, an apprentice, steps out and hands you a calabash, Koyaga. You take it in your two hands, chant some prayers, and spill the contents of honey and millet onto the peak of the termitarium-altar. Three other apprentice hunters lead a gazelle up, a gazelle captured that very day, and lay it down, holding its hooves and horns. You unsheathe your cutlass and slit the animal's throat. The blood spurts forth. The chorus of *sèrè* howl rather than chanting the *dyandyon*. You chant the prayer of the sacrifice in silence before the *dankun*.

> *Oh, ancestor Kontoron!*
> *Oh, ancestor Saane!*
> *Here are the libations of your hunter children.*
> *Take our gazelle, accept and approve it.*
> *We fete you, we drink of its blood,*
> *So that you will open the secret places across the extent of the*
> *bush,*
> *The totality of the infinite bush,*
> *So that you will gratify us with game, with game in quantity.*
> *We shall give some to the poor,*
> *To the orphans and the disabled,*
> *We shall offer it to our families, allies, and friends.*
> *Save us, preserve us from misfortune,*
> *From the fatal explosion of the chamber of our slave rifle.*
> *Save us, preserve our feet from evil wounds,*
> *The vicious lesions from logs.*
> *Save your children, protect them*
> *Against stings and the spittle of serpents,*
> *And from being crushed by pythons.*
> *Keep your children in the fraternity of the brotherhood,*
> *In the solidarity of union which is our authority.*
> *Let us encounter and vanquish black game*
> *In plenty.*
> *Let us come upon and kill white game*
> *In profusion.*
> *And as the second aim of this sacrifice,*
> *Oh, ancestor Kontoron,*
> *By means of the final position of the victim's hooves,*
> *Tell us without ambiguity what will be the game of this year,*
> *Much game, certainly,*
> *But also and above all grant long life and good health*
> *To all your hunter children.*

Let them keep the use of their legs
For many more seasons.

The prayers, chants, and music continue as long as the victim struggles against death, dragging on the ground, kicking out its hooves, and trying to shake its head. The *sèrè* stops and shouts with joy if the animal falls dead in its blood with its hooves in the air. An old master hunter peremptorily speaks:

"The positions of the sacrificed animal's hooves leave no ambiguity —our sacrifices have been accepted. Brother hunters, you will kill much game this year."

In answer, the earth and the forest suddenly tremble with thunder and a bitter cloud. The salvo from hundreds of hunters, their rifles loaded without bullets. A cloud of smoke envelops the entire valley. For long minutes, trees, men, and animals are lost in the fog.

The master hunters who are close to you, Koyaga, swarm around you and mutter:

"Thank you for your action. Thank you, great opener of the bush, thank you for your action."

Once calm has returned, another procession starts to be organized. It leads the hunters into the sacred forest. In the sacred wood where three concentric circles have been previously marked out. In the first circle there are the apprentice hunters, the neophyte hunters. In the second, the initiated members. At the center, in the heart of the forest, are the great master hunters, the *donsoba* seated about Koyaga.

A communion meal is shared by the brotherhood members belonging to each of the three groups. It is a meal cooked with the "vulture's wings," the dried or barbecued morsels brought by the hunters. The meal is copiously washed down with red wine, beer, and alcohol. It is shared in the joy and happiness of frank friendship and fraternity of the brotherhood.

Koyaga does not wait for the end of the meal; he disappears.

As soon as the sun begins to sink, a fourth procession takes the hunters to the public square. On the steps of the stands on the public square and between buildings, dense crowds, milling about impatiently, await the children of Kontoron. Songs and dances, interrupted from time to time by salvos, keep erupting on the public square and in the surrounding streets. Until dusk.

At daybreak, the hunters wind in a new procession, accompanied by a dense crowd, to Koyaga's residence. The dictator hunter makes a brief appearance that is saluted by a deafening salvo.

After dinner, the *sumu* begins, a *sumu* attended by numerous villagers, dignitaries, political figures, and soldiers of the country.

All night long, the celebrants sing, dance, and get drunk. The *sèrè* recite the praises of the association's mythical ancestors and Koyaga's own saga. All night long, dances and wild rounds follow one another, accompanied each time by dense volleys. Feasts, drinking bouts, and fervent speeches go on until the first crow of the roosters at four o'-clock in the morning.

At dawn, two military trucks arrive to transport about ten master hunters along with a few important dignitaries and invited guests of the master hunter. They join you, Koyaga, in the hunting preserve. That is the beginning of the *dankun* hunt.

The other hunters, the other hunters and the neophyte hunters together, their arms loaded with blanks, head for the plain, the large field for military maneuvers. The drummers and the *sèrè* chanters follow them. On the field, the pantomime of the *dankun* hunt is organized and performed.

In the woods, some novice hunters covered in animal skins have preceded them and hidden. The hunter who discovers them fires blanks from his rifle. The masks leap up and run full speed, stopping, whirling around, playing their roles as beasts, vicious beasts, flaying away at the aggressors with whips.

The young hunters, the young ones in particular, vie with one another in agility and mime. Before firing their blanks at the masks, they do little dance steps. The pantomime is carried out in an atmosphere of collective excitement that is accompanied by clouds of dust, the smell of powder, and cries of encouragement and admiration. The pantomime begins in the western part of the field for the games and finishes toward the east. Each hunter tries to grab one of the pelts with which the masked youth have covered themselves. Legend has it that the hunter who manages to steal a skin is certain to bring down a black game animal during the year.

At noon, on the public square, Koyaga and his guests present the game killed in the preserve. They offer game to the poor and to the widows of hunters. The hunters who participated in the pantomime present the skins they have removed. Presentations and distributions are followed by salvos. Dancing, feasting, and drinking continue the rest of the day. Until Tuesday morning at dawn.

Ah, Tiekura! Tchao, Koyaga's father, was an *evelema* (a champion of initiatory combat). His mother, Nadjuma, was an *evelema* (a champion of initiatory combat). Koyaga was a champion, many of the officers were *evelema,* the members of the presidential guard, the lycaons, were also *evelema.* All the close associates in whom Koyaga places his confidence are former *evelema.* The initiatory combats, the *evela,* the last celebrations of the good season, are the most important feast of the year; they are the only occasions more imposing and serious than the meetings of the hunters.

They are organized throughout the mountains of Paleo country. The combat competitions are organized at the village level in all villages inhabited by the men of the president's ethnic group. The village champions meet at the canton level; the best from the cantons meet at the seat of the subdivision; the subdivision champions fight at the seat of the circle; the best from the circles, less than one hundred and fifty, are summoned and meet at Koyaga's personal residence in his native village.

Stands are erected in front of the residence. In the stands, all the ministers, ambassadors, higher officers, top officials, and traditional chiefs from the entire country are assembled. Between the stands and surrounding the combat arena, the people crowd in with drums, dancers, and singers who howl as if possessed. To encourage their own champion, each community has brought its best dancers and sorcerers. All day, the champions engage in eliminatory combat before the president and all his guests. The thirty best fighters remain.

To ensure that those remaining are worthy champions, Koyaga, you yourself descend into the arena in costume and take on the five superchampions among the champions. To the applause and cries of admiration from the people and the dignitaries in the stands, you flatten one after the other in the twist of a wrist—you eliminate them. All the champions are polite enough not to resist you. You are the only undefeated champion on the field. Like your father, you are the best combatant.

For three days and three nights, you and some six old sorcerers of the country retreat with the thirty champions to caves in the mountains. Non-initiates know little about what you do during your retreat. Very little except that, for three days, you consume among you a great deal of dog meat and drink concoctions prepared by your mother and her marabout. The common consumption of the dog meat and the concoctions prepared by your mother, along with exercise, still in common, and other practices such as the blood pact may not be revealed in detail to non-initiates. The blood pact ensures, guarantees the champions' loyalty to your person. After the stay in the mountains, these champions are recruited and assigned to the corps of lycaons, the presidential guard. The best among them will become officers.

This is how the members of your personal guard are recruited. They are all great champions of combat. All have lived with you in the mountains for three entire nights and days. All have shared dog meat with you. Drunk with you the concoctions cooked by your mother. Mixed their blood with yours, and all have engaged with you in other practices that cannot be shared with non-initiates. Nothing to be said— they are loyal men, more devoted than dogs. They could not betray you.

The river always ends in the sea. Let us bring this fifth *sumu* to a close here. Explains the *sèrè*. The *koroduwa* erupts in his own manner—that is to say, with gibes, obscenities, and lascivious gestures.

Calm down, Tiekura, and let the listeners reflect on these proverbs.

The circling buzzard does not doubt that those who are below divine his intentions.

One does not forget the bush behind which one has hidden after firing at an elephant and hitting it.

The freshwater mangrove dances poorly because it has too many roots.

Sixth *Sumu*

"Everything has an end" will be the theme treated in the proverbs of this sixth *sumu*. Because:

There is not only a single day; the sun will also shine tomorrow.
If you can stand the smoke, you will be able to warm yourself over the coals.
A small hill brings you to the big one.

So announces Bingo, the *sèrè*.
He sings and plucks a few notes. The *koroduwa* responder, with unusual enthusiasm, goes wild.
Stop, stop, responder!

22

Ah, Tiekura, what did we not do to make the commemoration of the thirtieth anniversary a beautiful and fully successful feast?

For two full years, savings were put aside from the budgets of all holidays and all events. The funds reserved were credited to the thirtieth anniversary accounts that had been opened in the treasury and all the commercial banks in the country. Those accounts for the commemoration of the thirtieth anniversary of the assumption of power by the father-of-the-nation were, as numerous patriotic posters announced, referred to as the piggy banks of the entire nation and of the party. Public appeals had been made to businessmen, and public subscriptions were conducted in the schools, the post offices, the dispensaries, and at sports events. Schoolchildren had broken their piggy banks in order to send their savings to the father-of-the-nation so that he might have a fitting thirtieth anniversary. Prisoners had sacrificed meals for one day, officials, employees, and workers had given up a day's salary. All of these savings had been credited to the fund for the great feast of the thirtieth anniversary. Medals, pagnes, caps had been sold throughout the territory on all occasions. Private individuals had personally sent money orders to the president of the republic in order to participate in the collection of funds for the great feast of the century, the commemoration of the thirtieth anniversary. Never had such an important budget been created for a feast. The sums collected had to be significant. But nobody knew exactly the sum. Accounts for public subscriptions were rarely published in the Republic of the Gulf.

Six months before the date, the peasants of the least little hamlets, after hard days of labor, practiced marching in step for the parade of the thirtieth anniversary. Organizing committees for the great feast had been assembled within each canton and each prefecture.

The closer the date, the more tension and fever grew. The construction of viewing stands was accelerated; day and night, workers hammered on the gigantic stands all along the Marina (the Marina is the name given to the avenue along the seafront in the Republic of the Gulf). Soon, there remained only one week, and rail cars, convoys of trucks from all regions began to descend on the capital to unload the participants for the great parade.

Finally, the long-awaited morning arrived.

As for all feasts, the day began at four o'clock with collective ecumenical prayers over which you presided, Koyaga.

It was you, Macledio, you who were at the microphone offering commentary on the parade.

The sun rose over a Marina swarming with people. Peasants who had come from a great distance had piled in beneath tents erected as far as one could see on the beach. Other participants and curiosity seekers teemed in the downtown streets.

Seated in his command vehicle, Koyaga reviewed the troops and stopped in front of the reviewing stand. The chorale intoned a canticle.

And there is a sorcerer, in all of his sacrificial getup, coming up the middle of the boulevard on which the parade is assembling some distance away. He is pulling a billy goat by a cord and walks up to the foot of the reviewing stand. He stops. Assisted by a soldier, he makes the goat lie down between the stands and the command vehicle, on which Koyaga remains standing. He overpowers the beast. Then he turns toward the rising sun, waves his flyswatter, pronounces some ritual words, and leans over the struggling, bleating goat. He slits its throat. The blood spurts onto the tires of the command Jeep and the posts of the reviewing stand.

The decoration ceremonies could begin.

There were two: the ceremony during which some fifty decorations were presented to Koyaga, who, in the course of a long career, already had more than a hundred distinctions. He was standing. Standing in his marshal's uniform. Girls in white stood in two rows holding red baskets on which decorations had been stapled. Those who were awarding the decorations had come from all continents, from all countries, from all sorts of organizations. There were ambassadors or envoys from Kim Il Sung (North Korea), Nicolae Ceausescu (Romania), François Duvalier (Papa Doc of Haiti), General Augusto Pinochet (Chile), the Shah (Iran), Muammar Qadaffi (Libya), Mengistu Hailé Mariam (Ethiopia), and other saviors of this earth, each offering in turn another dithyramb on the merit of the Supreme Guide before hanging about his neck a brightly colored ribbon.

Then there were the prizes given by organizations in honor of his efforts for peace, the struggle against communism, the protection of life and the environment, international solidarity and cooperation: the Peace Prize (Pax Mundi) established by Dag Hammarskjøld, former secretary-general of the UN; the prize of Knight of Humanity given by the international White Cross; the prize from the Order of Malta, the sovereign order of Saint-Jean of Jerusalem; the prize of the Star of Asia from the International University for Complementary Medicine founded by the World Health Organization. There followed the Simba Prize for peace, given by the Simba Academy; the Man of Peace prize (a cross from the academy with a gold palm leaf) given by the Institute for Diplomatic Relations in Brussels; the International Prize for Progress, given by the Artefici del Lavano del Mondo Organization. Then there were prizes given by other organizations: the emblem of the international Gold Mercury; the grand collar of the Order of the Knights of Sinai; the Peace Trophy given by the International Institute of Private Law; the grand Prize of the Pléiade given by the Interparlementary Assembly for the French Language; the gold medal of European Excellence and the Statue of Fame of Mérignac given by the Committee for European Excellence; grand companion of peace of the Order Abdoulaye Mathurin Diop given by the Senegalese Association for the United Nations.

The sun is rising, and everybody who has been waiting to leave for two hours is getting restless. Koyaga understands and looks at his watch. They are already behind on the official program. The ceremony must be stopped. The representatives from small, insignificant organizations such as the Wives of the Blind or the Hunters of the Dekele Mountains and other leagues or international crosses can simply award their decorations during the dinner at the headquarters.

The second part of the awards ceremony begins. Accompanied by his military chief of staff and the grand chancellor, Koyaga swiftly presents himself before two rows of nearly two hundred people. There are calls for applause and calls for applause to cease. Between bugle calls, names and incredible exploits are called out and commented upon. There is a mother who is promoted to Knight of the Order of the Gulf for having denounced the husband with whom she had four children. Pretending to sleep, she overheard the subversive midnight conversation between her husband and his poker friends in the living room. There is that courageous peasant from the North who is becoming a Commander of the Order of the Gulf for having traveled eight hundred kilometers on foot to inform the president of a dream. The interpretation of that dream allowed the president's sorcerers and magicians to uncover a plot. There is the poet who received the rank of Knight of the National Order for having written and illustrated poems showing that Koyaga was clearly the envoy of God.

The awards ceremony, despite the solid commentaries and additions of Macledio, does not seem to interest the audience anymore. A muffled but increasing wave of sound is evidence of that. Koyaga understands. The ceremony is brought to a close. It will take place at the dinner for the high-ranking officers, after the public ball and the torchlight retreat.

A hubbub runs through the tremendous crowd stretching for more than five kilometers along the Marina. There are significant bursts of laughter: everybody laughs and applauds. By the minute, the hubbub draws closer to the reviewing stand. Finally, groups of children emerge and draw closer.

At the head of the troop, you can read on a sign, "Koyaga and his government." Bursting out laughing, Macledio comments on this. Parades always begin with children—boys and girls, all under twelve years old. They are all Koyaga's children, his own blood children, both legitimate and bastards. There are sixty-six of them. This is a pantomime of the regime, of power. The oldest boy among the participants opens the parade—he is twelve years old. He is tightly fitted into his marshal's uniform, cut to measure and copied exactly from that worn by his father, Koyaga, the Supreme Guide. His chest is bedecked with a row of medals made of chocolate. With talent and humor, he mimics the gestures of the dictator and even draws amused smiles from the dictator himself.

He is followed by a group of sixteen children—boys and girls—representing the sixteen ministers. Each child in the group imitates a minister to perfection, in both gesture and habit. For months, each child has studied and practiced the roles. The Council of Ministers—this is what the announcer calls the group of sixteen children—is followed by the team miming the officials of the executive council of the political bureau.

Following the political bureau comes the troop imitating the religious officials. A boy with a miter, a crosier, a short alb, and a large pectoral cross, sandals, and gloves is marching with one of his brothers in a beribboned burnoose on his right, and another covered with kaolin and bearing a fetish on his left. The mimes of religious officials are accompanied by girls miming nuns and Vodu fetishists.

Every category, class, and important organization of the country and the regime is represented, mimed by a troop of children.

Macledio describes and comments on the pantomime. He tells the significance and the importance of each scene. The first part of the pantomime is a small imitation of the parade's beginning; each group of children represents one of the important elements of the great parade of the thirtieth anniversary that is to follow. The pantomime is at once humorous, critical, and cathartic. It is not true that the regime tolerates no criticism or caricature. In what other regime could we see the chief of state's children publicly mimicking their own father, his power, and the entire country?

The abruptness, violence, and intensity of the bellowing, raucous cries, barking, and howls provokes a tremor of fright all along the Marina. The crowd holds its breath and wonders. The rhythm of the music for the parade quiets down and continues softly. The announcer at the microphone lowers his tone. One can barely hear him state that the wild animal cries are to announce the commandos of the presidential guard.

Koyaga rises and comes to attention. Everybody on the presidential reviewing stand follows his example. The Supreme Guide gives a signal, courteously inviting everyone to be seated once more. This is directed at the guests on the presidential stand, to those who have been summoned, to curiosity seekers, and to people in the other stands. The parade will be lengthy. Nobody knows how long it will last. Koyaga, you want to spare people a long and painful time standing. You alone will remain standing during the entire parade—you consider that the least of polite gestures you owe the citizens who have come from throughout the country to pay homage to you.

First, there is a pack of stocky, muscular fellows (quite naked except for the cords of their cache-sexe passing between their buttocks) smeared with white and red kaolin, bristling with heteroclite weapons, both primitive and modern: bows, quivers, daggers, and Kalashnikovs.

They trot along and nose about like packs of wild dogs on the track of a band of game animals. These are the members of the presidential guard, the ones who shared dog meat and mixed their blood with that of the Supreme Guide. They are called the Supreme Guide's lycaons or wild dogs. They have sworn to give their lives for the Supreme Guide, and they are always ready to sacrifice themselves for the Supreme Guide.

Macledio announces, in words that are at once mysterious and enthusiastic, the facts about the lycaons' attachment to the president. At night, they hide in trenches dug in the brush surrounding the president's residence. It sometimes happens that the lycaons refuse the rations served them for several days, and to harden themselves they eat only raw food: the meat and blood of the wild animals they kill and the green fruit they gather. Nobody knows their hideouts. One night, three careless plotters ventured up to the foot of the walls around the presidential residence. They ran into the lycaons: their throats were slit and they were hacked to pieces. It was only after some long *sumu*— and the personal intervention of the president—that the limbs, heads, and others parts of the victims were returned, sorted, and placed in coffins for burial. One of the lycaons whose own brother had participated in an assassination attempt against the president felt that his family was completely dishonored, and he decided to kill his entire family. With his own hands, the lycaon killed his brother, the wives, and all the children of the traitor, and then committed suicide.

Following the platoon of lycaons came the parachute commandos with modern uniform and equipment. They have great beards and the walk of wild animals. They chant in loud, strong voices. The music stops so they can be heard everywhere. They too are attached to the person of the president, and many of them have sacrificed themselves on different occasions to save the president—and they are all ready to do the same. They say so in their song. They have no father or mother except the Supreme Guide. They have no fetishes or prayers except from Koyaga.

Afterward there come the commandos of regiments from different corps, one following the other endlessly. Infantry, artillery, cavalry, engineers, sailors, aviators. There are all types of modern armaments. The Republic of the Gulf is an arms depot, an arsenal. The Supreme Guide is quite proud of his army's parade.

For an hour and a half, going on two hours, you remain standing like a pillar with your right hand glued to your ear. On the reviewing stand, many of your guests and your neighbors have lost interest in the procession of the arms of death on the Marina and have their eyes riveted on your hands and your trousers. They want to discern the least quivering of your legs, the slightest sign of fatigue in your bearing, a little distraction in your eyes. In vain, you remain like a rock!

The engines of war, of death keep passing endlessly.

"You have spent too much money on armaments, much more for defense than for health and education combined."

"That's false—spiteful journalists and liars are circulating those false reports." Replies Macledio.

Then, a fashion parade. . . . What followed resembled a great fashion parade of traditional costumes! Nearly one hundred young women passed in three rows, all elegantly dressed. They are singing. Each one is wearing the traditional dress of her own region. These are the heroines of revolution and authenticity. In his commentaries, the announcer explains that the heroines of authenticity are women who, by their heroic positive action, have demonstrated their attachment to the president, to the country, and to the revolution of authenticity. They are the women who will make of our country, one day, the Switzerland of Africa, a developed country in which security reigns.

"You knew it full well, but you are not saying it, Macledio. These heroines of the revolution and authenticity are simply the president's former mistresses, the young women on whom he has bestowed children. Some of them were offered to him by village chiefs in order to ally themselves with the Supreme Guide and to have a child of the father-of-the-nation in their village. These young women remain spies, intelligence agents for the regime."

"It's more than that. They are also heroines of the revolution of authenticity, important tradeswomen, important cultivators, great militants of the single party. Respectable wives, proper and hardworking mothers. Not all of them have slept in the president's bed." Replies Macledio.

There follows a heteroclite group of women and men. About fifty of them. They are strangely dressed and equipped—they march with exaggerated gestures, calling out prayers and evocations. These are the fetishists and sorcerers who work in the cantons and villages for the security of the president, for the protection and good fortune of the country.

Macledio comments on this. None of the sorcerers and fetishists sleep at night. From sunset to the first crow of the roosters, they engage in nocturnal combat against evil spirits and all the spells that impede the president's action. Evil sorcerers do not have time to act; they are systematically discovered and denounced as soon as an evil spirit takes hold of them.

A wave of white horses extends for some two hundred meters. Rows of women and men are progressing in silence and in a laborious manner as they lean on long staffs. A banner is displayed in front of them saying, "The wise who bless the Supreme Guide." Macledio explains why those who attempt to take Koyaga's life are wasting their time and their means. Why they will always fail and will never encounter anything other than misfortune and maledictions. Bokano and his secret Qur'an are not alone in protecting our president. It is not only Mama Nadjuma and her meteorite who save him. There is a rampart of blessing about him, thousands of old men and women who implore Allah for him every night. There are as many protective spirits, charms, words, and invocations as there are older people. They invoke the manes of the ancestors, and the manes of the ancestors will always be there to annihilate the evil intentions of plotters.

The parade continues, passing for four hours, five hours. The implacable sun, the stifling heat are relentless. Everybody is hungry and thirsty. Everyone wonders when this flood of men and women will cease flowing. None of your guests on the reviewing stand is keeping track of what is happening on the Marina. They are all looking at you, Koyaga, and you know it. You are the sole spectacle. You and the display of medals on your breast. Your left arm straight at your side, your left fingers on the seam of your trousers, and your right hand glued to your right ear. You are erect like a palmyra palm on the plain, unshaken by any wind.

You love being the object of all glances. That flatters your ego. You prepared for the parade, you drugged yourself. At breakfast, you took more than your usual cup of coffee; you stuffed yourself with meat *futu* and two gourds full of *bisap*. You want to show everybody—all your guests and your people—that you are still a rifleman.

Here come the delegations from the provinces, all the provinces, one after another. The authorities are at the head of each platoon. Then come the schoolchildren and students from secondary schools and institutes, young people and dancers from associations, the militants of cells from the single party, the monitors of shock groups, farmers, craftsmen, forest rangers, fishermen, and initiates from the sacred woods. Each group is announced by a sign. The craftsmen and farmers exhibit samples of their work and harvest. Macledio comments on everything. It is three o'clock in the afternoon; for eight hours, the flood continues uninterrupted. Officials, guests, curiosity seekers, everyone has had enough. Inwardly, each person was thinking that natural functions were going to get the better of you, force you to move, to tremble, to turn around, to give a sign, to give orders. A person can resist hunger and thirst for hours and hours, but one can never avoid taking care of certain natural functions. Once again, they were all mistaken about your character! In his commentary, Macledio imperturbably notes that the parade is not yet half over.

At that announcement, expressions of discouragement and exasperation break out. Loud exclamations erupt from many breasts, and the muted clamor waves along the Marina. You feign ignorance, hearing nothing. You are ever tall and motionless like the palmyra palm, silent as a rock, a wild animal on the alert. . . .

Fortunately, at that very moment, an incident happens that liberates everybody.

The dancers, drummers, and groups before the reviewing stand perform several minutes for the Supreme Guide. In that brief show, the performers demonstrate their talent. They have come from afar for this performance and have been waiting since four o'clock in the morning, for twelve long hours.

The *pokti* is an athletic war dance that is performed with sabers and tam-tam. The *pokti* is being performed for the dictator in front of the stand. The leader of the troupe has launched into a one-man show that is as thrilling as it is stormy: it is spectacular. A sharpened saber slides and fans over the dancer's back and belly without nicking him. By turn, he flattens himself on the ground and rolls as he brandishes the saber with diabolical skill. He throws the saber to a partner, bends forward, and walks on his hands as he rolls the tam-tam with his toes. He stands up and the partner throws the saber back to him. He catches it, jumps high, very high, and finishes his number with a movement that consists in waving the saber between his legs. But, instead of the usual landing on his feet—oh, misfortune!—he collapses like a sliced vine and falls stone dead. Stone dead—oh, irony!—in his multicolored warrior's costume, right in the middle of the pavement on the Marina. There is consternation on the stand, cries and sighs of indignation and protest.

The state minister, the only person in the country who would dare commit such an act, draws close to you and notes that the parade has been going on for eight hours. . . .

Only then do you unglue your fingers from your ear, raise your arm, and look at your watch. It is four o'clock in the afternoon. You give a signal and the parade pauses, but it only pauses. Delegations from some ten provinces have not yet been able to pass in review, and you consider it your duty, required by etiquette, to see everybody who has come from far away to participate in the commemoration of the thirtieth anniversary of your assumption of power. The next day, the parade resumes at ten o'clock at the headquarters camp.

For four hours, you remained standing with your fingers glued to your ear to watch the remaining delegations parade on the pavement of the Marina.

Let us imitate those who pound the millet. From time to time, they stop pounding in order to take a breath and empty the mortar. Let us also pause in our narration to take a break. Explains the *sèrè*.

He sings and plays his *kora*. His responder *koroduwa* lets fly gibes that are as crude as they are interminable. His master offers the following proverbs on the theme of precariousness:

He who lives a long life sees the dove dance.
Fate blows without benefit of the blacksmith's bellows.
The cow that stays still for a long time leaves with a dart.

23

Ah, Tiekura! The feast of the thirtieth anniversary was too beautiful. After such an interminable parade, the officials and employees of businesses and of the government decided that they were tired, and they did not go to their offices and workshops the following day. In the fields and villages, they took off for two weeks. Everybody forgot about their work until the end of the month, payday. A surprise awaited them. They did not believe their ears when the financial directors announced, "No money to pay salaries."

The union representatives become angry and go directly to the president's office. The president of the republic receives them during his public office hours, at four o'clock in the morning, listens to them, and immediately summons the president–director general of the Agricultural Marketing Board. The duties of this organization were to regularize and stabilize prices for raw materials. But, as in all African countries, the reserves of the board are a kitty that the president uses at his own discretion; that allows him to resolve minor problems of cash flow.

The director of the board comes in with the face of a nanny goat's behind that has been irritated and worn out by the bearded muzzle of a billy goat and speaks to you politely, Koyaga.

"The prices of cotton, coffee, and cocoa beans have fallen on the international market. Drought is ravaging the fields, valleys, and mountains. The board has spent a great deal to maintain prices. The remaining funds were drained to finance the ceremonies for the thirtieth anniversary. The board can no longer advance funds to the public treasury or to state enterprises and societies."

No one has ever used such talk with you. You did not believe it, and you understood only after he showed you the latest accounts. Everything was in the red, everybody was deeply in debt!

Immediately, you organize a hunting party for the French ambassador, and you wait for him to bring down a horse antelope before you mention your preoccupations to him. His reply astonishes you. In roundabout terms, he gives you an explanation.

During the meeting of French and African heads of state, at La Baule, the president of the Republic of France, President Mitterand, recommended that African heads of state change policies and cease being dictators in order to become angelic democrats. France used this enjoinder as a pretext and a date to stop the automatic emoluments for officials in the employ of francophone dictatorships where the treasuries had ceased making loan repayments. France requires that each dictator sign beforehand a SAP contract with the IMF.

What is the SAP (Structural Adjustment Program)? The president immediately summons the resident representative of the IMF (International Monetary Fund) and asks the question. But the banker-diplomat, instead of replying simply to such a lucid question with an explanation of the expression, pulls a thick dossier from his briefcase with great deliberation. Without raising his eyes, he leafs through it and begins to comment on the endless table in a manner so embroiled that it could give you colic. You have to cease and stop everything, interrupt or suspend all operations, reduce or trim away everything, renounce or sacrifice everything, close or suspend everything. You can no longer fund feasts and dances. You must reduce the number of teachers, nurses, women giving birth, children being born, schools, gendarmes, and presidential guards. Stop subsidizing rice, sugar, milk for nurslings, cotton and compresses for the wounded, pills for lepers and those with the sleeping sickness. Sacrifice the construction of schools, roads, bridges, dams, maternity wards and dispensaries, palaces and prefectures. Avoid helping the blind and deaf, paying for paper, drilling wells, consuming butter and cocoa. Reduce the number of people employed, close enterprises, etc.

"Stop that litany and get out! Quickly, or I'll break your neck, strangle you!" you yelled.

The diplomat gives a start, rises, and hurriedly leaves the office, forgetting his dossier on the table. He leaves with his tail between his legs, like a dog surprised in the process of stealing *sumahara*. Continually looking back, he scurries down the stairs, runs to his car, disappears into it.

But no insult or affront is going to stop the sun from setting. There was no money, salaries were not paid.

Requisite mediation and apologies allow negotiations with the banker-diplomat from the IMF to resume. After many sleepless nights and interminable talks, a minimal agreement is reached.

The secretary-general of the sole union participated in the negotiations, approved the drastic measures, and attended the signing of the SAP.

Up to this point, things in the Republic of the Gulf had been bipolar and quite clear; everything was discussed, organized, and played out between two partners. Power was authoritarian and the people submissive. At the top, you were the arrogant dictator with your army, your party, your chiefs, your intelligence agents. At the bottom were the patient, mute peasants, blinded by their beliefs, their misery. The disdainful dictator, a bloody emasculator, had declared himself anticommunist and had the West as a protector. The people had only lying and loquacious politicians, lying priests, marabouts, and fetishists as their allies.

It is that half-century-old partnership that ended with the entry of a third dancer into the circle. Let us bow very low before this third player, this intruder—a *sèrè* speaks of a hero only after having paid him great homage. We salute you, the new birds in the stormy skies of the Republic of the Gulf! We salute you who are of that race that can be killed without being reduced or suppressed!

This third partner has several names: lost youth, the regiment of the dropouts, loafers, pickpockets, and thieves. Koyaga, in one of your frightening and hateful speeches, you spoke of them as *bilakoro* ruffians, addicts, and homosexuals. We shall call them the *bilakoro*, the dropouts or the rock throwers.

What gave birth to them and tossed them into the streets and the marketplaces?

As soon as you took power, your white advisors inculcated in you the thought that the welfare of the fuzzy heads must be sought in literacy programs for the masses. They endlessly repeated to you that an educated people is a developed people. You believed them. That was more than an error, it was a mistake. You could not conceive that the forest of trees you were planting with your schooling would yield the wild animals that would bring you down.

From the first days of your reign, you had elementary schools built in all the villages and camps. Pupils abounded in the classrooms, were famished day and night, miserable in their homes and with their teachers, with no values, were often incompetent, lying, and slothful. Many children could not continue to the level of the *certificat d'études.* They left the schools but refused to return to the fields—we have to recognize that work in the African fields is among the most laborious and least profitable of human activities. They spread out into the markets and village streets, became the first truants, and made up the first gangs, the first birds taking flight.

A number of those who managed to get the *certificat d'études* found neither a position in the schools nor a job as a courier in public administration. Lacking any interest in hearing anything about a machete, *daba,* or fishing net, they joined their comrades in the marketplaces and streets.

Then came the crisis and the reduced budgets. A number of individuals with certificates found no place in secondary schools nor any clerical jobs in the public sector. They joined the truants in the markets and the streets.

Pupils with their secondary diplomas had no practical training, and the public sector organized no examinations for teachers and clerks; they were obliged or forced to take the route of the markets and the streets.

People with university diplomas and master's degrees got no scholarships to study abroad. Neither the École Nationale d'Administration nor the École Normale Supérieure offered an entrance examination. And since their parents could not continue to support them, the university students went out into the markets and the streets to swell the ranks of the truants.

The crisis got worse. At the last moment, all the young workers laid off through reductions of personnel, closings, and the restructuring of enterprises came to swell the ranks of unemployed school and university students. When the hour to jump from dictatorship to democracy came, this is the heteroclite group of people, hardened through trials, injustice, and lies, who took in hand the destiny of the Republic of the Gulf and all of ancient Africa, the cradle of humanity.

The dropouts are the needy, ready for anything, ready to do anything. Without morals or principles. At first, along with the unemployed youth, they had been at the service of the single party. They were the ones who chanted the praises of the father-of-the-nation and who carried out all the vile tasks of your tyrannical regime. They are the ones helping drivers park and then guarding their cars. They are the ones selling knickknacks at the red lights. They are the pickpockets in the markets and the buses. They are the ones who take aim and assassinate people.

When the first winds of democracy began to blow, they left their usual activities to join the revolution, hasten the fall of the dictatorship, and welcome democracy.

When political tracts came from nowhere and littered the sidewalks, when walls were covered with graffiti, there were clashes between these idle scholars and the forces of order. Our streets and markets became permanent spectacles with skirmishes and brawls.

The presidential guard changed duties and assumed a new mission. A mission for which it was not prepared. With arms strapped over their shoulders and buckets of paint in their hands, the fierce paratrooper commandos and the president's lycaons began whitewashing the walls to make the graffiti and insulting slogans disappear. As soon as they turned their backs, the idle scholars rushed to the walls with their fresh paint, markers in hand. There were high-speed pursuits in which the soldiers were quickly shaken off. High-speed pursuits with shouts and insults. All of that beneath the unbearable African sun and in the midst of bursts of laughter and spontaneous applause.

Then the idle scholars appeared on street corners, at market displays, and at the doors of shops, loaded with photocopies of tracts and forbidden publications, and began to sell them right under the noses of the police and the gendarmes. With clubs in hand, the furious police pursued and tried to arrest them, but only made themselves ridiculous in races they always lost. When one policeman was out of breath, three other idle scholars appeared from nowhere to taunt him.

At the entrances and in the halls of the Ministry of the Interior, there was another gathering, another to-do, another spectacle. People requesting authorization to create new parties, new unions, new publications were crowding and shoving each other. With loud whistling, the police tried in vain to make them line up and wait patiently.

In the National Assembly, an urgent special session is going on. The deputies are arguing day and night, carrying on an incredible rear-guard action. As with all African dictatorships, Koyaga had his own National Assembly. All the deputies came from his single party. Koyaga himself had had them elected—they had been chosen before being confirmed by popular balloting. They were old men, traditional old chiefs, friends whom Koyaga wanted to honor or for whom he had wanted to ensure revenues, caciques of the single party.

This extraordinary, special, and urgent session of the National Assembly had been called in order to examine bills on the multiparty and multiunion system. The session had been going without interruption for two weeks.

The first days of the session had been particularly deadly, suicidal, tragic. A multiparty, multiunion system spelled the end of the country for many deputies. Two of them died of a heart attack, two went insane, and two others committed suicide. For patriotic reasons. Autopsy reports by the coroners were clear: none of the suicide victims had been emasculated. The doctors had found their virile parts whole and in place.

As if all this misfortune and disorder were not enough, there were other strange phenomena: public rumors, disinformation, settling of accounts, and vendettas.

The idle scholars were making a living by selling photocopies of tracts. They spent entire days playing hide-and-seek with the police in order to deliver and distribute their tracts. When there were not enough tracts, the idle scholars began producing the tracts themselves to continue their daily games with the police.

Their tracts related the wildest stories. They were reproduced and commented upon by other publications, newspapers, and bulletins. The reprinting of the tracts in newspapers gave them credibility—made them into truth, reality.

The Blacks are an illiterate people. It was the colonialists, the priests, and the marabouts who taught them to read. These instructors inculcated in them a respect of whatever is written; paper became a fetish, a belief. A belief which, for the texts of holy writings and orders from the white colonizers, surpassed the Blacks' understanding and could neither be verified nor contradicted.

Thus, for the people, the wildest fantasies and gossip, the most hateful defamations that were printed and circulated, became believable. And the general disorder resulted in a situation where those who were insulted, defamed, discredited, and vilified had no way to contradict what was written, to defend or to justify themselves. They could not go to court. The police, their chiefs, the judges, and the ministers were all paralyzed and silent because they too were besmirched, defamed, and discredited every day.

Everybody became a dispenser of justice. The settling of accounts and vendettas grew more numerous. Those responsible for publications were attacked in the street. Those who were defamed and the journalists fought with each other in public places. At night, print shops and newspaper offices were bombed and burned.

You, Koyaga, carefully selected all the tracts demanding that foreign property be nationalized and presented them to the ambassadors of France, the United States, and the United Kingdom. These tracts were the incontrovertible proof that the idle scholars were in the service of international communism. This disorder had been initiated to push the Republic of the Gulf into the communist camp.

This was a useless gesture: there was no reaction, not a single echo. The cold war was dead, finished. The ambassadors did nothing more than remind you of that. As for Ramses II, Alexander the Great, and Sundyata, all regimes disappear. The Berlin Wall had fallen along with the communist world. The cold war had disappeared.

Discussions with the representatives of the IMF are dragging on, back salaries are mounting. The representatives of the sole union demand a meeting with you. You receive them. They tell you that a general strike of all workers is in the works. You must forestall that strike by paying all the back salaries. You are forced to give in to the demands of the IMF in order to get them to release the first block of funds.

The first measures required by the IMF for restructuring state enterprises are put into action. The first early retirements are decided for the railroads. This affected many railroad men, including Dalmeda.

Dalmeda was a well-known person in the country. His father, one of his uncles, and one of his brothers had been involved in several plots. They had been killed and emasculated. He had been imprisoned himself before receiving your pardon. Dalmeda had presented a request for the creation of an independent union. While waiting for the granting of the request, the independent union had set up a provisional bureau and named Dalmeda as its temporary secretary-general. In addition to the secretary-general, six other members of the provisional bureau were invited to request early retirement.

The railroad men considered these measures to be a veritable provocation and decided to prevent their being carried out. They voted to strike and to occupy the offices and workshops.

The idle scholars came to join the picketing strikers in order to prevent nonstrikers from entering the workshops and offices. Police, gendarmes, and soldiers intervened to preserve the right to work.

All morning, there were clashes and skirmishes between the forces of order, strikers, and idle scholars. There was general confusion. Idle scholars hurled stones, pillaged, burned, destroyed. The forces of order intervened by firing into the air, at first. But some gendarmes were wounded and killed. To extricate themselves, the forces of order began using real bullets.

That afternoon, the railway station and offices were in flames, and clouds of acrid smoke spread over the city. There were twenty-one dead: three policemen, one gendarme, ten railroad workers, and seven idle scholars.

It was a Tuesday, the tenth of October.

All Tuesday night, the idle scholars held a wake for their dead at Trade Union Center and the student residence. In defiance of the curfew. The forces of order had not dared oppose this wake; there had already been too many fatalities. Many idle scholars, soldiers, policemen, and gendarmes had died. The international press had given a great deal of coverage to these events. The whole world was shocked by the brutality and the massacre. They had to stop shedding the blood of the youth. To avoid new confrontations, the forces of order did not attack the wakes and did not try to scatter those people participating in them. They allowed friends and relatives to pray, sing, and dance for the dead.

At dawn, at the first calls of the muezzins, the demonstrators stopped the wakes, slipped away from the shops, broke up, and scattered into neighborhoods across the entire city. Each group knew its post, its mission, and its objectives.

As soon as the sun rose, the idle scholars returned to the attack, went into action. Fires arose in the four corners of the city, smoke rose and darkened the sky. There was the popping of grenades and rifle shots, like the previous night. The pillaging began once more, the ransacking of shops and public establishments, and the property of well-known people of the regime.

The idle scholars worked in gangs, like driver ants or termites. They swarm into a house from all angles and all openings at once—doors, windows, roofs. Everything that has not been consumed by the flames is immediately picked up and taken away. Everything, even electric wires, tiles, and bricks—everything is sold, traded on the spot. Clothes, electrical appliances, jewels, radios go from hand to hand on the spot. The forces of order disband the crowds with tear-gas grenades and fire real bullets at the pillagers, destroyers, arsonists. The demonstrators reply with salvos of rocks, bricks, arrows, and pitiful hunting rifles. Despite many fatalities, the idle scholars disband only to regroup in another spot. They are numerous, intrepid, drunk, drugged. The soldiers and the police cannot be everywhere at once. The progress of armored vehicles and tanks through the main arteries is slowed and hindered by barricades, hastily constructed but courageously defended. Burning tires cover the entire city with a blanket of thick, acrid smoke. It is impossible to see farther than ten meters. Similar scenes of pillaging, arson, killings take place in different sections of the capital all morning. Only toward two o'clock in the afternoon does a precarious calm fall over the city. The idle scholars leave their hiding places with their dead comrades over their shoulders. They pray as they carry the bodies to the embassies of France and the United States, lay them out in the gardens and adjacent streets.

Koyaga has been badgering the representatives of the great Western countries for two days. Koyaga solicits their assistance and their understanding in vain. He threatens to change camps, to become a Red, to have Cubans, continental Chinese, and Pyongyang Koreans come to Africa if the West does not come to his aid. The diplomats quietly ask him to stop the massacres and to propose a dialogue with the opposing demonstrators. The cold war is dead, really finished. The ambassadors simply remind you of that. As with Ramses II, Alexander the Great, and Sundyata, all regimes eventually disappear. The Berlin Wall fell just as did the communist world. The cold war has disappeared.

Koyaga decides to calm ruffled spirits—a gamble.

You asked your National Assembly to meet. The deputies had been chased from their luxurious villas and been deprived of their property. Their residences had been ransacked and the stolen goods sold, piece by piece. They had escaped with their lives only by taking refuge in the military post or at the presidential palace. The forces of order had picked them up one by one and taken them in armored vehicles, with a good escort, to the National Assembly. The president of the assembly managed to establish a quorum qualified to call an exceptionally extraordinary session.

Waiting for the Vote of the Wild Animals

All the bills that had been delayed for months in the assembly offices were hurriedly approved.

The constitution was modified. Laws instituting multiparty and multiunion systems were adopted. A law proclaiming general amnesty was approved by acclamation. The amnesty was extended to all condemned and exiled politicians.

Approvals for all publications, permits, and permission to print were granted.

These important measures are insufficient to satisfy the demonstrators and the idle scholars. They have other claims and demand other measures. The idle scholars, the union workers, and the political opponents form a League for the Coordination of Democratic Forces. The representatives of this new organization are driven to the palace. Discussions with the president begin to take place. Religious authorities serve as mediators. An agreement is reached to dissolve the National Assembly and to call for a national conference.

Islam is a religion born in the heat and the sand of the desert; Islam is the faith of men and women of the desert. It makes the faithful dream of paradise, a celestial dwelling, and the eternal kingdom; it makes the elect, those saved, and those thirsting in the desert seek salvation, hope. Islam's morality and ethics are virtues for nomads of the desert. For the Muslim, the supreme good and the greatest love require feeding and offering drinking water to one's neighbor. The Qur'an says this many times. The marabout Bokano, who titled himself the slave of the Qur'an, would have provided all human beings and animals in the universe with water if he had the means. He had had public fountains constructed in the streets and neighborhoods of the cities. He paid for the water consumed and the upkeep of the fountains. In many villages and camps, he had wells drilled, provided them with pumps, and paid for the maintenance of this equipment. Providing drinking water to humanity was his great charity, the most important of his works.

Nadjuma, Koyaga's mama, had conceived and given birth only once. Her labor brought her atrocious pain. She had terrible memories of it. For her, maternity was the worst of torture. God had willed and inflicted on woman a paroxysm of pain. Nadjuma dedicated the majority of her time and fortune to helping pregnant women and maintaining hundreds of maternity centers. If the resources were available, she would have covered the entire universe with maternity centers supplied with skilled midwives. This was her great charitable work.

The destructive fury of the idle scholars, during the skirmishes, had been directed at the police stations and certain public establishments, but especially against Mama's maternity centers and Bokano's fountains. The *bilakoro* (the idle scholars) arrived at a center, went into it, and removed the beds with the mothers and babies in them. They pillaged the establishments before setting fire to them. The fountains were systematically ransacked and destroyed. The *bilakoro* were not the only ones crazed with a spirit of vandalism and annihilation. The scholars lashed out at their school benches, their blackboards, their classrooms, and their teachers. Libidinous lepers raped the nuns caring for them.

You signed an agreement calling for a national conference in spite of yourself and with the conviction that you would never be forced to put it into action. You are a hunter, and you know the virtues of patience. The one who can stand the smoke definitely has the pleasure of warming himself by the coals. You want to let the situation deteriorate, and you know that the elephant does not decompose in one day. Unfortunately, one event was going to upset everything.

It was on the fifth of July that the terrible accident happened.

During the days of the insurrections, the idle scholars had been able to enter the imposing amphitheater of the single party and had taken over a large part of the establishment. They had made this their meeting place, the headquarters of their movement, the headquarters for the Convention of Living and Democratic Forces. The party building was covered with banners and graffiti. The forces of order had ended up tolerating this wildcat occupation. All the tracts and defamatory papers were being produced and run off in the party building. Following the *bilakoro,* the idle scholars, like flies swarming behind the boa, trailed all the street children who habitually sleep in the open in the halls and spaces in front of business establishments and market stalls. Several hundred idle scholars and all the street children, most of them under twelve years old, were sleeping, eating, and living in the party building. The building was a veritable beehive.

It was this beehive that was eaten by flames on the fifth of July during the night. What was the exact number of victims? It will never be known. No one had a roster of the children and young people living in the establishment. The international press was to publish reports on the criminal fire, reports with heartrending photographs that were to provoke the indignation of the entire world. The charred bodies of children in a fetal position by the hundreds. Hundreds of other burned and injured people.

The idle scholars did not wait for these reports. Starting at five o'clock in the morning, the insurrection erupted and inflamed the entire city. The *bilakoro* pillaged, burned, ransacked, and plundered in their anger. The forces of order attacked them, dispersed them, and made them flee. With grenades and live ammunition from weapons. With armored trucks and assault tanks. The *bilakoro*, the idle scholars, face the forces and defend themselves with volleys of rocks, the smoke of burning tires, the chassis of ruined vehicles, bricks, barricades. Insurrection, rage, massacre, cries, detonations, deadly madness—each stage more destructive than the others—continue the entire day.

At nightfall, a bit of calm returns. The mediators—priests and traditional chiefs, the dean of the diplomatic corps, the ambassadors of France and the United States—take advantage of this to take the representatives of the Convention of Living and Democratic Forces to the presidential palace of the republic. A roundtable is organized. A long discussion ensues. On one side, there are the *bilakoro*, the union workers, and representatives of civil society; on the other, there is the president, his ministers, and his army. The discussion continues all night and, at dawn, ends with a three-point agreement. The soldiers responsible for burning the party building will be hunted, arrested, tried, and severely punished.

The National Assembly is dissolved. The National Conference is to be convened. It will open in six weeks—just time to work out the practical details of its organization. It will open on the third Monday of the following month.

You cannot delay it this time, Koyaga.

When the barnyard chickens become too numerous around the women pounding the mortar, the women cease working. Let us follow the example of these women and reflect on the following sayings:

A far-off day exists, but the day that will never come does not exist.
When a bushfire crosses the river, that is cause for grave concern to the person who wishes to extinguish it.
The final limit for the difficult person is the tomb.

24

Ah, Macledio! I remind you that the National Conference opened one morning—one rainy morning. What an ill omen! The conference was supposed to be opened by the president of the republic in person. People waited until noon to see a substitute arrive. For security reasons, Koyaga asked to be excused. The meeting was opened in a conference hall of a large hotel in the capital. The hotel and the hall bore, like all great places in the country, the dates for two of the assassination attempts Koyaga had escaped. The speakers could not accept that their meeting place be designated by those dates.

So the first important question considered by the conference was to desacralize and give new names to the hotel and the room where the work was to take place. After two days and two nights of noisy discussion, an agreement was worked out on the name that should be given to the meeting hall—the "Hall of Martyrs"; but not for the name of the hotel. The meetings took place in a nameless hotel.

The second question that aroused passion in the participants was to specify the descriptive terms for the conference. Was it simply national or national and sovereign? This question drew in all the best orators for three nights and four days. In spite of the opposition of the government representative, the conference proclaimed itself sovereign and national.

The decision of the conference to proclaim and to qualify itself as sovereign and national was considered a matter of the greatest portent. It had to be feted, and in order to celebrate, an orchestra was brought to the Hall of Martyrs, and the participants jerked and twisted for an entire afternoon.

At the end of the celebration, certain participants noted that they had been relieved of their wallets while they were jiggling and wriggling. The *bilakoro* idle scholars had not abandoned their customs— the dog may become rich, but he never ceases to sniff around. They had not stopped engaging in their little pickpocketing activities, their favorite game. Some participants, those who were religious and the psychologists, admitted they understood, the pickpockets were right.

The conference should have begun with the essential matter: to set the amount of money to be paid to the delegates each day. Failing to have made this a priority, many participants, to the greater shame of the Sovereign and National Conference, made out the best they could, and they slept out in the open to survive.

Then it was realized they could not give honoraria without verifying the mandates and accrediting each participant.

Accreditation required an equitable representation from all social levels, all provinces, all ethnic groups, and all tribes in the country. That constituted an unresolvable problem in the Republic of the Gulf, for historical reasons.

It will be recalled that the colonizers had at first engaged in an experiment to exploit the territory of the Gulf. They had gone to Brazil to buy back black slaves who had been converted to Christianity. These converted freedmen were to serve as models for the Naked Black people, who were cannibals and imbeciles. The Brazilian freedmen were supposed to train their savage brothers, teach them to plant coconut trees, dig mines, adore the Holy Spirit, and cross themselves. Failing to understand or to accept their roles as pioneers, the freedmen wanted to continue the slave trade, an activity that was considerably more profitable. The colonizers strictly forbade the capture and sale of their indigenous brothers. To put the country to profitable use, the Whites were forced, obliged, to conquer and pacify the lands by armed means and to use forced labor and whips.

The freedmen were Christians and could not be considered as indigenous people; they were exempted from the burden of forced labor. Their children were allowed to go to church and to school. These children became the first literate Blacks in the country. The evolved Blacks, of course, constituted an intermediate class, between that of the civilized white Christian and the Naked Black, savage and stupid. Some of the officials from that intermediate class, who felt that they were at home, found the arrogance and scorn of the White toward the Black, and the exploitation of Blacks by Whites, hard to take. They became ardent nationalists and fought heroically against the colonial system when decolonization began on the continent. The partisans of independence threw the colonialists out of the country when the era of independence began to spread across the continent.

Quite naturally and obviously, they took over the furniture of the former white masters after the latter departed, and they assumed the vacant jobs with all the privileges, habits, manners, and mentality of the former occupants.

We know that Koyaga, the emasculating hunter of beasts and men, came to the South and chased the colonialists out after ridding the Paleo mountains of a few monsters. The descendants of the freedmen never accepted defeat, never considered themselves conquered, and the thirty years of independence were thirty years of continual struggle between the descendants of the indigenous people (with the Supreme Guide as their leader) and the descendants of the freedmen. Relentlessly, the descendants of the freedmen attacked the corrupt and bloody dictatorial power of the emasculating hunter of men and beasts. They were the ones who were continually organizing those assassination attempts that Koyaga had escaped and survived, thanks to his mama with her meteorite and to the marabout with his Qur'an. The descendants of the freedmen who managed to flee and to escape torture and death after the attempts remained abroad, living in exile. In France, they obtained French citizenship. They returned to the land of their ancestors with their dual nationality after the general amnesty voted by the provisional parliament. They were professors, doctors, lawyers, engineers. . . . They were intellectuals and capable managers. They were the ones who wrote the tracts and published the newspapers that the *bilakoro* idle scholars reproduced and hawked in the streets. Just as naturally, they had taken over the country after the departure of the Whites and assumed the direction of the insurrection against the dictatorship of the master hunter when they were returning from exile and disembarking on African soil.

As soon as they arrived, they created dozens of philanthropic, political, sporting, professional, and religious organizations; and other dozens of nongovernmental organizations for development. These associations and organizations were convened and admitted to the Sovereign and National Conference. As a consequence, the majority, the great majority of participants in the Sovereign and National Conference was constituted of black managers with French citizenship who had lived in France and had their property and families in France. They were foreigners, people alien to the men and customs of the country, and of Africa. They were told that they were removed from African realities and could not represent all the provinces, tribes, and ethnic groups of the country.

They replied that, during their long exile, they had lived with those realities day and night, and, having ingested and having been stuffed with humanism and universalism, they were quite capable of penetrating and comprehending everything African. They were quite capable of legitimately representing all ethnic groups and regions of the Republic of the Gulf. Peremptory and sure of themselves, they accredited each other. You could count as many as three delegate-deputies in the same family: father, mother, and son.

They set up a bureau of the Sovereign and National Conference and elected the members of the bureau. The president and all the members of the bureau were designated as people who had suffered from Koyaga's abuse of power. People who had in their own flesh suffered from the dictatorship. They were men blinded by resentment and the burning desire for vengeance. They were people closed to any compromise with the Supreme Guide. Between you and these people there had been deaths, and they were people with whom you could not and would not engage in dialogue.

The conference began. It assumed as its mission to try the thirty years of dictatorship and assassination. To exorcise the country, its people, its animals, its things, all of which had been subjected to the sorcery of Nadjuma with her meteorite and Bokano with his Qur'an. The conference wanted to build a new country on a new foundation. A foundation that would be solid, clean, and healthy.

At the beginning, the rules for the conference fixed a time limit for each orator—one-half hour maximum. This limit quickly proved to be insufficient, largely insufficient; the speakers complained. Since it was necessary to tell all, to reveal everything, to leave nothing in the shadows, to collect all testimonies and confessions, the conference voted for a modification—each speaker could, if he so desired, speak for up to a half day of the session, three hours without interruption.

They began with testimonies. The assassinations, violence, divestments, and lies that had really been perpetrated by the dictator during his personal reign of three decades. The speakers quickly clothed in verisimilitude the calumnies, fables, and inventions that had been circulated for months in the tracts distributed in the streets. None of that was sufficient. Each speaker felt compelled, in order to sustain the interest of the assembled delegates, to invent new revelations. The first speakers denounced the concentration camps where prisoners in shackles were dying of hunger and thirst in their own feces and urine. They denounced torture of indescribable bestiality; prisoners who had been cut up, piece by piece, or gently burned to death. Again in order to sustain interest, the next speakers demonized the dictator still more: they accused him of anthropophagy and gave proof. By means of sorcery and for ritual purposes—augmenting his vital forces—he ate the roasted testicles of his dead opponents for breakfast each morning. These were confabulations that went beyond comprehension and verisimilitude. Eventually, the national and international press grew tired and were repelled by these speakers. One must know where to stop. Once it has been said that the hyena's anus stinks, there is nothing more to say. Nothing is more putrid than the anus of that animal. To add anything else is futile.

For six entire months, the delegates released their pent-up rage in vengeful fabrication. Their speeches finally bored everyone. During the final days, there was no longer any audience to hear and applaud a speaker other than his friends and relatives.

Faced with the disinterest of the press and the public, the presiding prelate requested, one Saturday evening, that all delegates be present at a formal meeting to follow the Sunday Mass.

With an overwhelming majority—312 for, 30 abstentions, and 14 against—the Sovereign and National Conference voted, at the end of the meeting on Sunday the sixth, on the deposition and disempowerment of the dictator. Standing, in the midst of applause and vigorous hurrahs, the delegates acclaimed the resolution. The presiding prelate invited all the delegates to bring their wives, children, and friends to the hotel that evening, beginning at nine o'clock. In order to celebrate the national feast. The Sovereign and National Conference and the entire nation were going to fete the deposition of their oppressor and the advent of a new era for the country. Only the person who is unacquainted with the viper of the pyramids picks him up by the tail.

The financial difficulties that had appeared just before the unforgettable thirtieth anniversary parade were still there when the insurrection broke out. The insurrection with all the curses that followed it made the chaos worse and drained the country of its lifeblood.

The descendants of the Brazilian freedmen had not worried about that problem; at first, they had thought only of themselves and their own comfort. They were French, and they lived the life of developed countries. As members of the provisional assembly, they had set European salaries for themselves: sixty thousand francs per day. In a country where the minimum wage is blocked at thirty thousand francs and the salary of a soldier at twenty thousand! This was a scandal! The numerous extensions of the Sovereign and National Conference struck many citizens as scheming and subterfuge for continuing to live the high life.

The *bilakoro* idle scholars who had brought the dictatorship to its knees had presented specific demands to the conference. They were demanding that the system of scholarship assistance existing in the colonial period be reinstituted.

Under the colonial regime, a pupil without relatives in the area where he went to school was housed and fed by the administration. All secondary students, from the sixth class up to the *terminale* in the lycée, were boarding students with scholarships. All students had scholarships that were the equivalent of the salaries of government employees. The conference had noted these demands and had registered them in the register of claims for the future government of reorganization that would come out of the conference.

The delegates of the idle scholars *bilakoro* considered themselves rich with sixty thousand francs per diem, too rich from one day to the next. In solidarity, they had agreed to retrocede only a miserly part of their manna. It cannot be said that the idle scholar representatives had completely forgotten their colleagues. No, the *bilakoro* delegates had courageously fought and obtained the right for street children to be used as errand boys for the conference and a certain number as militia charged with maintaining order at the conference. The struggle, the insurrection had brought profit only to the delegates, the errand boys, and the militia: in the final analysis, a minority, a handful of *bilakoro*. The others, the hundreds and thousands of other idle scholars, continued to get along as best they could in the streets and markets. And the resulting situation was that the markets and streets, with endless strikes and social disorder, had become difficult, stingy, and heartless toward the street children. This situation led some of them, in order to avoid starvation, to return to the places they had occupied before the insurrection, on the sidewalks and streets leading to your private residence as Supreme Guide and rich dictator. Koyaga, you showed yourself to be more generous toward them, more openhanded than you had ever been. Their misery had broken your heart.

It is not true—it was a matter of calculation, to stem the tide, that he made gestures of largesse. The entire city learned of your generosity. Hundreds of starving idle scholars had taken to the sidewalks leading to your private residence as dictator. And to these hundreds were added all those who were unemployed as a result of strikes and social disorder. A compact crowd that made each of your trips out or back into the residence a manifestation of sympathy, a real feast. The people watched for your arrival. They applauded noisily and welcomed you with slogans as soon as your cortege passed. You showered them with coins and sometimes even with five-hundred-franc bills. They sang your praise and danced long after you disappeared.

The feast had been in full swing for three hours; it was midnight. The soiree had been officially opened by the presiding prelate of the Sovereign and National Conference. He had supplicated the faithful and had invited them to supplication. The soiree had been placed under the patronage of Saint Mary, the Mother of God. The new national anthem of the country had resounded, performed by two orchestras and sung by all who were in the hall, standing at attention. Tears had streamed down some cheeks. At the end of the anthem, spontaneous applause and hurrahs broke out. Three speeches, vibrant with emotion, had been delivered. They had underscored the historic importance of the vote for disempowerment that the conference had approved during the day. It was a new era of freedom, fraternity, and respect for every human being that was opening. The champagne dinner took place against a background of quiet music played by the orchestras. Dress for the evening had been prescribed. The descendants of Brazilian freedmen wore tuxedos with black bow ties. Their companions wore evening dresses. Their perfume wafted through the great hall, which was filled with some two thousand guests.

Even the delegates of the idle scholars had respected the recommendations for the event by giving up their filthy jeans. Guests invited included not only the members of the Sovereign and National Conference but also diplomats and all eminent persons in the country. Officers, ministers, and Koyaga's close associates had failed to reply to the invitations. The ball began: dancers swayed to the beguine on the floor.

It was at that moment, exactly at midnight, that the rattle of the first volleys of submachine guns resounded at the entrance to the hotel, followed at once by the explosion of several hand grenades. There was general panic, yelling! There were howls of fear and astonishment and a general rush for the exit. The firing continued crackling for five minutes: all around the hotel.

The muddle, the confusion, the chaos, the screams did not stop in the hall until two officers with six heavily armed soldiers appeared and took over the podium. The soldiers fired into the air; the officers ordered silence. It was the silence of the brush at noon at the height of the harmattan. The quivering lips of the weeping matrons was audible.

The officers explained and justified the operation. The military, the soldiers, had four months of back pay coming. The members of the conference had voted fabulous salaries for themselves and were indulging in feasting and champagne dinners. The country was fed up with seeing the Sovereign and National Conference living it up while everything else was going to the dogs. The army could hardly accept having strangers to the country come in to rob the founder, the father-of-the-nation. The army, accompanied by the repentant *bilakoro* idle scholars, pushed the militia out of the way, executed the stubborn rebels, and took the others prisoner.

The hotel is surrounded, completely hemmed in. All members of the National Conference have to remain in the hall. Only diplomats and women who are not delegates are allowed to leave. The deputies will remain hostage until the back salaries of the army have been completely paid. And, afterward, until the disempowerment of the father-of-the-nation has been voided. And, finally, until the liars, the spies, and the loudmouths have been denounced. They will be arrested, tried, and, if necessary, executed on the spot.

Bastard assembly! An assembly without power or means! This was the simulacrum of an assembly that had appointed the provisional prime minister and accepted his government.

The demands presented by the soldiers when they had taken the Sovereign and National Conference hostage had been almost entirely satisfied. The five principal players of the conference, all of them descendants of freedmen, had been able to leave the besieged hall and escape the military. They had managed by disguising themselves as women: they had donned wigs, glasses, dresses and had been able to leave with the women in evening gowns. In town, they had tried to live in hiding and to organize a resistance movement against the dictatorship. The project had fallen through. The soldiers had quickly discovered their hiding places. Two of those in hiding were found assassinated, frightfully mutilated and emasculated. The three others had fled, managing to cross the border at night in a pirogue over one inlet of the lagoon. They had taken off for France, where they are living in exile.

Almost a third of the representatives, deputies from the provisional assembly, had been uneasy, had feared for their lives, and had fled. The others organized this bastard assembly that had named the provisional prime minister. They had chosen him from among the descendants of indigenous people, not from the descendants of the freedmen. The mission of the provisional prime minister and his government had been specified and limited. They were supposed to cook up a new constitution within eighteen months at most, to get it approved by the country, and to organize presidential and legislative elections.

The provisional government had wanted to go a bit further and to apply certain decisions made by the Sovereign and National Conference. They wanted to reorganize the country's financial system and to replace the general director of the treasury and the president–director general of the marketing board. The president considered that the management of these two organizations was his private domain. The decisions had not actually been implemented. During the night, the soldiers and lycaons had seized power in a surprise move. They had shoved away the gendarmes charged with protecting the prime minister and his offices, had killed eight of them, and arrested the prime minister himself.

The goal, a pretext for this operation, had been to claim three months of back salaries. They had led the prime minister to President Koyaga by the ears, just as an unruly student is led before his father. You played mediator between the prime minister and the soldiers. The prime minister renounced his projects for reorganizing the financial apparatus and had agreed to have the troops' back salaries paid before the end of that month.

You regained all your popularity. The vicinity of the palace and the streets that led to it were never empty. Day and night, petitioners, flatterers, singers, dancers, disabled people, and *bilakoro* who were not in school pushed each other around. With men devoted to you at the head of the two principal state treasuries, you were once more able to be generous, to have a good heart, and to distribute prebends and charity.

The economic crisis, which had been aggravated by the social disorder, had drained the country and made money rare, more difficult than ever for the poor to obtain. And all those people began to miss the era of the dictatorship.

The idle scholars began to repent, the poor to cry. Opposition newspapers were forced to attenuate the sharpness of the insults and calumnies directed at you. The pen pushers who did not understand soon enough and who continued to spit out articles too critical, too insulting, and too scabrous with regard to the president were roughed up in the streets by unknown assailants. Some nights, they were killed by peaceful citizens who were sickened, disgusted, and revolted. Many of the victims were found emasculated. Even international organizations such as the UN, the IMF, Amnesty International, and the International League for Human Rights also tempered their criticisms of the regime and of the president of the republic.

The misery brought on by the democratization of the country became unbearable. Hospitals became dilapidated, schools were closed, roads were cut off; famine descended on cities when the crops rotted in inland villages.

In all certainty, even with honest elections, you were assured of being chosen chief of state during the next elections. You had become once more the Supreme Guide. You had recuperated everything: your lycaons, your arrogance, your hypocrisy, your lies, your flatterers, your mama with her meteorite, your marabout Bokano with his Qur'an. All your prestige and the former atmosphere of terror.

Only after the event did the inquiry reveal all that. The continuous presence of a crowd of beggars around your residence had facilitated the organization of the assassination attempt. The conspirators had the advantage of some months for placing, planting, posting, and organizing everything with patience and seriousness. They had been able to observe and take note of the habits, customs, and ways of the dictator over some weeks. With the complicity of two of the close guards, they were able on the night of the operation to follow the dictator's steps, to know about and survey all his gestures and movements in the palace. They learned through coded messages that the emasculator of men and beasts was going to spend that night in his residence, and they even knew in which room he was going to sleep.

Usually, no one could be sure of that. Each night, six bedrooms were prepared in the principal building and its adjoining structures, and he had hidden doors by which he could leave the residence at the last minute. That particular night, they thought they had seen his shadow through the windows of the second-story bedroom in the left wing of the main building. They had waited until he had put out the lights in the room. It was two-thirty in the morning. One after another they had fired; the shells had pulverized the bedroom. A fire had started but was quickly extinguished. Volleys of submachine-gun fire were aimed in the direction from which the shells had come. There was confusion, and the armored vehicles of the presidential guard quickly emerged from three guard posts and disappeared into the city. Then there was silence, dead silence.

The detonations of rockets and the crackling of submachine-gun volleys had awakened some of the people sleeping, but they had immediately fallen back into a peaceful sleep like other evenings. They were used to it. Nights had rarely passed since the beginning of democracy when distant and mysterious sounds of military weapons were not heard.

At six o'clock in the morning, the opposition radio from beyond the border broke the news. Immediately after signing on, the announcer declared, "Koyaga died last night, assassinated by patriots. He is really dead this time, quite dead."

The leader of the opposition abroad followed the announcer. He invited the people of the Republic of the Gulf to celebrate the death of their oppressor, the end of the bloody tyrant, and the liberation of the ancestral land. He ordered all dear relatives and patriots to go out into the streets in order to demonstrate their joy, and to occupy public buildings, the residences of the liars.

It was necessary to be vigilant and to prevent the dictator's collaborators from fleeing—they had to be arrested and held so that they would not escape justice and the punishment that awaited them.

Despite the emotion in the speaker's voice, despite the certainty in his affirmations, the appeals were not convincing. Many inhabitants shut their gates and closed their doors, and among those close to them muttered and asked a thousand questions about the event. A feverish uneasiness was noticeable in the few people who had dared go out to take a glance in the streets. But absolutely no one dared make a show of joy in public places.

For thirty years, at the rate of two to three times a year, there had been assassination attempts on the Supreme Guide's life. Each time the conspirators announced the dictator's death. Imprudent people went out into the streets, demonstrated their joy, and expressed their hatred aloud. Koyaga reappeared, came back to life. Those who had revealed their feelings and expressed all their hatred were pursued, arrested, tortured, and executed. They paid dearly, very dearly, for their haste. There was nothing surprising in the fact that everyone preferred to wait with prudent caution this time.

That created an atmosphere of uncertainty and of false rumors that circulated all day long. Nobody knew what was going on at the presidential residence and palace. The second day, forty-eight hours after the attempt, the expected and hoped for communiqué did not come from the president's office.

Abroad, the great international press rebroadcast with commentary the declarations of opposition Radio Freedom from the other side of the border. Radio Freedom was the sole source of information for the world about the situation in the capital of the Republic of the Gulf. Night and day, twenty-four of twenty-four hours, Radio Freedom confirmed, guaranteed, and swore that this time Koyaga had indeed been killed, liquidated.

It was the third morning after the attempt that you found out what was going on in your native village. Airplanes from all the African capitals were landing at the little airport. Groups of hunters from all regions of the country were swarming toward your home. Then you understood that you were mistaken, and that your strategy was mistaken. Then you decided to put an end to the uncertainty. Then you corrected the lie and published the communiqué announcing that once more the assassination attempt had ended in failure.

The conspirators were unaware that you had not been sleeping more than three hours in any one room. They did not know that you changed rooms, beds, mistresses three times a night. Half an hour before the attempt, you had fortunately left the bedroom on the second floor of the left wing of the residence. You had miraculously escaped and were indeed quite alive.

But you had conceived a ruse and argued this way: "I will soon be democratically elected and will have all my former power. My enemies are not disarmed. They are sure that they succeeded this time. I will let the doubt persist for two days in order to lead the determined opponents to show themselves in public and make their true feelings known. With my lycaons, we shall use the intervening time and the uncertainty to kill and get rid of all the opponents who are unmasked."

Waiting for the Vote of the Wild Animals

And, in fact, during the two days of uncertainty and confusion, many terribly emasculated cadavers were found in ditches.

But your feint turned out to be a bad idea in the end because you are the most envied dictator in Africa. Your despotic peers finally believed that the attempt was successful. Each dictator wanted to be the heir of the immunity and sorcery that had always saved you. Each one wanted to have your mama with her aerolitic stone and the marabout with his Qur'an, and every one of them had, on the third morning, dispatched to your native village a high intelligence official and the head of his police forces.

When you arrived, it was already too late. The spectacle was apocalyptic. It was a scene like those that took place at the end of the reign of all the great master hunters of the past: Ramses II, Alexander the Great, and Sundyata Keita.

To begin with, on the horizon, hiding the mountain chains and the setting sun, there was a gigantic brushfire. In the foreground was the airport. Between the airport and the brushfire, there were hunters armed with slave rifles, peasants with machetes, hoes, and pitchforks, and panicked animals (all the animals of the universe) running pell-mell. Beasts, peasants, and hunters were pursuing each other, fighting, and massacring each other on the plain and in the swamps.

On the airfield, the area of the airport was covered with little airplanes, each displaying its own colors and emblem. There were aircraft from Zaire, Côte d'Ivoire, the Central African Republic, Morocco, Guinea, Chad, Libya, Ghana, Nigeria, Niger, Cameroon, Gabon, Egypt, Ethiopia, the Congo, Upper Volta, Algeria, Tunisia, etc. All the African dictators—Africa is by far the richest continent in poverty and in dictatorships—had its team in action on site, a team with orders to get the meteorite, the Qur'an, and their bearers. And all the secret agents were swarming about your residence and the houses of your mama and the marabout. They were rummaging, searching, screening, bush by bush, tuft by tuft, anthill by anthill.

Beyond the airport, the hunting reserve extended to the mountains on the horizon. In that reserve, there swarmed delegations of all hunting organizations from all regions of all countries. Each group was preceded by tam-tam, *kora,* and dancing—dancers and musicians.

Hunters from all Africa had also believed the news of the death of their prestigious master, the greatest *sinbo* of all times since Ramses II and Sundyata. They were coming to participate in the three-month-long funeral rites due him. They came from everywhere—from lands as distant as the Wassulu, the Konian, the Horodougou, the Kabadougou, and closer regions such as the Bafilo, the Bassar, the Kabu, the Bafule, the Tamberma, the Gurma, and the Moba, the Kabie, and still others.

The hunters were astonished to find that all the animals in the reserve were, like themselves, headed in the direction of the residence. Mingling with them and accompanying or following them, there were herds of antelope, bubals, horse antelope, sitatunga, bongo, and all species of duiker—black, rutilatus, bay, Maxwell's, yellow-backed, and Jentink's. Mingling with them, accompanying or following them, were herds of great savanna buffalo, elephants, bands of warthogs, lions, leopards, dog-faced hyenas, and servals. And besides, mingling with all those species, accompanying or following them, there were colonies of flying squirrels, Egyptian rabbits, aardvarks, bushpigs. And besides, there were bands of chimpanzees, dog-faced monkeys, palas, mangabeys.

Crawling under the trees and along the roads leading to the residence of the greatest of all master hunters in our era were the tortoises (the *Testudo gigantea,* the *Kinixys belliana,* the *Trionychidae,* the *Cyclanorbis,* the *Eretmochelys imbricata,* the *Palusios subniger*); the serpents (the *Typhlops punctatus,* the *Naja melanoleuca,* the *Bitis gaonica,* the *Causus rhombeatus*); the crocodiles (the *Crocodylus cataphractus,* the *Crocodylus osteolaemus*); the lizards (chameleons, monitors, agamas).

Flying over the reptiles, the limbed animals, and the hunters were clouds and flights of gulls, sterns, terns, pelicans, cormorants, darters, gannets, phaetons, herons, ibises, marabou storks, *comatibis,* ducks, geese, rose flamingos, *rhynchees,* plovers, lapwings, snipes, curlews, pratincoles, oedicnèmes; rails, waterhens, fracolins, guinea fowl, quails; pigeons, turtledoves; secretary birds, vultures, falcons, eagles, kites, buzzards, harriers, hawks, goshawks; scops-owls, tawny owls; cuckoos, turacos; *barbas,* honeyguides, woodpeckers; martinets, goatsuckers; rollers, bee-eaters, mockingbirds, hornbills; crested *calious*; blackbirds, weavers, canaries, warblers, flycatchers, swallows, thrushes, sunbirds, crows, and still others.

The beasts were coming from the reserve. But where were they going and why?

The hunters had at first mistaken the animals' tears as mourning for their prestigious *sinbo,* their greatest friend, their protector and benefactor, and they thought the animals were headed for the funeral. That was not their reason or motivation.

Farther away, there was a gigantic brushfire that inflamed the entire horizon, masked the mountains and the sunset. The beasts were fleeing the walls of flame. The animals had been intercepted or chased by thousands of peasants equipped with various arms; the peasants were engaging in the greatest battue of the century.

These peasants were the former farmers and owners of these lands that had been taken for the reserve. They had been expropriated by brute force, and their owners had been dispossessed and expelled from their ancestral lands. They had not gone far; they had settled around the perimeter of the reserve, where they had been waiting patiently for thirty years. They too had believed the news of the dictator's death, had lit the brushfires, and had organized the battue in order to capture, kill, and eat the animals before reclaiming their lands.

The hunters had not hesitated when they found out the reason for the flight and panic of the animals on the reserve; they went to the aid of the beasts. They tried to encircle the fire and fought against the hordes of poacher peasants. That is why, across the entire plain between the airport and the fire, there reigned indescribable confusion in which beasts, hunters, and poachers were pursuing, fighting, and killing one another.

That is the spectacle you were able to observe from your command aircraft. That is the scene you found on the ground once you landed. The mess on the ground was indescribable.

You tried to make your way to your residence. There were dozens of airplanes on the ground. About your residence and surrounding the houses of your mother and the marabout, there were hundreds of secret agents searching and digging each tuft or parcel of ground. On the plain, in the reserve, the thousands of hunters, poacher peasants, and hooved animals, reptiles, birds were mingling in a melee, a pitiless combat. And, far away on the horizon, there was a gigantic fire obstructing the view of the sky, veiling the mountains.

Uneasily, you stopped, turned around, and asked a question:

"Where are my Mama Nadjuma and the marabout Bokano? Where are the meteorite and the Qur'an?"

No one was able to answer; no one knew; no one had seen them or found them. They had suddenly disappeared. Without speaking a word, giving a sign, or leaving the least little trace.

You smiled, and your uneasiness dissipated. You remembered. Your mama and the marabout had told you several times and had taught you long ago what must be done if you ever lost them: have your purificatory epic as master hunter, your cathartic *donsomana*, told by a *sèrè*, a hunters' griot and responder.

The responder will have to be a *koroduwa*. A *koroduwa* is an initiate in his cathartic stage. You know that once they have told all and that you have revealed and confessed everything, there will remain not the slightest shadow over your path: the meteorite and the Qur'an themselves will reveal to you where they are hidden. You will have only to go fetch them.

When you have recovered the Qur'an and the meteorite, you will organize democratic presidential elections. Elections with universal suffrage supervised by an independent national commission. You will seek a new mandate with the certainty of winning, of being reelected. For you know, you are sure, that if by chance men refuse to vote for you, the animals will come out of the bush, seize ballots, and vote for you.

The *koroduwa* Tiekura goes wild, dances, walks on all fours, and in turn imitates the gaits and cries of different animals. When the millet has been cracked, the pounders lay down their pestles and empty the mortars. They begin or recommence as long as there remain grains with chaff. As long as Koyaga has not found the Qur'an and the meteorite, we shall begin and recommence the purificatory *donsomana*, our *donsomana*.

Calm down, Tiekura. . . . The *koroduwa* refuses to obey the injunctions of the *sèrè*, who, amid the noisy howls, recites the following proverbs:

One cannot place cows in all the parks that the mind constructs.
Following patience comes heaven.
Night lasts for a long time, but at last day arrives.

Afterword

Ancestry and Life of Kourouma

Ahmadou Kourouma was born in 1927 in the town of Boundiali, some 445 miles (750 km.) northwest of Abidjan, the capital of Côte d'Ivoire.[1] Sixty miles to the north lies the border with Mali, and about 150 miles to the west is the border with Guinea. Boundiali is in the primarily agricultural country of the Senufo people.

Kourouma's grandfather was General Samori Brahma. Moriba Kourouma, Ahmadou's father, was a master hunter and descended from a princely Muslim family. His mother was a vendor who came from Guinea originally. Niankoro Fondio, Kourouma's uncle, who shares the author's dedication with Moriba Kourouma, was a master hunter, nurse, and fetishist who owned some farming land.

Kourouma spent part of his early childhood in Togobala, Guinea. He was sent to live with his uncle in Boundiali at age seven and entered the primary school there at that time. He went to the regional school at Korhogo with a scholarship and received a *certificat d'études* in 1943. From 1943 to 1945 he attended the École Primaire Supérieure in Bingerville, east of Abidjan. In 1947 Kourouma passed the difficult entrance examination and was admitted to the École Technique Supérieure in Bamako, Mali. Because of his participation in student demonstrations, he was arrested and sent back to Côte d'Ivoire in 1949. At some point, he was initiated as a master hunter.

Kourouma's deferment from military service was canceled and he was drafted into the army (*tirailleurs*, infantry) for three years. Although he went into training to become a noncommissioned officer, Kourouma met new difficulties when he refused to engage in the repression of anti-regime demonstrations. Demoted, he was sent to train in France for the French expeditionary forces. Kourouma was then sent to Indochina, where he served in Saigon (now Ho Chi Minh City) from 1951 to 1954.

After being demobilized in Côte d'Ivoire, Kourouma went to France to study at his own expense. He passed the competitive entrance examination for admission to the Grandes Écoles and entered the École de Constructions Aéronautiques et Navales (School for Aeronautical and Naval Construction) in Nantes. He was refused a scholarship because there were "no job opportunities" in Africa for this field of study. Kourouma passed another competitive examination and entered the Institut des Actuaires in Lyon. He was awarded an actuary's diploma and a certificate of business administration in 1959.

In 1960 Kourouma married a French woman of aristocratic ancestry before returning to Côte d'Ivoire, where he became assistant director of the Société Générale des Banques (General Bank Corporation) of Côte d'Ivoire. President Houphouët-Boigny had founded the Rassemblement Démocratique Africain (African Democratic Rally) in October 1946 at the Conference of Bamako (Mali), which brought together the deputies of the French Assembly from African states (Mazrui 175). Kourouma stated to an interviewer that he wished to get into politics around 1962 or 1963, saying, "As for me, I have always been in the opposition" (Kpatindé interview 119). Houphouët-Boigny had Kourouma arrested in 1963 on suspicion of participating in a plot against the regime. He was released because the president feared problems with the French government should Madame Kourouma complain. Kourouma lost his position with the Caisse des Retraités (Retirement Office) in Abidjan, however, and after a stay in France, he went to Algeria to work for an insurance company from 1965 to 1969.

In 1969 Kourouma received an offer to return to Côte d'Ivoire for an important position. He went to France to train in a French bank and returned to Abidjan in 1971, first as assistant director and then as director of the Société Générale des Banques in Côte d'Ivoire.

Kourouma's play "Tougnatigui ou le Possesseur de vérité" (published only in 1998 as *Le diseur de vérités;* The truth teller) was performed at the Institut National des Arts in Abidjan in December 1972. It was broadcast on national television in January 1973 and was suddenly considered to be subversive. At that point, Kourouma accepted a job as actuary with the Institut International des Assurances (International Institute of Insurance) in Yaoundé, Cameroon, and worked there until 1983, when he took a similar position in Lomé, Togo, where he remained until 1993.

In 1993 Kourouma and his wife returned to live in Abidjan, and since 1996 he has been president of the Conférence Interministérielle des Marchés d'Assurances (Interministerial Conference of Insurance Markets), which exercises supervisory control over the insurance markets of the international franc area in Africa (Kpatindé interview 119).

Afterword

Kourouma's Work and Reputation

In an interesting comparison between Kourouma and Sony Labou Tansi, Christiane Ndiaye notes that the Ivoirian novelist went outside the traditions of the European novel to tell his story through "the intermediary of language inspired more directly by African traditions" (27). Techniques and modes of discourse from African oral traditions are major elements in all three of Kourouma's published (adult) novels: the use of proverbs, the praise-song, funeral eulogy, protocols of greeting and conversation, traditions of the hunters' societies, Muslim prayers, and so forth.

Kourouma began to work on *Les soleils des indépendances* (published in English as *The Suns of Independence*) in Côte d'Ivoire in 1961 and finished it in Algeria in 1965. Two French publishers, Présence Africaine and Éditions du Seuil, refused the manuscript. In 1967 Kourouma submitted the manuscript for a competition organized by the journal *Études Françaises* at the University of Montreal, Prix de la Francité (Prize for French Culture and Literature). The prize was awarded to Kourouma, and the novel appeared under the imprint of the University of Montreal in 1968 (Nicolas 5).

Ironically, Éditions du Seuil then bought publication rights, and the novel was republished in Paris in 1970. It was awarded the Prix Maille-Latour-Laudry (best novel by a young author) by the Académie Française and also the Belgian Prix de l'Académie Royale.

The success of *Soleils* was rapid; however, Kourouma did not immediately follow up his initial success with the publication of a second novel. *Monnè, outrages et défis* (published in English as *Monnew*) was not published by Éditions du Seuil until 1990, over twenty years after the first edition of *Soleils* had appeared.

It is worthwhile to look at the scope of Kourouma's three novels because they constitute a virtual overview of French and Belgian colonialism in West and Central Africa and its aftermath following the independences of 1958–62. It should be noted that Kourouma inscribes the narrative of each of the three novels in a variant of oral discourse.

Monnè, the second novel published, is the first by dint of the setting, which takes the reader from the beginning of the French colonization of West Africa to the eve of the declarations of independence around 1960. The story of Djigui Keïta, king of Soba, is recounted as an oral epic by a griot. Disobeying the orders of Emperor Samory to destroy his village as the French colonial troops invade West Africa,

Djigui stays on, believing his kingdom will be protected by the magic of his ancestors. Djigui's faith in magic leads him to collaborate with the invaders with results that are at once comic and tragic.

The second novel, by chronology of scene, is *The Suns of Independence*. Again related by a griot, the story is that of the decline to poverty and impotence of a Mande prince following independence. The oral narrative is highly colored by the traditional praise of funeral song and narrative, which Prince Fama is reduced to reciting in order to survive once his traditional fortune and status have disappeared.

Kourouma's third novel, *Waiting for the Vote of the Wild Animals*, first published by Éditions du Seuil in 1998, brings his story of the effects of European colonialism in West Africa virtually up to the moment when he was composing the novel. The broad scene of the novel is that of the dictatorships during the period of the cold war, taking up where *The Suns of Independence* left off, in the 1960s, and continuing into the 1990s, when, following the breakup of the Soviet Union, France and the United States withdrew their funding from the dictators of West Africa and tried to bring them into line with international policies of liberalism and global economics. While it would be futile to tie every element of the novel to specific historical personages and events, a reading that combines analysis of Kourouma's structuring of the story and recognition of the numerous allusions to political events of the period will give a far better understanding.

The Shape of the Novel

The main characters of the novel are Koyaga, master hunter and dictator of the Republic of the Gulf, and his minister of political orientation, Macledio. The mentor-guides behind Koyaga's power are his mother, Nadjuma, who was herself a champion fighter in her youth, and Bokano Yakuba, a marabout of shady origins who saved Nadjuma from a fit of possession and subsequently became a guide for both mother and son. A numerous cast of secondary characters includes other dictators of West Africa, some named and others only lightly disguised by fictional names.

The novel is composed of six parts, entitled *veillées* (wake or evening social gathering) in the French text. The Malinke term *sumu* (ritual gathering of hunters' societies) has been used in the English version. With one exception, the parts are of roughly equal length; the exception is the fourth *sumu* (over half again as long as most parts), which relates Koyaga's dictatorial reign of thirty years. The principal part of the entire novel, the five-day series of *sumu* constituting Koyaga's *donsomana*, takes place in 1997 (the year in which Kourouma was writing, or finishing, his novel). The reader learns in the sixth *sumu* that Koyaga has been ousted from power, after thirty years, and that the *donsomana* has been celebrated in hopes that Koyaga will locate the missing symbols of his power—the aerolite and the venerable Qur'an held by his mother and the marabout Bokano—and will thus be enabled to present his candidacy for a new mandate.

Kourouma's Style and Traditional Knowledge

As with his the first two novels, Kourouma has made French into his own language in *Waiting for the Vote of the Wild Animals*. Instead of the griot or the funeral singer, who recite the history of a specific family or community, however, we have here the more specialized discourse of the *sèrè*, whose duty is to engage in the ritual recital of the master hunters' exploits at the annual gathering.

The traditions and rituals of the hunters' societies go back to the mythical figures Saane and Kontoron (see the fifth *sumu*), who figure in the origin of the societies. Kourouma, a master hunter himself, has inscribed the history of the dictator Koyaga in these traditions in which the very social organization of sub-Saharan societies are symbolized. The master hunter, who has demonstrated his courage by pitting himself against the great animals (the elephant, hippopotamus, buffalo, lion, horse antelope, hunter python), has earned absolute respect and obedience from the younger hunters and initiates seeking training and admission.

According to Karim Traoré, "*Kuma* is a general term that designates any articulated human utterance or thought." The normal use of *kuma* is in dialogue, and, "whether it is oral or written, literature is always a dialogue" (113–14). The hunters' society recognizes the power of the word in relation to the act of hunting: the *sèrè*, who alone is authorized to relate the exploits in the ritual *donsomana*, holds tremendous power in his mastery of the sacred word, the telling of which involves the coordination of the entire body. It is important to note that the *donsomana* is distinguished from other types of narratives in that it does not necessarily have a historical base (Traoré 163). Koyaga's *donsomana* contains elements of his exploits, but their veracity is frequently undermined by Bingo, the *sèrè*, by Tiekura, the *koroduwa,* and even by Macledio or other characters who occasionally interrupt the narrative.

The duty of the *sèrè* is to sing the exploits of the hunter and to praise him, but an essential aspect of the sacred power of *kuma* is that everything be told. In the prelude to the first *sumu,* Bingo tells Koyaga, "We shall tell the truth. The truth about your dictatorship. The truth about your parents and your collaborators. All the truth about your filthy tricks and your bullshit; we shall denounce your lies, your numerous crimes and assassinations" (4).

Each *sumu* is introduced by a theme, and from that theme come the introductory and concluding proverbs. These evocations of traditional wisdom are at once observations of the natural world, especially as it relates to the hunter, and expressions of a philosophical view of the universe. They likely have mystical impact in introducing and concluding each day's ritual gathering.

Because the entire discourse is presented as an oral ritual, Kourouma deliberately uses few and confusing indications of quoted speech. He has said that he consciously allows confusion as to who is speaking at times.

The Historical Background

There are historical models for all of Kourouma's fictional dictators: Nkutigi Fondio is modeled on Sékou Touré (of Guinea); Fricassa Santos is Sylvanus Olympio, the first president of independent Togo; Tiekoroni is Félix Houphouët-Boigny (of Côte d'Ivoire); Bosuma is Jean-Bédel Bokassa (of the Central African Republic); the leopard-man is Mobutu Sese Seko (of Zaire/Congo); the man of the jackal totem is King Hassan II (of Morocco).

If Koyaga overthrows Santos/Olympio, could it be that he is modeled on Gnassingbé Eyadema of Togo? The answer is, of course, a resounding yes. Kourouma has said that he was able to study Eyadema at leisure while he was living in Togo (1983–93): "The television and radio spoke about him all the time." At the same time, Kourouma insists that Koyaga is "an imaginary character" and that only some elements were based on Eyadema's career (Kpatindé interview 119). Koyaga is indeed a fictional character, but the parallels between his career and that of Eyadema are too many and too close to be dismissed lightly. The fictitious area of the Republic of the Gulf (56,000 square kilometers) is almost exactly that of Togo (56,790 square kilometers).

Afterword

Eyadema, whose given name was Étienne, was born in Pya, in the northern part of Togo in 1936. His mother was not sure which of the men with whom she had consorted was Étienne's father. As a gesture of Africanization, Eyadema later assumed the name of one of his mother's lovers, an old man named Gnassingbé (Bonin 39). He did not go to school until age ten and abandoned his studies after the third year of primary school (he later obtained a primary certificate) (Bonin 40). He joined the French forces and served in Dahomey (later Benin), Indonesia, Algeria, and Niger before being discharged in 1962. Like Koyaga in the novel, Eyadema led the protest of the half-pay veterans against Olympio. While it is not certain that Eyadema himself assassinated Olympio, as he later claimed, he was certainly involved in the plot (Toulabor 49).

In *Waiting for the Vote,* Jean-Louis Crunet assumes the presidency following the death of Santos. In historical fact, Nicolas Grunitzky became president of Togo after the coup. Like Crunet, Grunitzky was a mulatto, son of a Togolese mother and a German father (Crunet's father is a lieutenant of unspecified nationality).

Koyaga's second coup is the assassination of the president and the other two leaders of the first coup. This coup does not correspond exactly to Eyadema's seizure of power on 13 January 1967. Eyadema did not assassinate the other leaders, but he did put a new constitution in place, in May 1967, and set the army up to control all vital functions of the country.

The second attempt on Koyaga's life is the presumed sabotage of his airplane, which crashes close to the airport of his hometown. This is a transparent allusion to the crash survived by President Eyadema at Sarakawa (in northern Togo; he was en route to his home in Pya), on 24 January 1974. Eyadema was to milk this accident for every ounce of publicity value, claiming that it was the result of an assassination plot. He had a mausoleum constructed around the wreckage of the DC-3, and it became a shrine for pilgrimage.

Another clear reference to the historical Eyadema is Koyaga's policy of "authenticity," which was suggested to him by the leopard-man/Mobutu, the "chief of authenticity" (162). In the celebration of the thirtieth anniversary of Koyaga's ascension to power, the "heroines of the revolution" wear traditional dresses as a sign of "authenticity." Macledio explains to the assembled crowd that these women "have demonstrated their attachment to the president, to the country, and to the revolution of authenticity" (229). Fiction follows fact, once more: Eyadema actually followed Mobutu's lead, after the airplane crash at Sarakawa, and "authenticity" became the keyword. According to Comi Toulabor, "Authenticity is at the cultural level what the anti-imperialist struggle was at the economic level" (161). However, while the word may have denoted a true aspiration originally, it "was reduced in fact to a concept-slogan" (170).

The title of the novel comes from a reaction to Eyadema's dictatorial and self-serving regime. Kourouma says that, while he was working in Togo, the title was inspired by his "boy," who told him that "if, by any chance, the people did not vote for Eyadema, the wild animals would come out of the forest and would vote for him" (Kpatindé interview 119). This statement reflects Koyaga's confidence at the very end that his mystical tokens will be restored and that he will once more reign supreme.

Perhaps the most important question, finally, is why Kourouma has modeled Koyaga as closely as he has on Eyadema. A first suggestion is that Eyadema is in fact the only one of those West African dictators still in power at the time of the novel's (and this translation's) publication. He survived the National Convention of 1991 and has managed to push aside prime ministers who were on their way to usurping presidential power. Even as Kourouma's novel was in press, Eyadema was reelected once more (in contested elections) on 21 June 1998.

Aesthetic Functions of History and Tradition

Kourouma has been suggestively characterized as "the African Voltaire" (see title of Kpatindé interview). This should not be taken as limitative—there is an abundant and ever-present spirit of playfulness, of critical mockery directed at pretense and self-aggrandizement in African oral traditions. More specifically, Tiekura, the *koroduwa* or village buffoon, has complete freedom to mimic the obscenity of power in song and dance. The sacred quality of the word in praise of courage is counterbalanced by the license to ape authoritarian posturing. At the stylistic level of lexicon and syntax, Kourouma has chosen the discursive strategy of the *donsomana* as his own, casting himself as the *sèrè* behind the *sèrè* (Bingo).

The novel is provocative both of laughter—at the outrageous behavior of Koyaga and his brother dictators—and of anger if the reader pauses to reflect about allusions to historical realities in the discourse. It is reasonable, I propose, to assume that Kourouma intends his satire of abusive power to be directed at human folly and that he is confident it will shock and inspire reflection.

Afterword

The reasons for the sudden disruption of the *donsomana* for Koyaga by the secondary odyssey of Macledio are not immediately clear. At least two points can be made to show that the third *sumu* is only an apparent digression. (And, of course, the digression is in itself an ironic technique, brilliantly used by Aleksandr Pushkin in *Eugene Onegin,* to advance a major theme through affectedly offhanded and tangential anecdotes or discussions that are in fact deeply relevant.)

First, Macledio was predestined by the seers of his village to be an "eater of souls": "From the moment of his birth, Macledio was not only the bearer of an ill-fated *nõrô*, he was also a sorcerer and an eater of souls" (85). As the boy encounters one confirmation after another that he had indeed been born with the *nõrô* of misfortune, he begins to believe in his own destiny and goes in search of the "man of destiny" who will bring him to providential equilibrium. The boy was so intelligent that he instinctively understood and assumed the role thrust on him by sorcerers and tradition. (Kourouma narrates traditions; he does not believe in the supernatural aspect: "I do not believe in magic. If it worked, Africa would not have had such a tragic history. If slaves on the ships had been able to change into birds, they would have flown away" [Kpatindé interview 119].)

In addition, the direction of Macledio's career should be taken into account. Regardless of the sorcerer's power of prophecy, Macledio has indeed become an eater of souls. As a young man he refuses to accept institutional responsibility, as did Koyaga. For the dictator, the hunt was more important than school. Macledio's search for his man of destiny leads him time and again to discover and impregnate a new voluptuous woman. The recitation of Macledio's travels partakes of the picaresque tradition of *Lazarillo,* Fielding's *Tom Jones,* and Diderot's *Jacques the Fatalist,* along with Voltaire's satirical tales. But the quest for the fated man of destiny takes precedence when Macledio is mesmerized by Nkutigi Fondio's polemics on television. He immediately drops linguistic pursuits and his French family to become President Fondio's intimate friend and spokesman. This is the final stage before his talents are commandeered by Koyaga. With him, Macledio finally locates his man of destiny and becomes the factotum who can obliterate the distinction between truth and lies and carry out the master's every whim for thirty years. Macledio is to Koyaga as the *sèrè* is to the master hunter. Nothing in the series of six *sumu* is irrelevant—the digressive aspect of the third *sumu* is simply the superficial aspect.

What is the impact of the realization that the novel reflects in some ironic manner the realities of the African dictatorships following the end of European colonization and the declarations of independence?

Afterword

More specifically, has Kourouma taken Eyadema as the clear model of the master hunter Koyaga simply as an indifferent springboard for novelistic imagination? I would suggest the possibility that the novelist personally savors the obscenity of Eyadema's seizure of power and the support given by Western powers in their cynical efforts to stop the incursion of Soviet influence into Africa. The laughter provoked by proverbs on animal nature and behavior ("The civet deposits his offal at the spring from which he has drunk" [181]) stems from, among other possible emotions, incredulity, outrage, and a desire to correct.

There is an ultimate obscenity, not stated in the novel, since the survival of Eyadema beyond the terms (and lives) of most other dictators mentioned is not explicit: officially, at least, even at the turn of the twenty-first century he is still the president of Togo, who seized power through cold-blooded murder and opportunism and succeeded in prolonging his "mandate" well beyond a thirty-year term. He has survived assassination attempts and all forms of opposition. He appears to be incapable of comprehending that there might be any valid distinction between truth and lies. What is good for Koyaga/Eyadema is good for the country. Koyaga, in the final analysis, is only a pale reflection of the historical dictator in that, at the end of the novel, he is still hoping for the mystical tokens of office to reappear. To all evidence, Eyadema has found his aerolite and the mystical Qur'an.

Note

1. Biographical information has come from Nicolas, published interviews, and my own conversations with Kourouma.

Bibliography

Principal Works by Ahmadou Kourouma

Fiction

Les soleils des indépendances. Montréal: Les Presses de l'Université de Montréal, 1968. Prize: Prix de la Francité (*Études Françaises*).

Les soleils des indépendances. Paris: Éditions du Seuil, 1970. Prizes: Prix de la Fondation Maille-Latour-Laudry (Académie Française, for best novel by a young author); Prix de l'Académie Royale Belge. Trans. by Adrian Adams, *The Suns of Independence*. New York: Africana Publishing Co., 1981; London/Ibadan: Heinemann, 1981.

Monnè, outrages et défis. Paris: Éditions du Seuil, 1990. Prizes: Prix des Nouveaux Droits de l'Homme; Prix de l'Association des Journalistes Francophones des Télévisions et Radios; le grand prix du Roman de L'Afrique Noire. Trans. by Nidra Poller, *Monnew*. San Francisco: Mercury House, 1993.

En attendant le vote des bêtes sauvages. Paris: Éditions du Seuil, 1998. Prizes: Grand Prix des Gens de Lettres de France; Prix des Tropiques; Prix de France Inter.

Yacouba, chasseur africain. Paris: Gallimard (Coll. Jeunesse), 1998.

Allah n'est pas obligé. Paris: Éditions du Seuil, 2000. Prize: Prix Renaudot.

Theater

Le diseur de vérité. Chatenay-Malabry, France: Acoria, 1998.

Essays, Articles, and Interviews

Je témoigne pour l'Afrique. Grigny, France: Éditions Paroles d'Aube, 1998.

Kpatindé, Francis, Dominique Mataillet, and Valérie Thorin. "Kourouma, le Voltaire africain" (interview). *Jeune Afrique* 19 Oct. 1999, 118–21.

Mataillet, Dominique. "Interview: Ahmadou Kourouma, 'On ne peut plus gérer le pays comme un village. . . . '" *Jeune Afrique* Jan. 2000, 77.

Criticism and Background Studies

Alden, Peter C., et al., eds. *National Audubon Society Field Guide to African Wildlife*. New York: Alfred A. Knopf, 1998 (second printing; 1995).

Appiah, Kwame Anthony, and Henry Louis Gates Jr., eds. *Africana. The Encyclopedia of the African and African American Experience*. New York: Basic Civitas Books, 1999.

Baba Kaké, Ibrahima. *Sékou Touré, le héros et le tyran*. Paris: Jeune Afrique, 1987.

Banks, Arthur S., and Thomas C. Muller, eds. *Political Handbook of the World: 1998*. Binghamton, N.Y.: CSA Publications, 1999.

Bigo, Didier. *Pouvoir et obéissance en Centrafrique*. Paris: Karthala, 1988.

Bonin, Andoch Nutepe. *Le Togo du Sergent en Général*. [Paris]: Lescaret Éditeur, 1983.

Chipman, John. *French Power in Africa*. Oxford: Blackwell, 1989.

Cissé, Youssouf Tata. *La confrérie des chasseurs Malinké et Bambara. Mythes, rites et récits initiatiques*. Ivry, France: Nouvelles du Sud, 1994.

Geschiere, Peter. *The Modernity of Witchcraft: Politics and the Occult in Postcolonial Africa*. Charlottesville: University Press of Virginia, 1997. Originally published as *Sorcellerie et politique en Afrique —la viande des autres* (Paris: Karthala, 1995).

Hale, Thomas A. *Griots and Griottes: Masters of Words and Music*. Bloomington: Indiana University Press, 1998.

Hiskett, Mervyn. *The Development of Islam in West Africa*. London: Longman, 1984.

Hölldobler, Bert, and Edward O. Wilson. *The Ants*. Cambridge, Mass.: Belknap Press of Harvard University Press, 1990.

Hurault, J. *La structure sociale des Bamiléké*. Paris: Mouton, 1962.

Kelly, Sean. *America's Tyrant: The CIA and Mobutu of Zaire*. Washington, D.C.: American University Press, 1993.

Lusignan, Guy de. *French-Speaking Africa since Independence*. New York: Frederick A. Praeger, 1969.

Mazrui, Ali, ed. *Africa since 1935*. (Vol. 8 of the UNESCO *General*

Bibliography

History of Africa.) Berkeley: University of California Press, 1993.

Ndiaye, Christiane. "Kourouma et Sony Labou Tansi: Le refus du silence." *Présence Francophone* 1992; 41: 27–40. Reprinted in *Danses de la parole. Études sur les littératures africaines et antillaises* (Yaoundé: Silex, 1996), pp. 75–87.

Nicolas, Jean-Claude. *Comprendre "Les Soleils des Indépendances d'Ahmadou Kourouma.* Issy-les-Moulineaux: Les Classiques Africaines, 1985.

Okpewho, Isidore. *Once upon a Kingdom: Myth, Hegemony, and Identity.* Bloomington: Indiana University Press, 1998.

Ouedraogo, Jean. *Récit de l'indicible: Articulation, translation de l'histoire chez Maryse Condé et Ahmadou Kourouma.* New York: Peter Lang, (forthcoming).

Rosenthal, Judy. *Possession, Ecstasy, and Law in Ewe Voodoo.* Charlottesville: University Press of Virginia, 1998.

Rouch, Jean. *La religion et la magie des Songhay.* Paris: Presses Universitaires de France, 1960.

Senghor, Léopold Sédar. *The Collected Poetry.* Translated and with an introduction by Melvin Dixon. Charlottesville: University Press of Virginia, 1991.

Stoller, Paul. *Fusion of the Worlds: An Ethnography of Possession among the Songhay of Niger.* Chicago: University of Chicago Press, 1989.

Toulabor, Comi M. *Le Togo sous Éyadéma.* Paris: Karthala, 1986.

Traoré, Karim. *Le jeu et le sérieux. Essai d'anthropologie littéraire sur la poésie épique des chasseurs du Mande* (Afrique de l'Ouest). Köln: Rüdiger Köppe Verlag, 2000.

Waines, David. *An Introduction to Islam.* Cambridge: Cambridge University Press, 1995.

Westermann, Diedrich, and M. A. Bryan. *The Languages of Western Africa.* Folkestone: International African Institute, 1970.

Glossary

Words and expressions from various languages of West and Equatorial Africa are given here; languages other than Malinke are specified wherever possible. A limited number of terms pertaining to the French educational system and to the administrative system of the former French colonies are kept in French and explained, although capitalization of titles follows American conventions. Technical and rare English words found in standard dictionaries are not included. Some terms defined in Kourouma's narrative are included for reference. The spelling of non-English terms is simplified, avoiding most special characters and diacritical marks used by specialists of African languages: the "a" as in English "father"; the closed "e" (in English, a long "a" without diphthongization; French "é," as in "été"); only the open "e" as in English "get" (French "è, ê") will be marked with the grave accent, "è," to distinguish it from the "e"; the "i" as in English "street" (French "mille"); the "u" as in English "who"; the "g" is always hard as in "give."

Achura (Arabic)   act of expiation

agama   a family of lizards (common agama, tree agama) that ranges across West and Equatorial Africa

Allahu akbar (Arabic)   Allah is great!

apatam   rough shelter constructed by the people of the west coast of Africa

baccalauréat (French)   diploma given for those who pass the comprehensive final examinations at the end of lycée studies

balaphon   a type of African xylophone

Bibi mansa   the hymn of the royal eagle

bieri (Bamileke)   container for the ancestral skulls of a Bamileke chief

bilakoro   "lost youth," ruffians, addicts: young people living outside the system

bisap   a nonalcoholic drink having a hibiscus taste

Glossary

cache-sexe (French)   a small garment worn to cover the genitalia

Caravelle   a French commuter jet (originally, a medium-sized sailing vessel)

cercle (French)   an administrative region in the French colonial system of West Africa

certificat d'études [primaires] (French)   certificate awarded following successful performance in final examinations at the end of primary studies in the former French colonies as well as in present independent countries

certificat d'évolué (évoluant) (French)   Kourouma plays with the terminology of diplomas created by the Belgian colonial system for Africans who had gone through secondary schooling. The *certificat d'évolué* (certificate of an "advanced" or "civilized" person; French equivalent, *brevet de capacité coloniale,* diploma of colonial ability) was supposed to indicate the student had successfully completed secondary studies, but it was generally considered inferior to the French baccalauréat; the évoluant is a person who is becoming "civilized" but is not yet there.

chechia (French, *chéchia*)   a cylindrical, brimless hat of Arabic origin (often with a tassel)

CFA (French)   originally, the *Colonies Françaises d'Afrique* (French African colonies), an acronym that became the *Communauté Financière Africaine* following the declarations of independence: an association through which France invited its former colonies to remain in close diplomatic and economic ties following independence. The "CFA franc" was the basic monetary unit.

daba   a type of hoe in Africa

dahir (Arabic)   a decree of the King of Morocco

dankun   the crossroad marking the frontier between village and bush (according to Traoré, each village with a hunters' society has its own *dankun*); a formal meeting of the hunters' society, held at least once a year; the *dankun son* is a ritual of sacrifices at the crossroad

djadb   ecstatic dancing

djoliba   watering hole

dolo   millet beer

donso   hunter. Among the more important hunting-related terms used by Kourouma: *donsoton,* hunters' society; *donsokuntigi,* the chief of a *donsoton; don so ba(w),* master hunter(s) (*ba,* great); *donsodege* and *donsodenw,* a young hunter undergoing initiation; *donsomana,* the purificatory narrative; *donsotu,* the hunters' sacred grove; *donsobaw ka dunun Kan,* the voice of the great hunters' drum

dyandyon   hymn that extols the strength, coolheadedness, and moral uprightness of the hunter who has at least one of the six major game animals to his credit. Only the hunter whose exploits are recognized by members of the society is allowed to dance to the *dyandyon* (Cissé 148).

duga kaman   "the vulture's wings": Kourouma explains that these are the barbecued or dried shoulders of all the animals killed by the hunter a month before the annual celebration

École des Langues Orientales (French)   the School for Oriental Languages in Paris

École Nationale d'Administration (ENA; French)   the most prestigious of the *grandes écoles* (specialized institutions of higher education). A number of French presidents and higher-level government officials go through the administrative training of the ENA.

École Normale Supérieure (ENS; French)   a university-level institution for training teachers. The ENS, on the Rue d'Ulm in Paris, is one of the most prestigious institutions in France.

École Primaire Supérieure (French)   secondary-level schools under the older French educational system. As for the other specialized institutions, there is a highly competitive examination for admission.

evela   initiatory combat; from this term comes *evelema*

evelema   champion of an initiatory combat

Fa fòrò!   one of the most serious insults: Your father's penis!

fe'eh (Bamileke)   king or chief

Force publique (French)   the army created by Leopold II of Belgium to police the Congo Free State before he officially handed control over to the Belgian government in 1908

Fouta Djallon   a mountainous region of Guinea (an autonomous Islamic state from the middle of the seventeenth century to the 1890s)

futu   pastry or porridge made from flour of various tubers (yam, cassava) or crushed plantains, and served with meat

Glossina (Latin)   the *Glossina morsitans* is the genus of tsetse fly that inhabits forests and the banks of rivers and lakes in Western and Central Africa

gnwala'a (Bamileke)   the chief of the king's servants

Hauka (Songhai)   special group of mischievous spirits who began to possess the Songhai in the mid-twenties, when the French still controlled the vast territory called the French Sudan. The Hauka frequently take on identities that seem to be caricatures of colonial administrators, such as Gomno, the colonial governor, and Zeneral Malia, the general (of the Red Sea) (Stoller 153).

HLM (Habitation à Loyer Modeste; French)   originally, apartment buildings constructed by local governments for low-income families; now, simply low-rent apartment buildings

Holle (Songhai)   pantheon of spirits that are invoked by dancers of the Holle cult among the Songhai people, who live along the Niger River, principally in northeastern Mali and Niger. As in Vodu, the Holle "mounts" (possesses) the "horse" (the possessed person), who becomes the voice and person of the spirit.

icha (Arabic)   Muslim prayer

jebel (djebel; Arabic)   mountains, hills in North Africa (from the Arabic word for mountain)

jihad (Arabic)   sometimes defined as a Muslim crusade or holy war against infidels, but the more general sense is the necessity of seeking the way of truth (light)

Jula   Mandinga traders

juma (Arabic)   Friday; the principal public prayer of that day

kannari (a word of Caribbean Kreyòl origin)   clay pot used to store water

karite (Bambara)   the karite or shea tree belongs to the *Sapotaceae* family and has a hard, reddish wood used in construction. The shea nut yields oil for food, soap, candles.

kèn (Bamileke)   dance; ritual

kora   traditional West African stringed instrument made from one-half of a large calabash to which a long, hardwood neck is attached. Ten strings (right side of the bridge) and eleven (left side) stretch from the neck over the bridge to a ring at the base of the calabash. Strings are tuned by raising or lowering rawhide collars at the top of the neck.

koroduwa   village buffoon in the Mande social hierarchy; they play the role of responders in narratives

Kouhouha   although mentioned by Kourouma as a sura, this does not correspond to any sura of the Arabic Qur'an; could be a local West African term

La Baule   resort town in western France (Loire-Atlantique); the sixteenth Conference of French and African Heads of State was held here in 1990

Glossary

Labodite   the fictional hometown of the man with the leopard totem; Kourouma refers to Gbadolite (in northeastern Congo; called Lisala by the Belgians), where Mobutu was born

lali (Bamileke)   dance by warriors

lugan   place outside the village; a temporary residence for farmers during the rainy season

malaka (Arabic)   angels from Arabic myths associated with the Holle

masoh (Bamileke)   women's dance

mwuop (Bamileke)   dance

nõrô   destiny of an individual

nyama   vital power inherent in any living being or element. It is released with the death of that being or entity. The perpetrator of the death must take ritual precautions to prevent the released *nyama* from exercising revenge (Cissé 704). *Nyama tutu* is defined by Kourouma as the song of the "cocks of the pagoda," the young hunters.

nzima (*zima*; Songhai)   possession priest

petit séminaire (French)   Catholic secondary school

pieds-noirs (French)   French settlers born in Algeria

pokti   saber dance

Rassemblement Démocratique Africain (French)   African Democratic Rally; an African nationalist party formed at Bamako in 1946. Félix Houphouët-Boigny of Côte d'Ivoire was one of the founding leaders.

rhirib (Arabic)   prayer

Salamalekun! (Arabic)   "May peace be with you!" (polite greeting)

sama   spiritual concert of the brotherhood of marabouts

sambara   slippers

sarafulahi (Arabic)   pardon of Allah

sèrè   bard who specializes in the praise and exploits of the hunter

shock groups   groups of young people who were organized to act and demonstrate for President Eyadema in Togo

sicarii (Latin, plural of sicarius)   terrorists who attempted to chase the Romans from Palestine in the first century of the Christian era; used in the sense of hired killer

sinbo   hero of the hunt, a master hunter; the chief of a family is a *sinbo* (Cissé 18)

sumahara   food; spice made of fermented, dried grain

sumu   a ritual gathering; has come to refer to various social gatherings more recently

sura (Arabic)   a chapter of the Qur'an

Glossary

talibaa (Arabic)   young disciple of a master of the Qur'an

terminale (French)   the final year of study in the lycée

tse'eh (Bamileke)   a dance in which the *fe'eh* participates

tubab (from Arabic *tubib*, doctor)   ironic African term for a white or a European; used ironically to refer to westernized Africans

umrah (Arabic)   a pilgrimage that may be performed at any time of the year outside of the traditional season (Waines)

Vodu (Ewe)   a traditional religion found in a number of regions of Togo; also the word for a spirit in this religion

yovo (Ewe)   elegant gentleman (ironic)

CARAF Books

Caribbean and African Literature

Translated from French

A number of writers from very different cultures in Africa and the Caribbean continue to write in French although their daily communication may be in another language. While this use of French brings their creative vision to a more diverse international public, it inevitably enriches and often deforms the conventions of classical French, producing new regional idioms worthy of notice in their own right. The works of these francophone writers offer valuable insights into a highly varied group of complex and evolving cultures. The CARAF Books series was founded in an effort to make these works available to a public of English-speaking readers.

For students, scholars, and general readers, CARAF offers selected novels, short stories, plays, poetry, and essays that have attracted attention across national boundaries. In most cases the works are published in English for the first time. The specialists presenting the works have often interviewed the author in preparing background materials, and each title includes an original essay situating the work within its own literary and social context and offering a guide to thoughtful reading.

CARAF Books

René Depestre
The Festival of the Greasy Pole
Translated by Carrol F. Coates

Kateb Yacine
Nedjma
Translated by Richard Howard

Léopold Sédar Senghor
The Collected Poetry
Translated by Melvin Dixon

Maryse Condé
I, Tituba, Black Witch of Salem
Translated by Richard Philcox

Assia Djebar
Women of Algiers in Their Apartment
Translated by Marjolijn de Jager

Dany Bébel-Gisler
Leonora: The Buried Story of Guadeloupe
Translated by Andrea Leskes

Lilas Desquiron
Reflections of Loko Miwa
Translated by Robin Orr Bodkin

Jacques Stephen Alexis
General Sun, My Brother
Translated by Carrol F. Coates

Malika Mokeddem
Of Dreams and Assassins
Translated by K. Melissa Marcus

Ahmadou Kourouma
Waiting for the Vote of the Wild Animals
Translated by Carrol F. Coates